IN THE BEGINNING: CHOSEN

CORTLAND BONDS

CORTLANDJBONDS PUBLICATION

CORTLAND BONDS

ISBN:10:1479162310
ISBN-13:978-1479162314

"I wish to thank my family for believing in me, encouraging

me and telling me to always pursue my dreams, trust in the

Lord our God and never compromise who I am created to

be."

CONTENTS

I thank God for teaching me how to survive due

to tragedy, loss and abandonment. I am grateful to

be someone who forgives and above all to have

love in my heart toward mankind.

"Greater is he in me than he who is in the world."

NLT

CORTLAND

BONDS

IN THE

BEGINNING:

CHOSEN

First love is unforgettable…
True love makes you do the unthinkable…

PROLOGUE:

"I will face my weaknesses and overcome where fault lies

but how can I achieve such high objectives when I am in a

place of discontent and unruliness…"

FIRST KILL

The year 1973 proved to be my time to achieve more than I ever would have dreamed and as a result, face a future of solitude. I don't think there are many in the world like me but then I did find Murphy. The one who taught me to realize just how important my role in life is to those suffering including him, I guess that's why he wanted me to be the one to do it…

November, the winter cold came earlier this year but the coldness in my heart overpowered the air and the deserted path seemed strange and looked scarier than ever and yet it was all too familiar for I have walked it many times before. The trees hovered as though something eerie lurked around the premises and I cradled in the covering certain the air itself would shield me from the dangers it possessed. A thief would not have challenged this hour of darkness if it meant losing the most precious diamond of all because tonight was none like any other. The somber ambiance in the air emulates my heart in its loneliness and the loud screeching sound from the police siren is in harmony with the wind. I wonder if mom checked my room, became worried and called the cops. If they knew what I was up to would they detour and search for me instead.

I think about that day all the time and wonder why did I run Sara, why was I afraid to stand up for you, I had my chance and I let you down and my coward behavior ruined everything I thought I could have been to you but now is the time to redeem myself and

you and somehow I will find you. The wind blew hard and dirt brushed me in the face reminding me to focus on the task. There was a specific reason I had sneaked out of the house and it was not to focus on why I did not help her, for it was my duty to help her now. I must rid her and others of those taking advantage of kids and there was no room for pity and self-doubt.

I heard his steps as he unsuspectingly walked through the path where Lisa told him she wanted more of what he did to her and to meet her alone this time. He did not notice me hiding in the same spot he used when he and his friends attacked me. I waited patiently then he passed by and quietly I stepped out from behind the bushes.

"Is it easy to torment those who never wronged you?"

He jumped clearly frightened by the sound of my voice and turned.

"Who is that?"

He focused his eyes to see me standing behind him, covered by the shadows of the night, and alone. I stepped forward to reveal a small frame in comparison but his size was neither my concern nor my threat.

"…Hey, what are you doing in here you little freak? You want some more of what I started to give you before or did you like how I was taking care of your little girlfriend."

"Is it easy to torment those who never wronged you?"

My tone was firm, apathetic and it matched the unnatural setting just as death was about to approach bringing the cold air without regard to whom or what was out in it.

"Yeah, it is punk. Why do you care? You think that little whore you like so much never had it up her ass before?"

He stared at me then took out a cigarette and lit it. My eyes were burning and I began to squint. His boldness took me by surprise and simultaneously to his movements; I took two steps back when he approached me.

"What's wrong punk, didn't you stop me for the same thing I did to your little girlfriend or maybe you want to pick it up from the day we all met out here? That would mean I will have to leave for a short while and you would have to wait here while I go get the rest of the guys. But you don't want them do you punk, that's why you're in here in the dark alone, isn't that right?" He asked.

"Torment does something to a person when he only wishes to live in peace and accomplish the things he dreams of doing one day."

"Yeah and what kind of shit is that coming out your mouth?"

I remained like stone and repeated the phrase. He looked at me as though I was insane.

"...Yo man, I think you've been out drinking too much."

"Are you trying to reassure yourself you're not in any danger?"

"What did you just say punk?"

He started to move in closer but this time I did not move. I removed the gun from my pocket and shot him in the foot.

"Ouch!" He screamed. "You little fuck. What the hell's the matter with you?" He saw my cold, heartless glare piercing through him as though I had tapped into the core of what he fears most.

"...Hey, look man it was just in fun, nobody got hurt. Hey look I'm sorry is that what you want to hear?"

His desperate plea did not stop me and I moved in closer and

15

aimed the gun at him.

"No wait, what if I go and say I'm sorry to your girlfriend. I can get her some flowers. Hey man, you must know girls like flowers right?"

He kept talking but I was oblivious to his words more like I just didn't care something I'm sure was conveyed in my stare and he turned to run but felt the piercing pain as he heard the loud sounds roar through the trees and his flesh ripped off the back of his shoulder. He screamed for I had once again pulled the trigger and this time he fell to the ground.

"No! Please." He begged. "...You can't do this, I didn't kill anybody. Please, wait you have to listen to me please. I'll pay you." He offered.

I moved in closer and approached slowly.

"...Wait! Stop! Come on you can't do this!"

I raised the gun again and a third time I shot him only this time in the stomach.

"...Oh God, no, please stop, you can't do this."

I watched as he began backing away, dragging himself across the ground to save his life.

"You die, things change."

I raised the gun for the fourth and final time aiming directly between his eyes and pulled the trigger as he closed them knowing it was the last thing he would ever do. I looked at the body as it lay in a pool of blood and placed the gun back in my pocket and turned and walked away. The wind howled as it sent the autumn leaves and dirt to dance in an array of color swirling around me, blowing strong, effortlessly lifting me slightly off the pavement. Fearless, defiant, even cocky I walked along the path to go home

but made a stop on my way. I put the gun back in the brown paper bag and returned it to the freezer. All was silent except the wind. I had no trouble getting back home unseen and climbed my way back up the reliable method I used repeatedly and entered through the window.

I removed my clothes, got into bed, laid still, and listened as the wind blew methodically to the call of the night. Thunder began to roll, I got out of bed, went over to the mirror just as lightning streaked across the sky to see my reflection, a shadow of a phantom looking back at me, my soul had diminished, I was without feeling, without heart or was I. I stared at the mirror.

"...I will find you Sara." I went back to bed, lay down, closed my eyes and went to sleep.

REMEMBERING SARA

I wonder if maybe, I should take another shower; it would be the fifth time cleansing, scrubbing, and bleeding. The pain of raw skin still cannot subside the thing that's tearing me apart inside and cleansing is therapeutic but to hear her voice again after all these years, thirty-five years, it would be soothing, healing, and bring closure to a life spent alone. If only she knew about Mackey and that she was the reason why I burned him alive and what if she knows about her father it does not matter for she is my life, my reason to go on living, my downfall.

I'm determined to go to her house. I calculated what I would say preparing answers to questions she will ask but the answers would only frustrate her efforts to probe deeper. I've been there so many times before but didn't have the nerve to go to the door and ring the bell, what would I say?

'Hi I'm the guy who's been killing all those people who have been trying to hurt you.'

Should she know who I am that my search lead me to find her but the bloodshed had tainted my objectives, my very soul, and so I had to remain unseen, a secret love, her guiding light and sole protector, no, for she can never know who I am for she has already forgotten who I was...

I lay in bed, thinking, if I were to die tonight would people consider me a killer or hero but what would she think after all I did murder her father. I can't shake remembering the things she said

she had to do…

#

"I should have been there to protect you Sara."

"John how could that be possible we only just met this summer and how would you have been able to protect me even if you had known what was going on. Besides, we're just kids nobody's ever going to believe us and there is always the reality that I still live with him, you know."

Realization that her torture is not over hit me.

"Still Sara there must be something we can do."

"Since we've been talking John, I have to admit that a lot of bad memories have been coming to me and honestly…" She paused.

I watched her sad expression as we sat in silence and I hated her father and Mackey for what they were doing to us and what Mackey did to Sammy and his mom and Brian for knowing what was happening to me and taking advantage of it and of her. I was outraged and saddened by the things that came out of her mouth. I wanted to show her that I would put a stop to it. The only problem I was facing was how to do it. We finished our time in the park and again departed and went home. The stories Sara told me had me thinking of the experiences I suffered and though I wanted a solution to her fate thoughts of my own past dominated. I went to my room and avoided my nightly prowl to go see Murphy. I reached my hand under the mattress and with pen and pad, the words of that which were too devastating to speak came to life…

'As I sit an uncontrollable urge emerges, torrents of pain giving birth to grotesque amounts of mass only to think gluttony pays the price. The pain is excruciating, timing is critical, I move

to the floor, I feel the touch onto the back of my thigh, still I lay until a brief moment of agony subsides. The tangy mist, I wonder will I also vomit. I return to my seat to see my own disgust lying on the floor in front of me. It reminded me of the vivid images and that gluttony had no part in it, the invasion of cheap after-shave mixed with his bodily odors invaded my nostrils as though it was happening again and all I could think of is the putrid odors of a skunk overwhelming my senses. I tell myself to be brave, the ordeal has passed. I remove my shame off the floor and watch it drown in the undercurrent giving me some relief to the pretense that it never happened.'

I finished writing and placed the materials back under the mattress while thoughts of how to execute my plan was the only thing that made sleep possible. I woke the next morning looking forward to seeing Sara again and when our classes were over we sat in our place of solace. She lifted my arm and laid her head on my chest, I wrapped them around her, holding her close, never wanting to let go.

"I want to thank you." She said.

"For what?"

"For wanting to be my defender."

"This is insane."

"I know but it isn't over and even the dread of things at home follows me in other places."

"I..."

She looked at me. A tear fell from my eye.

"Don't cry, I'm strong, I'll get through this I know I will. Besides, I haven't been here a full term and that kid, the bully that you've been talking about and McIntire..."

"Wait let's talk about it later because I have something I want to tell you first."

"Don't worry, I won't hate you John, no matter what you tell me."

I remained silent and overwhelmed with grief and everything Murphy rattled on about was beginning to make sense to me.

"…I know it's been rough and incredibly emotional to be so young and have to suffer through stuff like this when we shouldn't know anything about it, but maybe one day things like this won't happen to anyone." She continued.

She looked at me and reached up to kiss me on the lips. We sat under the tree in the park for the next half hour making out. Gently holding one another and kissing. It was a gloomy Friday afternoon and rain began to lightly fall.

"…We should leave now."

"What if I were to take you away from all of this?"

She laughed.

We held hands walking to the bus stop. When the bus arrived, she kissed me again and entered inside.

"Uh, Sara…" I paused.

The driver refrained from rushing her and waited patiently.

"I know."

I saw a look on her face I was hoping I would never see again and I knew she was feeling sad.

She looked at me.

"John…"

Her remaining words were daunting but she would not let me dwell on them she immediately, gently caressed my face.

"Sara!" Again, tears filled my eyes.

"John, if you keep crying I'm going to be a mess by the time I get home. I'll see you Monday." Her tone was reassuring as she spoke smiling at me and that was the last thing I heard out of her mouth until…

SARA'S CONFRONTATION

"Everyone says that I'm an angry person. It seems to me if I was to leave the decisions pertaining to my life to everyone else, I may as well give up before giving myself the opportunity to try. Why do people feel they have all the answers to the dilemmas in other people's lives and yet they consciously refuse to see their own plight?"

"I don't know." She whispered.

I spoke while she was in the kitchen making a cup of coffee, it frightened her deeply, she dropped it and turned to see me standing in her doorway, revolver pointed to the floor and I couldn't take my eyes off of her as she stood before me frozen, terrified, beautiful.

"They think they have all the answers to my problems, well then, let's say they're right so you know what? I am angry, I am angry at the legal system, I'm angry with all those who think they have the right to persuade little kids to satisfy their own sick desires. I'm angry that they tend to get away with it, and angry with those who can live in a neighborhood as if they've done nothing wrong in society. I am angry I didn't have the nerve to speak up for myself, I am so very angry."

"Is this anger going to cause you to harm me?"

"What truly happens to those kinds of people anyway? Do they get what is coming to them, do they?"

We stared at each other clearly nothing like the gazes we

engaged when we were younger.

"...I hear of more cases than not how the sick fucks get away with it all. Is that right, do you think it's fair? Because I think, the twisted bastards should have lye poured up and down their genitals and then add glue to the area to make sure it sticks to them, that's what I think."

"Alright, I guess that's as good of a place to start as any."

Sara Moore was a respected therapist. She had a new life in a new city with a new name. She lived in a beautiful single story two-bedroom house modestly decorated and she dedicated her life to helping people with serious issues in order for them to continue with hope of a future without remorse.

Most of her clients were quite wealthy but had suffered from many different types of dysfunctional events over the course of their childhood and was trying to find some closure. Many of them felt lost or abandoned and buried their lives in work. Some lost out on relationships and others loss the family they had built. Sara was confident in her ability to assist those who were seeking guidance because she too had suffered so much in her past. She identified with many of the problems her clients had to endure and spent time doing all she could helping those who lost sight of their perspective while guiding others who had never taken stock in themselves. Now she was trying to brace herself through yet another unforeseen outcome, only this time a man was in her home saying things out of context to the appearance of what his intentions would do. She regained her composure and was desperately trying to speak calmly.

"I-I wasn't exactly expecting to have a one on one." She said. "...Especially, not with anyone who breaks into my home and

holds me captive at gunpoint."

"It's not how I planned it."

"And yet here you are. Well let's see if uh I can be of any help because something tells me you're not here to rob me are you? Please say you're not here to rob me." She whispered.

"…I help a lot of people, that is I try to help a lot of people and they keep coming back and so I guess I'm doing something right, wouldn't you say." She uncontrollably let out a slight giggle.

She tried to focus her attention to what she believed to be the needs of her uninvited guest rather than the situation at hand. She did not want him to lose control and start shooting just because he felt inadequate or misunderstood. She had no idea what to do and kept mumbling to him and to herself hoping to figure out something quickly to help her get out of the new founded problem he had forced into her life. She recalled how she had successfully sustained a poised position under her most awkward and difficult circumstances in the past and was hoping to bring that confidence thinking she should envision herself in her office with one of her clients where she felt in control but as she attempted to sound as though she could withstand her current situation, she realized she was failing miserably.

"…So what brings you here, are you a native of California because I'm not, ok that doesn't really matter I guess. Are you naturally black?"

"What?"

"Wait, that's not what I wanted to ask, well I'm part blac, I mean well, the gun and you've taken over and I ju-just well I'm not sure why, I mean are you here for a reason. I mean, ok, this is

not going very well, I need to know one very important thing."

A raised eyebrow indicated for her to continue.

"…I want to know if…well, DO YOU FE-FEEL YOU HAVE THE RIGHT TO BE THE JUD-GE, JURY AND EXE-CU-CU-CUTIONER? AND PLEASE FORGIVE MY TONE AND UNCHARACTERISTICALLY LOUD APPROACH TO THAT QUESTION." She continued nervously.

I tried to remain serious but a slight smile across my face was inevitable.

"Would it bother you if I was to say why not, don't you think life was designed in such a way that these types shouldn't live amongst those who haven't deviated from the plan and to make matters worse they get to go on with their lives and become successful while people like you answer to the needs of others AND GET NOTHING BUT A GREAT DEAL OF HEARTACHE AND DESPAIR IN RETURN."

She took two steps back, staring at the gun.

"I didn't mean to raise my voice."

"Is that h-how you re-al-ly f-feel, or is this some more of the anger you expressed earlier coming out of you again?"

"Earlier?"

"Well, yeah I guess it was only seconds ago but still earlier from now, I guess."

Sara knew her calm approach was not working and tried to stop her own wild imagination from taking over but the length of the silence was making her more nervous. She thought back to the work she had done with those in the field of law enforcement remembering the different types of stressful situations she encountered. She was hoping she had learned enough to be

effective to get out of the delicate and unfortunate dilemma she was facing, however, her thoughts regrettably guided its way to the one thing she was hoping she could avoid…

#

"Why do you have to jump? It is possible to face adversity with love and courage to beat the one thing you feel is tearing your life apart. There isn't anything, we, as human beings, and together as people, cannot get through and I know that I am right and though it's an unwritten truth, well actually it is a truth written in the Bible. It says that God wouldn't give us anything we can't endure, we just need to trust in him." The counselor said.

"Do you really believe there is a God?" The man asked.

"Absolutely, and do you want to know why? Well I'll just give you the reason I believe which is because he is a God of love and understanding and even if you don't believe in him he is someone who believes in you and he is patient and will wait on you until it's time to see him again and he is a forgiving God."

"So he can forgive me for cheating on my wife."

"Yes, he can and you know what, he already has forgiven you."

"Problem is that I didn't cheat on her, she was cheating on me, and do you think your God will forgive her?"

"Yes, I'm sure he already forgave her but it's you who must forgive her."

"I already did. I love her so much."

"Then why not put the gun down and come off the ledge, don't you owe it to yourself to give life a chance, can't you forgive yourself? What is it that you think you've done that's so terrible that you have to be up here? If you've forgiven her why not go

back to her, did you hurt her?"

"No, but I can't go back to her because she left me for the other guy but first she told me that she doesn't want anything more to do with me. She said that she thinks I'm weak, she said I shouldn't be forgiving her but that I should be mad at her but still I should love her so much that I should be wanting to go and kill the other guy."

"That's not a very practical way to look at things. Maybe you're better off without her."

"NO! Don't say that, how can I be better off without her when she is all I've ever lived for. She's the only one I've ever wanted in life and now she's gone. My life doesn't matter anymore."

"That's not true. Please don't feel that way. Would you tell me, what's your name?"

"Jumper."

"Excuse me?"

"My name, you asked me for my name, its jumper. That's what you can call me."

"Is there perhaps a chance you'll allow me to call you by the name your mother gave you?" She asked cautiously.

"I don't care."

They paused looking at each other.

"It's Peter."

"Hi Peter, I'm Grace."

Hesitantly, Peter looked up.

"Hi, that's a nice name. It reminds me of my wife."

"Really, is her name similar to mine?"

"I guess. Her name's Beth."

Grace smiles warmly.

"Peter you have a great sense of humor, I mean Grace and Beth doesn't even start with the same letter in the alphabet. That was very charming what you just did."

Peter smiled nervously.

"I meant your smile reminds me of her."

"Thank you, Peter, that's a great compliment, I really appreciate that. You Know, we're both up here, we're smiling and you're making jokes and complimenting in the same sentence and to bring a smile to someone else is such a gift Peter. You have more to offer than you give yourself credit for and you're truly worth a lot. I don't want you to feel uncomfortable but it would be nice if you were to, maybe, give me the gun and take my hand and we can get off this rooftop and go down for a cup of coffee."

Peter looked down at the firefighters and police below as the crowd stood around with concerned looks on their faces.

"You know they're going to take me away. I mean, I know that, so you must know it."

"Yes, I do but I have some connections and I promise we can first go and get that cup of coffee. All I want to do is help you Peter and help you realize that you have plenty to live for and much to offer, all you have to do if you will allow me to come closer to you and you can take my hand."

Peter did not respond but began to cry softly. Grace slowly walked over as though she would embrace a friend. She reached out her hand, he gently placed the gun in it, which she quickly put, in her back waist of her pants, he placed his hand in her hand, and stepped down off the ledge, the crowd below cheered.

The sirens from a police car pulled the attention of everyone

as the car turned the corner heading in the opposite direction and they could all hear there was a woman screaming from a distance. Everyone looked in the direction of the squad car and saw no one but everyone could hear the faint screaming, it was increasing in volume and someone looked up and softly uttered.

"Oh my God!"

The screams became louder and each person looked to realize that after Peter had taken Graces' hand and stepped off the ledge, no one but Sara knew what was happening. She watched from a distance, shocked, helpless and speechless remembering how Grace had explained to her the severity of saying the wrong thing before they went to the rooftop.

Sara was one of the chosen during her internship to continue her training on site on how to counsel the disturbed and suicidal that the law had to encounter. Peter gently leaned into Grace to hug her and in one quick motion; he grabbed her tightly by the waist and leaped over the ledge of the 40-story rooftop taking her with him. The crowd watched as they plummeted to their deaths and Graces' screams never stopped until they hit the ground.

#

Sara came back from the horrific visions of her past.

"I hope you're not my jumper." She mumbled.

"What?"

"Oh, I w-was about to make myself a c-cup of coffee." She said angry with herself for expressing her thoughts out loud and showing she was nervous by the tremble in her voice.

"I didn't come here to hurt you. I don't want to hurt anybody anymore."

"Have you hurt someone, recently?"

"Would it matter?"

Her head shook frantically.

'Of course it would matter!' She thought.

She contained her emotions but was angry that he could be so blatant. She knew trying to persuade someone about the value of life in his state of mind would be futile. So she tried a different approach all the while praying she wasn't insulting him.

"It sounds like a very hurt and scared little child inside of you has been severely damaged," She paused. No violent response, she thought and continued, "…And you don't know how to find the child to let him know that you as an adult will be the one to help restore the areas that all those bad people tried to destroy. It's okay to let go of what once hurt you and concentrate on the areas where you need to heal."

"I've been watching you for some time down at your office but so many people are there and I didn't want to attract the attention."

"Well there is certainly a lot of privacy here." She said quicker than she wanted to divulge. She swallowed hard and her eyes grew wider as she cut them to the weapon.

"Like I said, I'm not here to hurt you. I just need to talk. You are very good at listening and talking with people you don't know very well."

Sara breathed a sigh of relief.

"So why the gun?" She asked bravely. "…I usually do my job more proficiently when all parties involved are free of any artillery within arm's reach."

"You've always had a knack for bringing a certain humor into any given situation."

"How would you know that?" She whispered to herself.

I raised an eyebrow and slightly twitched.

"...It was rhetorical but I get it you said you've been watching me, but you couldn't have heard any of the conversations I've had with my clients. Did you interview any of them to get this information on me?"

"Interview them?"

"Alright, I want to know if you hurt any of them to find stuff out about me."

Blaring sirens rushed down the main street next to the block where she lived.

"DID YOU CALL THE COPS?"

"NO! How could I have when I've been standing here the entire time? Please don't hurt me."

The horn from the vehicle sounded and I realized the sirens coming from it were not from a police car but fire engines and the roaring piercing noise continued to go pass the street, only then I lowered the gun.

"Sorry."

Sara stood frozen, wide-eyed like a deer caught in headlights. She saw that there was compassion about his timidity when he apologized and found herself becoming more concerned for the person behind the state of mind he was expressing but quickly remembered there was still something deadly about him when he moved the gun. She reminded herself that the momentary regret he was experiencing was not something she could trust and she needed to get herself out of her predicament as quickly and safely as possible.

"...Let's go out back and sit on the lawn and I'll tell you what

I came to say and then I'll go and you can get back to your life but let me warn you unless it's absolutely necessary, I don't want us to be interrupted like before."

She nodded nervously although she had no idea what he meant by his remark and she did not want to rouse him any further by probing for answers to what he meant. It was hard for her to believe that right before her eyes she saw what appeared to be an introverted man who was lost and full of rage, unsure of what he should do, keep his level of anger somewhat contained and then in an instant become extroverted, violent and ready to take her life.

"...It's very challenging when one defies the purposes that were set in motion."

Sara listened and watched carefully as he took out a notepad and jotted something down.

GROWING PAINS

July 1972 Queens, New York, Saturday afternoon, I was ten years old, anticipating the day I was to turn eleven that summer and the love of my life was kicking me out of the house.

"John, John Chaney, do you hear me? I want you outside enjoying the day, it's too hot to be coupe up inside all day, no need to be mulling around go make yourself busy and do something constructive. Do you hear me, child?"

That was my mom; her indelible voice rang through the neighborhood or at least it seemed like it did. She was married to my dad Roger Chaney who had already deserted us.

"Yeah, I hear you, but it's too hot out."

I gathered the things I needed and climbed out the window. In the back of my house were two of the biggest trees in the entire neighborhood. One of the branches was long where it extended to the second floor ledge where my bedroom window was and the angle allowed me to climb out directly onto the strong branch which seemed it was as thick as the root of an oak tree. It was our apple tree and the other was a peach tree. It didn't make the other trees look any smaller and the one we had in our front yard didn't have any fruit but it was gigantic too.

I looked up and saw her in my room closing and locking the window. Clara Chaney, her smile could light up Broadway. She was sweet, kind to all, and very humble. What more could I say except for the fact that she was wonderful and I loved her dearly

and most importantly she was my mom. She smiled and blew me a kiss and went away. The heat was breaking all past records for being the hottest day in the history of time. The sun was intense and shining bright and to complain about it being hot would have been a waste of time because I had to stay outdoors. Luckily, for me, our block dominated than any other with big trees that kept it partially shaded. Almost each house had a tree in the front and back yards but the humidity is what nearly killed me.

The two-story house my parents bought was a single-family home and mom always told my dad she was thinking that they should convert it into a two family. The front door lead to the indoor porch and then the middle door lead to the living room, which was to the right of that door. In the living room was a half wall, which separated it from the dining room even though you could see everything in the next room. A door right off the dining room was the barrier that took us into the kitchen but the living room wall extended out to the middle walkway where a staircase leads upstairs where a room was located just at the top and to the right and opposite that was another room which was used as a storage area for extra suitcases and boxes with different items that mom didn't want to give away or throw out no matter how many times dad or her sister complained that she was just storing junk.

She always said that one day she would go through it all, clean the room out, and turn it into a second kitchen so that she would not have to go down stairs all the time when she wanted something as simple as a glass of water. Passed that room and straight ahead from the steps was my room and on the other end of the hall to the right of the stairs were my parent's room and a bathroom. The floor had an ugly brown industrial rug and the

walls were off white in color and in need of a new paint job, which was something my dad claimed often that he would do.

Every spring he promised to do it and every summer he complained it was too hot and that he didn't do it sooner because he got too busy with work. Well this time his excuse for the heat would have been right if he was still living at home but he left my mom and me when I was seven but like I said if he was around and complaining about the heat, he would not have been making any excuses this summer. I made it to the front where the other kids were on their way out and being cool as usual, Tommy was the youngest at nine and our pitcher Sammy was ten. Eric who usually liked to play practical jokes or try to get away with stuff was twelve and Warren was the biggest and the oldest at thirteen but he looked older and would hang out with us when his other friends his own age wasn't around.

"Hey guys look whose coming. Hey John don't trip over the air." Eric laughed.

He thought I was the most awkward if he were telling the story but still I tried to fit in even though Eric found nothing better to do with his time than to make fun of me for one thing or another.

"John maybe you should go back in and have breakfast if you eat 100 pancakes for the next ten years you might weigh a whopping 50lbs."

"Cut it out."

"Oh is little Johnny gonna go cry to his mommy."

Everything was a joke to Eric either I was too skinny, 'a goody too shoes,' a momma's boy, or I was too weak, not cool, too afraid, a baby, a tattle teller, too honest, too goofy, or a dufus and

on and on.

I didn't like the name-calling but he was nothing like the other guys from school that went beyond just being a bunch of teasers. They had more than their share of being vicious to go as far as to call me shit head, tar baby or bastard child of a whore. That's when it got personal but I wasn't in the position to actually defend myself so I ignored as much of it as possible.

I stayed around the local kids on the block even though they didn't try to stick up for me but I think it was because they didn't want to become the target of Eric's bashing and Warren just thought it was all in fun. It just happened to be at my expense but sometimes they included me in their game when playing sports, which was not my forte. We all stood outside looking as though we had been swimming in our clothes, something we would have gladly engaged in without a thought but the pool wasn't open due to repairs. I think they have been repairing that pool since they built it, there was always one thing or another wrong with it so why would today be any different.

"There isn't nothing wrong with that pool." Eric demanded.

"Yeah, I bet they just say that because they went to the beach and don't care if we suffer." Sammy added.

"Why do we have to be outside anyway, you know I heard my parents talking with some of you guys parents and they were telling one another about the heat and decided that we should be outdoors because they thought it was too hot for us to be inside all day." Eric admitted.

"Well that sucks." Said Warren.

When I saw Warren, Lil Tommy, and Sammy on their way out their door and Eric coming down the block and all of them

ready with their gear to play softball, I figured that was exactly what our parents had done.

"...They get to stay inside with the air conditioner and we are stuck out here forced to find a way to beat the heat and stay cool." Warren continued.

They talked about how it would have been better if we were inside enjoying the cool air coming from the air conditioner. It didn't make much difference to me because I could only imagine what it would be like to have air conditioning because we didn't have it in our home and the only time I did get to enjoy it was if I was staying at my Aunt Felicia's house. In my house, we had to soak a rag in cold water and wipe it up and down our bodies and stand in front of the fan.

At first, we were complaining about the cruelty our parents were subjecting us to and then we realized that only a half hour had gone by and we all were ready to go back inside to get something to drink. Eric started to walk away and then remembered to check his pockets.

"I almost forgot she gave me money." He said.

The other guys didn't bother to do the same because they admitted they were handed money directly, so I checked my pockets and saw that mom gave me money which was why she had already laid out my clothes the night before so she could slip it in my pocket just for this sort of occasion.

It looked like we were in the same boat when we found out each of our parents gave us money so that we wouldn't be trying to get back inside of the house for drinks or in case the 'Good Humor' man or 'Mister Softee' came down the street in their truck selling ice cream. Sometimes the trucks didn't show and if they

did and we didn't want to pay their prices, we had enough to go to the corner store to get sodas and 'Icee cups.' I never understood the concept of the 'Icee.' What was the purpose of a cup of ice with all that syrup or drinking a soda on a hot humid day. I always ended up being thirstier than before I had bought stuff like that and then I would have to spend more money for water if I couldn't go back in the house before dinner.

In the past during the spring, and all summer long when the ice cream trucks showed up we all would rush to buy one thing or another. Usually we were rushing to run outdoors with money we had to beg, plead and promise to do extra chores to get but not today, the parents welcomed the chance to give or slip the money our way just to get rid of us. It wasn't long before we figured out one summer day to buy the goodies we wanted and then ask for a cup of ice, which was free, and then we would walk down to the local park and fill the cup of ice with water from the water fountain. We had to figure out what we needed and then plan accordingly and the first summer our parents locked us out of the house, we came up with a solution.

Eric made us all feel stupid when he brought a pitcher with him full of ice from out of his house. Of course he didn't let us live that one down all summer even though the next day we all started doing the same thing. We turn on the garden hose to fill our pitchers and an idea came to life, ice-cold water without having to walk several blocks to the park.

As for our parents, all we had to say was that for old people they seemed to have thought of everything in advance to keep us from running back in the house for ice, cold drinks or even money.

"Look at this."

Eric pulled out a roll of toilet paper.

"You guys think you got it bad, my mom told me that I had to go outside in the backyard if I wanted to use the toilet right before she closed the door in my face and I could even hear her deliberately latching the door lock to make sure I couldn't run back inside until she was ready for me to come home for dinner."

We all laughed hysterically.

"…Yeah, she even said to make sure I dig a hole deep enough and to cover it back up thoroughly."

"Now that's a class 'A' bitch." Warren retorted.

"I'm gonna agree with him." Lil Tommy added then quickly stepped behind Warren.

"Yeah, I guess." Eric admitted sheepishly.

It was a harsh thing to say but Warren was the only one who could actually get away with it. We started a softball game and at one point during the game, the palms of our pitcher Sammy soaked the ball so much, we all got into arguments about him spitting on his hands. I tried to defend him but as usual our troublemaker Eric started in on him.

"Nah, I think he's just sweating from the heat."

"Yeah, and what do you know. You shouldn't spit on the ball Sammy."

"I didn't!"

"Yeah, that's gross." Warren added.

"But…"

"Next time bring a rag or something and wet it. We don't want your germs."

"But…"

"Yeah, man even I have to agree with Eric on this one." Lil Tommy added.

Poor Sammy, every time he opened his mouth to defend himself one of the guys brushed him off and ignored his plea of innocence. We continued playing, enjoying the wind that we created to blow against us as we ran to take base or after the ball and though warm, we had our water pitchers and would pour some of the ice water over our bodies but we had to use the pitchers of water within the first hour or suffer warm to almost hot water for drinking and pouring over our bodies. We must have visited Mr. Franks' store up at the corner about five times in the first hour of our game to get ice cream, cold sodas and lemonade and each time we went up there, he treated us as if we hadn't been there earlier. The funny thing of it all was that no matter how much we drank that day going to the bathroom never became an issue because we were sweating like pigs. I'm not exactly sure how much pigs sweat or if they actually sweat at all but it was a phrase mom always used and it seemed of all the phrases she used this one was appropriate on this day.

Our thirsts continued to grow as we continued to play our chosen game in the streets and each time we went to the store Mr. Franks continued to complain about the weather so much that he told us he had the notion to just pack up and go to live on the beach in Florida. We heard the same story from him for so long we would talk amongst ourselves and tell each other how he should just shut up and go. Today was no different and we had the pleasure of hearing him talk about leaving for Florida again and

again and every time we went to buy something he said the same thing about his dream of moving.

He must have told everybody in the neighborhood the same story but everyone kept quiet and listened, some offered their encouragement and agreed with him while others continued to smile knowing they heard it all before but in the end everyone treated him like they never heard his tale. The only thing about listening to the story of Mr. Franks' packing and moving to Florida that made it different from any other day, was that today the guys and I must have heard it about a million times. Still, we were always obligated to listen to him and be respectful because like mom always would tell me, when I had the urge to complain to her about Mr. Franks and his tales, was that he wasn't hurting anybody talking about his dreams whether they be reality of something he was going to do or not.

After she said that, I realized that it wouldn't have been so great if he had actually moved because it seemed as though every time we needed something, Mr. Franks' was the place to go. He had a nice store and for an old guy all by himself he kept it up even after some would be less then courteous after all his efforts of making the place clean and presentable for his customers.

He had a counter top made of a glass rectangular case with items for sale if there was anything inside of it and that would be the first thing noticed just to the left of the door. A door was behind that counter with a room to store the extra stuff Mr. Franks himself ordered. When he stood behind the counter, he could see portions of the store on the opposite side of the room where customers would shop. The far wall to the left of the front counter after the middle aisle had hooks vertically positioned for smaller

items and up against the same wall were several refrigerators. On the other side of that wall was a set of shelves and each row was parallel to the front counter full with one item or another. In the middle of the store was a small path, which divided the place into two parts. The first half had most of the soft goods like breads and cakes and flour, sugar and boxes of items to make pancakes, and cereal and baby food.

In the back next to the wall of refrigerators was an old rectangular shaped freestanding fridge with four legs grounding it to the floor and inside were small bottles of sodas, ice cream cups and popsicles. The aisle near the entrance at the counter was the first aisle, the next aisles had two and three marked on some white cardboard.

Mr. Franks would call out an aisle number and a letter to indicate which half of the store an item was located when people asked for things. He was an older man but his memory was as sharp as a tack when he needed to locate things in his establishment. It was too bad he never remembered that he was telling us the same old story about moving to Florida. I recall the first time I had to locate a very embarrassing feminine product for my mom a couple of years ago and Mr. Franks told me to go to aisle three (b) but it threw me off and so I told him there was no (b) listed in the store but he said that it would be the second half of the store. After that, I knew it was the aisle right before the refrigerators at the second half of the store in case mom had the notion to send me back for the same stuff.

She had no idea how that day mortified my entire existence, I was just happy I was able to get it to her before any of the guys came outside which would have undoubtedly lead to questions

regarding what I had in the bag. My first thought was is she kidding me, she just don't know how close she came to branding me something awful in the eyes of eight to eleven year old kids and the story would have made its way to school by the time I got to the front gate. I would have had to change my zip code and forced not to give it to her either but what can one do besides it was for my mom and I would have endured anything for her.

Sometimes we went around the corner to 'Lucky's' which was great because they were set up like a 1950's soda joint with stools in front of the counter. They served different types of soda drinks and even used a soda fountain and cool shaped glasses that looked like an hourglass when they made malts and ice cream sodas and they even had a jukebox. We heard plenty of stories about how a recording artist and her relatives used to hang out over there but we were skeptical about that because there was only one female artists performing with her brother and two male cousins that we knew of and they were really famous so we weren't sure if anyone ever saying that was telling the truth or not. Lucky's was popular and the place to go but the problem was that when we wanted to go there we usually had to be accompanied by someone older than us because the fire station was right next door and our parents didn't want us hanging around there without adult supervision. We never tried to push the issue because we didn't mind going to Mr. Franks especially since he was the kindest old person we had ever met.

...Our game was going strong but once again, we found ourselves going back up to Mr. Franks' store and like many times earlier that same day we knew we were going to hear the tall tales of his adventure to go to Florida. When we got there, it was to our

surprise the door was locked and Mr. Franks did not answer. We looked at each other baffled and our first thought was that something must have been blocking the entrance but it didn't explain not getting an answer when we called out his name. Eric started telling us how he thought Mr. Franks had actually left.

"I'm bewildered, he wasn't fooling; he was just waiting for the right opportunity." Tommy said.

First we looked at each other wondering how Lil Tommy knew such big words then we began knocking on the door some more and laughing telling each other he wasn't coming to answer because he was gone. We decided to act out a scenario and imitate how he would walk with his back hunched over and then we sat on the curb and started making up stories to tell each other about what he would do when he was there. We were wondering which way he went and asked each other if we could see him walking down the streets with his bags.

"No, he don't have a bag you guys, he's walking with one of those long sticks and one of them handkerchiefs tied around the end of it with a pair of socks and some bread." Eric said jokingly.

"Yeah I think he's still walking because everybody's getting a whiff of them old smelly socks of his and that's why nobody wants to give him a ride." Warren added.

We joked some more about how old and smelly Mr. Franks socks must be before we turned to see him standing at the door fumbling with the lock to re-open the store.

We all groaned.

"Ah, man I was hoping he was gone and fulfill his dream."

"Shut the hell up Eric what do you know about a dream other than a wet one." Warren interrupted.

"I'm glad he's still here, I'm thirsty." Lil Tommy said.

"...Mr. Franks you always talking about packing up and going to Florida that we all thought you left with your smelly old socks."

"Hush, Tommy." Eric whispered.

He grabbed him by the arm to pull him slightly back but Tommy just pulled away and stepped forward.

"What, that's what we all thought, so what's the big deal?" He added.

"Sorry Mr. Franks, we didn't mean no harm, we were just talking and some of us ain't old enough to know it's just talk and he shouldn't go around repeating stuff." Warren said as he looked at Tommy disapprovingly.

We all looked at Tommy and lightly shoved him to the end of the line one by one.

"Hey, you guys cut it out." Tommy said laughing while trying to cut back in front of everybody.

"No need to apologize young man. I guess if I had the gumption to sell this place and move on I would probably put some of this talk into action but I guess I'm just an old fool talking about things that will never happen. Don't have the nerve, I suppose."

Even though Tommy was the one to open his mouth and spill the beans about what we all said, Mr. Franks went around and passed us all up and gave him a lollipop for free, yep, Mr. Franks was alright with us especially after what Eric did a long time ago...

#

"Go take it back." Warren demanded.

"I can't."

Warren stepped in closer, towering over him.

"I said go take it back."

"I'm trying to tell you I ate it on the way down here I can't take it back." Eric explains.

"How much was it?"

"Fifty cents and I ain't got no more money."

"Okay, then we all go up to the store together and you tell Mr. Franks at first you were planning to pay for it, but you remembered you had to meet us for a game and forgot to pay and just ran out. After we tell him that you pay him for it, you got it; so how much you really got on you?"

"Okay! But I only got twelve cents left."

"Shoot I only got three cents. How bout you guys?"

"I got nine cents." Tommy volunteered.

"I got a quarter."

"Hey, thanks John. That's great! We got…uh, how much is that?"

"Forty-nine cents," Sammy said assuredly.

"Okay, we need one more penny." Warren added proudly as though he had no problems with the calculations.

We all looked at Sammy, shook our heads and rolled our eyes, knowing he was the one who had the mathematical skills out of all of us.

"Maybe he'll let it go for a penny."

"Maybe you won't do anything like this again or I'll give you serious brain damage."

Math may not have been Warren's strong point but we all knew who to turn to when we needed someone with muscles. He

was usually the one we went running to for help when we were facing some serious problems like the guys who enjoyed harassing us at school and would later come into our neighborhood and bully us when they figured he wasn't around.

The only reason they ever stood up to him once was because they were all together and thought they could take him down but Warren had his own group of friends he normally hangs out with and they were just as big as he was. One day those guys wanted to challenge him and he just happened to have five of his friends waiting in the back of his house and ready for action. It was funny to watch those guys walking very fast down the street and yelling back at him what they would do to him. In the end, it was just talk because they knew he and his other friends could beat them. After that Warren and his posse along with our help, have been the neighborhood look out team and he told us to let him know if we saw those guys come back. It was great to have that kind of protection.

…We only had the forty-nine cents but we all headed up to Mr. Franks' store and about ten feet away Eric tripped and claimed that when he looked down he found a penny. He didn't realize I saw him reach into his pocket and move his hand around to pull it out then look down and trip.

'No more money huh.'

I didn't say anything because it was the last penny we needed to pay Mr. Franks in full. Besides I would have been branded a snitch and I didn't need that title to add to the other crap I've been called and the main thing was that Mr. Franks wasn't getting cheated. We went in the store together nervous because we weren't sure how he was going to react after we explained to him

the story Warren coached us to say. Mr. Franks never questioned Eric or any of us about the matter he just thanked us politely for being honest and for paying him for the goods we were all sure he knew Eric had stolen.

"Well we all have our priorities, now don't we? I think it was rather nice of you to come back and face your responsibilities, young man."

"Oh, yeah, that's what I was telling the other guys." Eric said. Warren's eyes bulged so wide I thought his expression alone would give us away.

"Yeah, that's what he said alright." Warren added as he stared at Eric.

Lil Tommy was trying not to laugh and Sammy turned around altogether so Mr. Franks wouldn't see his facial expression. Mr. Franks continued to tell us that he understood how young folks like us are involved with our games and he knew it was easy to forget to do the right thing in a moment of excitement.

"It's an honest man that shows the character upon which we are made."

The way he was staring at Eric told us that he knew that Eric never did or had any intentions of doing what he was supposed to have done in the first place. He never mentioned it again and he didn't tell any of our parents about what he referred the whole thing as an innocent mistake. Yep, Mr. Franks was all right by us and we made sure no one was going to bully him around either and so we kept a watch out for his store too.

One day the guys who tried to go up against Warren came

back and they actually thought they were going to get away with stealing from Mr. Franks and push him around. It was a good thing Eric was on his way up there because he saw two of them go into Mr. Franks' place and quickly turned around to get help but one of the guys looked his way to see him turning to head back down the block. It just so happened that Eric was smart or scared enough to look back to make sure they were still going in the store and when he did, it was probably the thing that saved him from a bad beating. When he looked back, he saw two other guys running down the block after him and they gave him the chase of his life.

My indoor porch had a huge glass window and when I looked up after hearing one of the guys yell out to catch him, I saw Eric running faster than he had ever ran before. I thought man, if I could run like that when we were on the same team in our softball games we would never lose, at least not because of me. Eric made it down the block and in the backyard where Warren was with some of his other friends and before he was out of sight, I could hear him calling out for help. He was barely able to make it around the back of the house when the other guys went chasing in behind him. Whether Eric was able to tell Warren what happened or not didn't matter because the next thing I saw was those two guys running back past my house like lightning and there was Warren and three of his friends chasing them back up the street.

I had to run out of the house to see what was going to happen and as I had expected it was the biggest fight I had ever seen. I guess we all heard Eric yelling because all of us came out of our houses; Lil Tommy, Sammy and a couple of adults must have already been outside because they came down the street from a block away. We all went up to Mr. Franks' to see those two guys

and two more of their friends brawling with Warren and his buddies.

Our side did a good job beating those guys but it wasn't as easy as we all thought it would have been but in the end, we won and we haven't seen them back in our neighborhood since. Everybody praised Warren and his buddies for days and Mr. Franks gave all of us free ice cream and drinks for the whole week and he probably would have continued if our parents had not had their own little secret meeting that they didn't think we knew about to stop him. Sure enough without saying a word after one of our games, we went to the store and reached into our pockets to pay for our ice cream and drinks and we silently gave each other looks of understanding that our parents gave each of us the same speech.

#

...We finished buying our supplies and went back trying to keep cool because it seemed like the heat would never let up. Finally, we caught a break and a breeze blew gently across our bodies. Although it was warm, it was enough to cool us off because we were still drenched from our own sweat. We walked as slowly as possible to enjoy the breeze before we took to the streets to continue our game. When the time came, we all took our positions and Sammy was winding his arm ready to pitch the ball.

"Falk, falk that was a Falk," Eric screamed.

"And what's that?" Tommy asked.

"When you try to fake out the hitter and pretend to throw the ball but you don't that's like cheating."

"Well I didn't know that." Sammy admitted.

"Doesn't matter."

"It does matter." Warren interjected.

"…And the word you're looking for is balk. Cheating is when you're doing it on purpose like stealing." Warren emphasized as he looked back at Eric.

"…And if he didn't know it than it's not cheating."

Eric ignored him and shrugged his shoulder.

"I don't care I get to take a base."

"You can't take a base if all the rules aren't understood."

"Yeah, that's no fair."

"Shut up, Sammy." Eric bellowed.

"Let's look at it like this, Sammy was winding up for the pitch right?"

"Yeah, but he started to throw the ball and stopped."

"Right, but what's that, they don't have winding up for a pitch in real baseball, I mean not the way we do it. So now we all know the rules and if he does it again then you can take the base but for now it's a do over, okay, I mean that's fair, right?" Warren asked looking for everyone's approval.

We were not in the habit of disagreeing with those who were bigger than we were, agreed, and thought that Warren was being fair and even though we thought Eric would whine about it, he agreed without complaint.

"Yeah, okay, but if you do it again Sammy even on a different day we don't want to hear you saying you forgot, is it a deal?"

"Okay, deal now let's play ball."

Eric knew it was the best thing to do when he agreed with the rest of us considering the fact it was a good call and we all knew Warren could have made the rules any way he wanted. It was easy for me to agree with the decision because although we all tried to have some kind of camaraderie, keep a summer game going, and

maintain some degree of civility, there was a hidden reality that made me feel as though I was being left out. Some days I would watch from my indoor porch out the window as the other kids played. No one ever bothered to see if I wanted to play or even call me out to let me hang around as a relief player as they did with some of the others. I knew when they called for me to play; it was because they gave up on playing other games and finally decided after so many days without playing softball, thought it was better to have me than to forfeit another game.

I was told that picking teams was always one of the highlights but when it came time for the guys to pick their teams and I was lucky enough to play, I was always the one who they picked last and if Warren's pals came around and they all wanted to play, I had to wait to see if I was going to be on the team at all. Some highlight but I didn't let it bother me because sometimes I didn't always want to face the teasing because I made the wrong play or because I wasn't fast enough or whatever else they decided to pick on me and I wasn't completely without my wits and learned quickly enough that if I didn't make up an excuse that would be acceptable to them by their terms, I would get harassed for not joining in to play when they did ask me.

Overall, I felt like what I thought old man Murphy would be feeling if he knew what everyone had to say about him but I doubt he actually cared what others thought. I guess that was my downfall because I couldn't let it roll off my shoulders like oil sliding down a slope and I would take my revenge when I wasn't allowed to play and burn my G.I. Joe action figures and put a name to each one of all those who was teasing me.

One girl at school told me that I was the target of harassment

because I was a good student and that I used the manners my mom taught me.

#

"What the hell is that suppose to mean."

"Well, it's not like you're smart enough to be categorized a geek, or if you are that smart, you don't look like it. You know it's possible that I'm more of a jock than you."

#

...I had no clue what to do with that remark but she continued on by telling me that I wasn't considered to be one of the 'cool kids' and the way things were going I probably wouldn't find my niche at least not at that school. I couldn't hate her because I felt everything she said was true. I was doing what I thought was my best to fit in but that always landed me sitting alone on school grounds during recess. It was beyond my understanding as to why a few of the teachers were constantly trying to encourage me to make an effort to get involved with the activities when one girl was able to figure out everything about me in an instant.

Sometimes I wondered if the teachers were on the same planet I was on or at least if whether they taught at the same school where I was attending because they didn't seem to get that none of the other kids wanted to cut me a break and I just never knew where I actually fit in. If I was clever enough to slip away from the nagging teachers, I didn't have to concern myself with anyone asking me to participate so I would find a tree to sit under, dig small holes, and bury the ants that crawled into it.

I was after Eric and at the plate ready to swing and praying I would hit the ball and make it to base unfortunately today, I was about to get my prayers answered and find out a little bit more

about who I was and how I was truly different from everyone else. Old man Murphy's peculiar behavior left him to be the one everyone called odd, weird, demented and bizarre. It just seemed a little more possible that the things said about him were true when the parents started putting in their two cents about what they thought of him and no matter how it was expressed about the old guy, the consensus was that he was definitely strange and an outcast. Yep, Murphy was that guy.

One of the strangest things about him was that he never associated himself with any of the parents and yet he knew almost everything about everybody and the frightening thing of it all was that I was about to find out how much he and I had in common.

OLD MAN MURPHY

The ball came toward me heading over the cardboard we had cut out of a cereal box to make as our home plate. Sweat came down my forehead but I waited until just the right moment. Bam, it went sailing over a house, it was the first time I actually hit the ball without somebody easily making the catch or it not bouncing on the ground first and one of the guys getting it and tagging me out before I could make it to the base on time. All the kids roared.

"Wow!" Sammy said.

"Oh my..." Eric started in disbelief.

"Hey, John that was great!" Warren said excitedly cutting Eric off.

"Man that ball is outta here." Tommy said as he imitated a referee kneeling down on one knee and pulling his forearm back with his thumb extended up copying the motion of a hitchhiker.

Everyone was telling me how great it was that I lost the ball over the house. We all took off running to see where it might have landed and hoping that it didn't go into old man Murphy's yard. We prepared for the worst but no matter how much we braced ourselves it wasn't something any of us was ready to face when we came face to face with the difference between hope and reality but I never would have known of my true potential if it wasn't for that damn ball.

We went around the corner toward the direction we all saw it last flying and to all our dismay and of all times for our ball to go

into the yard where the house stood on the corner lot several feet from the chain linked fence with a hallowing weeping willow in the front yard towering over the rooftop, there it sat. The area added a certain chill from a horror flick where all other places and things seemed as though they did not exist. The unnerving desire to enter the most terrifying place was too inviting to resist but it was not the place as much of whom it was that lived there.

The ball was waiting like a dog sitting for its master to retrieve it only without the heavy panting and drooling saliva. We stood in front of the house looking through the fence and then at each other trying to give the other the eye to go in and get it. No one wanted to face the old man just in case he came outside, but they didn't have to because as fortune would allow it I had to show the rest of the guys I wasn't afraid to go in the yard belonging to the old grumpy outcast.

Actually, I was the unlucky straw who was fortunate enough to win over all the votes to go get the ball because everyone else said that I was the one who lost it in his yard. I was facing the opportunity to show all the others that I wasn't the wimp they all thought and made my way to enter old man Murphy's yard.

"You're not going to chicken out, are you?" Eric said tauntingly.

"No, I'll get the ball, it's no big deal."

I stood for a moment and Tommy came close and stood next to me.

"You show em, John, you're no chicken, right?"

We looked at each other.

"...Man, talk about earning brownie points the hard way."

"Yeah, tell me about it." I whispered.

I went up to the fence and of course I was hoping to get in and run right out. However, life loves to play its tricks on people and kids were not exactly life exempt or from being known as people and lucky for me I was a full-blooded living and breathing person. I climbed to the top of the fence and jumped down crossing over to the other side and when I hit the ground, I saw a pair of feet in front of me. He watched me as I stood up watching him bend down to pick up our ball. He stood outside at the other end of the yard where none of us had noticed him and I'm thinking he had to have moved as soon as I was making my efforts over his fence.

He looked at me for every moment he was picking up the ball and when he stood, he was partially straight because he had a hunch when he was standing his version of upright. He started tossing the ball a couple of inches into the air and catching it as he continued to stare me down. I knew everyone like me was frozen, but what I wanted to know was how in the hell did that old man travel from one end of his yard to the other so fast without being detected by any of us?

"I take it you're Chaney's kid right, John Chaney, isn't it?" He said.

I stared back at him.

"Yes sir."

"Chaney and Company," He added.

I could hear the guys scatter away from the fence.

"Huh! Oh, yeah we were playing soft…"

"I know what you were doing, young man."

I knew the lecture was coming and it was going to feel like a slap across the face. Nonetheless, I had to be polite as I had been taught because mom always said if I was faced with getting caught

doing something I wasn't supposed to be doing I was to be as sweet as pie and perhaps the punishment would be less if any at all. Nevertheless, my mind continued to wander and one of her phrases popped into my head on cue when it seemed like I was in trouble and I could hear myself whispering...

"If someone slaps you across the cheek then turn the other one to let them have at it on the other side."

'What the hell did that have to do with my situation at hand was beyond me, so why was I thinking of it; I have no idea but one thing certain was that mom's phrases came to me at the most inopportune times.'

"May I have my ball sir?"

"Well, I must admit you kids are from a litter who knows how to show some manners, at least to the older folks around here that is to say." He said.

'Great, someone else is adding his memory of phrases that will never leave my mind. It always seem to be the case when you don't want to see someone there they go and ruin your day by showing up like you're their best friend or in my case just in time to be caught where I wasn't supposed to be.'

"Here it comes another life long story I'm going to have to listen to." I muttered softly.

"You have to speak up young man the hearing ain't what it used to be."

"Oh, nothing sir."

"Well you know why I chase all of you boys away when those other boys come around here don't you?"

I knew he meant the kids who liked to come around just to start trouble with us.

"No sir."

'Would it be because you're a mean old dog and don't want anyone else to have any fun.'

"It's because those guys are so much trouble and I don't want them thinking I'm playing favorites. It diverts their attention, they can leave you, and your baseball buddies alone. You weaker ones, at least for the moment, so to speak." He grinned.

'Okay, he's got a point but I just want my ball back, I mean after all I got a game to finish.'

"Well now Mr. Chaney, I guess you want your ball back is that not right? Of course you do. Why else are you here? It's not to listen to the ramblings of an old man, now is it?"

I shook my head, and then nodded, my eyes widen and Murphy smiled because he could see that I was confused.

"Hey kid I got something for you. Wait here, I'll be right back." He grumbled.

He tossed me the ball and turned to go up four steps leading to his porch before entering inside the house. I stood looking bewildered.

'I got my ball back so why should I wait around.'

"Hey, John what's up?" Warren whispered.

"Yeah, did you get the ball or what?" Tommy asked.

"Got it but he told me to wait here."

"Why? You got the ball so let's go." Eric snapped.

"Because if I don't and I lose the ball in here again he might not give it back to me, besides he's not quite the mean old fart we all thought."

"He's just messin with you, let's go."

"Just wait! He's kind of cool."

"Cool? You mean as in creepy, might kill you and stuff you in the refrigerator, cool?" Eric continued.

"No, I don't think he's like that, just hold on a second, it won't take long."

Eric had no idea how close he was to the truth when he made that remark. Neither did I for that matter. Murphy returned and again the guys scattered. In his hands, he had a slingshot, switchblade, and two brown bags. He kept his eyes on me.

"Come over this way a bit and keep your back to the fence. Now these two items you can see for yourself what they are because I didn't put them in a bag but do you want to know what's inside the bags?" He asked, lowering his voice so no one else would hear him for he knew the crew was standing nearby.

I moved closer towards the items wanting to find out what the mysterious objects the old guy was keeping a secret to the point he would put them inside brown bags. He placed the bags carefully on the ground and put the knife in his pocket. He moved the slingshot from one hand to the other and turned it over and back again then he rubbed it gently before pulling the thick elastic band back and releasing it.

"The slingshot is good when you want to protect yourself from a distance but if somebody breaks a window everybody's going to believe you're at fault just because people don't know the history about the nature of the slingshot and we all know how those old fogies are and how they like to point the finger at young boys with slingshots now don't we?"

The twitch on my face was involuntarily, I don't know if I actually smiled or just looked deformed but curiosity exuded from me and I continued to watch as he removed the switchblade from

his pocket.

"…And the switchblade, well, it can be concealed but if the blood drips it could lead a trail to you. But I guess you could wipe the blade off but what happens if some blood gets on you or your clothing, and if there are no visible cuts, everyone will ask why your clothes are bleeding and you're not." He added.

'This guy is crazy, what does he mean if the blood drips, does he think I'm going to go around stabbing people?'

I was confused about the topic but chalked it all up as old man Murphy's way of showing himself to be incoherent. I thought that perhaps it was why people teased him behind his back but more importantly it was fascinating to see the different items the old man brought out of his house and I wasn't as concerned with the things he had to say as much as what was in each of the bags.

"…And now the brown bags," He continued.

He reached into the first bag and then stopped himself.

'I was becoming annoyed because he kept staring and now Eric's phrase of this old guy being creepy was starting to make sense.'

After taking a moment, he closed the bag and smiled.

"…Curious or just tolerating the whims of an old man."

My mouth opened and I knew he could tell I was showing interest and I could see that he was amused when he saw the look of disappointment on my face as he closed the bag and put it down. The spark rekindled in my eyes when he took hold of the other bag but again he stopped only this time he moved closer to me as I reached out to take hold of it indicating I wanted to see more.

He extended the bag so I could touch it and the coldness of the object through the brown sack sent a thrill of delight through

him, I could tell because of his reaction when he saw mine after I touched it and the fact that I had the same thrill. We were bonding and I don't know why or how but his trust in me was something he knew I would never betray and in that moment I wanted to know everything, the old guy had to offer.

"What is it?" I whispered.

Murphy reached inside and retrieved a 32 revolver. My eyes opened wide. It was intriguing to see such beauty. I felt scared and excited at the same time.

"Go ahead and touch it. I took out all the bullets."

I approached the seemingly deadly but for the moment, harmless weapon and Murphy asked me a question. I paused as he reached out and took hold of the gun.

"Well?"

I looked up at him.

"Can you shoot or not, boy?"

He seemed as though he was in a hurry.

I shook my head.

"No."

I was in awe by the object in his hand, then my focus deterred, and quickly, I turned my head in the direction where I heard one of the guys.

"Hey man, are you coming or what because at some point I want to go home and have dinner tonight."

I recognized Eric's voice.

"Um, yeah here I come."

"Well since you don't know how to shoot a weapon I guess it can get pretty dangerous for you even though it's a good way to protect yourself against the bullies in the world. You're probably

not ready for this kind of firepower because you would have to train yourself and you would have to be diligent about practicing regularly. I guess it wouldn't be a good idea for you right now to have such a powerful tool, besides I might need it in case somebody tries to rob this old fool."

The old man stared devilishly as he watched my reaction after he took the weapon out of my hand and returned it to the brown paper bag. He was elated and then he said something I found curiously intriguing.

"...I thought I found my protégé when I first saw you but couldn't tell until I saw that the gun had an appealing quality to that young mind standing before me, just as it had captivated me the first time I had ever seen a gun up close. Well, I guess you better get back to your friends, but so things don't look too suspicious maybe you better take what's inside bag number one."

As though I had been running in a race, my mouth had become dry. I would think on his words later but for now the original bag he had started to open was once again in his hands and I stared at it anticipating what was inside.

'Could it be the bullets?'

I licked my lips and swallowed hard trying to catch my breath as I spoke.

"What's inside?"

"Fireworks and lighting strips." He said flippantly.

"Fireworks, is that all, what are lighting strips?"

I asked curiously and yet disappointed that it wasn't something as intriguing as the gun.

"First we must see how well you handle yourself with the use of the fireworks. It is imperative for you to sustain your ability to

keep certain information pertaining to the whereabouts of your supplier under wraps. If you can pass the test without caving into the pressures of those with the power to take them away from you, only then will, I think you to be ready to expand your knowledge about the lighting strips. Beware, young Mr. Chaney, as far as anyone knows you just have fireworks in there, which most will seemingly think are harmless, you got it?" He retorted.

"…I put the strips way down at the bottom and whatever you do after today don't keep them together until you need them and the distinctive flashy color will let you get away with telling people you need them for a science project for special effects if anyone happens to find them. They'll never figure out what the real purpose they were created."

"Then how am I supposed to know what to do with them if I can't figure out what their use is for either?"

"I wouldn't worry about that if I was you young man because the clue is not far from your grasp." He said. He leaned down to whisper in my ear then he pulled away still staring and grinning.

I took the bag.

"Thanks!"

"Make sure all these other items here are never mentioned other than between you and me. I'm going to teach you how to take care of your momma being that you're the only man in the house, we wouldn't want some young punks like those bad ass kids hurting her now would we young man?"

"No sir."

"It's always important to take care of the women who brought us into the world, don't you think?"

He never released his menacing stare or grin at me then he

started backing up, turned and walked closer to the steps where he left the slingshot and the bag with the revolver. He put the bag inside his pocket with the knife, picked up the slingshot and went up the steps to his porch.

I took an immediate liking to the old guy, something was drawing me to him causing me to want to know more and oddly, obey. I turned to walk towards the fence where the other guys had been waiting and I could hear them trying to get my attention because they wanted to know what it was Murphy gave me. I was in another world and captivated by the gun and lost in my thoughts by the time I reached the gate. The resounding noise of the door startled me out of my trance, I turned to face the direction where Murphy had been standing to see that he was no longer in sight and the door was closed. I was slightly disappointed that the old man had disappeared. I paused for a moment waiting to see if the mysterious man I had just encountered would return but the anxiety prevailed and with no more patience, I began to search through the bag to find out what different types of fireworks he gave me. Murphy re-opened the door, I looked up, and he spoke more audibly because I was standing further away from him.

He blurted out what he wanted to tell me without regards to the other kids hearing what he had to say because they weren't aware of what he had whispered to me. I could barely see a figure standing behind the screen door at the top of the steps, and though difficult, I could tell when he finished talking that it was moving and fading away until once again he closed the door shut. I was confused but convinced I would understand when the time presented itself that I would properly know how to use all the things given to me.

JOHN'S DIALOGUE

Sara was fearful but becoming more bold when she spoke out because she was tough and not easily pushed around something she had proven over and again during her life but everything has a time and place and this time belonged to me to savor everything about her and what we once shared.

"Why do you keep writing, what do you want from me? Please just tell me and go, please. At least say something, this silence is killing me."

I lowered my eyes and continued to write.

"...Fine, then I'll start, what do you believe about the challenges in your life?"

"I bet you would never guess that some consider me a breed of vigilante."

"I wouldn't take that bet if I were you."

"I guess I have a certain need to give more details about who I am and my need to fulfill a promise I failed to uphold so long ago."

"I'm sorry but you're not making sense, what promise?"

"So many challenges along the way."

"Yes, you said something about the challenges and people defying some purpose, what does that mean?"

Our eyes met again and I could see she was annoyed and intrigued but what would she think of me if she knew of the many who have lost their lives because of her, it would be pointless if I

was put in the position to get rid of her, it would have all been for nothing. She watched my every move from the gun in my hand to the rhythmic pulse on my temples and I couldn't help but remember what we shared.

"I'm not at peace, so much rage inside."

"You don't appear to be someone who is full of rage, well except for the whole pointing the gun in my face and threatening to kill me, other than that you look like you know exactly what you're doing and seem to be quite serene about it."

"It comes about during moments when all appears to be going well, silent screams craving to express the wrath of my inner core forces me to submit when I accept the fact that there is self-rage causing all the rational thoughts to subside when the overpowering will envelops my soul."

"What does that mean, are you saying you're ready to hurt me because it looks like you won't, I don't buy that you have the gun, so I'm thinking you're prepared to do exactly what you intended." She cried.

I looked at her but it must have been with cold intent and again she stepped back.

"You don't have much further to go; you don't have to back away. I mean where do you think you're going?"

"Why are you doing this, who are you and what do you want from me?"

"I became his prodigy but then it evolved into my way of life to secure a future I had not known would be a destined reality."

"I don't understand."

"I didn't realize there was potential good inside me or that I would be willing to help those weaker than the ones who had tried

to oppress them. I learned that it was instincts as to why I became the defender of the weak, their defender without mercy, without remorse."

"It's quite evident that you are extremely intelligent."

"Intelligent? People aren't aware of the darkest realm of my psyche, I know it is there where I am obliged to beat out the aspects of every possible failure at arm's length waiting to cripple my intentions and decapitate the birth of realizing its dream."

"What dreams?"

"I understood the things I did didn't come without a price to pay, a price most would shudder to think about much less consider to be their desired opportunity in life. It was a price the majority would think unimaginable and perhaps unreal to accept that another human being could actually have the ability to subject himself to live in unconditional surroundings. They could not accept not knowing where it would be safe to lay one's head for the night. The price of an unforeseen truth was an inconceivable thought as an unattainable fate to live unsure if that life would still be a part of the human race as though it was just the roll of the dice, hoping to awaken the next morning."

"That was an elaborate response but I'm not sure you answered my question."

The hardened look across her face became soft.

"…Why are you here?"

"Why not?"

Her eyes widened.

"Because you don't…"

"I didn't finish what I was saying."

She looked at me with contempt silently daring me to

continue.

"Holding someone against their will is a crime you'll have to face."

The smirk caused my eyes to squint as my lips tightened and my stare continued to look through her as she returned a seemingly devious stare as water filled her eyes. I continued.

"Paying the price for what is right is something far beyond the ability of most to understand. Besides the price was the least of my worries because there was a trauma I had to submit myself to then experience that unattainable truth within myself, and look the other way as if nothing had ever happened."

"If you've suffered an injury let me call an ambulance." She said, tears flowing.

"Not necessary and stop the tears, I haven't hurt you, I'm just here to talk."

She wiped her face and nodded.

"...The one thing I've learned about myself is that I became a machine with the highest levels of apathy and no one's emotional deformities could break through the barrier that I chose to create."

"People have choices and whatever this barrier you created its forcing me to give up my choice. You don't have to do this." She stopped pleading and the tears evaporated but her tone though suggestive, was apparent that she was demanding me to leave.

"Too many people think their future is a decision they choose, they believe it is something no one can take away or that no one can change it for them but for the few, the rare minority who cannot escape that dark path, a path with an unseen outcome; beware, for not only can the unsuspecting who's future looks bright be changed; it can manifest into the one thing no one ever

thought to be possible."

"Manifest to what?" She whispered.

"When the truth is unveiled, power emerges, reasons forfeit rational behavior, and one begins to believe that it would be impractical to give it all up. I quickly learn that each time it happens; it is the only thing worth making the survival of the best desirable."

"Once again you're touching on my point, but not answering my question. What reasons caused you to come here?"

"Listen, it's what you do and though your insight is helpful right now I just need you to listen."

She nodded.

"...I know the source of true dominance and what means of authority can take it away. I know what it is like to feel the cold hard component opposite my face and wake up unafraid knowing the possibility of its uses and the harm it could inflict. I understand the fear it can strike into a man's soul and what causes satisfaction many believe to be real and the superficial conception of power one thinks he is experiencing when giving into its façade, when knowing the motives of its use is to terrorize the helpless by those less than brave.

...I have watched some cower and whimper before my very eyes as I gazed upon the one thing that has a fleeting moment of influence to stand between them and life itself as others defied their very own existence with meager thoughts leading them into hopeless efforts, giving reason to why they had fallen into the dominion of nothingness.

...I have learned to respect its presence and appreciate its beauty. I can manipulate the hand, which passes it from position

to position, and I marvel at the ability to open its chamber, clean its drum, and manage the device that one can deplete its source and replenish its needs. It allows me to choose at will to give or take away the possibilities of what many believe is a given gift that should be cherished more than what all the riches in the world can buy."

"Are you talking about…?"

I raised my hand to indicate she was interrupting and she remained quiet.

"Its many uses can assist or destroy and the dark round eye is as threatening as it seemingly gazes into the dark void of my own curiously piercing glare during the midnight hour which only drives the unconscious realms that has been created within this void being. All doubts wanting to surface and prevent my inevitable from taking its rightful place toward this quest was something I had to eradicate and use what I possessed to conform those who test my authority. I am to move forward and at best seek what passion that can never surface through the eyes of a silent walker who is destined to help fulfill an unspoken truth.

…I learned that the meaning was for me to stop those who try to prevent the inevitable when such objectives are more crucial than the few who were forcing me to cause their disappearance or more likely causing them to cease to exist. I found others to cross off their disruptive path that prevented the meek from finding a better way to sustain their existence. My training kept all deviants from interfering and made them submit to their fate when my true desire was hoping they too would follow a road less inviting of someone like me who was and still willing to show them the aftermath of adverse decisions made on their behalf.

...I have learned to admire the only power I have lies within my passionate heart, a heart that has been strengthened to achieve the unthinkable, a heart that will do things beyond my own thoughts and yet not far from my grasp which lives within its center. I have no regrets for a heart that although unforgiving in nature, is one that has not escaped my unconsciousness and reminds me all too often that still it is a heart that possesses the capacity for human desires. However, my decision cannot be moved, my quest must remain, and those in opposition of the path I must follow will only know that same heart as one to be as cold and dark as the depths of the ocean floor..."

MISSING SAMMY

Jake drove down the block. That was his name, Jake
McIntire. He stood five feet nine inches tall and weighed one
hundred and eighty five pounds. He had a solid build, was in good
shape with brown hair and brown eyes. He had a mustache as
thick as the bristles on a broom and it was black which didn't
match his hair color. He looked strange almost demented and the
scent from the aftershave he wore was so thick it was as though the
clouds from a cartoon came to life to fight the odor from raising
any further pushing it down causing it to linger right below the
nostrils of anyone within a few yards from him.

He wore suits that gave him the appearance of a stereotype
television pimp and the only thing missing from his attire was the
wide brim hat. The polyester pants with the bell-bottom legs and
the tight fitted jeans he wore that looked like a crow bar was in
need to peel them away along with his cocky attitude made it too
easy for us to ignore considering his last name when we secretly
nicknamed him Mackey.

Some of the other kids heard about the new teacher who was
going to be starting at our school that summer and that some of us
would get to meet him at that time because there were a few who
would have to endure summer school. I was one of the unlucky
ones and of course since our summer school teacher was pregnant
and thought to go into labor sometime during the summer session,
we were going to have to get used to another teacher for the

remainder of the term. I also had to endure the lack of a birthday party by the time it happened in August because my dad didn't show up, give my mom money for me, send any type of gift and with mom struggling to do her best but unable to do more; I turned eleven in summer school.

Mid August 1972, the school administration decided to give our teacher the time off and Mackey started right away. He had been introducing himself to some of the moms even though not every student was going to be attending during the summer. Some of the kids said that they knew of a man who had met Sammy and his mom but no one concerned themselves about the guy when we first heard of him and when Mackey did start teaching he told us that he would also be remaining with the school as one of our regular teachers throughout the year.

The first time I saw a glimpse of him was when the car passed by me after he called one of the kids over and I couldn't see who he was talking to. I was looking on from a distance as I was heading back after retrieving the ball to finish the game and when I reached everybody I saw Sammy pass by in the car with the man, no one else had actually met. At the time, no one figured he was the new teacher Sammy and his mom had met. Tommy was standing nearby when Sammy got in the car with Mackey.

"What's going on, why did Sammy get in the car with that guy?"

"Tell him Tommy." Eric encouraged.

"Well I guess that guy must be Sammy's relative or something because I heard him say that Sam's old lady had to go to the hospital and the ambulance was already at her house."

"So there goes our pitcher, huh."

During the summer of Mackey's first year at school seemed fine. What we didn't know at the time was that Mackey was with Sammy's mom when she had the accident. He was taking him to go see her and we didn't know that our new teacher had been making himself at home in their house since June. We had no idea that the man entrusted to watch over us was making up stories just to get Sammy to go with him to his own house and taking over in their lives as though he was Sammy's dad. What we did notice was that after it was clear to us that Mackey was the new teacher and not related to Sammy, how very different Sammy started acting towards us and in less than a month after Jake McIntire started teaching at our school, Sammy didn't want to hang out with us anymore. He always checked with Mackey before he came over to talk with us and then he would give us some excuse to have to hurry home.

One day early October 1972, Sammy saw me in the hallway at school and rushed me over to the door of the stairwell leading to the basement, he opened the door and we went inside to stand at the top of the stairway landing. He looked scared and kept looking around before saying anything to make sure no one was coming. It was dark on the staircase and the only light minimally coming through the window of the door was from the hallway.

"He's doing stuff to us John." He whispered.

"Who?"

"Mackey but it's not just me. He's doing stuff to my mom too but she won't say anything and she's different now. She doesn't seem like she's my mom anymore."

"What kind of stuff?" I knew the tone of my voice must have come across demanding but it seemed as though Sammy was

acting paranoid but he was looking bad.

"Something's happening to me and I can't stop this pounding in my head."

"You having another headache, what does your mom say about them?"

"Don't know!"

"You haven't told her, that's not good."

"He tells me I'm just whining and to take it like a man. That's what he always tells me when I tell him to stop."

"Stop what?"

"Look John Mackey ain't..." He paused, looking as though he didn't want to say anything more.

"You got something to say just say it or it can eat you alive Sammy, at least that's what mom always says." He went over to the door and looked through the window to make sure the coast was clear.

"Stay away from him John I've been down here with him before don't let him bring you down here. I don't know exactly how to tell you but he's doing stuff to my mom and she don't like it either and when he comes around the house she goes into her room and stays there because she knows he wants her to leave him alone with me. At first I didn't understand why she was leaving the room and then one day I learned why."

"Why Sammy?" My curiosity was peaked.

"It starts and mom doesn't come out until he leaves unless he calls her out to do stuff but I don't know what because that's when I'm sent to go to my room and most times I'm forced to leave the house. I can see how sad she is but she won't say anything to me about it and the weird thing is that he acts like he belongs there and

like he's her husband, I mean don't you think it's strange."

He looked to see the shadow of someone coming in our direction, opened the door, and took off running. He never said what it was he learned about Mackey. I looked out the window of the door into the hallway and then I heard a sound from the bottom of the stairs. I turned around and tried to see if I could see anything but decided not to stick around. I opened the door making sure whomever Sammy saw wasn't still coming. I didn't see anyone, stepped out, quietly closed the door and left.

A man stood at the bottom of the steps watching the door close behind the kid he now knew as John. He listened to the soft whimpering sounds in the background and faded away in the darkness.

GUARDIAN DEVIL

Soon after our conversation, we learned that Sammy was in the hospital and had lost a great deal of blood. Doctors were saying that they did not know what was happening to him and before Halloween 1972, Sammy was dead. Mackey told us stories about how Sammy was in need of help to deal with the fact that his dad was no longer in his life and said that he was a troubled kid. We were all very sad about his death and Mackey took advantage of our emotional state and continued telling us what he thought we wanted to hear to justify what had been happening with our friend. He was good at making us hear what he wanted us to believe and he even came up with a story good enough to satisfy our need to understand why Sammy went home immediately after school and didn't play with us anymore.

#

"Sammy's been going home to care for his mother because she needed him to be the man in the family and that's why he was skipping out when it came to hanging out with a lot of you here at the school."

#

Everything he said made sense and it affected us deeply. It was after Sammy's death and before Thanksgiving that I was destined to find out the things that happened to him and the truth about Mackey. At first, everybody liked him and he gave us no reason to suspect him of doing malicious things. He was smooth

with the female teachers, played softball with the students on the school grounds and even helped the janitor a few times with the trash while talking with him. He befriended everyone and it would have been hard especially for the kids to get any of the adults to believe an accusation as strong as the one that I was going to learn that would cause me to take action. He spent less than a full term at school getting to know who the kids were but he was selective when it came to being friendly with some of us. He found out the most intimate details about the kids he wanted to spend time with and figured out or manipulated others to get information on them. He watched us to see who played together and who was quiet.

I was a quiet kid just like Sammy and I did not try to be involved with much activity unless it was required to do so for gym class. Sometimes the teachers would be talking amongst themselves and then one of them would urge me to be more active and join in the games the kids were playing but I enjoyed spending most of the time I had during recess to myself. It wasn't easy being a kid and having your own individuality. It's the genetic make-up for being the target of harassment, which later I learned from Murphy leads to feelings of anger due to the torment of others. I understood that there was a lot of resentment inside of me but I coped by keeping to myself whenever I thought I would become a target for those who wanted to tease me.

Mackey was very observant and sometimes when others were not around; I got the feeling he was watching me. He always came at the right time to put a stop to others heckling me or to stop any adverse situations involving me. He always had a strange look on his face when he looked at me after coming over to stop the other kids from harassing me and his smile was creepy too but he

claimed he only wanted to make sure I was okay.

#

"John, it's okay if you don't want to play with the others and it doesn't give them the right to harass you because of it. You let me know if any of those guys are causing you to feel inadequate."

'Feel inadequate; what the hell does that mean?'

It was nice that he would get involved to stop the other kids from picking on me but the constant hand around the shoulders and the eerie smile was beginning to annoy me.

One time Mrs. Hawkes came over to me after noticing Mackey diverting some kids away from me.

"John, don't you think it's nice to have Mr. McIntire here to stop the bullies from harassing you so much, I mean it's like he's your guardian angel, don't you think."

"I guess. Mrs. Hawkes don't you think he smiles too much, I mean he always has this weird look on his face when he smiles at me."

"Mr. Chaney I should write you up and call your mother talking about poor Mr. McIntire like that, he's the only one that notices you enough to make sure no one bothers you, you should be ashamed of yourself talking about him like that, besides I think he has a wonderful smile. I wish I could wake up to a smile like that each morning."

I watched her for a few seconds as she went off into dreamland and I walked away wondering if she even noticed me leaving. It didn't matter to me what she said about him and although he always insisted that I let him know if the other guys bother me, I couldn't shake the uneasy feelings I had when he smiled at me, touched my arm and for some reason in addition to

that; patting me gently on my lower back. After the teachers started encouraging and more likely insisting me to join in the softball games as always I would try to bargain my way out to no avail because after much persuasion from them, I would end up listening to the roars or discouraging phrases from schoolmates when I ran out to the mound to find out what position I was playing.

#

...I noticed how things were changing because I think Mackey must have had a talk with the teachers because they weren't getting involved as much trying to encourage me to play. I thought it was as mom would say a blessing in disguise because sometimes the sounds of despair would be overbearing of how nobody wanted me to play to the point I just wanted to bury myself in the back of the school but if I had to I wouldn't give up especially when I didn't want to play. I would keep making the effort to prove I could learn the game and be one of the gang. Well, today and to no surprise to me, the consensus was that no one wanted me to play on their team but I noticed that Mackey was in the bleachers so everyone kept their opinions to themselves. I hated to think that in addition to being forced to play, the dirty looks from the other kids was because of him. The usual group of teachers didn't have to coax me to play this time because Mackey took care of everything. One of the kids was sick from something he ate and someone had to cover left field and because of Mackey once again I involuntarily volunteered. One of the guys hit the ball and it was sailing toward me. It should have been an easy catch but I didn't catch it in fact it went right between hand and glove and then continued to roll away from me. I ran and picked up the

ball and threw it as hard as I could to first base but I should have thrown it to second base and the fact that my throw was wild and off target made it easier for the runner to make it to home plate and the roar of disappointing screams was clear to me that not only did I miss catching the ball but I made the wrong play.

"Man, I knew we shouldn't let him play."

"Yeah, this sucks McIntire." One kid screamed.

"We're gonna lose the game because of him."

"I don't even know why they let him go to this school."

"Hey man, ignore those guys they probably wouldn't have caught it either." Another kid offered.

"Yeah whatever. Who are you, his mother?"

"Maybe she should teach him how to sew."

"He's the reason why we lost the last time he played."

The same kid that made the last remark threw down his glove and started running toward me. It was like lightning to see another figure come into my view as Mackey raced across the field, grabbed hold of the kid who was only a few feet away from me and ready to pulverize, by the shirt.

"Get off me!"

"Stop it!"

"Get off me!" The kid demanded.

"I said stop it, damn it!" Mackey insisted.

He jerked the kid's shirt collar.

"…If I have to tell you again."

He cut himself off because Mrs. Hawkes was making her way toward us fast.

"Behave yourself young man." She said.

Several of the other teachers came out to help calm things

down and later Mackey saw me in the hallway and called me over to him.

"Hey John, I think it would help you out if I showed you how to catch a fly ball. I've been studying the way you play and it's not good enough to be on the team with some of these guys. You know kids can be quite vicious if you don't know how to catch a ball or pitch or make a good call to force the other team out."

"Yeah, tell me about it. They always have some kind of problem with the way I play."

"Well let's see if we can get all that to change. You don't have to be afraid of the ball John, you have to attack it. It's no different than the things you want in life. You know what I mean." He said confidently and winked.

"I guess."

Mackey spent a week teaching me how to throw a ball and catch a high fly and some afternoons he would have me eat lunch on the way to the field to prevent losing time he wanted to spend with me in order to show me some eye to hand coordination techniques. He called out commands to help me make the correct play based on his simulated team and what plays he created to help me play better.

"John, you should always try to get the ball to the closest person on your team when faced with an uncertain decision and that way the pressure would be on the other guy and taken away from you."

"Oh, cool, I like that."

"Yeah but just remember that just because a teammate is close enough to get the ball, it might not be the right decision to throw it to him."

"Oh, great, it just seems like there's always this stuff you have to know and I can see the other guys doing it but sometimes it doesn't make sense to me."

"That's not altogether a problem John. You know some people don't have the talent to play sports. Maybe you have a hidden talent and should try to start developing your abilities in the arts. I teach piano lessons and if you want you can start learning to play and perhaps you'll find out that your talents within might be for you to become a great pianist perhaps one the world have yet to discover."

"Yeah everybody tells me that I might develop into one thing or another later on in life but what do I do until then." I whispered.

"How about I keep teaching you how to play ball and you develop your hidden talents as a pianist." He said.

I looked at him wondering why he had answered my question but left the matter to rest. It all seemed harmless enough and Mackey got in touch with my mom and convinced her to let him give me lessons for free in order to build up a clientele. Mom thought it was a good idea for me to see if there were other talents hidden inside of me and agreed to Mackey's offer. The moment he found out my father was no longer in our lives; he took every advantage to become more of a trusted friend to my mom. He told her that he was watching and listening to how the other kids were treating me and I could probably use more of a male role model in my life. He also said that he thought it would help me if I had someone to talk about the things that bothered me. If that wasn't enough, he started encouraging her to go out and he even suggested that she start dating. He seemed to genuinely care about her well-being and mine so there was never any reason to doubt his

motives when he suggested that I should stay at his studio learning the piano in order for her to go out and have fun. It was all too good to be true but it was free, it's just that I found out that the price was an unspeakable amount more than any dollar could have paid and the damage, irrevocable.

Mom thought Mackey's decision was good when he suggested that she should get out more and she took his advice and started to go out occasionally. At first, she would pick me up two hours after school ended so by 6:00pm we were back together. It wasn't altogether horrible as I thought it would be because Mackey never let any of the other kids notice that he was giving me a ride from school to go with him to his studio. I guess mom wasn't used to going out much and so she would come to pick me up early because she would only treat herself to a matinee or just spend some time shopping. I don't know what came over the woman because she started coming to get me as late as 8:00 o'clock at night. It wasn't often that she would go out or stay that late but occasionally she wanted to stay out to treat herself and a few times she actually went out on a date. I think the defining moment my mother decided she wouldn't go out on dates as much as she thought she might was when she was invited to double date with one of her friends. Mom wanted to go and she deserved it and although I wasn't' happy about spending more time with Mackey, I wanted her to be happy because it was a long time since she had actually had the chance to go out and truly enjoy herself for her birthday.

The problem I was facing was that I was learning about the things Sammy was talking about when he said Mackey was doing stuff. When he first started teaching me to play the piano, things

were normal but when he saw that mom was taking him up on his advice, he would excuse himself to go to the bathroom and then return with his zipper open. He would shift his body next to mine on the piano bench causing our thighs to touch claiming he wanted to show me how to do something he was teaching me to play. At first it was just the zipper and the close sitting but sometimes he would leave the room and return and his zipper was still down but his underwear would be showing with his manhood pushing through the opening of his pants. He actually started changing his clothes from the pants or jeans he was wearing when my mom dropped me off and started giving him an approximate time to when she would pick me up which he encouraged at every chance.

I overlooked a lot of the things he did and concentrated on learning to play the lessons he had for me to learn but the more I concentrated on what I was there to do the more I became distracted. He started using an excuse to go into the other room at his studio and tell me to keep practicing because he was going to do some work to prepare for class or whatever else he came up with to leave the room and then return in sweatpants making sure I could see the protrusion in his pants. When he realized I wouldn't pay attention to the things he was doing, he started watching movies and turning up the sound. I wasn't exactly sure what was going on at first but then one day I got up to look to see him with his back to me in the room watching naked people engrossed into one another. When I saw what he was doing, I started to close the door but when I reached to grab hold of the doorknob, he turned and looked me right in the eyes.

"Caught you."

I was startled and frightened as if I had done something

wrong and when I backed away, I left the door opened, went back to my seat, and began playing the piano.

"Hey John."

"Y-Yeah."

My voice was trembling.

"Maybe you should have just stayed in the room playing the piano, you probably shouldn't be sneaking around to try to spy on adults when I clearly gave you the lesson you were suppose to be practicing. Now what am I going to tell your mother about all of this."

I jumped up and went to the door. He was fully dressed.

"No! Wait, you can't tell her, I didn't do anything, I mean, I didn't see anything please you have to believe me, I was just closing the door, I just got there honest, I didn't see anything."

"You sure about that?"

"Yeah!"

"I don't know it looks to me that you caught an eye full." He gently manhandled his crotch when he spoke.

"…I tell you what, you don't say anything and I won't have to tell about you spying, deal." He winked and grabbed himself again.

"Y-Yeah , I mean because I was just closing…"

He cut me off by raising his hand and shaking his head. I began to feel uneasy more and more when I was around him after he caught me watching at the door. I wasn't sure if he was going to tell on me. I kept trying to convince myself I didn't do anything wrong but it didn't matter I felt as though I was trapped. I didn't want to continue with the lessons but I didn't know what I would say to my mom besides I was the one who stopped playing the

piano to go to the door. I was terrified after that and my next lesson made me so nervous I thought I would vomit.

He sat next to me and I thought he would touch me or make me touch him but he started asking me questions about what I heard while he was watching the movies. I was more uncomfortable with his presence than his questions and when he wanted to know if I enjoyed watching him, I licked my lips involuntarily out of fear and not knowing what to say. He made a move that surprised the hell out of me and made me fall off the piano bench and hit my head, which ultimately stopped him from making his advance.

"John, John are you alright, here take my hand, what happened, how did you fall off the bench?"

He knew what made me fall because I wouldn't have moved at all if he had not…he must have thought I was interested, that's the only thing I could think of as to why he stood up, reached inside his pants, removed his swollen flesh, and tried to push it onto my lips.

"Ha ha ha, what did you think I was serious, come on John it was a joke, we both know you're an alright kid. Hey look I didn't tell on you right and this was just kids play that's all, nothing to it, right? I mean you know the guys at school already tease you, you wouldn't want them to think you're some kind of pansy, would you. It's a guy thing, don't overreact, okay, it's nothing."

He made sure I was alright and when I tried to be the cool guy and laugh it off with him, he could see I was about to have a nervous breakdown. He kept playing it off with different situations he recalled being in camp and the male bonding games that the guys did but he said that nobody ever tried to hurt the other

one. He didn't make any approaches or ask me anything for a couple of weeks after that but he must have thought I was back to my old self again because he began to probe me for information about the movie I saw him watching and told me it was normal to like those kinds of movies. I never answered his questions and he kept on asking me about the other types of things, I saw and if I liked it. He said that it was evident how much I enjoyed watching what he was doing.

"Why would you say that, I didn't…"

Again, he raised a hand to stop me from continuing.

"You're lying."

I froze, staring at him thinking he had caught me in a lie.

"…You know, I'm glad you want to deny seeing anything. It's a good thing, to keep something like this to yourself just goes to show you how cool you really are and how the other guys got you all wrong. You know, I knew you were at the door when you got there, I just wanted to see how long you would watch but I didn't expect you to want to shut me out when you tried to close the door. I just wanted to test you, you know because pals like to see how each other react to stuff like that and if the guy can keep a secret, you know like you, John, that's the true mark of a real cool guy."

At the time I didn't know he had deliberately made sure I saw him shift his body a couple of times so I could see his shoulders moving in an up and down motion or that he purposely positioned himself in a way so I could see that his hand was down inside his pants. Everything was a set up and I'm sure he was hoping that my curiosity would peak to the point that I would try to see what was going on in the room. My fault was that I let curiosity take

over and now I am paying the price for it.

He repeatedly asked me if whether or not I liked what I saw in the movie and my silence seemed to fuel him more because he kept trying to assure me it was harmless. He went as far to tell me that he could even show me in person, how men go about doing necessary things to themselves when they don't get dates with women and that again it was okay and that it was something I would grow up doing.

"You know, John I'm not the enemy. You don't have to be afraid of me. You will learn that this is normal and you will grow up doing this sort of thing all the time when your dates leave you wanting."

"Wanting what?" I was mad at myself for asking that but he just looked at me.

"I bet your dad have movies like the ones you saw me watching but I'm thinking you never caught him so he probably have a stash hidden away somewhere."

"My dad is gone."

"Yeah, I know, but when he was at home with you he probably had them but he was just clever enough to keep it from you and your mom."

He even asked me if I had ever seen a grown man naked and continued to explain how guys liked to touch themselves for fun. He went back into the other room and I thought at last I could go back to concentrating on the piano lesson but his motives weren't that pure.

"Hey John, why don't you stop all that racket in there and come in here with me."

I didn't move.

"John, get in here I got some more lessons for you to take out to the piano." He bellowed.

I got up and went inside the room where he was sitting. "Go sit over there on the chair and watch me while I sit on the couch." He ordered.

I sat on the chair and watched nervously as he reached down in his pants again and pulled himself out and exposed what he had but this time he started to play with himself. He ordered me to keep watching so I could see the release of the substance escaping his body from his private part. After that, I always felt strange, enraged when I was around him and he kept watching me at school but it felt more like he wanted something from me and that he wasn't worried if I would tell on him. He went about things in a normal fashion when other people were around and I thought that perhaps he was right about me being paranoid when some of the kids at school told me what they thought about what happened at the studio between Mackey and me.

PEERS APPROVAL

I was sure trouble was about to start when I saw some of the guys who never wanted me in their games coming toward me during recess and as usual, Mackey was lurking around. Mixed emotions flooded through me; do I call out to the guy who tried to shove his manhood into my mouth or do I let the kids pummel me. I decided that because he was there and I didn't want to call him to make him think I would rely on him for anything that if they did want trouble it would only be a short beating.

I stood determined to face what was going to happen unaware where the strength or stupidity came from and when they got right in my face, my vote was stupidity. I was scared shitless. They circled around me and each patted me on the back.

"Man, I didn't know you were like that, John. We all got to hang out some time."

"Yeah, good job, man." Another kid said.

"Wow, I'm shocked." A different kid added.

"Yeaaah, that is so cool."

I was confused.

"What are you guys talking about?"

They all laughed.

"Oh, right we got to keep quiet about it." One kid said.

"Yeah, right but Mackey told us what happened at the studio. Didn't think you had it in you."

"What? He told you!" Now I was shocked.

"Yeah, it's no big deal. We do it all the time."

"You do?"

"Yeah that's how we learn about girls. We get right in there and smell them when we're up close or gently press up against them."

I opened my eyes so wide to what I was hearing I thought they would pop out. They knew what had happened and they did it all the time. Some of them began elaborating with certain gestures as each of them took a turn telling me about the girls they liked and what they wanted to do to them and how they enjoyed smelling their scent when they hung out with them. Everything they were saying was normal but different from what I had experienced and the more they talked the more I realized nothing like what they were saying happened at the studio. One thing I thought was right when they told me that what we were talking about and the things at Mackey's studio should remain between the guys because parents didn't understand and other adults would probably freak out too. I also told myself to make a mental note to stay away from a bunch of perverts who thought I was cool because Mackey wanted me to touch his privates.

Mom's voice kept coming up inside telling me that I should listen to my inner voice, another one of her phrases but this was one phrase I decided to keep on high alert. I was never like most of the guys at school or in my neighborhood and I wasn't going to start to try to be like them now especially if I was suppose to sit around and learn how to be a guy by watching other guys play with themselves. Another troubling thought came to me while the guys were talking. I kept thinking about Sammy telling me that I shouldn't be around Mackey if it wasn't necessary the problem is

that it had become necessary because it was all for my mom that he would be watching me. She was very happy when she expressed how lucky we were to have someone in a respectable position to offer to help us out the way he was doing and I wasn't going to disappoint her when it came time for her to go out for her birthday.

I kept hearing Sammy's voice but mom was more important and she needed me to stay with Mackey in order to go out with her friend. Shirley was nice and very energetic and she convinced mom to go out on the town. She came to our house with the two guys they were dating for the evening and Mackey came over to watch me until she got back. I wasn't happy about the arrangement but I couldn't spoil her evening. She deserved one especially after all she had been through with my dad and my Aunt Felicia. I wanted to do all that I could for her because she deserved so much more than just working at a fancy hotel for low wages cleaning up behind other people.

Sometimes when things were rough, she had to take a second job. I was fortunate Mackey was on his best behavior that night. I was becoming more confused about his actions and thought that maybe all the guys were right. I told myself that I was making myself paranoid because of Sammy's words but still the one thing that continued to haunt me about it all was that even if Sammy was also paranoid, there was still an eerie fact about the whole thing. Mackey was befriending my mom as Sammy said he had done with his mom. Mackey was doing stuff and it was now evident about what that stuff was even though Sammy never spoke the words and no matter what I convince myself to believe, the undeniable truth is after spending time with Mackey, my friend Sammy is dead.

MACKEY'S LIE REVEALED

Mom came home looking depressed, she thanked Mackey for watching me and offered to pay him but he told her to consider it as her birthday gift. She told us that Shirley ended up ditching her and she was with a guy who had enough money to buy two six packs of beer for him to drink and hang out in the park with his friends.

"I can't believe she actually left me with this dead beat. He expected me to pay for dinner for him because he didn't have any money which I had no choice because we already had our food. Then he takes me to a park to hang out with his friends and expected me to buy their beer."

"I'm sorry that had to happen to you Clara." Mackey expressed.

"Yeah, me too and to top it off he said I was the one complaining because I suggested that I didn't want to stay in a park while he reminisce about his glory days when he was a big man on campus with his friends."

"Well, there's always next year and for what it's worth Happy Birthday." Mackey said enthusiastically.

"Thank you, Jake that's very kind of you and thanks again for staying with John."

"Anytime, see you at school, John."

"Yeah, ok." I said, hesitantly.

Mackey left and mom expressed how disappointed she was in

Shirley but knew she shouldn't hold her responsible for what happened. It was the right thing to do to accept Shirley's apology along with some flowers after she had been trying to reach mom for over a week with no success. Shirley explained in the note that came with the bouquet that she wasn't trying to ditch her for the hell of it but had an opportunity to go with her date and was hoping she was going to have the same great experience she had. I was glad mom didn't hold a grudge after that because she knew Shirley had always been a good friend to us for years. I wasn't happy about her having had a bad date on her birthday but it left me feeling good knowing that she wasn't going to be leaving me alone for too long with Jake McIntire anytime soon but I still had to endure the time spent with him during the piano lessons. A week later Mackey gave mom enough money to pay for her birthday disaster and bought her a bouquet of flowers.

She was convinced he was a man who was respectable and trustworthy. I couldn't be the one to tell her of all the things he did especially since he was so good to her and though I wasn't sure, what was going on in his head and what motives he had for her or me I paid close attention to how she reacted when he was around. I didn't forget Sammy's warning that Mackey was doing things to his mom to make her sad but at the time, mom was very happy with him and though he wasn't forcing me to do anything, I couldn't let what he was doing continue.

I thought Mackey told the other kids the truth about what he was doing but later I found out that he made up a story about me and some girl he claimed was learning to play the piano and how he caught us making out. He lied, which made me wonder what his intentions were to go so far to conjure up a story. He kept his

movies and actions of what he liked to do away from me for three of the sessions after mom's birthday but I was unwittingly his target. He wanted to make sure I wasn't aware of his next move when he came out of the bathroom naked. I continue to suffer from the constant nightmares of the endless torture that did not stop from all the things that he was doing to me and with every waking moment of haunting anguish, a tear fell endlessly submersing me under the torrent rush of eternal pain when I would awake during the late night hours as I remembered what he did.

This time he walked up behind me. I could smell his aftershave as he spoke in my ear while pulling me closer to his body and I felt the protrusion up against me.

"It really hurts, you know." He whispered. I didn't know what to say, I couldn't say anything. I had no idea what he was planning to do to me.

"…Let's pretend you are my private nurse which is why you can take care of my private part." He laughed. "Come and put me to bed in the next room." He breathed hauntingly.

"M-maybe you should c-call a doctor." He laughed and then he rubbed his face up against mine moving his lips closer to my ear.

"No need for a doctor while you're standing right here ready to supply me with what I need."

His naked body trembled against me and then he took hold of my arm and asked me to touch him between his legs as he pulled my hand closer to his hardened flesh. I tried to fight him off but he was too strong pulling me in toward him forcing me to grab hold of him. No matter how much I kept struggling to break free, it was no use he was much stronger and he would easily hold me close to

him and take me down to the floor and roll on top of me.

He made sure I was face down and he put my arms over my head, held them there with one hand, and strip my clothes off with the other. He moved so quickly switching the use of his hands it almost seemed as though he had more than two. He shoved himself inside of me while forcing my head into a pillow so I could not scream aloud. As he forced himself in and out of me, I could feel the inside of my body split apart. He spoke softly into my ear and told me how much I was going to help him to feel better. All I could do was cry into the pillow from the increased pain I was feeling as he gyrated himself in and out.

He would stop only to tease me and when I thought he would be pulling himself out, he would stop himself from removing it out completely only to reenter inside of me forcing it to go deeper while he continued to grow wider as he breathed heavily in my ear. I can still smell the odor of his cheap after-shave lotion and the roughness on the side of his face in need of a shave as he brushed up against mine. What seemed to be an eternity would finally end as his breathing began to increase. The sounds grew louder in my ear than when he first started and the intensity of the pain within grew until I could feel intervals of a wet substance enter inside my bottom and his gyrating motions became less and less until he had stopped moving completely and lay on top of me motionless.

His hardened flesh subsided and then he pulled out the entirety of what was left of his erection but he continued to take heavy deep breaths while remaining on top. His entire body and mine were wet and cold. I could feel the sticky substance inside of me, it felt disgusting, and when he decided he was through with me, he got up and told me to pull my pants up. Every part of my

body was wet from the back of my neck to the bottom corner of my ankles and inside I could feel the thick mass of fluid move as I moved to get dress. I quickly ran into the bathroom with my clothes to release into the toilet what was ready to escape from within me. It felt like it was ready to rush out of me without any regard to my ability to control the mass amount of fecal matter wanting to part from within my system. Streams of tears fell upon my cheeks as my hand wipes them away. He tells me to hurry up and his voice is cold and apathetic when he speaks because he is no longer concerned for my well-being, as he had pretended all this time. He was only concerned with his own pleasures, which he had achieved, and I was no longer of any use to him until the next time. Finally mom came to get me and Mackey offered us a ride home. I'm sure I was in shock. I kept quiet, went to my room and softly cried until sleep was the savior of the night.

FIRST LOVE/TRUE LOVE

June 1973, Sara's parents wanted to get her started in school right away after they had moved close to my neighborhood. It was a year after Mackey arrived, and it was rough because I was missing my friend Sammy and Mackey was invading his life into ours. By the time, the New Year rolled in I found out that I would have to go to summer school again. Two years in a row only this time, it was because of the things that were disturbing me why I did not keep up the grades expected. I didn't like school very much and to be facing a reality of summer school wasn't something I thought I would enjoy.

The building itself had no life to its stature. It was a tall four story high square in diameter structure with bars over the windows. The bricks were old and had a dusty orange color that at one time was red and they were chipping all over the building and falling down onto the property. A black gate imprisons the place when it is not open during the weekends and holidays and it appears to want to trap anyone going pass them to lock them inside the gated bars. It always looks deserted even when the building is full of students and the walls inside are bland; painted dull cement gray. They wouldn't speak to a medium if the soul of someone murdered were stuck behind them. It was usually cold during the winter seasons and excruciatingly humid during the late spring as the weather reached its peak closing in toward the summer days and on top of it all, I had to face the fact that I would be there during the entire year with perhaps a couple of weeks total as a vacation.

I had to spend twelve weeks there and that's where we met. I was about to have the summer of a lifetime and a lifetime of change that I was not prepared for and I could not ignore.

She was walking down the hall on her way to class and I was on my way to mine when our eyes met and there was an immediate attraction, silently we knew we wanted to hang out with each other. Sara Plimkin was her name and she wore glasses and had the most beautiful smile. Anyone could tell that she was going to be a model with or without the glasses; at least that was what I was able to see when I looked at her. I was not sure of her attraction to me because no other girl at school liked me except those who considered me a friend. Even they did not associate themselves with me but still they were kind enough to say hello and didn't fall into the group of merciless teasers.

Sara and I met at lunch and I told her how I would hear about the girls saying they thought I was too skinny but that although modest in my appearance I had to admit, I was cute. She thought I was charming and it opened the floodgates to the first of many discussions. However our ethnic difference was never an issue between us. In those days, a black man dating a white woman or the other way around was problematic enough for the adults but we, as kids never thought that we would have to concern ourselves with the issues of the world. We didn't think of it as being a time where segregation was something people thought was a thing that should remain active. We didn't let our ethnicity hinder us by the same theories most engaged in by holding on to anger toward another human being for the ridiculous reasons of having a different skin color. Although silently people were not satisfied with a lot of different political and personal decisions made in their

lives, there was the satisfaction of knowing there were those fighting the peaceful war to change such issues and teach people to accept human beings of all color. Still some people carried their personal phobias and the stigma of embarrassment was not something anybody wanted hanging over their heads. People didn't talk about many things while I was growing up and many things were in the minds of others as a forbidden topic.

"Why do people hate so much and separate themselves from one another, John?"

"I don't actually know but I was told by some very old men who sleep here in the park and drink their nightly dinner of 'Night Train' that no one wanted to have to face the fact that bad things were happening in their own families. Sometimes people needed an outlet and blaming their problems on others whose skin color was different from their own was a way of releasing their frustration."

"I guess a lot of people from our culture suffered from the hate of others."

"Yeah, and sometimes that hate was amongst ourselves and we ended up destroying each other because of it. Did you say our culture?"

"Yeah, I'm part Black too but no one can tell because of my skin color."

"Oh, okay, doesn't matter to me!"

"I know John I think that's why we met and just like we don't care about the difference of our skin color and get along with each other, there are things in life people do to hurt others and it doesn't stop them even though the skin color is the same of the ones their hurting either."

We knew that racial issues wasn't the only type of suffering going on in the world and Sara's life was no different because she was mixed, having a black, white and Indian background from her mother's side of the family and French white descendant on her father's side. She had a light complexion and thought to be white by many but she never tried to lie or hide her heritage and she wasn't prone to having an antidote because of her light complexion especially by those who knew of her true heritage. She and many other girls suffered the same ordeal and in some scenarios so did the boys. This was something we began to discover during our time together.

We quickly began discussing things in our lives that were supposed to be a secret and beyond our years. We didn't know it but we were making a clear statement that there should be nothing known as a color barrier between two people that would keep them from being together.

We simply had a way of knowing that we could trust one another and we had a unique unspoken ability to tap into each other in such a way that it ultimately became our talent to help each other out when things were stressful. We studied together and learned that history taught us about the different tragedies in people's lives during their hard times and the studies of current events proved to be just as resourceful in sharing the troubles people suffered in our own time. The two of us believed that as the younger generation, it was our obligation to stay in school and perhaps one day we would become the voice to help change the way people treated each other or at least become the type of professionals in order to help those within our own generation to get over past hurts and problems.

Our goal was to conquer the problems of the world by helping others get out of their tragedies but first we had to deal with the unknown truth that we needed to find a way to help ourselves because there was much that we had endured. It was in a very short time we did just that for each other.

FIRST DATE

Sara and I didn't pay much attention to the kids who snickered or the teachers who looked on with disapproving eyes because we were happy and some teachers smiled while talking to each other calling it puppy love. No mattered what the consensus, we chose to be together and we did not let anyone discourage us because we knew we were there for each other for life. Sometimes we secretly held hands and contagiously we enjoyed sneaking a look at each other when the teachers who did not approve were around and looking to see if we were ogling one another but most times we settled with giving each other a smile as we walked the hallways when we were on our way to our next class.

We spent lunches together and at recess, we were inseparable. We laughed about having to go to recess during summer school because we only had one class left after it was over. The teachers claimed they had to follow a certain format and that it would be against the law not to take some form of a break even though the day was not as long of a day as it was during the regular school year. Summer school was out by 3:15 in the afternoon but sometimes the teacher would let us out fifteen minutes earlier. One day we decided we were going to meet every day in the park after school and talk. She thought it best to get permission from our parents to stay longer to hang out in order to prevent her parents picking her up too early. We told the same story that we just wanted to hang out with our friends but neither of us gave in depth details because we wanted to keep what time we had with

each other a secret but the secret did not keep for very long. I started dressing up for school on a regular basis but the day I went to school in my plaid shirt and polyester suit with platform shoes, was our first official date. I think I had on every color on the chart. Mom suspected I was up to something and decided to show up at school that same day. I saw her leaving the area before recess was over and knew she knew why I was dressing up daily but she never brought it to my attention that she had spied on me and was aware of Sara's existence. She treated me with dignity and respected my privacy at least to the point where she didn't tell my dad or aunt and I pretended that I had not known she came to see why I was dressing up to go to summer school.

In hindsight I probably looked like a clown lost from the circus but it didn't matter to me even when others pointed and laughed and some told me that I looked nice but they still snickered. Lisa said that I did look nice but it wasn't the right time of the year for what I was wearing. She also admitted that she knew the reason why I was dressing so nicely and said it was admirable that I thought highly enough of someone to put myself through the torture of sweating all day like a pig for someone I liked.

'Lisa's been talking to my mom or her mom's been talking to my mom or how else would she know about the phrase sweating like a pig.'

I shrugged my shoulders.

"Thanks for not making fun of me."

"No, I'll still make fun of you, you just won't hear it." She said smiling, winked and walked away.

I smiled at her remark and went on about my day. Lisa was

right about the torture, I was hot but it didn't matter because I wanted to hear what Sara had to say and when we saw each other in the hallway as we were passing each other to go to our next class we smiled as usual. I was a little disappointed that she didn't stop me to tell me what she thought of the way I looked, I guess it wasn't the right time but when we sat together at lunch she told me she thought I looked handsome.

My smile was bigger than I thought possible and my expression came across with pure satisfaction that I had made the right choice. We both agreed the day before that we were going to skip eating lunch in order to share lunch privately when we were to meet later for our date.

I took Sara out to the school park after our last class and we had our very own private luncheon. I brought sodas and chips, four sandwiches each because I didn't know how much she would eat. It wasn't easy but with a little pleading and agreeing to take on an extra chore over the weekend, I even got my mom to help me make the potato salad she used to coach me in making when the holidays came around. She said there was no way she was going to make a small amount of potato salad just for me when we could have enough for the week and after peeling what seemed to be about a hundred potatoes, I finally had the dish I eagerly wanted to share with Sara.

I was not the only one prepared for our picnic Sara also brought plenty of food for us to eat. She was smart and had a picnic blanket and some potato chips, cupcakes, sodas, two pieces of apple pie and some hot dogs. It looked like we had enough food for the whole school. It was a success and the time passed quicker than we both had wanted and her parents were due to pick her up

by 4:30 and that gave us an hour and fifteen minutes after our regular school session was out but I was counting on us leaving the fifteen minutes earlier. I learned that things do not always work out and instead of letting us out early we got a surprise quiz and ended up leaving 15 minutes later than normal. After our quiz, it gave us only an hour but then we had to pick the spot, set up the area, place the food and actually eat. My hopes of an hour and a half changed to about 45 minutes but then we cleaned up five minutes early so that her parents would not have to look for her when they arrived. I thought it was the greatest 45 minutes of my life because we were still together during the clean up and to me no one else in the world existed.

When the time came, we walked out to the front where her parents saw and greeted me politely as her mother smiled warmly, her father tried not to let us know he was aware of our attraction and that he was not pleased. He grunted in a parental gruff kind of way as he moved his daughter along into the car so they could be on their way. The car pulled away, I started toward home and from the remarks, I heard from those passing by in their cars, I must have been smiling the size of the Hudson River.

I was sure they were right and I could not remove the incessant grin plastered on my face nor was I going to try although I was trying not to smile as evidently as I walked down the streets so that people would not notice my internal joy. I gave up because I could not stop myself for I was very much in love with Sara, Sara, Sara Plimkin and her name was all I could say when I opened my mouth. I wanted to convince myself I only thought she was nice and I liked her as a friend and nothing more but Sara plimkin, was smart, independent, and I could see that her eyes sparkled like

the stars above through the glasses she was so conscientious about having to wear. The only thing I noticed was that she was the most beautiful girl in the school and everyone had a right to be jealous of her and of me because she was mine.

She wasn't in school long before I became aware of some of the other girls teasing her for being awkward and clumsy but I knew she wasn't those things, and if that wasn't making her nervous enough if she occasionally had a misstep, it was because of the other girls who were purposely knocking her books out of her hand. They enjoyed tripping her when she walked by or deliberately bumping into her then screaming at her to be more careful. It was because of these things they did to her to be the main reason why she kept to herself. It seemed to others as though she was clumsy but the reality of it was that the other girls were forcing her to feel self-conscious about what she was wearing or about her looks. Sometimes she would involuntarily trip when she noticed the other girls standing around pointing at her but I knew the truth.

I saw her for the most beautiful and kind hearted person any of us had ever known. I knew their reasons were unjust against her and it was probably because one of the greatest things about her was the fact that she had independence and a high regard for the educational system. The sad part of it all was that none of the other girls ever wanted to give her a chance and decided who and what she was to them because she was new, quiet and different.

They were all cruel to her except for Lisa, Val and Roxy, her two girlfriends. They did not befriend Sara but they were not cruel to her either. One day when Lisa was walking in the halls and saw some of the girls picking on her; she walked over, took Sara by the

arm and escorted her out of their line of attack and then she went on about her business. Lisa may not have considered herself Sara's friend but she did not let the other girls get away with their cruelty. The girls did not like it when Lisa got involved because she was tough and though she knew they whispered about her too, they made sure they did it when she was not around because two girls at school had already been in a fight with her and they were not looking for a rematch.

I wanted to be the one person Sara could escape to without fear and when she was with me, she knew I was not going to judge her. We continued to meet for lunch, recess and after school every day during the summer and each time she would bring me something to eat. I also enjoyed bringing food for her, especially sweets and I thought it was intimate when we would share our deserts, feeding each other and sometimes purposely making the other miss a bite so the desert would go on our chin or the side cheek of our face. We did it for fun and then would tell each other what was going to be for lunch the next day and how the other should have a bib in case we could not find our mouth. One month of school went by fast and we laughed a lot and had the perfect romance but we only had eight weeks left and then our grade school romance was going to end. We would rekindle what we had back in September because Sara was leaving for Disneyland with her family to enjoy a two week vacation before school started again. I did not want to think on it but when I did, I reassured myself knowing I would be with her after Labor Day and to celebrate with her on her birthday in October. I tried to make her think I had something exciting to do so I told her I was also going to go on vacation.

"My mom and I are going to see my family some place great because we can take the train that takes you all over the place maybe even the world."

"Oh, really John, and does this train of yours have a name? The one that takes people all over the world."

"Now Sara how can you ask me that? Sure it does, well, I don't exactly know what they call it or if it can actually go all over the world but it can take you a lot of places."

"Come on John, there's no train to take you all over the world. My dad travels all the time and lots of times he takes me with him and we haven't been on this train of yours."

"Well it's not my train Sara but it's real."

She gave a seemingly knowing look.

"So where are you really going?"

I tried to keep up the charade until finally I had to confess where I was actually going to be for the rest of the summer and thought to myself that if I were lucky I would get to go to Coney Island.

"Okay, okay you got me, we might have been going to my Aunt Felicia's but mom says we can't go there because…well this year we're just staying home."

"I figured it was something like that otherwise you would have known if you were going to be taking Amtrak which is the train that takes you many places within the United States. You're such a little sneak."

"Yeah I guess, but it was just teasing, you know that right?"

"Of course I do John. So why can't you go to your aunt's house?"

"I don't know." I said shrugging my shoulders.

"Maybe you'll get to go to Coney Island."

Sheepishly I agreed and the two of us laughed.

"I think it's great you're going to get to go to Disneyland. Wow, I wish I was going there but we can't, well, in the past my mom always wanted to stay and visit her sister."

"I think that's great John. I wish I had an aunt I could go visit and maybe I would have someone I could talk to sometimes."

"What about your mom, you can talk to her right?"

"Can I tell you something?"

"Sure!"

"No John, I mean really talk to you and you talk to me. I mean I know you probably don't think you can trust me, which is why you don't want to talk about why you're not going to your aunt's house. I feel I can trust you John, and we have to be honest with each other okay, that way we will be able to face anything together."

"Okay, whatever you want and Sara it's not true that I don't think I can trust you, I just feel why should I burden you with boring family problems that's all."

Sara started the conversation and we talked about everything. We were able to get through the next two weeks pouring out of us everything we could think of and there was a lot said and more to come. We continued to spend our time with each other and said things neither one of us ever should have known, but we continued confiding in each other in ways we were too young to understand. We didn't know just how scary the things going on in our lives were or at least in Sara's case it was still part of her nightmare.

The two of us knew how close we were becoming, the discussions we engaged were in depth and quickly reached a point

beyond turning back, it was a realization for the both of us, and we understood the fact that we truly were soul mates.

TRUST

I was deeply saddened as Sara silently wept when she explained how she repeatedly did things for her dad's clients. She said there were times her mom was too busy and she was to fill in for the long moments in between sessions. She explained in detail that her dad told her how he thought it would be best if he could use her for little things when her mom was occupied and of all the things she had to do for the men that came over to her house.

"It was all because of my dad. He said it was okay and no one had to know as long as no one was being mean to me. He said I had nothing to worry about because he would be there to protect me. Everything was a game to him and he acted as if he enjoyed playing it. He had to know that he too was hurting me, is hurting me," She continued.

"…Each time he did it he said let's do something we've never done then he would continue to do the things he had me do for him in the past. Sometimes before he continued I would tell him that we did it already and he would say pretend we've never done this before. He kept doing the things he wanted to do, then I would hear him laugh about the stuff he did to me to some of the other men while making deals with them so they could take pleasure in fulfilling their needs.

…I wanted to say something to make it all stop but I didn't know how to tell anyone and I felt as though my mom didn't seem to care. The scariest thing of it all is that he knows what he is doing is wrong and that's why he never wanted me to talk about it

with anyone.

...I don't know why I'm telling you all of this but you have to swear to me that no one and I mean no one will ever know what I am telling you John, swear it!" She cried.

"I promise Sara I won't tell a soul. You can tell me whatever you want and no matter what happens I will never tell anybody about what we talk about for as long as I live, I promise."

I looked at her with tears in my eyes, we assured each other we could tell one another anything, and it would remain between the two of us always. It became more shattering to hear what she had to say but I managed to keep my composure and brave through what she needed to get off her mind.

"The things he wanted me to do for him and the different things he enjoyed doing with me wasn't normal and I didn't think it would ever end. He had more than one way of wanting to do the same thing and he just kept doing them over and over again no matter how much pain it caused me or how difficult it was for him to perform the act."

"That's not right Sara, our body is too...I mean your body is too young for that kind of stuff and besides he's your dad. He should be made to pay for what he did to you."

"Oh, John no, I can't bear to think what life would be like without my parents."

She looked deep into my eyes and I could see that despite what her dad did to her he could not strip away her soulful innocence.

"...Please tell me you do understand." She cried. I reached out and she allowed me to hug her letting her know I was her friend and was willing to continue to share with her and keep all

her secrets to myself, as I knew she would keep mine.

"No matter what happens Sara we will be friends forever and I will always understand anything you do or anything you say, no matter what, I will always be there for you."

"I trust you John and I'm glad we're friends."

She wanted to say more but could only weep. We went our separate ways only this time before she got into the car I was staring at her dad with contempt in my eyes. He stopped, gave me an odd look then hurried Sara into the car and pulled away. I went home thinking about the things she told me and I shared her pain. Sometimes late at night I shiver in my bed at the thought of the different experiences she had to endure and I was at a loss at how anyone could have survived what had taken place.

We met in our spot under the tree the next day and from that day on the stories became more intense and I could not believe I was hearing the things she was telling me. It was disturbing that she did not have her own mother to defend her. I had a vivid image that her mother was ignoring what was happening to her. We shared a long silence but it was more because we were draining high levels of emotions causing ourselves to the brink of exhaustion due to the discussions extracted from the memory of our young minds. She looked directly into my eyes.

"I used to go to bed terrified of being touched during the night and unconsciously I had no idea the things happening to me was connected to all the things that started happening but I couldn't control myself.

…I became something so embarrassing I thought I would kill myself if my dad ever told anybody at school and that was also one of the things he used against me to get me to do what he wanted."

Sara leaned into me and whispered.

"...I was wetting my bed at night. I knew something was wrong with me because I would dream about being on the toilet but I would awaken in my own urine. I always bathed at night before I went to bed and then I would wake up the next morning and my bed would be completely drenched. My mother decided she would take me to the doctor to see what was wrong but she said in her opinion she just thought something was making me nervous.

...I was so scared of someone taking me away from my family because my dad used to tell me how bad people would take me away from him and mommy. I guess it is hard to tell people someone is hurting you when the person you're going to expose is your own parent. I don't get why my mom said to the doctor in her opinion she thought there was something causing me to be nervous, she was there, wasn't she paying attention to all the things going on in the house, why wouldn't she protect me, John, does my mom hate me that much?"

I could not answer her because I did not know just as I didn't know about my own father and the way he treated me.

"...The truth was never revealed to the doctor and so he only had his own views of what he thought might logically be causing me to do that and he told my mom perhaps she should try giving me liquids before a certain time of the night and thought it would help me."
Sara moved closer to me as we sat in the grass.

"...They tried the Doctor's advice and stopped giving me liquids to drink late at night but it only worked for a short time. I used to get thirsty, go into the bathroom, and run the water lightly

so no one could hear and let it run into the palm of my hand. I kept sipping it to keep my throat from being dry but no matter how little I would take in, I woke up wet. It never seemed like I had much but I guess a few times in the hand could amount to a full glass of water or more when you keep sipping."

I could tell she had been deeply troubled and she was feeling ashamed of herself but I would not let her feel ashamed. I wanted her to feel secure when she talked to me about her secrets. Sara was good and pure in my eyes.

"I used to wet the bed too."

She looked at me amazed that I confided in her the same thing as she had in me.

"…Some mornings I would get up early enough to run to the bathroom and wash up so I wouldn't smell like pee. I would dress before my mom got up to call me for breakfast, it never mattered because she would see the wet spots on my sheets and confront me about it when I got home from school. I never knew what to say but she didn't hold it against me. One night my aunt stayed over and she caught me in the bathroom the next morning running the water at a low pressure because I was hoping no one would hear it going in the tub and she asked me what I was doing and saw the wetness on my pajamas. She went to my room, turned the covers back, and brought the sheet out from off my bed.

…She made a big deal of the situation and I begged her to keep her voice down but all she cared about was to let everyone in the house know I had wet the bed. She kept yelling out that, she had proof and that I was trying to sneak in the bathroom to bathe. Mom and dad came out of their room to see me crying, begging my aunt to stop talking so loud but all she did was point and laugh

at me and kept raising her voice. Mom ran over to me and took me in the bathroom and opened up the valves to let the water run at full force and she put bubble bath in the tub. She looked at me and told me I was the love of her life, she told me to take my time and she would have breakfast ready for me when I was through.

...I asked her to stay with me until I was finished and she sat on the bathroom floor and washed my back and hair. It's funny how family like to make claims that they could be trusted and they would pretend to be loving and concerned for my well being when in reality all they wanted to do was point, ridicule, blame and tease me just like my aunt had done. But mom showed me no one could hold a candle to the true love a mother holds in her heart for her child. I could see there was more than love coming from her because she had the soul of an angel when she spoke to me and it made the things I thought were devastating appear to be like nothing and she showed me a level of her patience and kindness I thought was only there when she was helping someone else. I thought she liked others better than me but in that moment I realized I had always been her favorite and no matter how many people she helped in her life, I knew it was me she loved, her son.

...My aunt stayed over at different times and her numerous threats to tell everyone at school about catching me wet the bed was my biggest fear because I believed she was mean enough to do it. One day my dad whispered something to her in her ear and I never heard another word about her threats again. She actually helped my mom get some plastic bed sheets to put under my regular sheets to protect the mattress that had already suffered numerous amounts of stains."

Sara touched my hand gently.

"I know the feeling." She whispered.

"Yeah, it is scary, huh? Another one of my biggest fears happened when they made the decision to get rid of the mattress. The day of despair arrived when finally mom told me to help my dad when he got home to remove the old mattress from my room because he had picked up a second hand mattress and was on his way home. It was a second hand bed but it was new to us and there were no ring stains from urine covering it. I didn't want the old mattress to go outside on the streets because the neighbors were going to see the rings on it. All the guys I was trying to get to accept me would have known even though we were younger I knew that was something they wouldn't have forgotten, I just know it and you won't believe what my aunt did?"

"What did she do John?" Sara eyes widened.

"Well, she started covering the stains with black nail polish so that when the garbage man came to pick it up not even he would have been able to tell I had wet the bed, boy, it shocked the hell out of me and my dad smiled. Mom didn't say a word but I could tell she was pleased with her sister. I always thought my aunt hated me and then she did something nice to keep me from being exposed."

"Wow, John, I never would have thought she would have done something like that after all the things you said she did to you."

"Yeah I know, I thought perhaps my mom was rubbing off on her but she had her own reasons and it had to do with the secret she was keeping from my mom about my dad and the other woman but we didn't know that at the time."

"Oh John, you don't mean to say your aunt knew about your

dad and didn't tell your mom. I'm sorry; it's just that I mean, she was your mom's sister, are you sure?"

"Yeah, unfortunately it all came out in the open and it devastated my mom."

"I bet it did but maybe she already knew it would hurt your mom to that degree and that's probably why she didn't tell her."

I lowered my eyes and hesitated.

"I think maybe you'll still be my friend after knowing all of this about me but I don't know for sure anymore."

"You know what I think John?"

I looked up at her waiting to hear what she had to say and she pouted her lips playfully.

"...At least we were able to ward off evil bad guys with our powerful spray when we went to sleep at night."

"I don't believe you said that Sara."

We looked at each other and laughed. She smiled at me as we got up, folded the blanket, and packed away the remainder of the sweets we did not eat.

"I had a wonderful time with you again John and we can talk some more tomorrow if that's okay with you."

"Sure we can, anytime and I don't want you to worry about anything Sara because I'm going to look after you I promise."

We walked out to the front of the school grounds where we saw her parents pulling up in their car ready to take her home. We said goodnight and looked at each other convinced our discussion was safe with one another. I watched as the car pulled away. I felt alone and fulfilled as I looked until the car disappeared and then walked home.

DADDY'S GONE

I saw Sara in the hall the next day and we smiled. One of the girls deliberately tripped her and immediately a rage surged up, I started to head over toward her, and a teacher stepped in my way. Luckily, Lisa came up behind the girl and knocked into her and for the second time, she took Sara by the arm and moved her along. I saw what happened and kept still while the entire time the teacher was staring at me. I shrugged my shoulders, smiled and when she turned to see nothing had escalated, I walked around her and went to my class.

Sara and I saw each other at lunch.

"I'm sorry I couldn't get to you in time but that teacher…"

"I know, John, I saw her. I guess she doesn't approve of us hanging out."

"Yeah, but that's her problem."

"Yeah, but right now I have to go do something, I'll see you after school, okay."

"Yeah, sure, no problem."

I watched her leave the cafeteria anticipating the time we would hang out after school. When lunch was over, I got up and looked down where she sat and noticed a speck of red on the seat. It looked strange but I didn't give it a second thought. We met at our usual spot after school.

"What did you have to do earlier?"

"See the nurse. It's nothing my mom wants me to get a check up every now and again and they didn't want to pull me out of

school this time but nothing to worry about, I got a clean bill of health."

She said as she lowered her eyes.

"You know since you're always telling me about your life, I can tell you about my dad if you want."

"I think it would be a nice change from everything at the moment."

"I didn't mean to go on about my mom but where you lack the love from your mother is the same for me with my dad."

"I'm sorry John, I didn't mean to make you think I'm not happy about your mom, I think your mom is great, I wish she was mine. I guess we have to deal with what life throws at us. I wish my parents didn't even meet."

"But then you wouldn't be here and we wouldn't have met."

"After you tell me about your dad, I could tell you about my parents and how I wish they weren't together."

"You know what, I think we're going to be together forever to tell each other everything we want."

"You're right because I'm not going anywhere at least that's what my mom told me. She said this time we were staying right here so you're absolutely right because we'll be here forever." She said smiling.

I had a need to protect the people I loved and still had not learned what it was going on inside of me. I had no idea how far I would be willing to go to ensure their safety but Murphy said I had to be patient because of the type of characteristics that make up my genetic substance. I spent many days questioning him about the things he was saying but I always ended up leaving him more confused than when he first started talking to me.

It destroyed something inside and angered me to see Sara in tears and it hurt even more to know she had to endure so much without having anyone she could lean on for support. I made sure she knew I was going to be there for her to lean on and she did the same for me. She remained poised as she listened and I didn't know why I would share such intimate details about my life with her but I could not stop and she proved to be the one I was to trust.

"What's your dad's name?"

"Roger. Why?"

"I don't know I just wanted to know I guess."

"Well, he made it clear that he didn't want me and he was always doing stuff like starting arguments just to get away from us. I don't think I would care if he was dead. I bet you think I'm strange for saying that, don't you?"

"No, I don't."

"Sometimes after an argument, he wouldn't return until late at night or the next day. I learned that cruelty is just that and whether it's coming from an uncaring mother or an insensitive father, the pain is devastating. I can't compare how your mother made you feel but my dad was just as heartless when it came to me."

"I believe you."

"One day I guess he finally had enough pretending and just decided to leave for good. The sad thing is that my mom and I watched him walk out on us when I was only seven years old and the woman he was leaving her for sat in the car with her hat covering the side of her face as she smoked a cigarette. My mother knew he was no good for us but still she was deeply hurt and it wasn't in her genetic make up to want anyone to suffer no matter how they treated her but somehow I knew it was in mine."

"Why would you want him to suffer, John?"

"I guess because of the hurt I saw my mom going through and she never did anything to hurt anybody. It shocked me when she lashed out at him when she learned of his betrayal but I didn't care because he deserved it…"

#

"I hope you rot in hell Roger Chaney. I curse the day you ever entered my life. No I take that back."

"I figure you would take it back cause I was good for you baby." He said with a smirk.

"I curse the day after I conceived my baby John that you stayed in our lives."

#

"She knew she struck a chord in him when she spoke those words because it was true. He was no good as a father and he never could stop the cheating.

…Roger Chaney, my dad, a cook in a downtown restaurant and had served his time as a cook on a naval ship. He claimed he could not work out the differences he and mom were having but in reality, he enjoyed sleeping around and having another woman he could go to and pretend that his life was free of responsibility. He never wanted any kids and it was his excuse to blame mom when things weren't going his way especially when finances became a problem or when he was suppose to use the money he had to buy me clothes for school instead of spending it on other women."

"Did he tell you and your mom he was leaving or he just left?"

"No, I don't think he said anything to her but I wasn't always around every time they talked but he might have said something

but all I remember was seeing him pack his suitcase and without regards to my existence he walked right out the door and got into the car and drove away. Sometimes I would hear mom crying and she would say that at times she didn't feel like she wanted to live knowing he was remotely happy while living with another woman. But there was nothing either one of us could do about it, at least not for the moment."

"What do you mean John?"

The dauntingly thing about her question was the way she wasn't surprised at what I said. It was almost as if she was interested in knowing what I was capable of doing and furthermore condoning the execution of my thoughts.

"I don't really know right now but I'll just tell you what happened and how we found out who it was he was sleeping with thanks to my aunt. She came over to see us and I suppose she thought she was cheering mom up but as usual she crossed the line when she opened her mouth to say something about me..."

#

"You know Clara if that bastard son of yours wasn't born you would probably still have your man and you wouldn't be here now dragging your feet and feeling all sad as if the world was coming down on you."

"Let's get one thing straight you old cow. Don't talk about John like that ever again. My child is the best thing the Lord has blessed me with since I was born. And yes sometimes I'm sad mainly because Roger is not here to be a positive role model for his son but I am happier than you will ever know that he is out of our lives!"

"Well if you ask me..."

"Well no one is asking you. Why do I bother trying to talk to you Felicia Clamrod, you think you have all the answers anyway."

#

I looked at Sara still remembering seeing myself standing behind the door listening to what my aunt had to say.

"The funny thing about Aunt Felicia was that she didn't think mom knew she was acting to care about me when she was around. Sometimes I think she forgot I was mom's son when she blurted things about me out to her and other times I thought that she didn't care and said nasty things about me anyway."

"What kinds of things."

"Not important now. I was sad but also satisfied the way mom showed her love for me. Nothing else mattered because she could lift my spirits when I was feeling down and she would talk to me as though I had a right to live in this world even when I made mistakes and she wasn't against punishing me when I did wrong but I understood her love for me would never die."

"That's a special thing to have John."

"Yeah, and I know they kept talking but I left from behind the door because I didn't want to hear anything else my aunt had to say about me. The only problem was that it didn't matter that I left because when I went to the living room I had to hop behind the couch which was about two feet away from the wall because they continued their conversation as they were entering the room and I laid on the floor quietly listening."

#

"...Alright girl, don't get bent out of shape. You know I'll do whatever it takes to see that man of yours is taken care of for what he has done to you. I mean really girl the bottom line is we are

blood relatives and no man has the right to treat my sister like the way he's doing you so tell me what you want done." She continued.

"Why Felicia, you know I don't run in them kind of circles. I don't want anything done he just needs to be gone and stay gone."

"If you say so girl but you know who I know and who I know don't play no shit and I can see to it that he can be gone for good."

Clara looked at Felicia disapprovingly.

"...Alright, alright whatever you say, now I expect you and John to come and spend some time with me. You should come for dinner and spend the weekend. The two of you haven't been out to the house in a while." She said, pouting her lips.

"Well it has been a while hasn't it? Alright I'll make some arrangements and we'll come out soon."

"Good, now I've got to be going but you call me and let me know when you comin, you got it. And you better be comin too or I'm comin back out here with a broom stick."

#

"I wasn't sure what she meant by having dad taken care of but it felt right when I heard it. It seemed the one thing I didn't mind agreeing with my aunt about but I didn't quite understand my mother's need to be with her sister because Aunt Felicia was sneaky but I couldn't say anything because I didn't have proof. I remember my dad walking out like it was yesterday in July 1968 but as Aunt Felicia requested, six months after my dad left, we went to her house for a barbeque. She lived about forty-five minutes away by car and what seemed to be about three hours by train. Everything was nice and we would visit her from time to time over the next three years but I had to go more than mom did

because she would need me to stay with her sometimes. What I remember was that my aunt always made sure mom understood to call first. I thought it meant for her not to just drop me off unannounced but I'll never forget the day my mother saw the betrayal she had never thought could happen in our family but we didn't find out until three years after my dad left. It was two weeks after my tenth birthday but that was two years ago even though I'm eleven now because in a month I'll be twelve." I said proudly.

Sara laughed.

"Yes it would mean you're eleven now even though you turned ten when it happened two years ago because most of this year is already gone and your birthday is coming up, John I get it." She said jokingly.

"Oh, right, but I'm going to be twelve in another month so I could say…" I smiled.

"So did your aunt and…" Sara cut me off.

"Just wait, I'll tell you. It was a sunny August day and mom and I had been out shopping to see what she could find for me to wear. We went to the second hand store because many times people got rid of their clothes and other stuff they used only a few times. Sometimes some of the things people had were in their possession for years and in good condition. It amazed me how there were things there that were still brand new, and people had decided to donate them.

The main strip on Junction Boulevard was one of the busiest places on earth especially during the Christmas Holidays but during the summer it seemed to be just as crazy. People were all over the place and one time it was so busy I got lost in the crowd.

I knew enough to stand up against the window of a store until mom found me and in that case, it only took about five minutes later. Most people walked by but a few asked if I was lost and thought I wanted help locating her but she always told me that if we ever got separated to find the spot we were last seen together and stay there because she would always retrace her steps. Shopping with her was fun because I always got something out of her for going and helping with the bags."

#

"Hey mom, can I get a quarter for a bag of candy."

"No, but you can have a nickel for a couple of pieces." I didn't like the compromise and looked at her as if she was some kind of cheap skate.

"…You have to remember John I only get part time work here and there and your daddy ain't helping like he should."

I knew she was right and nodded in agreement and though disappointed at the small amount of change I would get, I quickly shrugged it off, happy with the fact that I was about to get some candy and it was all because of my mom. It seemed as though we would be shopping around forever and after looking at all the expensive clothes and things, we walked to the less expensive area to buy me a pair of shoes and if we didn't have enough money we bought a used pair. Sometimes she would go to the shop and get me a pair of pants if the dealer was feeling generous and marked the price down a little more.

The man at this one shop always had this twinkle in his eye when he looked at her but she never looked at him in the face. She would ask for what she wanted and most times, she was asking how much something cost. I never knew what was going on with

those two after we walked into his store but I did notice he made her very nervous, so one day I asked what was going on.

"How come that man always marks the price down for you and he looks at you funny too?"

"I don't know John, I guess he's been smitten and wants to do us favors so I would turn my eye his way."

"What's smitten?"

"It means when somebody likes you and they want to do nice things for you hoping you'll like them too. But I can't be involved with him because I'm still a married woman."

I left the matter alone after she answered me because we always went there and he was never disrespectful to her but I didn't trust the man.

#

"You do understand all of this was before I met you Sara."

"John, we just met this summer of course I know John, now continue." She urged.

"Okay, okay." I said smiling. "Where was I?"

"The store and the man liking your mom and getting you some shoes."

"Oh yeah, but it was pants."

"Whatever, keep going."

"Okay!"

#

...The day arrived and we were going to Aunt Felicia's, it was the Labor Day weekend in 1971 and Aunt Felicia said it could be a party for that plus my tenth birthday all in one. I was playing in the park for a few hours before I asked the park attendant for the time. It was close to 4:00pm and mom was going to be home by

4:30pm. I continued to play until I realized that I had been there for some time and I rushed to get home. On my way, I could see her coming down the street with a package in her hand. I ran faster to meet up with her.

"Mom, mom!"

I was running to her and she looked up and caught a glance of me rushing her way. I could see a big smile came upon her face and she waved, as I was getting closer. She signaled me to make sure no cars were coming before I crossed the street. I was frustrated for having to wait and checked heeding her request, I looked both ways to ensure no traffic was coming then ran right into her open arms.

"How's my wonder boy, did you have fun at the park?"

"It was fun. So what did you buy me?"

"Oh no, not this time mister, you got yours a couple of weeks ago for your birthday, I bought this for me. You remember we're going to your auntie's for a barbeque and I wanted to go in something she hasn't seen me in before."

We walked a few blocks and made it home. We packed some luggage to stay a couple of nights and my aunt had already arranged to have one of her friends come and pick us up because we didn't have a car. Although we were only going to Far Rock-Away, Aunt Felicia did not want us riding the bus and then taking the nightmarish train ride besides she said someone would have had to come and pick us up from the train station after we got there anyway and she didn't want us to arrive later than six o'clock in the evening.

"Mom isn't it a bit late to be having a barbeque at this hour?"

"Well now, you know your auntie and when she wants to do

something she goes for it. Besides, you know she got a couple of them track lights out in the backyard so it doesn't matter what time she starts a barbeque and we are going to be spending the night remember and I get to spend some time with my favorite sister." She said as she playfully tapped my chin with her finger.

"Mom she's your only sister so how can she be your favorite if there isn't any others to compare her to."

"Well, don't you never mind that. You heard what I said didn't you and besides that should make her your favorite aunt."

"Yeah, I guess."

"Yeah, you guess, huh, get over here."

"No, stop okay wait please mom stop I'm gonna throw up. Okay, okay."

"Say it. Come on and say it or I won't stop."

"Yeah."

"Yeah, what, I didn't hear you say it."

"Yes, she's my favorite aunt. That's not fair! You know how ticklish I am."

"Well I guess I have to level the playing field when I want my way."

We continued laughing, went to the front porch, and sat. Our ride arrived and when the car turned onto Aunt Felicia's street, we could see as we were riding down the block that there were plenty of people enjoying the festivities. She was friends with musicians who brought their instruments for live music and people were dancing, drinking, talking and smoking cigarettes which made it look more like a nightclub.

Once we got there, we could see there was a nice big front yard. It was a four-story house with plenty of rooms and four of

them were bedrooms. One of the times, I was there, no one was renting the upstairs, and I went around counting all the rooms. I could not believe how big it was with two living rooms, two full kitchens, two full bathrooms and a basement with enough space to put a bed and there was another bathroom with a toilet, sink and a raggedy excuse for a shower, which sometimes she rented out. She has a family room and an extra room she uses as a walk-in closet, which also doubled for the laundry room.

After I counted those ten rooms, I added the four bedrooms to equal fourteen. There was one kitchen on the second floor and one on the main floor and two of the bedrooms were upstairs for the tenants but my aunt's section had the space for the laundry room, family room and the basement with the toilet room that had the crappy shower. It was clearly more room on the main floor because of the basement. She usually rented out the upstairs to a family but this time she told mom she had rented the upstairs to only one person who had been there the last three years and we could use the family room and the big room in the basement. Some of the guests were in the living room on the first floor and others were using the big room downstairs. People were standing at two of the bathrooms one on the main floor and the other in the basement and there was a long line of men downstairs waiting to use the facility and when I passed the wall to that bathroom I could hear an occasional thump and wondered why it was only men waiting to use it.

All the women who saw the line were frustrated and went back upstairs to see if the bathroom was available but I thought there must have been more to it when some of the guys were telling women it was a full house before they made it down to the

third step. I had to push my way through the crowd of people to get back upstairs and out the front door. Some were blocking my path because they were heading up to the bathroom on the second floor. It was right at the top of the stairs before the door leading into the living room of the upstairs apartment. One person had gone upstairs and used it so other people started doing the same thing.

I heard someone tell another they should all try to be quiet so they would not disturb the tenant but the reality of it was because they did not want the tenant to know they were sneaking upstairs to use his bathroom in case he was home. I finally made my way outside to the side of the house where I laid on the ground to peek inside the window of the basement bathroom to see why some of the guests were not able to use it. The room's design was in such a way so that anyone who was using the toilet would still have complete privacy but if anyone was over by the sink, you could see everything that was going on.

I saw why there was a hold up and knew that all the men were waiting to see who was going to come out. My eyes witnessed all the pleasures of two adults because of this man who had some woman up against the wall next to the sink having sex. The side of the house had a small area between it and the fence dividing the next property that I didn't think anyone would ever catch me but a drunk was stumbling by and saw me.

"Hey boy what you doing looking through that window get out of there you little pervert. You shouldn't be looking at people. Go on and get lost."

I did not stick around to let him see my face. I took off running as he was still talking and when I looked over my shoulder

to see if he was chasing me I noticed he had stooped down to look to see what it was I was looking at. It didn't take him long to get comfortable and pull out of his pocket the bottle of liquor he had in order to drink and watch the show. The two inside were so engrossed in their business that they never noticed the drunk or me. I thought it was only fair for the one who reprimanded me to have to answer to somebody too.

I went over to my aunt and asked who was the big fat man wearing the brown polyester suit with the white tie around his neck and the yellow stained handkerchief sticking out of his pants pocket. She told me he was the Reverend Johnson and he and his wife were visiting from Georgia. Well it wasn't the nicest thing for me to do but I could not resist finding out where I could find the wife of this fine respectable old fart. Surely not at this large family oriented event. All I can say is who can resist the eager yearnings of a young child wanting to learn more about God. I'm sure not the wife of a Reverend and it was my duty to make sure she knew in what vicinity I thought I saw him last where she could go get him so he could speak to the hungry young youth with all those spiritual questions.

The next thing I know the Reverend's wife was doing her own share of pushing, hitting and yelling, and the words coming out of her mouth was not the kind of language I thought I would ever hear from the wife of a man pasturing a southern church. She started flailing her purse up against his head, he was running toward the car and everyone watching was laughing.

Some of the guests ran inside to get others to watch the spectacle. It was truly a sight to see. The two of them headed for the car respectfully saying their goodbye's to my aunt as she stood

outside watching them and wondering what was going on. We all gathered around to see the show and I listened to people trying to figure out all the different scenarios they gave to one another as to what they thought could have possibly been the reason behind her actions. Some of them looked my way and gave their opinion. I just shrugged my shoulders and walked away. I could hear the women talking.

"He don't know he's just a kid."

I went inside laughing to myself, knowing I had started this particular bit of commotion. I looked over passed some of the people milling around and saw my friend Beanie. She was the girl who lived down the street from Aunt Felicia's and each time I saw her she had a bag of jelly beans and I decided since I had to ask her to tell me her name every time we were together, I thought it was only right to call her Beanie. We hit it off right away and when I would stay over for the week or just for the weekend, Aunt Felicia would call her over to watch me so that she could go out for a night out on the town, as she would always call it.

It was not so much of a problem having Beanie over but the fact that she was there specifically to carry out the job of babysitting was never an idea I liked to consider. I made my case to her one night when she came over to watch me.

#

"Well, that's normal for a seven year old…"

"Eight!"

"Okay, eight but you just turned eight, right?"

"Yeah, last week." I said proudly.

"Okay, so how about this, how about I treat you like you were just coming over to hang out and as long as you mind your

manners and don't get into mischief, we can be two friends of different ages just kickin it, deal?"

"Deal!" I said smiling. We sealed the deal sharing her jellybeans. Beanie kept her word and for the next two years after that when I had to stay over at Aunt Felicia's we just hung out and I did my part and remained respectful and didn't get into any mischief. On some occasions Beanie would leave me for up to an hour to be on my own but I thought I noticed someone lurking around the tree watching the place a few times each time she left but it was fine and a lot different from the year prior to those two years when it felt like I needed a babysitter and it was cool feeling like I had the place to myself.

#

...We had lots of fun together and we talked about when we would get the chance to go to the next party given by the famous Felicia Clamrod. We enjoyed talking about all the things that happened at the last party my aunt had, and we were always bringing up the events that took place to see if one was better than the one that happened before. The funny thing was that anytime there was a party at Aunt Felicia's there was always going to be some kind of uproar to spice up the evening. We reminded each other of the two women that got into a fight over some man they both liked and the whole time they were cursing at each other, throwing drinks on one another and pulling off each other's wigs, the man left with some other woman and drove off.

I told her what I did about the Reverend.

"You should have seen them I think together they must have weighed about twelve hundred pounds."

"John, hush before someone hears you." She laughed.

"...I'm sure they didn't weigh twelve hundred pounds."

"Maybe not but it was something high because they were big." I said as I expanded my hands and opened my arms wide. She pushed my hands down quickly looking around and ushered me into the kitchen.

"...I know it was mean but the way I figured it, he was bound to get busted sooner or later so why not now besides how often do you see a Reverend run from his wife screaming, baby it didn't mean nothing, I was just looking."

"Shush, John, you stop that right now." She laughed.

"Hey it's not often we would see two out of shape fat people barely able to run two feet ahead of them wearing clothes that made them look like a psychedelic light show."

"Be that as it may somebody might hear you and then we both will get into trouble for talking about people, especially a reverend."

"Well, okay but it was a lot of fun getting the old timer in trouble with his wife."

We whispered and laughed some more reminding each other how we always looked forward to getting together to watch the different people and secretly point out how they walked or danced and even how they chewed their food and the bizarre ways they expressed different things they were saying. We looked at each other knowing we both could smell the aroma that was in the kitchen and the wonders about Aunt Felicia's parties, which were the deserts and the way she always had her kitchen smelling as though it was Thanksgiving. Every time there was a party, it would get later and later before anyone was able to enjoy the many deserts, she had in the kitchen. Sometimes when we found her, she

would still be talking to her friends. She was always the life of the party and it would be almost impossible to get her to go inside to start serving the deserts. By the time people started to leave, the deserts were still in the kitchen untouched. Most of the time the people who knew her really well would go in and cut themselves what they wanted before they left and of the many different cakes and pies my aunt baked, bought or had someone bring with them, there were plenty to make a healthy choice.

Beanie and I would get together when we thought we had enough time to map out a game plan to see how long Aunt Felicia would be out of the kitchen in order for us to dig our paws into the long awaited deserts. We thought it was only fair to partake in the endeavors of pulling the wool over her eyes considering she was always taking too long to serve them. First, we asked her when she would come to serve the sweets and when she agreed to come with us, she always managed to get busy socializing with one or more of the guests. It was always the same no matter who was having a party. First mingle then we would have to eat dinner before we could have any deserts. Beanie and I thought Aunt Felicia always took much too long to get to the desert part and we chose never to wait at least not at her house.

I guess my transgressions of what I did to the reverend were catching up to me because it was a close call this night when we were acting out our need to eat some of the sweets before it was time to be served. We stood in the kitchen with a piece of homemade chocolate cake sliced to perfection, ready to eat with savory delight and my desert cohort was such the professional she showed me how to slice the amount of cake I wanted and then refill the empty area with frosting so no one would realize any was

gone. Surprisingly an unannounced Aunt Felicia entered the living room through the front door, our eyes widened and it felt as though we were caught stealing from a Jewelry store with a precious diamond in our hands. We looked at one another and quickly stuffed the cakes into our mouths, laughing and nearly choking without any time to enjoy the theft we had just committed. Aunt Felicia almost saw me when she walked up to the indoor bar she had in her living room.

I had dropped low to the floor where the counter of the bar blocked the view of the desert table and from a low position with the entire cake and tin foil in hand, I tried to wrap it back quietly while Beanie was lucky enough to move and stand in front of the sink. A wall was partly extended from the sink counter blocking the view of anyone coming through the front door. The back portion of her body was in view from the angle she was standing and it could easily look as though the person standing there was washing dishes. She quickly thought to turn on the water, as I stayed unmoving because I thought the foil made too much noise and without suspicion Aunt Felicia yelled out thanks for washing the dishes.

She was going into one of the rooms to get someone's coat and never bothered coming into the kitchen. She didn't see me but I thought it was only fair to Beanie that as partners in crime I should stay and help her and for the next forty-five minutes we were stuck doing the dishes but it didn't matter to us because we thought it was worth it.

A FAMILY AFFAIR

Staying at Aunt Felicia's started out great but it did not end that way and it was not long before the laughter turned to dismay at my mom's expense. I never thought I would see the sparkle leave her eyes and experience her heartache, which took over her life as though she gave up believing in the goodness of people. All the guests left for the evening and we were down in the basement where my aunt set it up nice for us. Mom was feeling a little hungry and there was plenty of food in the fridge for a late night snack. I didn't think there was much because many people took two and three plates full of food home. She told me that Aunt Felicia already prepared the event for such gluttons and had a stash of food enough for us to eat for a couple of days that she moved to the main refrigerator out of a spare fridge after the guests left. She went upstairs to the kitchen to get something to eat and after a few minutes I decided I too wanted something and figured I would join her but when I got close to the entrance I could hear sounds coming from the other side of the kitchen which was my aunts bedroom.

I kept quiet and knew that mom was trying to be quiet also by the way she was rushing and looking to see if anyone was coming from that direction. I saw her look up a couple of times while trying to get what she wanted but the sounds were getting louder and there was no getting pass it other than for her to leave the kitchen and wait awhile before returning.

She quickly returned the plate and started putting the food back into the refrigerator. She rose up from putting the last pot back into the fridge and I had to duck behind the wall fast because I saw the bedroom door open. I heard the door to the fridge close, looked around the corner of the wall and that's when mom and I both saw Roger Chaney, my dad standing naked and fully extended. My aunt came out of the bedroom in sheer lingerie but not paying attention to the fact that I was kneeling in the doorway to the kitchen.

"Did she leave yet?" She was saying as my mother stood there completely shocked at what was happening.

I watched my dad grab hold of my aunt and kiss her passionately in front of mom and then grab her by the waist, turned her in the opposite direction, and playfully pushed her to go back into the bedroom. I will never forget my aunt turning back around and looking into my mother's eyes and the words she repeated after my mother told her never to speak in such a manner.

"...I told you girl, if it wasn't for that bastard child of yours you'd been able to keep your man." She said.

Mom tried to run out of the kitchen where she and everyone would have seen me but my dad stopped her, held onto to her, and playfully suggested that they all have one big happy family night of fun. He was extremely drunk. In his condition, it might have explained his behavior if he and my mom were still together, the party was at our house, and it was some woman he just met. I was stretching my ability to find just cause for his actions along with other unrealistic reasons I came up with to excuse his behavior. Regardless of what the reason or how much we tried to lie to ourselves, Aunt Felicia knew what she was doing and my dad also

knew that he was deliberately leaving us for my aunt, my mom's flesh and blood sister and that made it all inexcusable and unforgivable. When he had hold of her, it was my cue to run down the stairs and hop into bed because I did not want them to see me. I could hear my mother demanding my dad to let her go and something I never thought I would ever hear coming out of my mom's mouth. She was using a series of words that not only did she scream out in succession but spoke so quickly and eloquently I had to stop to think if she had actually used the terms I heard her say, accurately.

She quickly broke free, I guess the phrases surprised my dad too and she came running down the stairs just as soon as I got into bed. I quickly put myself under the covers so I would be invisible to her and my dad in case he came down after her.

"John, John get up, we have to get out of here. Let's go, now." She said sweetly but with anticipation.

"What's going on?"

I tried to act as though I did not know what was happening but the look she gave me told me she knew I had seen what happened. I didn't say another word and I got up and quickly got dressed and we rushed out of there like a bat out of hell. It was one long night and mom was so upset, she cried and cursed, prayed and laughed all in one breath. I looked at the clock before we left and it was three in the morning when we embarked our way out and we walked until we had made it all the way home. It must have taken us about seven hours and by 10:00am, we were at our house, and by the time we got inside, the shock of it all had her lost for words and too angry for tears. She never talked about it with me and never spoke to her sister again. She never accused my dad

of doing anything wrong when she spoke to me about him and that was only if necessary however, whenever she remembered what happened she would slightly cringe, close her eyes as though she was replaying what she saw in her head and her body would tremble. It looked as though she was shaking a bug off her and then she would continue the task of what she was doing without saying a word. We did not settle things by going to court. We just settled them and we did it without letting or wanting everyone knowing our business. We were never the type to make things a public display and since my dad had left three years earlier, we didn't have to worry about moving him out because all his things were already gone.

I did not want to add any more heartache to her but I wanted to understand why he would be living upstairs from Aunt Felicia's during the three years I was going over there when Beanie was watching me and never let me know he was around. I kept quiet about it but it did surprise me when mom told me that he did not want her to close him out completely and still wanted to see me. They arranged a time when he could call when he wanted to spend time with me which was something mom always suggested should happen anyway because he was my dad.

I didn't mind the arrangement because I was sure she knew as I did that his phone calls would be few and far enough in between that she wanted me to get whatever time I could with him. She never said or did anything to anyone for someone to misconstrue her words or actions to be insulting or purposely to harm them and she did not try to act like a saint either nor did she ever bring up the bad things about anybody, at least not in my presence. She always loved her sister dearly and for Aunt Felicia to do that to her

made the betrayal even more devastating.

When dad would finally come by to take me to the movies or to the neighborhood fair when it was in town, mom would get me ready and made sure I was sitting inside of our indoor porch so that I could see him through the window and go out to meet him when he drove up. She never tried to see him again and there were plenty of times when he tried to apologize and ask me to tell her that if he had not been drinking that it would have never had happened. I never delivered his messages. I just let him stew in his own pot of mess he created with my aunt.

#

…I had almost forgotten I was spilling my life story because I wanted it to be something that was happening to some other family but it was my reality and I had all the emotions behind it. I was lost in my past visions in a trance that overwhelmed me until I heard the loving tone from Sara's voice.

"Oh John, it's as though you've been through one problem after another and nobody was ever there to hear what you had to say about any of it except for your mom but you never told her any of this stuff you've been feeling have you?"

I stared at the ground and waited until once again our time had ended. It was Friday and we were not going to see each other again until after the weekend.

"I'm going to miss you Sara."

"And I'll miss you too John, but we'll see each other in two days okay and I'll be thinking good thoughts for you." She said.

"Yeah, okay. I'll do the same for you."

Once again, we walked to the car that pulled up to the side of the curb and both parents stayed inside waiting for their daughter

to enter; Sara got inside and rolled the window down.

"See you Monday."

THE BULLY

Autumn 1971, Brian's school reputation caused us to fear the one person we did not know if actually existed. Brian, Reggie, Todd, Derek, and Melvin whom everyone called Mel were the band of thieves harassing the neighborhoods one way or another. Brian and Reggie were twelve both younger than the other guys but only by a year or two and it was clear that Brian had proved to be the ring leader over the guys who were thirteen and fourteen years old.

At twelve, Brian looked as though he was sixteen years old, he was very big, mean, and ornery and he used his size to dominate over those he thought to be weaker. Reggie was nowhere near Brian's size and looked to be more like his younger brother. Brian did not like it when someone opposed him especially from those he felt to be inferior to him, which in most cases he thought that of everyone including the teachers. We heard that he was transferring to our school and by the time we got through the first half of the fifth grade and he had not arrived we all realized we practically worked ourselves into a pointless panic for nearly a year. The rumor was out that he was a bully beyond the meaning of the word. He did not use his time constructively because he was too busy causing havoc in the lives of others and he usually skipped school. His teachers thought he was a lost cause and most times, they checked him in class as present because they felt it was time to get him out of their school before he became more of a problem. He liked to smoke cigarettes and drink beer which he kept inside a brown paper bag and hidden in an ice tea bottle. He kept other

innocent snacks like brownies and chips in the bag in case
someone wanted to stop him on school grounds. He was clever,
sneaky and did what he wanted during the regular business hours
of the day because he learned he could get away with things that
most people would not believe anyone would be so bold to commit
such acts in daylight. Sometimes he convinced his friends to cut
classes but most times, they waited until they were out for the day,
off school grounds and harassed one kid after the other. Most
times when they were stealing from some poor soul trying to get
home trouble free they ended up convincing the guy to give up his
sneakers in exchange of experiencing a severe beating and threaten
that he would have to walk home completely naked. When the
unsuspecting prey agreed to give up his sneakers, they would
torment and tell him next time not to punk out and that he should
have defended his right to keep his property. Once they were
bored with the kid knowing he was completely terrified, they
would spend a few extra minutes shoving him back and forth and
then push him in the direction he was originally going, threatening
him to make sure he did not squeal on them.

Derek enjoyed unstringing the sneakers they had stolen and
sniff the inside and complain how the kids' feet had some
horrifying odor. Then he would try to stuff the shoe in the other
guy's faces to make them take a whiff, laugh it off and then thread
the string through one of the holes of the other shoe in order to tie
them together and throw them up high to hang from a street light.
If the sneakers were new, they sold them to some unsuspecting
parent who was on food stamps for as much cash as they could get.
Their usual hunt and prowling of the night getting into mischief
had become a regular habit from sneaking into nightclubs to

stealing. They enjoyed spending their weekends taking from local liquor stores but always went to other neighborhoods if Brian wanted to take more than just a few snacks. He let the other guys take stuff like chips, sodas, cigarettes and beer but sometimes he got out of control and would pull a nighttime heist with a gun, harass a clerk and take cash from the register.

One Friday night Brian was becoming restless so by 11:00pm they all went to a liquor store where a student worked the night shift. The place was closing by midnight and Reggie knew that the owner would return by 11:45pm to close the place up for the night. Reggie had known Brian the longest and used to steal with him before their grade school years and though Todd, Derek and Mel were just as roguish, Reggie was a little more subdued and usually wanted Brian to keep things on a level that didn't get out of their control. Brian tolerated Reggie because he knew Reggie wouldn't tell on him but he was frustrated on several occasions and didn't want a recurrence of what had happened a year earlier, which is why he suggested that Reggie stand outside the convenient store as the lookout man while the others went inside to hold up the place. Reggie was satisfied with that idea but could only hope things did not go sour indoors.

Brian liked taking chances and he enjoyed including everybody in what his tactics were going to be for that particular night. After hanging out with his new friends for a year he decided at the age of twelve that it was time to let them in on a little secret he enjoyed using from time to time. He reached in his pocket while the others were down the aisles stuffing snacks into their pockets and pulled out his little surprise in front of everyone. Reggie could see the look of concern on their faces and thought

Brian was becoming a little careless in letting them see how overly enthusiastic he was capable of being. He preferred it when only the two knew of his fascination with weapons during a robbery and now he involved the others. Brian knew Reggie did not want him to use any weapons in their current heist while they were with the others but did not think it was serious the time he pulled the trigger on the old man they held up in the past, so he thought it was time to have some fun. He did not want Reggie to overreact so he showed the entire group that the gun was not loaded. The rest of the guys thought he only wanted to scare the clerk so they laughed it off and unanimously agreed to join in for the fun and games by nodding and giving the thumbs up. Although Reggie was relieved, he knew Brian came prepared with bullets. He kept quiet and hoped for the best but he was still apprehensive and wanted them all to get out of there as fast as possible.

Reggie's first encounter with Brian's armed robbery was when they were nine years old, but he only carried a bat, a nightstick and sometimes a slingshot to threaten but as the years passed Brian became more aggressive when he pulled a heist. At eleven, Brian asked Reggie to get his cousin to loan them his motorbike. He had proven himself capable of handling the mini cycle by the time he was nine years old and so his cousin had no problem handing him the keys. The two of them had planned to skip school but Reggie had to wait until school was officially over before asking his cousin for the keys. Brian's dad was no longer in his life, his mom was an incurable alcoholic and it was easy to use the weekend at Reggie's place and make it the excuse when he wanted to get into mischief without being questioned.

Reggie paced back and forth outside the convenient store and

was having flashes of the past incident when he and Brian rode across the 59th street Bridge, locked the motor bike in the city and took the train into New Jersey. He was already nervous that someone would steal his cousin's bike but that was of no consequence when he found out about the crazy stunt he did not know Brian had planned. Brian had been drinking but that was as usual to Reggie, it was midnight and the place he wanted to rob did not close until 2:00am. They sat on a street corner going over a plan Brian devised to get in and out of the store with what they wanted to steal.

#

"It's no different than any other time Brian so what's with all the deep cover black opt shit."

"The difference here shit head is that this old fart has a rifle and security cameras so we have to make sure that our faces aren't seen by the cameras when we go in and without arousing grandpa of suspecting something's up."

It seemed forever to Reggie but finally at 1:50am Brian walked up to the front of the store from around the corner.

"Hey what did you say?"

He had timed it perfectly when he saw a man and his girlfriend pull up to the side of the store where just the taillights could be seen out the side corner of the window if the old man was suspicious and decided to go from behind the counter to look out to see if Brian was with anyone. He kept his face out of view of the camera and walked in backing up as he was yelling out in the direction of the car knowing that the two were there to make out. Reggie came from around the corner running in past him tripping and excusing himself as if he did not know Brian and kept his head

down with the hat covering the bulk of his face. Their entrance was smooth and unsuspecting of their original intent. The two got in with their faces unseen by the surveillance camera at the front of the store.

Reggie went down the snack isle, ducked low and stuffed his pockets with different cakes and cookies as Brian made his way over to the refrigerator where the beer and wine were located knowing the old man would focus his attention on Brian. He then moved over to the other refrigerator with the juices, sodas and bottled water. He knew the old man was watching to see if he was going to try to buy the alcoholic beverages. He went to the sodas, picked up four, grabbed a few snacks and then made his way to the register. He approached the counter, and placed everything down respectfully. The cameras were now behind him and he could see the reflection of the taillights from the car and needed to play it cool. The old man started ringing the sodas and Reggie came up to the front with some products just like Brian had done.

"Add those to the groceries please."

"You two together?"

"No, I just like paying for strangers stuff."

"Alright, alright it's just that you two didn't look like you were together when you came in." The old man said.

"We were racing, trying to see who could make it in first." Reggie added.

"Alright, well then your total is $11.63."

"Take it out of this." Brian handed him a twenty. The man took the bill and handed him $8.37 change. He closed the register, Brian reached into his pocket and pulled out a few more bills, noticing that the car lights outside were getting faint from the

reflection, and then they were gone. He displayed the hundred dollar bill on top of the other bills and added his change to the rest of his money. The old man looked curiously at the amount of money the young boy had in his possession.

"Go get some more drinks."

Reggie left the area.

Brian put all the cash away, then shifted the change into his other hand, and calmly reached in his other pocket, where he released the coins and pulled out a gun.

"The cash old man!" Brian ordered.

Reggie returned with two six packs of soda.

"What the hell are you doing?"

"Shut up! What does it look like I'm doing?"

"We can't do this!"

The old man opened the register and put the money on the counter.

"Shut the fuck up, I said, now grab the money and let's go."

Reggie hesitated.

"...Do it or I'll fucking put a bullet in your mother fucking head bitch."

Brian turned the gun and pointed it in Reggie's face.

"Here, here's all of it, I don't want any trouble, take it please," The man turned his attention to Reggie.

"...I think he will shoot you and then he'll turn on me because I'll be a witness so please take it, this way you take it and no one gets hurt."

He put more money on the counter pushing it forward toward Reggie. He watched the two as they squared off at each other and thought it would be a good time to make his move, he reached

below his waist to get his rifle.

"…Look I have more here. Please I don't want any trouble." He continued.

Brian turned as the man raised his arms lifting the rifle up to point over the counter. He pointed his gun and shot the barrel of the rifle knocking it out of the old man's hands. He fell back up against the shelves behind him, grabbed his chest, and fell to the floor. Brian pushed Reggie toward the door and grabbed everything they had actually paid for and the money.

He ran out ushering Reggie as he headed toward the door. They left the store unaware if the man had died. It was not until a week later when Reggie saw on the news about the old man of the New Jersey liquor store, who was robbed by two unidentified youths, and was in the hospital with a report to be in fair condition. The reporters stated that the bullet never hit him but he suffered from mild bruises and an anxiety attack. They added how lucky the man did not suffer from a heart attack from all the excitement at his age.

Reggie went back to the store two weeks after that to find an older woman tending to the store and when he asked her what happened to the old man she began to cry, excused her behavior and told him she had to close early. Reggie never mentioned it to Brian but thought that perhaps the old man died but he could not be sure if that was actually true.

#

…He stood outside convincing himself the kid would not be so stupid to try to go up against a gun for a store that did not belong to him and risk his future for a few bucks.

"Hey you, how long you've been working here?"

"I don't know. I guess about two years."

"What grade you in at school?"

"Eleventh, Why?"

"Just want to know if you're good in math."

"I guess."

"Well take this equation, what if I take this gun and put it in your face. How much money would you have left in the cash register?"

The clerk's eyes grew wide and he took two steps back staring at the gun.

"Is that real?"

Brian took a bullet out of his pocket and opened the gun to put it inside the chamber. He successfully loaded it without his friends seeing him. He closed the barrel and pointed it back in the clerk's face.

"What do you think and you didn't answer my question."

"I guess nothing." He said nervously.

Brian's friends came up from the aisles and stood there laughing when they saw him look over and wink. They enjoyed thinking the clerk was scared for no reason but they were unaware the clerk knew differently. The three of them kept stuffing treats in their pockets while Reggie paced back and forth outside and finally he went in front of the car and then in front of the door of the convenient store smoking a cigarette, lighting another before finishing the first.

Every chance he got he kept motioning for them to hurry up. He shrugged his shoulders lifting both his hands with the palms up to the sky. He was impatient long enough and stuck his head in the door of the store.

"Hey Brian let's go I think someone's coming."

"Nobody's coming you little punk, you just scared just like the last time and what's going through your fucking mind, man? What you giving out names for now he knows who to finger."

Reggie could tell Brian was angry with him and retreated to the car to continue his post but Brian remained calm when he turned his attention back to rob the clerk.

"You guessed right. So why don't you come closer here to the register and open it up and give me all the money out of it."

The clerk followed orders, opened the register, and handed Brian the bills and started to close it.

"No, all the money, I want the coins too."

The clerk placed the coins in a brown bag and gave it all to him paying close attention to the gun Brian was pointing at him.

"Very good, now what are the chances I or my friends here will come back and hurt you and your mom if you point the finger at me?"

The clerk stared at him unable to answer.

"Come on, come on I don't have all night I got to run, I just robbed you, remember? Let me make it easier for you. I don't think those guys have girlfriends and they might make your mom do some stuff while you watch and if they're feeling drunk and wild they might make you join in, you know what I mean." He said and winked at the clerk.

"...Now what are the chances that you would point the finger to me when asked about this robbery?"

"None! I, I, I think they were um, I mean they all had um, ski masks?"

"You know something kid you are good in math and you

create stories quite nicely too. Just remember that story the rest of your life. Got it!"

The clerk nodded as Brian leaned in closer to him pointing the gun and pushing it into his nose. He backed away watching the paralyzed kid who stayed behind the counter amazed at what had just happened to him. Brian knew the clerk was wondering what he could have done to him. They all left the store and got in the car. Brian turned the gun on Reggie.

"You got a death wish?"

Reggie stared at Brian and nervously shook his head. Everyone kept quiet.

Todd started laughing.

"Hey Reggie, relax man, the gun's not even loaded, so chill man."

Brian opened the barrel and removed the bullet clearly for Todd to see it and placed it in his pocket, closed the barrel and put the gun in his front pants at the waist.

Todd's expression went from light hearted and carefree to seriously scared and bewildered, each of the guys became serious wondering when Brian had actually loaded the gun, Todd swallowed hard, nervously keeping his mouth shut so that Brian wouldn't get any ideas to reload and turn the gun on him. Brian turned to look at Reggie.

"He's right, chill, gun's not even loaded!"

BRIAN'S TRUE NATURE

The different stories about Brian told to us at school did not seem possible for any one individual to have committed all the crimes he was accused of having done and everyone telling them was getting out of control to the length they were expressing of what had happened. Some of the kids started talking about how they found out about Brian following some girl into the women's bathroom at the movie theatre and threatened to kill her if she did not perform oral sex on him. We began brushing all the stories off as something someone made up just to get a rise out of all of us and there was still the fact that we did not know if he was real.

We made it through the first half of fifth grade without him and soon after, all of the things said about Brian seemed to be a little more than possible when he appeared at our school. They waited until after spring break of 1972 to transfer him at thirteen into the second half of the fifth grade from his school to ours, the kid we heard so much about was standing before us looking a lot tougher, and he was definitely a lot bigger than anyone of us could have imagined. I was turning eleven that summer, Sammy was still full of life and Mackey didn't show up until the summer of that year and Sara had not yet entered into my life but we all had to face the fact that terror was going to rain down upon us when Brian arrived. We could see by his size he had to stay in the same grade more times than he could probably count but that was an assumption judged by most of us. The irony of it all was that he was very smart. He proved to be one who never wanted to

conform to the rules of education. He started out showing the teachers that he was very intelligent, went to all his classes and did extremely well when it came time to test his skills.

He managed to convince the teachers his lack of interest in school was due to the teachers' at his old school, inability to educate him at a level beyond their training which he expressed was clearly not up to his level of understanding.

He was a straight 'A' student and administration was convinced the teachers at his other school were out to get him because he was probably smarter than their aptitude. He had the book knowledge he needed for the school system to promote him in order to catch up with his proper grade but the fact was that his poor marks prevented administration from placing him in a higher grade and so he had to complete the program. Brian did everything that was in expectation of him because he was learning about his new surroundings and he was learning about whom it was he thought to be inferior to him. Some of the students tried to get on his good side and spoke to him of Lisa, telling him that she was the girl at our school who had a reputation for making out with boys. When he saw her, he wanted to get to know her better. He watched her and studied whom she hung out with and where she liked to go after school. He was relentless and one day followed her and her two best friends Valerie and Roxanne to her house. He learned everything he could about her and tried to figure out what he could do to impress her and he talked to some of the boys at school about his infatuation. He spent a week daydreaming and thinking of what he could do to get her to like him.

One day after school, he went up to her to ask her if she would like to go hang out with him and perhaps go see a movie.

His approach was awkward and he came across nerdy, she gave
him the finger and told him to fuck off in front of her girlfriends.
Some of the students whispered amongst themselves and one guy
mentioned that she walked away saying he probably had a small
penis. A girl said she did not hear that and that he just wanted to
start trouble but it got around the school quickly and to Brian. He
met with his friends regularly and for days we would see them
walking and waiting across the street from school looking to see if
he could see when she left before they would leave. We did not
know it at the time that he had his own hell ready to break loose
and torment the girl he once tried to impress and as for the rest of
us well, we were about to have a reign of terror come down upon
us and the fact that he would be in a lower grade didn't matter to
him. It was one more year of terror for others as far as he was
concerned. Many began to see just how sneaky and ornery Brian
was as he started his silent rampage that no one could prove or
control. Some of the kids who thought they would be hanging
with him found out he had no use for them and he would push
them around knocking books out of their hands and stealing their
items he didn't know half the time what he was taking.

He was letting his anger vent out on the boys who told him
about Lisa. He was calm in front of everyone watching and
walked away from her when it occurred but a month after, the
word got around that he and his four friends went to where she
lived one late night. The story was in depth how they went into
her bedroom through the window she usually kept open, pulled her
out of her bed and raped her. Everyone's whispers suggested that
his friends held her down in the alley behind her house and that
when he was done with her he let them take part in their demented

sex play. It was extremely graphic what the kids were saying they did to her from the five of them having spread her legs wide open and having their way with her to them bending her over and entering inside her rectum. There was no room left to the imagination by the time word got around the school of what had happened to her and they even said Brian and his friends urinated in her face and mouth. Each person had a different variation after a certain point but all said that one of the boys stuffed her panties she was wearing in her mouth after she bit his hand when he tried to stop her from screaming. Some claimed her brother heard the noise and went to her rescue but they over powered him, ripped his underpants off and bend him over and started chanting for Brian to do the same to him. No one ever said anything about the matter when we saw her and her brother at school but we all thought there was something very strange going on when we noticed Lisa changing directions when Brian came into the cafeteria or when they were walking down the halls coming from opposite ends.

Whispers were suggestive to the fact that it must have been true and others said she was just being the bitch she can be and was continuously snubbing him. Lisa held her head high and never let on that she or her brother had been victims of abuse at the hands of Brian and his friends. Brian was relentless and he knew she was avoiding him and one day Lisa turned to go in another direction after they saw each other and he decided to follow her.

Brian, Mel, Derek, Todd and Reggie were outside and spotted Lisa as she turned to go in the other direction. "Mel, Derek, you see what I see? Go cut across the street and get ahead of her to cut her off."

"Hey Brian come on man we're in front of school, man."

"Look Reggie it's harmless but I just want to remind her, what happens if someone decides to embarrass me in front of um, anybody or nobody." Brian said pointing his finger at Reggie and laughing as he nodded for the other two to take flight. He moved through the crowd of kids who were blocking his path pushing some out of the way without regard to their existence, with Todd hot on his trail.

Mel and Derek made it down the street and crossed over to the side where Lisa was walking before she noticed them ahead of her. When she saw them she stopped and turned to go back the other way as Brian and Todd stood boldly in front of her. She froze wide-eyed watching to see what he was going to do.

"Got anything to say?" Brian asked. He stared into her eyes and started licking his lips but she stood still not saying a word and yet the rage inside of her caused her eyes to well up with tears.

"ANSWER ME!" He shouted as he moved in closer to her drawing the attention of some of the students.

Lisa backed into one of the guys and screamed.

"NO, LET GO OF ME!" She yelled as she dropped her books. One of her friends called out that she was going to get a teacher.

"I'M OK!" Lisa yelled. "I'm okay I just dropped my books, forget it, it's nothing." She continued.

"Hey man, back away she said she can do it herself." Brian said as he backed away with his hands up to show he had not touched her.

Valerie and Roxanne had heard of the stories told about Brian and what he did to Lisa but they did not question her about it. They figured if it was true and she wanted to tell them then she

would tell them in her own time. They also felt that maybe she was too ashamed to say anything to anyone especially if they did to her brother as some insinuated.

"Hey Lisa, we'll help you." Valerie said.

They went over to her having to pass by Brian, and they clearly expressed politeness by excusing themselves. They did not know if any of it about him was true but the way things were unfolding, it seemed more conceivable to them that it was probably real and they did not want to take any chances of him coming after them. They kneeled down to join their friend.

"No, wait," Lisa whispered. "…Let me just wait here until they leave." She pleaded.

She did not want to rise for she had urinated in her panties and did not want anyone to know. She wore jeans but she could feel the warm wet substance spreading through her pants and getting cold fast. Brian nodded to Mel and Derek and turned to face the direction where he and Todd came from and the other two followed where they all walked up to Reggie who stayed behind. The girls could hear Brian yelling at him.

"What you stay up here for we didn't hurt the girl, why you always wanting to punk out bitch." Brian said and continued to walk by brushing up against him. Reggie kept silent and their other three friends looked at him and kept walking following Brian without saying a word.

Students walked by Lisa, Valerie and Roxanne, some offering to help Lisa as they got closer and others staring at the misfortune they felt had taken place. Other students whispered to each other and giggled and Lisa thanked those who tried to help before sending them on their way and ignored those that were being rude

and childish. Valerie and Roxanne were the two best friends that Lisa could have ever wished for and when everyone left, she felt that she had to confess of her current situation to her girlfriends, clearly embarrassed by the whole ordeal but she swore them to keep her secret.

"Everything's true she said as she kept her head low and her voice even lower. Those bastards did everything you heard." Lisa admitted.

"Are you shitting us, girl you've got to tell somebody you can't let him get away with this kind of stuff?"

"Girl, please, what am I going to tell the cops that I was forced to do what half this school says I do just to get a good grade? And we all know there are names that want to remain unmentioned and besides those bitches who think they're better than me would have a field day. Right now they can only speculate and if I hold my head up high, the only thing they can do right now is wonder if it's true or not."

"Alright, I hear you girl but we need to do something. What if he decides to come after me or Valerie?"

"He won't, neither one of you mouthed off at him in front of everybody like I did."

"That don't matter, he might hate the fact that we're friends and want to make it round two and three." She said pointing to Valerie and then to herself.

"Give it a rest Roxy, I doubt he's going to come after us and Lisa just because you mouthed off, it don't give him the right to violate."

"That's alright you know they say hell hath no fury like a woman scorn and that is something that motherfucker will surely

learn the hard way."

"What you gonna do girl?"

"I don't know but until that unknown event against him is to take place at the moment my biggest problem is a little more personal than that right now. I lost control when he came up to me."

"Girl who can blame you, that motherfucker was all up in your space." Val said, turning and lifting her head making sure he and his friends and nobody else could hear what she just said.

"No, I mean I lost control. I need a sweater to cover my pants."

"Oh shit, are you kidding me. Well, I can't say I blame you because I was about to lose it myself; and he wasn't anywhere near me. Oh shit and I ain't got a thing with me, oh, wait, here, I brought my sash it's big enough to cover a cow."

"Thanks, Roxy I've always wanted to be compared to a heifer."

"Girl, hush, you know what I mean, besides, it'll look real cute with what you're wearing." She reached inside her bag, unfolded the garment, and held it out so Lisa was able to stand without anyone noticing the wet spot on her jeans. The three girls had been friends since kindergarten and told each other everything. Including the things they had done with boys and the experiments with drinking they had tried but Lisa was the queen of them all when it came to the sexual experiences and they all knew it.

Lisa developed at an early age and by the time she finished putting on makeup and dressed herself in tight clothing she managed to get herself into the underground nightclubs that were clearly the establishments for twenty-one and older. That didn't

stop her because she knew those who were sixteen to twenty could get in if they knew somebody that would vouch for them knowing that only the discreet would be let in the club. If the bouncer was feeling generous and he knew there were some younger than the required age he would sneak them in for a small fee. Lisa was barely twelve and managed to manipulate the things she wanted because she learned plenty from her mother who brought men to the house who on many occasions wanted to have their way with her too but she stayed away. She focused her attention on the men who could benefit her academically and financially and she wanted to stay away from the same men who had been with her mother.

She was exceptionally choosy but also took care of the few she befriended for letting her in the club who also slipped a few bills into her pocket. She was not too far from achieving the same reputation her mother had acquired but she felt that her mother did what she had to do to support the both of them and she understood and felt that what she was doing was what she had to do to get ahead at school and in life. She learned from her mother that she could use her feminine attributes in life to get ahead and saw herself much like her mother and never having any problem following the example set before her but it was not until she met Larry when she learned that the things she was doing in life could get risky.

THE CON ARTIST

September 1971, Larry, Caucasian, genius who graduated
high school at seventeen, a financial tech business school at
nineteen and at 20 years old landed a job in the financial district as
a junior accountant. He lived near the train tracks about an hour
ride out of Manhattan and enjoyed the daily commute to and from
Long Island. He spent his mornings reading the financial section
in the newspaper, walked by the lingerie store at lunch time and
visited the porn shop after work where he frequently purchased a
new movie. He flashed and spent his money to impress the ladies
and many times on his way back home, he and some of the other
passengers on the train got a bit wild, drank too much, and partied
hard in the bar car as though they own the place.

The drinks on the train were expensive but he would buy one
or two to keep things from looking suspicious and after that he and
others provided their own personal stash of alcoholic beverages
and that way he would have the needed cash flow to buy some of
the women a few drinks and then try out his advances on them but
usually with no success. He would always leave very horny and
unsatisfied. Lisa took the train for a week and spotted Larry,
monitoring his behavior and tactics. She figured if she could get
one of the more cash indulgent men whom lived out of her district
things would go a lot smoother when it was time to break it off and
she could gather the much-needed cash flow her family lacked.

He was medium build, brown hair with a bit of a small round
belly but nothing she thought to be disgusting and it had not

phased her one bit that he was eight years older. She was watching him shell out some cash repeatedly and offering to join different women on the train who were gladly taking his offer to buy them drinks but were not interested in him for anything else. She did not take the chance of someone recognizing her for any reason in case things did not go as she planned. Each day her hair was up in a ponytail and she wore light colors and looked the part of a school girl but this night she wore a dark trench coat over a long jean skirt and a black turtle neck sweater, hat on her head covering most of her face and sat ignoring her prey reading a newspaper until it was time to get off the train. She knew he was drunk and exited before him but waited to see which direction he would walk. She followed immediately when she saw him heading in the opposite direction the train was heading and ran in front of him when they got near a park. She stepped out of the long jean skirt to reveal a mini, took off her hat, quickly released her hair out of the ponytail, removed her coat then dropped the paper when he was only a few feet away waiting until the right moment to seductively bend over to pick it up.

She could clearly see he was willing and he could not do anything to control himself. He slowed down as he got closer staring at her and swallowing hard. She timed her movements perfectly turning slightly making sure her face was right in front of his bulge when she went to get up. She rose slowly and upon reaching his ear, she whispered to him giving her innocent helpless act of needing money for her mother so the bank would not take their home. She elaborated more than needed but it did not matter because she could tell he was generous and she wanted to secure the deal for some immediate cash that night. He gladly gave her a

hundred dollars, she touched him leading him into the darkened area of the park where by 7:30pm it was late enough during the autumn months for all who understood that if you went in there past a certain time during the evening, you were more likely interested in the same type of one on one action with your unknown partner as everyone else was with their newly found friend. Men were with women and men on men and mostly the loners who watched their newly interested buddy for the comparing and mutual ejaculatory episodes.

After Larry and Lisa finished their business, she explained just how old she was and that he needed to be prepared to shell out a few hundred more dollars and by the time she left him, she had five hundred dollars in her hand. She left the park first only to follow him to see where he lived. She stalked him reminding him of her age and desperation and how no one would ever know if he agreed to meet her mother and start helping them out at home. Her mother was very young when she gave birth to Lisa and many times when the two were together people thought they were sisters.

Lisa told him if he continued offering to help with any financial overload, they were experiencing she would continue to be a part of the deal as a bonus and they would keep it a secret. When he agreed, she arranged for her mother to meet him and explained to her how lonely and financially capable he was to help the family out. It was the first time she ever shared a man with her mother and felt no shame in being a lifeline to helping their needs. She was sharp and very much aware of what she was capable of doing and within two months, Larry had shelled out a substantial amount of money in return for his fulfillment. By the time she was done he paid the amount of several mortgages but their house was

already paid but Lisa's con was thick and she gave him the impression that it was all for her mom to help them get out of the financial hole that was about to cause them to lose their home.

The Christmas holidays were over and Lisa saw to it that her mom and she had a lucrative one but she was getting bored and it was during one cold snowy day in February 1972 when she met Larry in the park and told him she thought it was time they went their separate ways.

"It wouldn't be wise of you to try to end this between us because I'm sure your mother and neighbors would be glad to know what a little whore you are and how you use men to get what you want. I'm sure suing your mother for everything she's got would keep you and her on your backs for several years to come."

"You wouldn't dare."

"Oh and what about the cops knowing how your mother used sex against a young man to get all the things she wanted and then threatened me with rape if I didn't continue to give her money."

"You did what you wanted and you're old enough to know what you were doing you won't get away with that kind of a lie."

"Oh, no and how about all the money withdrawn out of my account where did it go, you think there won't be an investigation? And what about me, telling them that she threatened me to say that you were sexually abused by me, the way I see it my hands were tied and I obeyed the cunning threats and was manipulated by the desires of an older woman."

"You're always trying to pick up on women and you would be exposed for a sexual predator."

"You said it yourself, I'm always trying to pick up on women and how would you know that if you weren't stalking me which

means you lead me on to believe you were of age and your mother knew all about it. I'm respected in the world of business and lewd approaches are not my style of operation." He said he could prove that he was always respectful and never tried to force himself on any of the women his own age when he approached them. Larry continued to tell Lisa that although she was cunning and looked innocent he was able to monitor her and her extracurricular activities with pictures of other older men she was flirting with sexually and allowing them to grab her playfully.

"Look, what do you want? Please I'll do anything."

"Oh, yeah you will and this time it's not going to be your mother that will continue to please me in every way I can think and I have a few surprises that whether you enjoy them or not, I'm definitely going to be looking forward to them."

Lisa pleaded with him not to expose her and she told him how she would continue to do as he wished as long as word never got back to her mother. She was persistent when she begged him to make him feel as though he was in control of the situation. She let him give out his demands of what he expected from her and she continued to seem helpless and ended their night pleasing him orally. She watched as he left feeling victorious, went home and called some friends who were grateful for her services in the past and they were more than willing to help her out during her desperate time of need.

LARRY'S DILEMMA

Larry laid on his couch in the living room one night with a beer in one hand and his other hand down his shorts. He was watching a movie from one of the many videos from his porn collection. There was a single tap at the door, sounding as though someone had thrown something up against it. He looked over toward the window near the front door when he heard it. He got up to check but did not see anything out of the ordinary when he looked out the window. He could not see any movement indicating that there was anyone at the door nor were there any more sounds so he decided it was nothing and went back to continue watching his program. He watched the people on the screen and after about ten minutes, the man in the movie was ready to reach his climatic experience, he removed himself from the woman as he moaned with anticipation.

The man in the movie moved his hand up and down himself frantically, and Larry sat there making each movement in rhythm to the man on the screen thinking about Lisa and what he would have her do for him. It was his lust for her that brought him trouble he did not expect...

The ride to Long Island was not one they thought to be pleasant. It was snowing most of the day and the cold was biting through every garment worn by the people who had the desire to be out from the warmth of their home. The stars shined bright lighting up the sky, it was clear and the air was crisp as if one could snap it in two like a twig. The clean fresh scent had a

lingering aroma indicating that the heavens were descending to cleanse the filth in the earth.

The wind blew causing the soft white flakes that fell from the sky to fly recklessly into the faces of all who braved the night. Each one stared into nothing and took a sip of scotch to help warm their bones, as they stood unspoken and without regard to each other's presence.

They had to wait for the train that was late arriving and causing them more frustration because the cold was in the night where one choosing to wear gloves was not an option but a necessity and impatience won over those who had a mission of refuge for their damsel in distress. The train ride alone was not one the young men wanted to take and they constantly thought about the young white boy over twenty that they were about to meet. The four men were in their early to mid twenties, the first man was the leader at twenty-four and the rest were about twenty-three years but not older. The second in command had the nickname the butcher, and the last two were part of the posse as extra muscle.

They all had one thing in common other than the ride they were taking and that was to visit Larry because their needs has also been satisfied by the one they were going to defend. They were heading to the house of the one who thought he would take advantage of their friend but unknowingly was about to meet the four who was ready to dismember any necessary parts they deemed appropriate to take from their unsuspecting opponent.

…The man let out a bursting yell and the woman screamed at the same time as Larry was about to join in with a shout of pleasure from his own rhythmic movements. He continued to

watch his porno, when suddenly the four men bust in his front door and charged him, by the time they reached him, they were ready to bust his head wide open with a crow bar one of the muscle men was holding.

"Hey motherfucker, we're gonna break your fucking neck, you think you're the man fucking a young girl, barely turned twelve, you son of a bitch." The butcher said.

Larry was terrified and tried to run out the back door. They grabbed hold of him and punched him around, placed him on his knees and tied his hands and feet.

"Where are the pictures?" The leader demanded.

"What pictures, I don't know what you're talking about I don't have any pictures." Larry insisted.

"Don't lie to me, man, the pictures of Lisa with the other men you told her you had, where are they? And I'm not going to ask you again."

The butcher went into the kitchen and came out with a pot and a butcher knife. Larry tried to beg for mercy but the third man got behind him and started strangling him.

"You like that hot black pussy, don't you, and now you want to blackmail the girl to staying with you, man you should have just walked away."

The fourth man came in close as Larry was trying to breathe and pulled out a pair of girl panties and stuffed them in his mouth, then he strapped a thick piece of rope around his partially opened mouth and the one strangling him tightened it to gag him from screaming for help.

"Now how you gonna go and gag the man after I asked him a question?" The leader asked.

"Well, he can answer you, all he got to do is nod his head, ain't that right, man?" The fourth man asked.

He was holding the crow bar as he looked at Larry and Larry nodded.

"...See what I mean," he looked back at Larry. "...Do you have any pictures of the girl you've been fucking?"

Larry quickly shook his head, no.

The fourth man looked at the first.

"...Think you can handle it from here."

The leader gave his partner an indignant look and began questioning Larry.

"So you telling us you were lying to her when you said you had pictures." Again, Larry answered quickly, this time nodding his head, yes.

"...Are you lying to me now, cause you know what I'll do to you if you're lying and we find out later there are pictures." Again, Larry responded quickly shaking his head, tears falling from his eyes.

"Not so manly right now are you, motherfucker. You like sticking your white cock in little black girls, now you see, what I'm thinking is that maybe you should donate what you got down there to her on a permanent basis." The butcher said.

He had the pot and the knife with him and kneeled down next to Larry.

"...You know what's going in there my man."

Larry's eyes widened as he looked at the man who revealed the butcher knife and shook his head frantically trying to back away. The butcher moved closer to him digging his right heel into the carpet and dragging his left knee in order to keep up with him

from getting out of his reach with the knife ready to make his incision. Desperately Larry tried to make sounds of screaming while jumping up and down on his knees, his body twisting from left to right. He fell over onto his side hitting the floor, his hands tied and feet bound. His movements were out of desperation as he still tried to scream through the gag. His actions looked as though he was having convulsions and the tears flowing blinded him, the moans coming from him were non- stop until finally he laid still sobbing uncontrollably, his body trembling.

The butcher took no concern to Larry's emotional state and moved in closer, Larry tightened his thighs still trying to fight himself away but the man grabbed hold of his underwear and began to saw away at the material until Larry was exposed and still he tried to move away pleading through the gag in his mouth.

"Wait!"

"See man, I knew you were gonna do some shit like this, let me just cut his shit and that'll teach him not to go around messing with young girls not old enough to be played."

"Well let's look at the situation the way it happened, he looked down at Larry, lucky for you man, we know who it is you been messing with and she told us everything."

"How am I to keep my rep as the butcher if you keep doing shit like this?"

Larry laid still looking back and forth between the man with the knife and the one who was in charge.

"We gonna look at this from my man's point of view, for the moment."

He knelt down next to Larry.

"...Let's see now, a hot young thing come at you over and

over and you're in a weakened place and she swears to you no one would ever find out and be it told, I believe the first time, you were practically falling down drunk."

"Don't matter, back the fuck up, cause I gots to cut his shit."

Larry was nodding in desperation and then heard the butcher speaking, and desperately started shaking his head.

"So you're telling me that you weren't drunk?" Larry shook his head, and then nodded, and then he stopped and looked at him with wide eyes. The leader smirked.

"...I know you were drunk and not only that, she hooks you up with moms, and being a generous white boy you think you're helping them from their financial mess and stop 'The Man' from taking their home." Larry looked at the butcher and nodded frantically.

"...You could say he was their shinning white knight helping to save the day, so we got to give him that." The leader said as he looked at his cohorts. The two other guys nodded expressing their agreement and agreed with each other acknowledging they were right to agree with the leader. The leader watched them and shook his head.

"...Unbelievable." He whispered to himself as he moved in closer to Larry.

"...Let's see if we can put this in a way you can understand." Larry's eyes were wide and he was nodding to everything he heard trying silently to proclaim his attempts to stay out of range of the butcher.

"...If we leave what you got alone, you promise to break it off with her mom and never bother Lisa again." Larry nodded to show he was willing to obey and relieved they gave him an option.

The leader put on a thick black glove and reached down to grab Larry between his legs.

"...If we come back, we take this with us." He squeezed and Larry moaned in agony.

"...Remember, break it off, you have until 7:00pm tomorrow night, you do like we say and you'll never see us again. It's not like we actually travel in your circle, and technically nor you in ours, if you know what I mean, so it shouldn't really be much of a problem for you, am I right my man."

Again, out of gratitude and desperation Larry nodded frantically, the leader nodded to the butcher and the man moved in closer to Larry who started to scream again through the gag, the man turned him face down on the floor and cut the twine they had used to bind his hands. He left his feet tied, the other two men kneeling, rose to their feet, and the four of them watched over the frightened young man staring at him as he sniveled on the floor covering his manhood, elated with the fact it was still there. The four turned to leave. One of the men picked up a watch as they were making their way through the door. The leader took it out of his hand, threw it back where his friend took it from, and pushed him out the door.

The butcher still had the knife and was the last to leave. He walked to the door and turned to face Larry who was still on the floor, he pointed his finger at him then through the knife causing it to land in the carpet next to the pot and where Larry laid then he turned and walked out closing the door gently behind him.

Larry breathed deeply rolling onto his back and untied the rope from across his face, he removed the garment they stuck inside his mouth and before he untied his feet and out of pure

gratitude that he was still able to perform the act, he reached down and masturbated in the panties they had left behind.

FELIX THE SNITCH

…The girls composed themselves and started on their way and though talking, nervously laughing about some of the things they had been through together as they walked off from the area where Lisa had the encounter, they were grateful they had each other.

At first, it seemed strange when the story about Lisa reached us but then after seeing her reactions to Brian, it became more suspicious that the stories were true. Still it was uncertain if everything was in fact the way it unraveled because we all knew she embarrassed him and it was easy to make it seem as if it were true. When word surfaced that one of the boys who lived near her claimed he could hear and see what was going on from his upstairs window overlooking the back alley, the gossip quickly became factual news worthy. Now we had a witness and that changed everything and that bit of information not only spread like wild flowers but the school was aware that there was more than the impression of probability.

Felix never liked Brian mainly because Brian took a pair of his glasses and broke them intentionally and then immediately apologized when he saw a teacher coming in their direction and tried to act as if it was an accident. He brought the whole incident regarding Lisa up to Brian a few days after he was telling everyone he was able to see everything from his back window. Tuesday afternoon during lunch, Felix told everyone he was going to get the information he needed from Lisa and her brother because they

were his friends. He tried to rally others to join his personal
protest to help vindicate Lisa's reputation and expose Brian. Three
days later two boys were waiting at the bus stop where Felix got
off to walk home. The driver noticed some other kids with their
backs to the bus but a couple of them kept looking up and over
their shoulders. No one knew if the driver was curious or had
good instincts but considering his route did not consist of picking
anyone up at that hour, he pulled the bus up further away from the
normal drop off point then opened the door. The mob rushed
toward the bus, as Felix was about to get off but the driver closed
the door fast and pulled away from the curb as the kids started
screaming obscenities to Felix and throwing bottles and rocks at
the bus.

They chased after the bus screaming.

"You think you're going to tell." One yelled.

"Yeah, I'd like to see you squeal with a broken jaw." Another
said.

The rest of them started chanting.

"Broken jaw, broken jaw, broken jaw!"

The driver looked at Felix.

"Those guys want to give you a serious beating."

Everyone on the bus moved to one side where they could look
out the window and see the gang running and yelling after them.
A girl on the bus admitted it was frightening to see so many people
chasing the bus to cause harm to one kid. Felix was terrified. He
was a good kid and one who never had any trouble with anyone in
the past. He just happened to choose to go up against the wrong
person.

The driver drove straight for two blocks then turned the

corner and went back to the stop where he normally let Felix out only this time he turned the corner and drove further up the street where Felix was only less than a block from his house. He wanted to take him closer but he could not travel down the block where Felix's house was because it was a dead end street and with the two motor homes parked there would have made it difficult for him to back out and the fact that Felix's house was on the opposite side of the street was only going to allow the mob to catch up to them.

The crowd was still behind the bus but about a block away. Felix started to get off and start running but first turned and said that he was hoping the close proximity to his house gives him more of a chance to make it unscathed. Some looked at each other not understanding what he meant but yelled for him to go. We watched as he ran. Most of us on the bus were cheering for him to get home safely.

"It's so close Felix, you can do it." One girl encourage

"He's a geek he could be two houses away and wouldn't make it." A guy added.

"Whose side are you on?" She retorted.

We continued to watch as Felix was running so hard one of his sneakers came off but without missing a step, he kept his intention on getting home. We all watched in anticipation as Felix ran for his life desperately trying to make it to his front yard. The crowd was closing in on him and two of the guys were about one house away from catching up to him when one girl screamed when she saw him open the gate to his yard and ran out of sight.

"…He made it, he made it." She cried.

It was clear to me that Brian was behind the sudden interest of

Felix when those boys showed up wanting to annihilate him. Brian was nowhere around when the event took place and so no one could point the finger at him but the whispers traveled and we could tell that this kid was a professional bully and had been getting away with this sort of stuff for years. When we went back to school Monday the word had already gotten out that no one should try to squeal on Brian and as a rule on anyone else either.

It was crazy how so much chaos was taking place once Brian arrived. He put Bullies to shame. In fact, he bullied some of the bullies. Some of the boys would talk about standing up to him when he was nowhere in sight but they would get shut down when one of them mentioned that all those who wanted to go up against Brian should go for it but not to expect anyone else to help them.

"Hey, you want to be stupid enough to go after that big scary son of a bitch you're on your own." One would say.

"Yeah, he has an entire football team on his side." Another added. Other boys would agree not to get involve and everyone acted as though no one ever mentioned it. Brian had the place locked down to the way he wanted things and he was usually hanging around outside after school to make sure of it. Most times, he would have at least two of his four friends from his other school hanging out with him. News traveled fast when all four were outside waiting for him. The word would go around as if it had to be on the front page of the morning newspaper the next day that everyone would be talking about it before the last bell rang. When they were all together, we would wonder if whether or not Brian and his friends wanted to beat someone up, chase some poor kid mercilessly, grab his shoes or his books and whatever cash he had or some other form of torment he and his friends wanted to

perform on some poor soul.

Some of the kids referred to him and his friends as the five assholes but none of us would ever say it aloud especially if we thought anyone would repeat it to him or his friends. No one wanted to get beat up but there were those who did not care if blood was shed especially when the blood was not their own. One day some kid who did not like this other kid told some big mouth girl that the boy said Brian was a jerk and word got back to Brian. He found the girl and whatever he said to her, she confessed who it was that she thought made the remark and it was to no avail that she repeatedly told Brian that it was just hearsay based on some other kid telling her but it didn't matter to him and the kid never knew what hit him. He suffered from a broken jaw by the time Brian was done with him and no one was ever able to connect him to the incident. The kid was scared shitless and never told anyone who attacked him. The worse thing about the ordeal was that it was all a lie in the first place. That kid's parents were so mad at the school board they pulled the boy out of school and transferred him somewhere else.

"We're going to get to the bottom of this!" The principal said.

We would always have to endure the usual speech when they spoke those words but this time they were scared of a lawsuit. I think every kid in school had to submit to an interview to see if we had any involvement or any information leading to the expulsion of all of those involved. Like everything else, the word spread and everyone was talking about how the kid's parents were going to sue the school and probably have it shut down. Fortunately, the parents never sued but the cops were involved and no one ever

pointed the finger at or even suggested that Brian or any of his friends were involved in what had happened and we never heard of the matter again.

Somehow, when it came to Brian things had a way of disappearing as if they never occurred. He was a terror ready to pounce and everyone was afraid of him. He attacked and did not care of how far he pushed someone, completely oblivious to the fact that he might be pushing too far and that there could be someone on the other end ready to retaliate.

I guess Brian was not ready for the lessons in life that could destroy a man, at least that's what Murphy always had to say about any given situation forcing one to defend himself and though I had to wonder where he learned to convey his messages, sometimes the words he spoke needed no explanation.

#

"It's not until one is cornered does the hidden strength from within is truly developed into manifestation."

NEW PREY FOR BRIAN

…Monday morning and we were back at school and the anticipation I was feeling without fail diminished when I saw her in the hallway. Sometimes Sara had to leave on time to meet with her parents and if that was the case, she usually met me at lunch and would explain why she could not meet with me after school but most days we were able to meet as usual to continue talking about the different things that happened in our lives. We continued to meet at our favorite spot under a tree on the school grounds. The day was warm and sunny and I started talking about Brian searching to see if he could trap any of the kids he enjoyed harassing. I told her how I had happened to be one of the fortunate ones clever enough to dodge him but that it did not last long.

"I didn't think the weekend was ever going to end Sara. I didn't have much to do."

"Well didn't you play with any of your friends over the weekend?"

"I usually don't bother trying to play with them because I've been meeting with my uh neighbor well he's more like my uncle. It doesn't matter now I'm glad we're back in school."

"I've missed you too John." She smiled and touched my arm.

I told her how Brian had made me his target before she started attending our school and how he caused havoc in my life. He was making sure things were as uncomfortable for me as possible.

"As far as I'm concerned he and his friends were the daytime version of a nightmare in my life."

"Yeah, he's definitely a bully and takes what he wants, doesn't he?"

I missed the innuendo and continued to share details how he would tear up my papers destroying homework or notes from previous lessons and push me back and forth threatening me to keep my mouth shut or else.

"All chances of studying for a test would be lost if Brian stole papers unless I was able to get someone to let me copy their notes. Most times the ones who did not mind helping me took lousy notes and the ones who were straight 'A' students did not want to associate themselves with the target of a bully. After taking the heat for so many destroyed works that were scheduled for the next day in class or having to do homework in a different class to make up for what Brian had taken, I made sure that I started doing all of my work in duplicates."

"John that's a lot of work, he was really mean to you."

"Yeah, I was always scared he would take all of my books the way he did when he picked on Alvin."

"Who's Alvin?"

"Alvin was this kid who did his work and mind his own business and tried desperately to stay out of anything that involved other students. One day he was going home after stopping off at the post office and at around the same time I guess I decided to take a short cut through the alley to go home after having dropped off a package to one of my mom's friends. I found Alvin trying to catch hold of what looked like to be every piece of paper known to the universe."

#

"What happened here?"

"I'll give you three guesses, or I should say guesses involving 5 assholes."

"You mean they took all your papers and just threw them across the alley."

"Yeah, they said if I didn't want to get my teeth knocked in I had better hand them my book bag, so I did and this was the results."

"Man, that's rough."

I helped Alvin pick up all his belongings and a woman drove in the alley to turn down the pathway to get to her car garage.

"What the hell are you two doing making this mess?"

"We didn't make this mess lady some guys stole his book bag from him and threw all of his things on the ground and I'm helping him pick them up." I said indignantly.

#

"What I didn't know at the time was that Brian was watching me, something Alvin told me later, about a few months later after I had fallen victim to his abuse. He said that when I was explaining what had happened to the mean woman, he noticed Brian and his friends standing at the entrance of the alley looking in. When he saw them looking down the alley that was the reason he took off so fast and he didn't have time to think about telling me what was happening. Ever since I helped him, he noticed Brian would wait outside the school to find out when I was coming out of the building, what I was doing at lunch and that he waited so long to tell me because he did not want to try to go up against Brian and his gang to warn me so he always chose to take a different route home. I could not blame him and I told him it was understandable of him doing so and admitted I was tempted plenty of times myself

to find a different way to go home."

I know Sara would have been understanding but I decided to keep to myself that it was during the time Brian was finding out what my schedule was like when he found out something very incriminating against me and did everything in his power to use it to his advantage…

THE BASEMENT

Sara listened intently as I explained to her how I found out about what had been happening with my friend Sammy and our so-called fine upstanding teacher Mr. Jake McIntire.

"I have to tell you something about Mr. McIntire John, he's not who he says he is. He's an evil man."

"I know Sara."

"But people seem to think he's a good man but they are confusing someone who has an upstanding position and the quality of the man and this man is evil," She continued.

"…Wait," She paused. "…How do you know?"

"Remember when I told you Sammy took the kid to the top of the stairwell in the hall that day."

"Wait, John you didn't tell me about that, I'm getting confused, did you really because I don't remember."

"Okay, wait, maybe I didn't but it doesn't matter because I'm about to tell you now. I believe you Sara about Mackey but that's what I'm trying to tell you about him."

I felt as though I was having flashbacks as I continued to talk to her about Mackey and what he was doing to Sammy and his mother and that Sammy died.

"I'm so sorry John, you must have felt awful."

"Yeah, I think I can deal with it better now anyway this kid thought the day was gonna be normal and right before lunch Mackey took him to the side and told him they had to discuss his grades and how poorly he thought the boy was doing. He

promised to get him back before lunch was over and led him to a door, he opened it and quickly grabbed him by the arm, looking behind him making sure no one saw them going in, he closed and locked the door behind them. When they got inside he grabbed hold of the kid's waist lifting his feet off the floor, it was dark but Mackey had been down there many times before so he knew exactly where he was going without risk of falling. He moved his hands like lightning covering the boys' mouth to stop any potential sounds from coming out of him while he quickly ran down the remainder of the steps holding him close to his body. He rushed him over to an area forcing him by his neck to bend him over an old table as he pulled both their pants and underwear down to expose their nakedness. He maneuvered his hand into a jar of Vaseline he had already set in place in order to spread up and down his protruding flesh until he was able to push himself inside the tiny frail bottom of his victim. He breathed hard into the kid's ear and then he said…"

#

"Sammy tried to warn you about me but he didn't last long enough to tell you and he should have told you when the two of you were at the top of the stairs. I didn't realize before then that I had forgotten to lock the door that day but he got scared and ran away. You heard the noise of the one I had down here but you could not see in the darkness and I was hoping you would come down to investigate.

…After I heard him talking to you, I had to increase my surveillance on you to find out more so I got you to start taking lessons at my studio. I thought maybe you really enjoyed hanging out there listening to the movies but I couldn't get a read on you

but I bet you enjoyed it the first time we were there didn't you.

...I saw you with those two kids in the boy's bathroom. I listened at the door at first and there was one behind a stall that had no door while the other two were making fun of him. I opened the door and I could hear that they were grunting out sounds and they were acting as if they were trying to use it too when I peaked inside. What gets me is the kid wasn't trying to tell them to get away so I'm thinking whoever it was must have liked the fact they were watching him."

The boy listened to the teacher and tried to utter out the sounds to deny what he was hearing but Mackey added more pressure to his mouth to keep him from saying anything.

"...And the most interesting part of it is when he got off the seat one of the other boys laid down on the floor with his pants down and guess who step out from behind the stall, yeah, you're right, and nothing was done to try to stop it, not even a protest."

Mackey pushed his face closer to the boy's ear.

"...You were waiting to get on top of him weren't you?"

"No, I..."

"Don't say another word. You were clever the way you got your mom to let you stop playing the piano but I was prepared for that and if I couldn't keep tabs on you at my studio well as you can see I have a nice little nest down here waiting for all those like you who know the curiosity within is waiting to be unleashed."

#

I looked at Sara void of any feeling and continued using the third person of the one I was describing in the basement with Jake and spoke carefully choosing my words...

"He told his victim that there was no need to try to deny what

he was saying because he had the story of the two kids who were willing to tell the school principal and his mother the whole thing was true. Mackey told him about the legal system having the right to take him away from his mother if he told anyone what he was doing to him because he would bring out proof that she was an unfit mother."

Sara sat emotional as she listened to the story I had told. She touched my hand.

"John, was the kid in the story you."

"What makes you say that?"

"I guess, well I don't know, I'm sorry I shouldn't have asked, I didn't mean to imply…"

"Don't worry about it, it's no big deal. Let's go, I think your parents are probably out front." We got up and walked to the front of the school but we had another fifteen minutes before her parents were due. She took my hand knowing there was more going on inside of me than the impatient behavior of waiting for her parents. She tried to get me to think of something else.

"Let's take a walk to the corner and back. You know you've been doing all the talking, not that I mind, I love listening to your voice but maybe we should find out what's been going on with me, and me again and then maybe some more about me." She said smiling. We laughed and I asked her if her dad had ever taken her to Disneyland before. She was excited to talk about something she thought would take my mind off what I had been telling her in the park.

She talked and laughed as though she was reliving the time she was there once before and how much fun she had with her dad and right after mentioning him she suddenly got quiet and squinted

her eyes like she was seeing something distasteful and then she became sad. By the time I was asking her what was wrong she noticed her parents pulling up to the school and we ran back down the block. Before she got in the car, she whispered in my ear.

"I'll tell you all about it, later."

Sara got in the car and her dad drove away leaving me standing there to my own solemn thoughts. She was insightful enough to know that even after I had tried to deter her from thinking I was the kid in the story, she was right to have asked. I went home and lay on my bed after getting clean and then spending time with mom and eating. I lay there going over my day and continued remembering how Mackey had turned his attention to me after Sammy had passed away and at the same time how Brian was terrorizing me.

He had already succeeded once at the studio and now he was making bold choices to advance himself on me at school. Mackey finished what he started and then he let me pull up my pants and told me to wipe my face in the sink over by the steps. I was in shock and uncertain why he wanted to continue to do what he was doing to me. I thought I had managed to escape his urges after what happened at the studio when I convinced my mom I was not the piano playing type but now he had figured out a way to trap me at school. I did not know if I had encouraged him not having told anyone about him coming out of his room naked at the studio and what he had done or if he was acting out his own sick desires and trying to make me think it was something I wanted. He reminded me of how he could convince the courts to have me taken away from my mom if I got any ideas about exposing him.

He also said that if I were to tell anyone he would find a way

to get her to want him to do the same to her. I was shocked frozen for a moment and looked at him wide eyed immediately thinking about Sammy telling me how he felt like his mom wasn't his mom anymore. He pulled me toward the stairs and we went up. He walked ahead of me, listened at the door, and then looked through the small pane window making sure no one was walking by before opening it. We went out into the hall and he shut the door behind him staring at me. He took me back to the cafeteria and told me to go in and get some food so I would have energy to get through the day. He acted as though things were as usual before his act of violating me. We went to the cafeteria, he left and I stood at the entrance waiting. It looked as though everybody was laughing at me. They were eating and having a good time with their friends but it seemed to me they all knew what Mackey had done and was whispering and laughing about it.

One student came up behind me knocking my books out of my hand. He turned to face me and I heard him say…

#

"Get out of my way or I'll take you down there and fuck the shit out of you like that teacher just did."

"What, what teacher, did what, what are you talking about."

In reality, his phrase was nothing like what I thought he said and it was hard fighting back tears in a room full of people. Somehow, I managed to keep myself in control as I kneeled to pick up my books and one of the teachers monitoring the cafeteria came over to me and knelt down next to me.

"I hope he apologized for knocking your books out of your hand." She said as she handed me a book.

"What, oh him, yeah he was um," that's when I recalled what

he had actually said.

'I didn't mean to get in your way and knock you and your things down there, ah fuck, shit and that teacher saw what I did.'

"...Oh, yeah, he said sorry, I think."

"Honey, are you alright?"

I looked at her for a moment, wanting to tell her everything but I could not face the possibility of losing my mother.

"I'm fine thank you. I should go get something to eat if that's alright."

"Well of course it's alright. You go right on over and get you some food." She smiled genuinely at me. I finished gathering all my things, left, and got a tray to get lunch.

I tried sitting down at a nearby table only to feel the intense pain shoot through the inside of my bottom. I could not sit without remembering what had happened to me. I could taste his cheap after-shave in my throat and feel the gushy stuff still inside my body. I tried sitting on one side of my cheek to prevent applying pressure to the area but to no avail, anything I did helped. I was in too much pain to sit and the feeling of his liquid mass inside of me moving around when I moved was disgusting. That day was hell and I could not wait to get out of there. I did not feel as if I could eat anything and the sight of the food made me sick. I still had three more classes so I left my lunch and got up to leave.

"Wait a minute young man, you have to remove your tray and throw away what you don't want." A woman said.

I looked over to see a different woman talking to me. She wasn't as nice as the first one who helped me with my books. I picked up my tray, went over to the trash bin, emptied it, and placed the tray on the cart with the other trays. The cart was full

with plates, cups, utensils, napkins, food and other trash on it. I stared at the mess thinking how my life was just as jumbled. I left the cafeteria to go to the boy's room. It always amazed me that the bathroom next to the cafeteria was always dirtier than any other boy's bathroom in the whole building. I went inside, went behind the stall, and closed the door. I was frustrated to see the feet of someone in the stall next to the one I was using but he was having his own personal dilemma and the smell was overbearing. I covered my nose with my shirt and sat waiting, after a few minutes only the sound of passing gases escaped. I cleaned myself and could feel the mass of gooey matter I wiped onto the toilet paper as if I had diarrhea. The lunch bell sounded letting us know we had only three minutes to get to our next class.

"Shit!"

An appropriate term used by the kid in the stall next to me. I finished wiping myself, pulled up my pants, and left the stall to wash my hands at the sink. I washed them thoroughly hoping nothing got on my fingers and then washed them again. I splashed water on my face and dried my hands and eyes.

There were three classes left, two after lunch, recess and then the last class and they all were inescapably long. I wrote everything I saw on the blackboard from the first class and somehow managed to write the same thing repeatedly until finally I noticed my entire page consisted of the first two lines of information from the blackboard.

The bell rang.

I asked some of the other kids about homework and they looked at me as though I was from another planet. They laughed and one of the girls told me we had played charades in the first

class using material from previous class lessons and the other class was dedicated to do whatever homework or studies we had because it was a substitute teacher.

I was not thinking clearly, I couldn't believe I actually completed two classes since lunch but remembered that both those classes was in the same room and only the teachers changed but I knew most of the time we would not get homework from those classes and the teachers would just let us start on our homework from the classes we had from the earlier part of the day. When the school bell rang, it was finally over for the week but I was certain I was going to face more heartache and despair when I saw Brian leaning up against a car lighting a cigarette and staring at me.

I swallowed and continued to walk because if I had tried to run he would have chased me to where he and I both knew he would have been able to cut me off and then no one would have been around to help me. He wasn't too far from the school entrance and I took it as a sign that he would not bother me. I lowered my eyes, didn't look up at him, and kept walking knowing he was watching me. He got off the car he was leaning on and when I got close to him, I could see him grab himself between his legs.

"You like that don't you?" Mel was with him smiling.   I didn't say a word and walked passed him.

"Cheetah, cheetah, cheetah, yah, yah, yah," Mel yelled. He was trying to get my attention but I refused to look and I wanted to run but I just kept the same pace I was using when I walked passed them. I didn't know what was going on and I couldn't believe after everything that happened to me today, Brian was there telling me I liked what he was doing to himself, but I didn't have the

strength to deal with his childish games and I wanted to get away from there as soon as possible. I didn't feel comfortable about him being everywhere I turned but I thought it was because of what Alvin told me about him seeing me help him when he and his friends threw the boy's papers in the alley. I thought he wanted to intimidate me to make me think twice about helping someone he was bullying.

I was grateful that when I first got home to see mom was not there. I was one of the many known as a latch key kid. People knew latch key kids existed but we never were to mention it to anyone because someone of my age wasn't legally supposed to be home without adult supervision. I was never home for longer than an hour to an hour and thirty minutes and on rare occasions, I would be there for two hours before mom returned. I was familiar with who to get in contact with if something came up that needed an adult. I had all the numbers to the neighbors whom my mom trusted and would cover for her if there was a problem and I had the right information to call an ambulance or the police. From time to time, my mom's friend Shirley would check in on me to make sure things were okay. I quickly rushed to the bathroom and took a shower, I must have stayed in there an hour using soap between my legs until I was itching to the point I had to let the water rinse over me for a while before the itching stopped.

After the shower, I sat in a tub of warm water full of bubble bath my mom bought. I was certain there was a stench I smelled on myself and I wanted to get it off my person. The water drained from the tub and I watched hoping any foul odors on me were draining into the sewer. I successfully cleaned the tub and went to my room minutes before mom walked in the house.

I couldn't say anything to her or anyone and I had to continue my day as if nothing had happened. I knew she would want to know about school and when she asked, I had to lie and tell her I had a special homework assignment to complete because I wanted to go to my room and not be disturbed. I thought if I could just be by myself, I would figure out what I should do next.

Mom was very emotional, her life was in enough turmoil and I had sat in the back seat of Mackey's car and pretended I was asleep after the first encounter at his studio, at that time he offered to take us home because it was so late and so I didn't say anything to her then. Overall, I wasn't going to put her through the heartache of possibly losing her son, she had already lost a husband and a sister and I wasn't going to be the reason behind any more suffering in her life. I had to figure out a solution and make him pay for what he had done to me but I had no answers for the moment and I had to wait until a breath of insight was revealed to me, keep things together and go about life as normal as possible. I forgot that I had asked her to make my favorite dish, baked beans and hot dogs, and she knew I could not resist the sweet savoring flavor baked into the beans and hot dogs and the dripping sauce it made after she put in the syrup and brown sugar. It was the best dish she made and my favorite and I requested it every time she asked me what she should make for dinner. She laughed every time I answered her and she would know something was wrong if I did not have an appetite for the meal I waited five months to get. I didn't want to eat but I could not afford any suspicion of what had taken place at school to become evident. In some ways, I was hoping she would know something was wrong and start asking questions. She had no idea I was no longer pure. It was baffling to

me because she did not think I looked strange.

"Mom, do I look different to you?"

"No, precious why, should you look different?"

"Oh I don't know. I just thought maybe I looked different somehow."

"Are you getting sick? Come over here. You are looking a little flushed. What did you eat today?"

"Nothing, I just thought, never mind. I'm fine."

My whole world had crumbled and my mom had no idea what was going on inside of me. I managed to finish eating.

"Sweetie, maybe you should go to bed and get some rest and don't worry about your special assignment because I can write you a note." She said lovingly.

"Yeah, alright, but that's okay, I'll finish it, goodnight mom," I kissed her on the cheek.

She didn't know I only told her about a special project because I wanted to rush upstairs but I had to face her when she fixed my favorite dish. I lied. I headed up to my room.

"Goodnight dear, sleep well and let me know if you feel any different through the night," She said.

"...John, momma's always here for you, baby, you remember that." She added.

I turned to look her in the eyes to see the most loving creature on the face of this planet and again thoughts of destroying the knowledge of her son was no longer the same as she imagined was not an option. She had to believe that who she was speaking to was the same child she had raised.

"I love you mom."

"And I love you too, baby."

I turned away and headed to my room feeling the tear fall from my eye just as I had started walking away. I walked inside my room and turned the light off at the switch on my wall by the door. I walked over to my bed in complete darkness.

#

This is where I now lay across the top comforter in my shirt, jeans and sneakers and as I lay here, remembering what he did to me and how he made me lie to my mother, again. I felt a rage surge up inside of me and silently cried myself to sleep.

TEACHER'S PET

I went to school and found Sara in the hallway just as we had always seen each other in the past. We met in the park after school as usual and I talked more about some of the trials I encountered with Brian and his friends before she arrived. I thought for a moment before continuing what I would say to her about the winter of 1973 in January. Our Christmas vacation from school was over and a little more than six months had passed after I had the encounter with Murphy, a few since the death of Sammy and only two since I learned about Mackey's desires. For some reason I left out telling her anything I did with Murphy but I continued making frequent visits to see him usually before the weekend but then I started spending as many weekends as possible with him. I kept our meetings secret, which was not hard because most times the other kids did not notice or care that I was not around. Murphy showed me other items he had collected or that he had from his earlier days from his youth and told me the reasons why he had used them and the different situations he had encountered in his life that he believed will be some of the same that will encounter mine. I don't know what it was but he talked to me in riddles and as much as he confused me, the more I liked what he was saying. Even though I could not explain why or what he meant by most of the things he said to me, there was a connection I did not see as one I wanted to break. He was amazed at the strength I possessed that most considered my long thin frame was too inadequate to endure when it was time for any type of

physical training. I overwhelmed even myself at the diligent fortitude I embraced to countless hours of repeated exercise. He could see the determination was far beyond fitting into my environment but a need of self-acceptance. Murphy was teaching me about the need I had to be myself.

#

"True acceptance from others was an extension you couldn't bear to allow yourself to embellish. I went through the exact same thing."

"Murphy, what does that mean?"

"You know more than you're allowing yourself to accept at the moment but when the time is right you'll figure it out just as I did. This is why you must continue your training even after me, John. The art of martial arts is a balance of the mind, body and spirit. It is a freedom from captivity and a way of escape while ultimately giving you the tools to annihilate your opponents.

…Do what you have to do to make things right, emotions are a waste of time and nobody wants to hear anyone's complaints and despair, and always understand this, John, life has a way of teaching us the things we think we don't understand in such a way that causes us to know we had more insight than we were willing or ready to acknowledge. It is a tough battle and everyone in the game has to be tougher in order to survive."

#

Murphy always acted as though he knew something was different about me but he didn't declare what it was he may have known. In hindsight, I am sure he would have known what to do because he always said emotions were not a luxury people like me

were able to indulge. His innate sense was eerie to say the least, probably the defining factor of why so many branded him as weird and treated him like an outcast. He used his bizarre trait to give me insight that Brian and his crew would be searching for me.

Sara listened as I told her how I started taking a new route to school, which added an additional fifteen minutes to my regular time but I didn't care because I wasn't able to deal with the harassing Brian and his friends enjoyed inflicting upon me. I had a successful week without them knowing how I was getting to and from school and I did not have to face Mackey because I wasn't assigned to any of his classes and that was a relief in itself. I was free of torment by the infamous five assholes. In fact, I had made the phrase my ritual song as I walked along my new secret path and I sang it each morning before I reached school. It was a time of bliss my first week without anyone knowing of my new route and as time progressed I was certain no one would ever learn of it. I sang until my heart was content and no one could hear me.

"The infamous five assholes,

you won't find me so try if you dare.

The infamous five assholes no longer

do I care, with Brian as your leader and

he's dumber than mud, all of you are jerks

and nothing more than thugs.

My path is secluded and you're all so very stupid

is why I've eluded the infamous five assholes.

Brian, Reggie, Todd, Derek and Mel the name asshole fits

you all and it's true you all smell."

It was a song I created, enjoyed singing to the trees that I passed and sometimes I would pick up a branch, use it as a

microphone, and address the bushes as if they were my audience applauding my awesome talent. The street had a split in the road and in the middle of the main block was a median. Across from the median on one side were houses that stretched down the length of the block. The entry on the other side was full with trees and weeds and that was the point where I separated myself from the actual street where cars drove down occasionally. The block always looked as though anyone who might have lived there was always away from the house or occupied by the elderly who couldn't do much to help anyone else but even at night it seemed that the area if inhabited at all was by the deaf because no matter the hour the entire block appeared to be deserted. Most of my haven overshadowed me by trees and the high bushes and weeds was an escape from anyone traveling on the other side of the road.

There were many bushes clumped together opposite the median and though there was not a sidewalk, a fence partitioned the road where trees and bushes occupied the empty lot. It was its own miniature jungle. It still took me to the main road onto 24th avenue and from there I was just a few blocks away from the school. I would cut down 97th street and go through the alley where Brian and his boys harassed Alvin but they never thought to go back to the same area. As Murphy indicated during one of his sporadic senseless speeches, he was giving me a safe route to travel. I remembered his words as I embarked on my new route and came out to the place where the five assholes saw me helping Alvin.

'Why do you think the safest place to hide is at the scene of the crime?'

I was always amazed at how his sayings would come into my thoughts and most of mom's sayings were diminishing. The old man was definitely a force in my life I had only yet to discover. Usually after exiting the alley on the opposite side at 98th street, I would walk in the school unnoticed from the side of the building. For some reason one day the clouds up above seemed to be speaking to me in my head in the same random way Murphy blurted something out at me and be it luck or captivated by the strange way the clouds rolled across the sky, I was happy I had not been singing the song I made up. I was looking to see how the clouds were passing by and from behind the bushes three of the most frightening faces stepped out one by one.

First Mel, Derek, and Todd of the four of Brian's friends and they were pounding their fists ready to hurt me. I stopped to turn around to go back around the median and the remaining two of the unfolding nightmare appeared in the form of Reggie and Brian who stepped out from behind the fence where there were weeds and more trees. I didn't like that area for the same reasons I felt safe and now the unthinkable was before me. I could only think of what had possessed me to take that route in the first place and now I was trapped in my own devious plot to escape and in the area where no matter what happened, no one seemed to be aware of what took place. They surrounded me all grinning and ready to cause damage. They started picking up rocks and throwing them at me. They ran up to me from behind knocking my books out of my hand, pushing me back and forth. Mel shifted his eyebrows up then pushed me so hard after he saw Derek drop to his hands and knees in order to cause me to fall backwards over the human obstacle that I hit my head on the ground.

#

"Hey you bastard freak, your mom ever tell you she fucked the garbage man while your daddy was at work."

He got off his hands and knees quick to stand over and kick me. He started thrusting his hips forward toward me and balled his hands into fists pulling his elbows back then stretched his arms out in front of him while pushing his hips back again then thrust his hips forward again as he pulled his arms back and repeating the motion with his fists and elbows to indicate he wanted to hump me in the face.

"Oh no, man I heard she was with the mailman." Todd added.

"Impossible, because I saw her with the delivery man." Reggie said.

"All you guys are wrong. My dad and uncle had her tied to a tree in our backyard making her beg for it, and you know what? She did. She was begging and pleading for some of the biggest hot dog this side of the East coast." Mel said.

"Why don't you assholes stop fuckin with the kid,"

'Funny he should use that term,' I thought.

"...Can't you see his old lady had to go through as many guys on a football team before she shitted out this fuckin piece of shit, ain't that right, fuck face?" Brian said as he moved toward me, towering over me and raising his fist. "...ANSWER ME!" He screamed.

I stayed still shaking my head, lowering my eyes and desperately fighting back tears knowing if he saw any coming out of me they all would have beaten me mercilessly.

"That's not true." I said, gritting my teeth.

"Well I know she likes to take it up the ass, doesn't she tough guy?"

"Hey John, you know why you look like you is black as burnt leather?" Mel inquired as though he was asking a broker for financial advice and placing his index finger on the side of his chin.

"Hey John, how come you not as dark as yo mama? " Derek asked.

"Yo man, you gots to pay me to keep them other guys from hurting you." Todd said.

"No, he likes it when it hurts. Isn't that right Johnny boy or maybe you like to be called teachers' pet!" Brian said.

The other guys started chanting teachers' pet repeatedly. They weren't sure, why Brian had said it but they probably all thought he was referring to me being a good little boy to all the teachers. I became more aware of why he used the term when he looked over passed his friends who were going around me in a circle and I saw him grab hold of himself between his legs and lick his lips at me. That was the second occasion he had made the same gesture. I realized he was there somewhere watching Mackey do his business. Derek saw Brian grab himself and licking his lips while looking at me.

"He shouldn't have to pay you Todd because I think maybe he wants the protection Brian can give him. Ain't that right?" Derek said smiling.

"Wait! It must run in the family if yo mama like white dick then her bastard son must like it too." Todd encouraged. I got up from the first time Mel pushed me over Derek and now the guys were in my face only this time Brian shoved me. The impact from

the push made me hit the ground like a sack of bricks crashing down into a pile of dirt.

Mel and Todd quickly grabbed my legs spreading them open as they continued to taunt me. Brian stood over me and dropped his pants down to show he wasn't embarrassed to let his friends see that he had a bulge in his shorts.

All the guys started chanting.

"Do it, do it, do it!"

"No! Get away from me! Let me go!"

The guys continued to hold my legs and Brian walked around them, went over to stand directly over my face, then kneeled down, and started hitting his erect manhood on top of my head, face and lips.

"You like that, don't you, Johnny boy."

It didn't matter how much I tried to move my head to keep him from touching me, the other guys held me tight to let him do what he wanted and I could hear the other guys laughing and chanting. I was angry and frustrated that I couldn't get up and tears began rushing profusely from my eyes. Brian stopped and pulled himself away from my face and lowered his lips to my ears and whispered so the other guys couldn't hear him.

"I saw you in the basement with the teacher so I'm thinking you must really like what I'm doing to you, don't you Johnny boy?" He whispered.

"Get off of me."

"I wouldn't advise you to go telling anybody about this because all the girls think you're a little punk anyway and it would be very easy to convince my boys here to spread the news about you and the horny teacher and we could have the whole school

knowing what you like to do."

"No, it wasn't me, he made…"

"Shut up you little bitch and stop your whining or I'll turn these guys loose on you."

They all continued to tease me and started poking me in the side and up and down my stomach and chest. They grabbed hold of my ass and pinched me, and continued their untiring way in which they taunted me. It suddenly stopped when we all heard a noise and like a breath of fresh air, some women with their husbands and dogs were walking from around the corner. We could hear them before they turned to cut through the path, the guys quickly left me, and took off running.

Brian was still trying to fix his pants as he ran off with his friends and all of them were moving fast and ducking into the brush behind bushes and trees around the median so no one would see them. I picked myself up quickly and brushed off, wiping tears and gaining my composure. I gathered my books and things before the people got close enough to see what happened. They walked by completely oblivious to what had occurred. They continued minding their own business and the men pulled on the dog's leashes as the dogs barked unaware anyone traumatized me. I stared at the dogs almost in a trance and they stopped barking and returned the gaze equally hypnotized. The two dogs continued their blank stare into my eyes as though they were telepathically telling me what I needed to do. The men tugged on the animals causing the three of us to break our gaze. I took off running, made it to school, tried to shake what had taken place just moments ago, felt sick, ran to the boy's room, and vomited.

THE SUICIDE ATTEMPT

I didn't want to have to face anyone after what happened but I braved through my classes until it was time for a break. I thought about going back to the basement at lunch but was too scared since it was during lunch when I was down there last time. I waited until recess, went over to the basement door and shuttered right before I checked to find again that it was unlocked. I went down the stairs slowly making sure I did not make any noise and being careful enough not to bump into anything in the dark.

I wanted to see if it was true about what Brian said or if Mackey told him. I went over to the area and looked around then noticed the glare I had not seen before, looked up and saw the window. I froze in the light shining inside as I looked into the eyes of Mackey. He bolted and I immediately took off for the stairs running as fast as I could until I was out the door before he could get there. Once in the building, he was quick enough to make it down the hall and just as he turned the corner, he reached out to grab me, I ducked low enough causing him to miss getting hold of my jacket and ran to an exit at the other end of the building and outside. I could not stop from breathing fast, my heart was thumping uncontrollably and I could not help thinking that Mackey must have been outside looking in to see if anyone could see inside that basement window. I was trying to catch my breath when I saw some of the teachers standing not too far from me. I went over to them but I couldn't think of anything to say as I was starting to see that one of them was Mrs. Hawkes. She called my

name and I snapped out of the temporary daze as she was explaining the rules of going out a side exit when school was in session. I made some excuse of not paying attention and found myself outside, which seemed to settle well with her allowing me to escape any punishment but she saw to it that I made it to my next class without interruption. I was relieved because my plans were to leave and that would have caused the principle to know that I skipped class, and ultimately they would have called my mother. After school I walked down to Ditmars Boulevard to the pedestrian crosswalk on the bridge where people could get to the other side by walking or bicycling without having to cross the highway below. The area had bushes and shrubs large and thick on the hillside of each side of the bridge where one could easily hide. I stopped at the railing and looked into the distance.

Cars were driving fast in both directions and I could not stop myself from crying. Murphy's training to void certain emotions and having the ability to conjure any strength on command that I needed didn't help me in this situation and I felt like a failure because I couldn't explain or understand what was happening to me and trying to grasp at any of the things he said in that moment were too confusing. Though I could not piece together what he was teaching me, I knew I had an unbiased focus that would not shake loose. I decided to let that focus be the strength to carry out what I needed to do in order to accomplish the one deadly thing that would put an end to the suffering.

I stared into the traffic and unconsciously focused my attention on the speed the vehicles traveled to calculate and execute my next move. The trance felt like the one earlier when the eyes of the dogs met mine. I thought about how Murphy was

215

probably teaching me to be strong to make the decision I was about to endeavor. I grabbed hold of the railing and rose up to cross over and heard the sounds of the cars' horns as they approached the bridge. The blaring noise was loud and piercing and yet I could hear nothing. Time stood still though I could see the movement around me. Nothing made sense and everything was in order. I let go of the rail, a hundred foot drop and I would meet the ground below in time for the traffic to mall and crush my frail body into nothing.

The feeling of the air and wind blowing gently across my face was soothing and the movement of falling was in motion only I was no longer falling but standing back where I started after I felt hands release my shoulders. I turned to see no one was around and I had no possible solution for whom or what saved me from jumping. It was evening and getting colder as I stared over to the bushes wondering and trying to see movement. I was sure someone was there waiting, hiding and then I heard the low grumbling of what I thought was a dog. It was not strange to find strays down in that area because people would let dogs out of their cars late at night on the highway and they would climb up the hillside to the top of the brush of the bridge for safety if they were lucky enough to make it. The wind continued to blow as it picked up speed and it was cold. I went home and made some excuse to my mom about staying at the park giving reason to why I was an hour late. She knew I would stay at the park longer during the summer but I needed a valid reason because it was now the middle of January. Once again, I lied to her, knowing she would accept my reason of having wanting to see the Christmas lights that were still up on some of the houses before they were completely

removed from that area, I excused myself and went to my room where I stayed until it was time for dinner and then back to my room when I knew she was going to bed. I quietly went out the window down the tree and walked to Murphy's house still confused because I thought that perhaps something in the old man's riddles would explain what happened to me. I entered to see the front room was empty, looked over at the collection he had on the human psyche and noticed a great deal of books about death.

"Was your journey successful, John?"

I turned to find him mysteriously sitting in the chair I thought was empty when I first entered the house.

"What Journey?" I whispered.

I returned his stare and it was at that moment I began to feel dizzy and stepped back shaking my head, grabbing hold of it. I didn't know if whether I had tricked myself into believing I made the jump when I was in that trance or if I had, actually jumped but moved backwards onto the pavement out of fear or was Murphy there to stop me? I thought long and hard on the failure and odd feelings of triumph.

"…Am I losing my mind, what are you doing to me, old man?"

"What are you doing to yourself is the question you should be asking."

"Stop talking to me like that, what's happening? Am I going crazy or am I finding ways to help loosen the connection that's inside of me causing me into submission of emotional turmoil?"

I paused.

"…And what the hell did I just say, I'm sounding like you, I don't even know what I'm talking about."

"You know more than you want to admit John. It's been more than enough time now John and soon you're going to realize you also know what you have to do. They can't get away with it and you know it."

"They, who, what do you know, how can you say I know stuff when I don't know the stuff you're talking about, and what do you know to say they can't get away with it, get away with what?"

"Stop talking like a kid, John, those days are gone now. It's time for you to go home."

He explained nothing more, offering no words of advice nor did he try to help me understand any of it. I began to breathe calmly instinctively emulating him. I felt a triumphant feeling overwhelming my senses, which told me I figured out what had happened and what Murphy's role was in my life. I walked to the door; eyes fixed on the entrance different from the one I entered and continued to move without addressing him and walked by with assurance, without a single doubt. My movement was bold, smooth and direct were my steps my demeanor almost grateful. Although I had not mentioned what happened to me to old man Murphy, I had the impression he knew what was going on. It was his gift and strangely, I thought somehow it was his way of teaching me things.

I walked out the room, passed him again and walked out the front door. The next day I walked through the path on my way to school and void of any emotions, prepared to face the gang if nothing more than to prove I had gained the fearless stability or mental stupidity, to make a stand as to who I was, at least who it was I unknowingly was becoming. I put my hand on my pocket and felt the cold object.

SARA'S WISDOM

I told Sara more about some of the trials I encountered with Brian and his friends before she arrived.

"So John, Brian was doing all of this to you and then it just stopped?"

"Yeah, first he tormented me and it was no fun either but for some reason right after summer school started this year, he stopped bothering me and yeah just this year around July he started harassing some other poor soul."

Sara got quite and lowered her head. She quickly changed the subject.

"I couldn't imagine having to face those dogs the way you did. It's a good thing they were on leashes and the bridge, that's just eerie. Oh John, you must have been feeling truly alone to even think of such a thing."

I failed to tell her she was right to have asked me if I was the boy that Mackey had in the basement. For some reason I just needed that to remain a secret but somehow telling her what happened to me between Brian, his friends and the bridge was satisfying but still I made sure I omitted the part where Mackey was involved. She looked at me with her deep soulful eyes as though I was her hero and showed no disgust or disappointment toward me when I finished talking.

"…I'm glad you weren't able to go through with it or even if someone did mysteriously stop you, I'm happy the outcome is the same, you're here with me right now because of your courage to

face your fears otherwise we never would have met."

"Thanks Sara, I am glad it wasn't a success too but I still can't figure out what happened."

"Well, maybe it's for the best, you know John, sometimes we don't realize the problems we have can be solved by having someone listen to us. We think we have the ability to work them out ourselves and keep whatever we are dealing with a secret, but the secrets we keep could lead to something terrible. I know because I have to face my own demons and I think we just need to understand we're not always at risk of losing the one we admire most just because we tell the person what has been happening to us. No matter how terrible we think something is in our lives, sometimes the one we fear we're going to lose is the only one who will take a stand and support us."

"Wow, I never thought of that."

"Yeah, it's not easy but when we have people in our lives that are willing to help us it gives us inner strength to endure a little longer that is if we can get past our own fears and share what's going on inside to someone we trust."

"You really are smart, Sara."

"Thanks and don't dwell on it John, the main thing is now you have the knowledge that there is inner strength within you to control and eradicate potential dangerous behavior." She continued.

"Okay, Sara how do you know this stuff? I mean you're sounding very much like an adult and it's a little weird but it also seems like it's what I expected you to say."

"I watch a lot of talk shows with psychologists and they were saying stuff like that, I usually write stuff down so I can practice

talking to imaginary people when I'm in my room by myself. I was just waiting to be able to use it."

We laughed and made our way back to the front of the park.

"…My parents can't pick me up today so I have to take the bus if you don't mind, I mean, would you walk with me?"

"Of course," I said enthusiastically.

Sara's words were impressive to me and clearly they were words beyond her years and I wanted to hear more. I think I wanted to use any excuse to be with her. We made it to the bus stop walking down to 94th street and Astoria Boulevard holding hands the entire time. We arrived and almost simultaneously, so did the bus. I told her that I thought the driver knew she needed to take the Q19 bus because he arrived within moments. It was not in the stars for me to spend much time with her after we walked down to the bus stop because usually it takes that bus an hour before it shows.

She kissed my cheek gently and got on the bus. I stayed watching as though I was back in a trance but this time it was a trance of being on the bus with her and I was fully aware of what I was daydreaming as the driver drove away. It seemed as though my life's mission was to watch her as she was leaving me, but still I was grateful for the time we spent together and the kiss meant more than she would know, I happily turned to walk home.

I saw her the next day and she looked very sad and told me she wanted to share something with me and said that she thought it was time to tell me what she whispered to me one day a couple of weeks ago.

"John, I don't think we're going to be able to laugh our way out of this one." She was serious and in tears before she started.

"Sara you don't have to say anything if you don't want to."

"No, it's okay John, besides I can't tell you to trust me with the things that have happened in your life and not trust you with the things that have happened in mine."

"…At one time my mom and dad was a very happy couple and for some reason they decided they wanted to have a child, a child who also experienced some happiness for a while, for a very short while. I guess that's where it all began…"

I could picture everything she was saying as we sat on the lawn in the park at school. The day was getting hotter and becoming more humid and as though the heavens above were telling us her past was her present, overcast began as the clouds rolled in looking as though there would be a summer thunderstorm.

PART 2

SARA

THE BIRTH OF SARA

Lightning flashed during the midnight hour striking a portion of the house and the lights went out in four of the seven rooms. The phone was still working and his fingers were dialing frantically. A woman answered the phone; she was still groggy when it rang awakening her from her slumber.

"What, oh no, not now, yes, yes of course I'll be right there. I'm going to need…"

The phone went dead.

She ran down the stairs while grabbing her coat off the banister. She was only ten blocks away but it was enough to seem like a lifetime giving the present condition of the weather.

Janie screamed and the sounds of thunder roared and James dropped the phone as lightning struck the telephone pole causing it to crash through the window in the hallway when he was trying to get the information Nora was going to need.

Thunder continued to roar and the brilliant flashes of lightning streaked across the sky. On this night only the emergency crews were out but Nora Hill was a great friend and was there when someone called her no matter what time of the night or the condition of the weather. Rain poured down hard and she could barely see where she was going. It looked as though a tidal wave was hitting against her car causing her to swerve to one side of the road. She prayed there wasn't anyone out on the streets crossing or on the sidewalk, hoping she would not be the cause of a fatality, as she was on her way to try to prevent the inhumane

acts of her friend, she held the steering wheel with a tight grip.

Janie never experienced such pain and was not aware it would be something she would ever have to endure and nothing prepared her life for such an extraordinary sensation; it was tearing through her from within causing her to think she was going to burst. She writhed back and forth in bed, yelling, cursing; it wasn't like her to be so forthcoming. James ran back into the room when the phone went dead but he did not know what to do other than try his best to hold her down.

"Stop it, stop it!" He snapped.

"Fuck you, you fucking asshole I'll kill you myself for what you've done to me. Get away from me. Help me!" She yelled. "...Nora! Please, come in here, now. Get him away from me please, he's killing me, why won't someone help me, oh God please."

Nora drove as quickly as the weather permitted. It was blinding by the amount of rain pouring down on her windshield. She hit a bump in the road, her car skidded across the pavement, and she turned the wheel, screaming at the loss of control. Certain she was going to die on her way to help a neighbor, her friend, she tried easing her grip off the steering wheel allowing the car to go where it led, releasing only a small amount of control until finally her technique worked allowing her to regain power over the vehicle.

She could not see where she was going, all seemed hopeless to be so close and not know of her location. It was only ten blocks but the rain, the bump, the swerving, then she turned down the wrong block, tried to retrace where she went wrong, turned back around and then turning down another block trying to remember if

she went left or right after she made the wrong turn. She turned down another street, lost track of her bearings, and realized she was lost in her own neighborhood. She stopped the car after pulling over what she hoped was the side of the road. She sat inside waiting, hoping and a few moments later the answers came to her prayers. The overbearing down pour eased away and she could see she had pulled onto the side of the curb two houses away from James and Janie.

She ran up to the house checking the door to see if she could get inside but to her dismay it was locked. She rang the bell unaware the lightning had knocked out the power, banged on the door just as thunder erupted from the sky, banged again screaming; hoping someone would hear her to let her in the house. She saw no other choice but to pick up one of the bricks from the yard, hit the window on the side of the front door and reached her hand through to unlock it. Once inside Nora could hear Janie as she tried to break free from James' grip. She ran up the stairs into the room to help her. Immediately, she was able to assess the situation and knew she had her work cut out for her. James was helpless, desperately trying to control his wife.

"Please Mrs. Plimkin you are making this into much more than what it is."

"What? Are you mad woman?" Janie bellowed. "…Get away from me. You're both stark raving mad. I can't do this."

"Stop it!" She snapped. "…Mr. Plimkin you have to hold her please. You must tie her hands together or she's going to cause irreparable damage." James wrestled Janie's arms over her head as Nora fought desperately to open her legs. Janie kicked, screamed and writhed back and forth like a woman possessed.

James snatched the bedside lamp and pulled the cord out of the wall to tie one of Janie's hands to the bedpost. He moved his hand down slightly to get hold of one of her legs to hold it in place. Nora simultaneously reached up to grab Janie's other arm and held it down while maneuvering her other hand to grab hold of her friends' other leg, hoping that together James and she could pry her, Janie's legs open. Nora kept talking frantically trying to coach Janie reminding her to push, breathe and to help make her job easier by thinking of her role and what joy she was about to expect. It was mind boggling to Nora. All her years as a nurse she did not know of any pregnant woman trying to prevent her own birth.

She fully understood the fear Janie was experiencing but quickly tried to convince her to relax and allow nature to take its course or she was going to cause both the baby and herself considerable harm. Three hours passed and at 3:30am, Wednesday morning October 31, 1962 the storm was subsiding when Janie heard the sounds of her newborn baby girl.

"Let me see her." She said. Nora brought the newborn to her mother just freshly cleaned from the blood and the aftermath. The little girl screamed loudly and defiantly echoing the sounds off the walls of the room.

Nora stood proud with a big smile on her face.

"She has your eyes Janie."

"How come when you're scolding us it's Mr. or Mrs. Plimkin but when all is calm you use our first names?"

"That would be the inevitable charm of our Nora Hill, my darling." James interjected.

The three smiled happily at the success of the arrival of the

new sounds piercing throughout the room. Janie looked at her baby wondering if she actually looked like her or was it too soon to tell.

"Does she really? It looks like she has more of her dad than me."

Janie started grinning from the joy she had bursting from within until she could no longer contain it. She was a very proud and happy mother and she felt as though she was the luckiest woman alive. She gently enveloped what she referred to as her little precious bundle into her arms as Nora passed her carefully over to her mother. Nora could no longer contain her curiosity for a minute longer.

"What will you name her?"

James stepped up behind her smiling and in awe of the birth, he had just witnessed.

"You've done a magnificent job Nora how can we ever thank you?"

Tears fell from his face. He was a very proud dad and his emotions overwhelmed him. He moved in closer to Janie and looked at his wife with loving eyes.

"…She seems to have your mouth." He said.

Janie cut her eyes sharply yet lovingly as she smiled at his remark.

"Let's name her Sara."

"You know something Mrs. Plimkin that's a beautiful name and I think you did a beautiful job."

"Thank you kindly Mr. Plimkin but I had a little help."

"Oh really, anyone I know?"

"It's possible. My husband played a part in this wonderful

occasion. I think he's a wonderful man."

occasion. I think he's a wonderful man."

"Are you telling me that he's not the man you wanted to kill only moments earlier?"

"Oh no, not my husband, I could never hurt him." Janie said, playfully.

"Well he sounds like a man I'd like to meet."

"Maybe later but right now come give mommy a kiss."

"And what about that wonderful man of yours."

"Under the unique circumstances, I'm sure he won't make any complaints."

James moved in slowly and carefully making sure, he would not harm his newborn baby, leaned in as he gently, and lovingly kissed his wife.

Sara stopped crying and was peacefully asleep as the two parents stared down at the new life in Janie's arms. They were silent and pleased knowing it was the two of them who had been a part of bringing Sara into the world.

SPYING EYES

After Sara was born, James moved his family to a three-story seven-room house in Astoria Queens, New York. Two bedrooms, a living room, a dining room, kitchen and two bathrooms, and a basement with a large open space they used for entertaining. He was relentless as the years passed, wanted to get things started right away in their home and felt they had waited long enough, and though Janie wanted to be supportive, his demanding ways bothered her. At first it wasn't what she wanted but could see that she had no say over what he had decided when he wanted to do something and wanted things a certain way in their home and in their lives. He became a strong demanding force over the five years they had been raising Sara. The level of control increased and his ways of persuasion became a tactic Janie was too afraid to try to fight. If he thought, she was saying something that was contradictory to what he wanted she suffered a slap across the face or he would punch her in the stomach.

Once he thought about suggesting they change the décor of the basement to set the tone for his plan but as he sat in the living room imagining how he thought Janie would complain about his wishes, he became angry. He went in the dining room and then upstairs searching for her, his anger increased when he did not locate her immediately and then returned to the dining room and opened the door leading to the kitchen where he saw her at the stove making dinner. He stood with an intense look across his face and stared at her with piercing eyes. He spoke slowly with tension

in his voice.

"What are you making?"

"I baked chicken and steamed some vegetables."

"And that's your decision; you didn't bother to ask what I wanted."

"I thought it would be a nice meal."

"I don't believe I asked you about what you think, shouldn't everything be a matter of joint decisions including what I'm going to eat."

Janie's confusion did not allow her to see in time what his mannerisms were projecting and she did not know what triggered his behavior.

"Sorry, James but you never showed any interest in what I made in the past, I thought you would like it."

"Are you mouthing off at me?"

Janie's eyes widened.

"No, of course not."

"So what you're saying is I'm too stupid to know when my wife is being flippant."

"I'm not, what are you talking about I didn't do anything."

"Then I must be a liar. Is that it Janie, you're calling me a liar."

"No!"

He walked up to her and grabbed her by her throat choking her hard. Janie accidentally knocked the pot of vegetables off the stove; they splattered up against his leg. He released his grip backing away from the hot water and vegetables that landed on him. His anger increased as he backed away brushing his leg. He knew his actions caused the chain reaction of the pot to fall, but it

did not save her from his fury.

"Pick that shit up you fucking whore are you trying to burn me alive." He shouted.

Janie bend down to pick up the mess on the floor, James moved in closer and kicked her in the stomach forcing her to fall to the floor in agony. He stood watching her for a moment then turned and walked out. Janie lay on the floor crying. She never knew what would trigger his anger and always in fear, she might say something wrong even though she never believed she was at fault.

He needed help, he was drinking more and more and she saw him put some pills in his mouth a few different times but she did not dare bring up anything she felt would set his anger in motion. It was a delicate situation and the topic of suggesting him in need of professional help put fear into her because she thought it might set him off to kill her. She knew what she had to do to help him become more satisfied with her and their family. He was in the living room lying on the couch and she went to him, sat on the floor at his feet in tears, and told him she would agree to do whatever he wanted from her to help him be a success.

She knew it had to do with the way he wanted to setup their basement and use her to entertain certain guests and she feared that after what he just displayed, if she didn't agree to his wishes, things would get much worst. James sat up on the couch and reached for Janie's hand and she timidly gave it to him to join him on the sofa. He hugged her gently and slowly kissed her on her cheeks and lips. Disgusted by her own actions Janie laid on the couch to let him have his way. Each night after that James made his arrangements to get the basement the way he envisioned and

Janie was happy she decided to do things his way only because he refrained from beating on her while he made things the way he wanted them. They entertained as the weeks went by but things were slow at first but within a few months James had build a small clientele.

One late night a few months after James built a steady routine and had some regular patrons coming over for his new venture, Sara awakened by the sounds of strange muffled noises and got up to go find her parents. She continued to hear sounds she could not make out but heard them more distinctly as she walked out of her bedroom and down the stairs.

People were laughing and she could still hear the whispers but the sounds though unclear were loud. There were no creeks in the flooring and the doors did not squeak, something Sara felt was to her advantage. The closer she got to the door the more she could hear the muffled noises. She opened the door leading to another set of stairs that led down to the basement. She slowly walked down the stairs until she reached the bottom. There was another door at the bottom of the stairs leading into the basement portion of the house. She still could not figure out what the different types of sounds she was hearing. She opened the door very slowly turning the knob making sure no one heard her while she peeked into the room. All the lights were out, at first she thought her eyes were playing tricks on her, it looked as though there were only figures entangled in different directions and the uncertain movement was disarray.

Shapes and shadows were moving from one place to another as she continued to peer inside, her eyes began to focus more into the darkened arena. She witnessed one of the largest orgies

anyone could have in a private home in such a small area. Men were wrapping themselves around other men, women were rolling back and forth on top of each other, men were thrusting in and out on top of women and other women were bouncing up and down on top of the men. One man was on top of a women and another man was on top of him while yet a third man was standing over the first man and was thrusting himself into the mouth of the second man.

She could not make out any faces and she saw that there were so many bodies moving in so many different ways it seemed almost impossible to accomplish the things they were all doing. Her innocent frail mind was confused and she did not understand what was happening.

She never counted on anyone having to leave the area to go upstairs to the bathroom so she remained in place watching but as she stood there looking inside, a voice was heard from behind.

"Sara, honey what are you doing?"

She never flinched but gently closed the door so no one would hear them.

"Daddy what's going on in there I can't see anything."

"Everyone is just playing a game. Why don't I take you back upstairs and you can get some sleep."

"But I was sleep and all the noise down here woke me up."

"Well I'll tell everyone to keep it down next time so you can get some rest."

He picked her up gently and carried her upstairs through the living room and then up another flight of stairs into her bedroom. He laid her down onto the bed and decided to lay next to her under the sheet and blanket. He was already dressed down in his sweat pants and a tee shirt.

"Alright daddy, I won't tell."

"Are you sure? It has to be our little secret game, okay my little princess."

"Okay, daddy, I'm sleepy now."

"Alright you get some sleep and we'll get you off to school bright and early so you can have fruit and cereal with your friends."

He kissed her goodnight and returned to the activities down in the basement.

DADDY'S LIL GIRL

James worked with the advertising department for a beer corporation and he enjoyed his job a great deal. He would spend his time drinking a different beer at lunch on a daily basis. He did his job well and always wanted to impress his boss with ideas he had for the products.

Mike Peters, his boss was never interested in what he had to say and James wanted to discover a way to get him to one of his soirees' without coming across as a pervert or giving the impression that he thought his boss was one even though he knew the weaknesses that Mike possessed for the ladies and thought Mike would be a perfect candidate. Mike had no idea that James knew his secret of sneaking women into the men's bathroom at office parties and occasionally, James saw him going into the men's room with a porn magazine and figured he was going in there to relieve himself of the pressure building up inside his pants.

He did not find him to be much of a challenge and figured he would get the opportunity he needed to move up in the company. One day James arranged for Janie to visit where he worked when he knew she was going to be out shopping with Sara. Janie decided she and Sara would spend the day together and then wait for James until he was ready to leave, and perhaps they would all go see an off Broadway show. Mike noticed Janie as soon as she walked into the room. He could not believe James was with such a beautiful woman and he watched the two of them as they talked. He paid special attention to Janie especially when she laughed.

James told her to make sure she followed his instructions to the letter when she came to visit.

#

"I want you to tilt your head back ever so gently to show off your beautifully sculptured neckline."

"Got it."

#

Mike was unaware he was being set up. He enjoyed watching how she slowly licked her lips as she began to tilt her head sideways something else James encouraged her to do. She wore a low cut dress to show her perfectly shaped breasts that Mike had only seen in magazines. He believed photos in magazines like that were purposely tampered with in order to get a rise out of men, causing them to purchase their products, a tactic which received no argument from him, for he gladly bought everyone who sponsored such a thing of beauty. Now before his very eyes stood a woman who could have been the poster girl for all the others he had seen in the past. It was an autumn day and the tan color knit dress fit every curve, she wore boots with a medium length heel and the length of her dress partly covered the top portion of her boots and she had on a leather maxi coat which she took off when she knew Mike was watching.

Mike thought she deliberately wore that dress knowing it would accentuate her figure beautifully. He could not resist his bulge from growing and used a newspaper to cover his area where he would not appear to be so obviously attracted to her. As he watched Janie say goodbye to James, he could only imagine her warm mouth over his extended flesh as he gazed upon the kiss she sensually gave her husband. When she left Mike walked by James

with the most intense bulge in his pants that James could only imagine to be possible when he saw the animated porn that some sketch artists exaggerated. Mike requested James to follow him and James knew the bait he used caught his boss' attention and Mike played right into his snare. He began acting as though James was his best friend because he wanted to find out all he could about the woman that was causing the protrusion in his pants. Although he already knew who the voluptuous beauty he saw talking with James, he wanted to get on James' good side.

"I hear you have parties for those interested in something new, fun and different James, is it something you and the lovely Mrs. Plimkin do on a regular basis."

There were occasional conversations James timed out perfectly knowing Mike was in ear range in order to get him interested without ever mentioning the type of events he offered or suggesting them directly to him.

"Yeah, we host a number of parties you've been invited to on several occasions." He lied.

"I don't actually recall ever being invited but how about the beautiful young lady I saw you talking to this morning has she ever attended one of your gala affairs?"

"I hope so considering she is the lovely Mrs. Plimkin."

"Really?"

"We like to host parties for friends who like to extend their wealth with the other guests."

He looked down to see Mike's bulge then looked up at him and winked.

"…If you know what I mean." He continued.

He turned to leave the room.

"So how does one get himself invited?" Mike asked.

James knew he was interested in Janie but wanted Mike to suffer a little leaving him hanging like a puppy wanting a bone.

"One must wait until one gets an invitation if one decides to give it." James added.

He never liked Mike and thought it was a daring attempt for him to try to invite himself to one of his private events after snubbing him from all the ideas he proposed for the company. He figured that perhaps Mike would be willing to listen to them giving him a way of getting a promotion if he presented his boss with an immediate invitation. He thought of something better, for he knew Mike would want to keep everything secretive.

After work, James met with Janie and Sara to have dinner but plans had changed when James asked Janie to join his boss for dinner and he would take Sara. Sara had not heard the conversation between the two but she could tell that her mom didn't want to go because it was a long time since the three of them had spend any time together. Although reluctant Janie agreed to meet with Mike before he left the building and invite him out for a good time. James, Janie and Sara stood across the street until Mike came out of the building in a rush after receiving a call from James about the set-up with Janie.

Sara was not sure why her mom had to leave but she was okay with spending time with her dad out in public. Soon enough she learned that her dad had an insatiable appetite for dangerous situations. He made her wait up against a wall and went over to a man he thought would be about the type of kinky behavior he himself enjoyed. He talked for only a few minutes and showed the man the amount of cash he would receive. The man paid for a

ticket and went inside the cinema. James and Sara walked around the corner into an alley; there waited a man who had the back door opened and his hand out.

James handed him some cash and the three went inside. Sara had to go to the bathroom and James took her to an opening behind the ticket booth. They went down the steps unseen by the clerk. He left her alone behind the stall in the men's room but never left. She noticed through the crack of the door that her dad was busy by the urinal with another man. She stood there watching the two of them play with each other the same way he had her play with him the night of their party. She stood still confused and did not know what to do. They both quickly turned away from each other when someone else walked into the room. They flushed the urinals and James went over to the sink, waited for the other man to leave after the first man took off and then went over to get Sara.

"Are you through pumpkin?" He whispered.

"Yes, I'm all done." Sara responded.

"That's good because we don't want to miss our movie."

"Okay, what are we going to see daddy?"

"We're going to watch all the nice people help each other like the way mommy is going to help daddy's boss tonight. Remember how you helped daddy feel better before?" He whispered.

"Oh, yeah." She said disappointingly.

"Well, we're going to see a lot more people do the same thing for each other on the movie screen."

Before the movie started, it showed different previews of pornographic scenes for future showings and the title for the current movie appeared.

'Daddy's Little Girl.'

Again, her dad made her fondle him and the many different perverts enjoyed watching the little girl play with the man's big private part inside the theatre. He did not let the other men touch her but he liked it very much to watch them masturbate next to her and to see others turn around in the row ahead of them, pull their pants down, and join in the sick twisted game he thought to be fun. When the movie was over James and Sara went back out of the movie theatre the same way they went in undetected by anyone except those who were inside the theatre. They went home and still Janie was out with his boss. Sara was able to take a bath and her dad left her alone from any further advances for the rest of the night. She lay in her bed with a saddened expression, exhaled quietly and went to sleep...

JOHN'S DILEMMA

A sliding door leads outside from the kitchen to the backyard where the lawn was full, green and beautifully tended and where Sara planted some of her favorite flowers. I was guessing the lawn chairs and table were there for entertainment. We were out back and things felt different and yet familiar when she sat before me once again on the lawn, and I knew she was capable of making things right.

My life could never be as it once was before but to capture a small amount of what we once shared was all I needed. I knew my actions from the past had changed things considerably and my life was doomed to heartache. I had to grasp hold of what was familiar to me anyway I knew how and find a way to make it last. It was my way of holding onto the past, and at the same time, I was not to forget the time that brought me to a place in life where I inevitably was doomed. I could see she was uneasy and wanted to break the silence by starting the conversation, I was guessing to try to keep her wits about herself.

"Haven't you tried to do something in life that would bring you some level of normalcy if I may be so bold?"

"A path of loneliness is the only one I know and bits and pieces is all I am allowed to put together in order to have some measure of this normalcy as you so call it. But what is it anyway? It's a word so many hold onto in order to feel better about their own useless and pathetic lives. These are the ones who are truly lonely. Have you ever wondered why so many sit before their

beloved and have no idea who it is that sits across from them?

...They fill their lives with false doctrine and lies only because they have the financial means to get the things in life they believe to be worth living for in this world but what are they truly searching for? Is it to get up day after day to go to the same work place, to greet the same people daily only to be stabbed in the back?"

She cut her eyes to me quick.

"...Metaphorically speaking, just in case you were wondering."

She swallowed and nodded.

"...If they only knew what it is that will happen to them and the world they have built on lies."

"Not everyone is like that. There are people who believe in one another and the possibility of happiness."

"Sometimes I don't know what to think about it all but what I do know is I can't stand to deal with the monstrous thing living within me. It waits to come out, and then like the roar of thunder and the speed of lightning it causes untraceable damage to anyone in its path."

Once again Sara thought he was rambling about things not pertaining to what was immediately being discussed and her words seem to have no affect on him but his words definitely caught her attention and the 'untraceable damage' phrase was not pleasing to her ears. She had no hint of him suffering from multiple personalities, in her opinion it was as though he stopped dealing with reality and was trying to find a way to convince himself of his own actions as being righteous.

"...It seems almost unreal that I haven't taken the lives of so

many others by now."

"What is that suppose to mean?"

"Just as it sounds."

"I hate to think what it sounds. You do understand the words you speak are far more deadly than the outcome you propose."

"And yet you're still alive."

"For now." She whispered.

"I heard that."

"What do you want from me?"

"I am tired of hurting people."

"Then don't!"

"It's what I'm good at."

"Take up bowling."

"What?"

"Bowling, you can throw the ball as hard as you like and knock down the pins. It's a great way to get rid of frustration."

"Bowling, that's good."

"I'm glad I amuse you."

"When I express my wrath its passionately destructive urge that I think is the only way to get my point across when I am pushed to the point of feeling this amount of rage."

"This amount of rage, as in right now, WHAT DID I DO TO YOU?" She screamed.

"…I don't feel as though I have the ability to control it."

I raised the gun admiring it and looked at the expression on her face.

"…Perhaps the need to be believed would be much more convincing to you without this in my hand but so much has happened and I am scared of the end result."

"And what would that end result be exactly. I mean does it involve me?"

The way she looked at me I could tell of her concern for her safety but wondered if she thought I was telling the truth or if she thought I was using a way to detach her from suspecting a more dangerous fate. I chose to focus her attention to one thing that caught my eye when I said it. I knew she thought it was strange for me to say such a thing.

"Yes, Sara, I too become afraid. So much rage against others takes over to the point I feel as though all hope in accomplishing anything poignant is demolished by my own actions. It seems as though no matter what I do, something always goes wrong and no matter who I try to help someone else tries to create some ulterior motive that was never a part of my agenda and they too suffer for it..."

"And what do you do when the outcome occurs differently than you had expected?"

"I always expect the unfavorable outcome but I am filled between a hope that doesn't make itself known where I can only imagine if there truly is hope and the despair that presents itself showing me there is no hope at all. I'm left with the question of what exactly should I believe?"

"I don't know." Sara said timidly.

"Do I have the control to make the things I want in life come into existence or am I fooling myself to believe there is something available to me when the reality has already proven to be different, you see I have chosen my path and I'm sure it is one I would repeat given the opportunity."

"I don't have any answers for such a question, but why would

you repeat your choices if you feel they have lead you to this point."

"Probably because I don't know what I'm truly looking for in life. I haven't fulfilled dreams and accomplished the different things you like to consider 'normal' people perceive as accomplishments."

"Isn't that the real dilemma you're having? You're wondering if there is a God out there directing your path or at least the path of others and if he was so inclined to leave you out then why, where is he and why haven't he presented himself to you in your travels?"

"I understand there are plenty of questions without answers and perhaps none of them are ever to be answered. I don't want to go backwards and fall into the same trap that led me to where I am now and yet I don't understand how I can feel like that when I've already admitted I would make the same choices."

"If you know you would do the same thing where is the emotional upset you're experiencing coming from?"

"Emotional, you think I'm emotional, doesn't that border on the lines of being human, someone caring? Something tells me you don't think I have the capacity for this type of human quality. I am in a place further than where I once was or perhaps I have moved on to do things I wanted to do when at one time of dreaming of things seemed absolutely impossible."

"I'm not sure that actually makes sense but are you telling me you dream of things, a better life for instance, what kind of things, do you hope in these dreams, is it to be someone else?"

"Why should I want to be someone else when I am satisfied with who I am."

"Well if you're happy with who you are then why are you tormenting yourself, what's stopping you from moving forward?" Sara demanded.

"I don't know. How do I pursue the whatever it is factor to move forward, actually I think I do know how to pursue it but what I don't understand is how to go about accessing the pursuit?"

"Okay, first why do you keep talking in riddles? I'm sure I could possibly begin to help if you actually made cohesive statements."

"Do you think it's within your power to help me?"

"Do you think it's within your power to allow me to help you?"

"Well put."

"Have there been opportunities you feel you missed out on?"

"There have been too much interference, and how exactly does someone get on with his life when in fact he has dedicated everything he has ever learned to others, getting them ready for what they are destined to do."

I was feeling more the way I used to when I was back with the Sara from long ago. I did not interrupt her as she broke it down mainly for herself to understand what I was going through.

"I don't know if you have exhausted everything there is about yourself to the degree where you should be feeling you are no longer worthy to others."

"I think perhaps there is a purpose I have in helping others, and I don't have any idealistic approach to how I can correct any of my past mistakes. As you have learned, I have had an incredible journey, but now I am tired."

"I see a man once confident and certain of his choices and

motives, now, no offense, perhaps broken with a past undeniably sorted by the kind of torment he is displaying before me. Have you ever felt as though your life meant nothing more to anyone than whatever it is they can get out of you?"

The look I gave her showed her that I was disappointed in what she just asked and it seemed as though she had slipped away from the matter at hand. Her words had proven she lacked the insight to what has happened.

"...There is always the question of which way do I turn and how can I fit in a society that has no place for me." She continued.

"Then the question still remains the same doesn't it?"

"And that question would be since I made it this far isn't there something of value I have inside of me that I have used in the past and if so it must have been worth something to at least one person and if so couldn't it be of some value to so many more?"

I breathed gently relieved to know she was showing everything about herself to be who she was all the days I knew her once upon a time ago.

"Sara." I whispered.

She looked at me and I could tell she was wondering what was so intriguing. I watched her as I remembered the young version of her and the last day I saw her when she got on the bus unbeknownst to us both that we were having our last encounter together as kids.

"...So many times fear has turned into terror which could have come from my own self induced unconscious behavior having a need to attract attention."

"Don't you find the method of your choice to be a harmful way of getting attention or anything else in life?"

"I don't in any way feel sorry for myself because I have come through hell to advance to a place of peace in my own head. But sometimes I feel the peace I am having inside isn't real but was created in me by Murphy."

"Who's Murphy?"

"And then I guess I have learned how to generate that peace into a reality to create my surroundings in order to get me from a place of discontent and move on without the pressures of guilt."

I knew she was getting frustrated when I ignored her question but I had to continue to discuss the theories without showing any regard to what she was asking.

"...Maybe there are plenty of people who have as many questions as I do or perhaps they have already asked themselves the same questions and worked through the trials and errors I still have yet to face."

"Why? Why now have you reached this place of moral standards that makes you want to change whom you've turned out to be?"

"That's the easiest question of all for me to answer. You see Sara; I know you no longer have any need for me..."

RAGING WITNESS

November 1973, three months passed and Sara was nowhere in sight. 'Something happened, did her dad suspect she was telling me his secrets or was she hurt, dead; no, someone would have mentioned it at school, they would have known about it. Why did she have to leave? Did she hate me, of course not; it has nothing to do with me. Then why is she gone? Too many questions, too many possibilities but the fact is undeniable that Sara is no longer here and I have no more excuses.'

I was sure to catch the one who had stalked so many before him. The storm from the skies above, the crisp cold air, the darkness was an expression, an extension of who I was and there could be no regrets, only anticipation lingered inside like a hungry wolf ready to feast.

I waited three hours in the night and what would have felt like an eternity to most was only a moment in time. It was clever how Lisa lured the victim to the very spot he once waited for me. I could not discourage the thoughts as I sat in the dark waiting, patiently wanting it to be over and my mind wandered reminding me why I was there...

\#

July 1973, I was waiting for Sara one Monday afternoon but she never showed up and I was filling up with anxiety in hopes I would be able to spend time with her but as I waited in the hallway time stood still. I had to come to terms with the fact she was not going to be there. I thought perhaps her parents took her away for

the weekend and she would return the next day.

I checked with one of the teachers from her earlier class and she had been there. I figured whatever happened it was urgent enough that she had no way of telling me that we would not be meeting today. This was an unsettling interruption but one I told myself I would recover.

I passed the basement door and noticed it was slightly ajar. Slowly I walked toward it and I could hear sounds from below. I closed my eyes knowing who it was down there with some helpless, defenseless kid. I could not stand around so I crept down the stairs hoping that my presence alone would be enough to stop the man violating the innocent. The sounds became clearer as I approached and I could tell the whimpering was from a little girl and I became enraged by the boldness and audacious behavior this man was displaying.

I heard the whispering threats of Mackey as I walked closer to where the sounds originated. There was a pink scarf tied around the girl's neck and Mackey was tugging on it causing her to lose the little air she was trying to breathe. He maliciously thrust himself inside from the rear. He turned to look over his shoulder to see me staring in complete shock, it wasn't Mackey, it was Brian who stood in front of me looking at me unfazed by the fact I was there watching. The girl remained faced down crying into her own underwear that Brian had stuck in her mouth.

"Hey!" He whispered. "…If it's good enough for the teacher, then I know you want to be next that's why you're looking so hard at what's so hard."

He pulled himself out of the girl, licked the palm of his hand, and started to masturbate in front of me. Quickly he moved toward

me but I turned and ran reaching the stairs before he could reach me because he still had his pants partly below his knees slowing down his momentum. I ran up the steps and out of the basement quicker than I had ever moved and I kept running out of the building passing a teacher without noticing whom it was watching me run so fast. The teacher stared suspiciously, as he watched me run pass him then he turned his attention to the direction from which he saw me coming. Mackey headed in the direction of the basement where he stood in front of an open door. He stepped in behind the door, closed it quietly, and locked it. He walked down the stairs slowly all too familiar were the steps he walked and knew he could quietly approach. He watched as he looked at Brian pushing himself up against the little girl only this time Brian did not notice anyone else because he wanted to finish quickly and get out of there.

"...Hurry up and fix your clothes and put your underwear back on and let's get out of here before we get caught."

"I think it might be a little late for the clean get away Brian."

The voice startled him but he was defiant to see Mackey standing in front of him while he fixed his clothes. Mackey looked at the girl and watched her as she shook with fear and though timid, she still tried to show some dignity and dress herself quickly to get out of there.

Brian looked at Mackey.

"What makes you think because you're a teacher you have the right to have all the fun down here."

Jake McIntire knew he was cornered.

"What are you talking about?"

"Okay, teach if we're gonna play that game but just so you

know you can kill the innocent act, it's only fair to warn you I don't think your favorite little student is gonna like the fact you forgot you brought him down here while I watched you from up above."

Brian pointed to the window but Mackey did not bother to look up because he was there the week before when he saw me in the basement alone. He stood there in deep thought but only for a moment knowing the stories about Brian and the many times people tried to accuse him without proof in order to catch him. He had to be cleverer than Brian and the girl went to leave but Mackey stepped in front of her and turned her around as she started to cry out. Brian quickly grabbed hold of her and held her as Mackey began covering her mouth.

"Put her underwear back in her mouth." He encouraged Brian.

He then forced himself inside of her. Both Brian and Jake were laughing and speaking obscenities to her. They remained engrossed in their sick game, neither paying any attention to the window above where I looked inside to see the two of them having their way with Sara.

#

...A roar of thunder brought me out of my past and the emotion was overpowering as I thought about the abuse we had suffered at the hands of these two perverts. I waited for Brian in the deep of the night knowing he would be my first kill.

MACKEY'S TURN

…The next day I had the urge to walk through the path on my way to school, where I killed Brian but there was no body, no trace of blood in the area. I was baffled, I clearly left the body unattended and though I did not want anyone to catch me, something in me wanted his body discovered but nothing was there not even footprints in the dirt or leaves bunched together as though something was hiding underneath. I did not understand and then it occurred to me.

I went to school as usual only there was nothing usual about the days without her. Sara was gone and I had no idea why she was no longer in my life. Mackey was lurking about and Brian was dead.

'Who would be the next victim? No! These people were the predators and no one had the right to think of them as victims and they secretly had a wish for extermination.'

That was something Murphy always used as an analogy when it concerned the well-being of those who were innocent compared to those who were hurting them. Mackey was next, the only problem I had was to figure out how I was permanently going to get rid of a teacher without suspicion. The days grew into weeks and still I had no idea what I could do to get rid of the man who portrayed himself as decent and wholesome.

It was a mission to stay away from him and with every waking moment, I calculated his next move in order to figure how I would execute the one who without a doubt abused many more. I

was certain of everything I did and was determined to honor my word to protect her. I was going to make sure that Sara and neither I nor anyone else had to fear Mackey just as Brian was no longer a threat. Mackey was next on the list.

I became obsessed, desperately wanting to expose the deceit of the man pretending to be upstanding but I wanted it in the form of him joining the dead as soon as possible. It was three weeks later and the morning of the day he was to meet his demise, I didn't know the request made of me before going to school was a death sentence for Jake McIntire.

"John, I want you to stop at the grocery store and pick up some eggs on your way back from school so take this money with you."

"Mom, I can come home and get the money and then go to Mr. Franks."

"I don't want to pay those prices, it's much cheaper at the grocery store besides most times nobody wants to go to the grocery store so they go to Mr. Franks and by the time I want something like eggs, he's usually out of them anyway."

"Okay, but just for the record I don't want to go to the grocery store either."

"I know you don't baby, and that's why you're my favorite son."

"Mom, I'm your only son, just like Aunt Felicia is your only sister."

The silence was clear and without the effort, I had brought a sad memory to life for my mother.

"…You know what mom, you're my favorite mother."

I kissed her on the cheek.

"Thank you, baby."

"And don't you worry I'm going to pick out the best grocery store eggs in there because you deserve the best."

I saw a tear fall from her face. I wrapped my arms around her and she held me tight.

"…I love you mom."

"I love you too baby, now off you go, don't want to be late for school."

It was a long day and I still had to figure out a plan of action but teachers annoyingly kept asking me to answer questions I either did not know the answer or knew it and did not care to participate. Everything was a nuisance but the scholastic endeavors were important to mom and I would do everything possible to achieve greatness. Again, words spoken by Murphy, he was an intelligent old kook. As much as I hated school, I did not have a legitimate reason for failing out and I could not afford to risk the school administration expelling me. I tried hard and focused on doing the best. The last class was only fifteen minutes away from ending and when the bell rang, I jumped up and left the building. I was on my way across the street to go down 98th street to walk to the grocery store but noticed Mackey going in the opposite direction from his usual path. He was heading toward the direction of my house. I followed him to see he took the fork in the road that split 101st street and 102nd street and figured he was going down to Lucky's store. I watched him, kept my distance to see him pass the store, continued onto Astoria Boulevard, and turned left to go toward Mr. Franks' store.

I had no idea what I was going to do but it felt right so I ran over to the door when I saw him go inside the store. Mackey

walked over to aisle three (b) to look at the different styles of condoms next to the feminine products along with some parental pamphlets and self-help books in the little Planned Parenthood section. He must have thought that no one would suspect anything if they entered the store and saw him near the self-help books but he had a thirst for taking risks, he enjoyed testing fate to see how many times he could get away with stealing condoms he liked using to satisfy his perverse appetite.

He did not want to buy them in case anyone wanted to accuse him of sexual abuse because he would not have a justifiable defense if there were questions if anyone found out about him buying condoms, was not married, and did not have a girlfriend. He made sure he used them when he was with little girls but did not care one way or the other with the boys. There was no one in the store except for Mr. Franks and Jake saw that he had his head down and was busy with his daily routine. He knelt down low and secretly started taking condoms off the rack and putting them into his pockets. He stood up and looked toward the front of the store to make sure no one was coming when I noticed he saw me at the door so I pretended to drop something and then I entered the store. I acted as though I did not know he was in there and Mr. Franks continued to be engrossed with what he was doing while sitting on his stool with some papers in his hand. I realized the old man was sleep in the middle of his task.

I had my backpack and inside was the lighting strips given to me by old man Murphy that I started carrying ever since I made my unknown plans to eliminate Mackey. He watched me from across the room and still he could not keep his attraction from swelling up inside his pants. He kept staring at me as I walked in

the front of the store pass the third isle where he stood not knowing I was aware of his presence the entire time or that he was stealing. He was no longer a threat all that has now changed and no longer was the fear of when the next time he was going to strike or to whom was going to be his next victim to suffer at his doing. Vengeance was playing its role in his life and I was the one used as the vessel to execute that in which he was going to suffer.

Though I was ending the injustice, it was because of her, my only true love, why I took the initiative to stop him from hurting others and me and when I saw what he was doing to her, I knew she was the last person he was ever going to touch. There was no remorse in my heart nor did I find it difficult to sleep at night. I suppose I could say the uncanny relationship I had developed with Murphy was a factor that didn't allow me to slow down but it was helping me filter out everything and though nothing truly snapped inside of me until the day she unknowingly had to leave me it was then I knew things had to change and I was no longer going to tolerate the injustice. It was to my amazement that my plan was being formed with every step I took and I knew it was Mackey's turn to die and that somehow I was going to make sure he died in that store before I walked out. It was thrilling to me to know that his safety was no longer secure. I was doing my own version of surveillance and hoping no one else would come in and interrupt my newly formed idea. Mackey thought he was getting my attention for the first time and cleared his throat after I walked over to the last aisle and down passed the middle where I took a dozen of eggs out of the refrigerator in the back half of aisle four.

I closed the refrigerator and turned to see him having no shame standing in the middle of the store at the entrance of the

fourth aisle masturbating. I panicked and froze for a moment, showing some concern, I did not have the gun and I was amazed at the bold risk in public he displayed. I channeled the concern to be successful to execute my not so planned out plan. I moved quickly further to the back where I turned around the corner and ran over to the shelf between the first and second aisle where I stopped at the end shelf, which was wide enough to hide a person's body.

I leaned up against the shelf between the two aisles where Mackey also made his move in the middle of the store and went over to see if I was on the second aisle. I moved closer into the first aisle and then slowly made my way back to the end shelf to hide when I thought he was moving over to check the first aisle. I went into the second aisle and slowly raised my head to look over the shelf and could see the top of his head. Mackey was heading down the first aisle to the back wall where he would have seen me once he turned the corner to check the second aisle so I went back to the back wall of the second aisle and moved over into the third aisle. He turned out of the first aisle as soon as I disappeared into the third aisle and he went up the second aisle back to the middle of the store, turned to go to the third aisle. I back tracked and went back over to the second aisle but for some reason in his sneaky demeanor had the notion to stop in the middle of the store and back up where he stopped and saw me squatting low in the second aisle, as I looked up at him. He pointed to me then to his crotch and then placed his fisted hand up to his mouth indicating he wanted me to gratify him. I moved around the shelf to go to the first aisle but stopped at the end of the shelf knowing he was going to follow from the middle section and I quickly ran down the length of the back wall and made it back down to the fourth aisle.

I went to the middle section of the store of the fourth aisle and peeked around the shelf to make sure he would not see me and I could see he had entered the first or the second aisle. I ran across the middle section of the store straight up to the first half of aisle four before he could see where I had gone. I was hoping he would check each aisle at the back half of the store and was right which allowed me to make it to the front door. I saw that Mr. Franks was still asleep.

I had to act quickly and thought the timing was perfect so I kept low and went down the first row away from the front of the store and grabbed a small hammer and placed the eggs on the floor at the middle section. I could hear him in the second aisle coming from the back half of the store and started to go over to where he was to lure him out but when I saw the back of his head something told me I was not ready and then he turned and I ducked back into the first aisle. He went to search the front half of the store and I rushed over to the shelf between the third and fourth aisles.

He came back down the second aisle and went further to the back of the store to cover his tracks. I had moved into the third aisle and in my haste, it caused me to bump into a can which fell off the shelf onto the floor. He heard the sound and headed over to see if he could catch me. I ran up the aisle back to the front of the store and over to the fourth aisle. I could hear him taking slow and deliberate steps into the middle of the store and up the third aisle heading to the front so I moved out of the fourth aisle into the middle of the store to hide between the third and fourth aisle. I kept low and ran over to the second aisle and down to the back half of the store. Mackey reached the center of the store and moved over to the first aisle and started making his way to the back wall.

I made it back over to the fourth aisle and up to the middle of the store. I gently slipped out of the straps of my backpack making sure to leave a portion of it extending into the fourth aisle. When I heard Mackey in the fourth aisle as I was slowly making my way down the third I could feel his movement thinking he would catch me in the middle of the store where I left my backpack. I was able to sneak up the fourth aisle with the hammer in my hand behind him as he walked toward the middle section, the movement would be swift and no doubt, the blow would be deadly. I ran up behind the man who violated me, Sara, and he being the same man that I was sure he was the reason that caused the death of my friend Sammy, and with a forceful strike, I cracked him over the head.

Jake felt the blow and grabbed the back of his head not knowing what had happened. His face contorted and mouth opened to scream yet no sound came from him. He felt the blood trickling from the back of his head as he watched his hand covered in the red substance that came from his body drip between his fingers and fall to the floor. He followed the movement of the blood and began to fall as his knees collapsed first causing him to go down almost gracefully without a sound. I stepped passed him and grabbed my bag and got hold of the lighting strips.

I searched through the items in the bag and took in a deep breath remembering all the times I and others like Sammy were the victims of his mistreatment of our youth, our innocence and now the man, who mistreated Sara, was reaping what he sowed from the one who appointed himself as young defender. I was ready to implement the death of those who felt they had the right to violate the many they thought to be helpless. I placed a lengthy portion of the lighting strip onto the floor and extended a length of it from the

last row over from where he was laying then I dragged his body by his feet to the back part of the fourth aisle and then continued over to the third where there were some cans of flammable liquids. I loosened a container of kerosene lightly tilting the can to let some spill onto the container and the shelf, grabbed another can and poured it onto the floor continuing a path from the back of the third aisle to the back of the fourth where Mackey lay. I returned the can back to the shelf also leaving the lid on slightly loose, took two more cans and poured the contents out around and on the body. I removed the knife from my backpack and stabbed him right through his esophagus then ripped part of his shirt to stuff it in the hole where the blood was quickly regurgitating, sealing the area but causing the substance to ooze out of his nose and mouth. I took another piece of the lighting strip and placed one end underneath some of the kerosene cans then I ran over to the middle section of the floor and wrapped the other end of the strip around into the fourth aisle so that a piece went from his body in one aisle to the cans in the other.

Mackey's eyes were trying to fix on his murderer but he was losing consciousness fast not knowing where I was but I went to him, looked into his eyes, covered his nose and mouth to suffocate him and watched intently. I photographed every struggling move he made wanting to feel the full measure of the life that was about to expire before my eyes.

"You die, things change, and this is for Sammy."

MR. FRANK'S TIME TO GO

I looked up to check to see if Mr. Franks was still sleep. I took a deep breath, grabbed a box of matches and right before striking it someone entered the store. I rushed to the middle, grabbed my backpack, and headed down the fourth aisle keeping low until I was at the back of the store. I could not wait, did not want to but knew it would be best not to take any unnecessary chances. I remained silent, slowed down my breathing and listened to the conversation the man was having with Mr. Franks. I held my breath as he was heading in my direction. I grabbed hold of the hammer ready to defeat all who was going to interrupt what I had plan, including Mr. Franks if it became necessary. The man noticed what he wanted in the third aisle in the last half of the store right opposite to where I was kneeling, found the item and left turning away from my view.

He was stepping on the strip never noticing it and for his sake; he never knew I was kneeling below staring up at him with the hammer in hand ready to strike. The man paid for his item and left the store and Mr. Franks went back to his tasks. I got up, went to the first aisle in the back of the store, took a dishcloth and some rubbing alcohol, and went back over near my prey. I poured the liquid into my hands and wiped the blood away then poured the alcohol over the top of Mackey's body. I used a second bottle to scrub away again the feeling of stench that I felt coming from my person. The blood that was oozing out of Jake's mouth made me feel as though I was defiled once again by a substance coming

from his body. I laid the hammer down and went back down the back half of the store to the first aisle and walked over to the front half and made it to the door sneaking past Mr. Franks, and opened it as if I was coming in for the first time remembering that he did not realize I had come into the store earlier.

"Hey there, Mr. Franks, I just came for some eggs for my mom."

"Hey John, how are you young man. Well, you know where they are. You know I was thinking that perhaps I would take that visit to Florida to see if I can find somewhere, maybe I would like to settle. I think all of this is getting to be a little too much for this old man and I need a change of scenery in order to rest these old bones."

"That sounds great Mr. Franks."

I knew I would not get another chance like this and needed to get away from him to finish what I started but I didn't want anything to appear to be out of the norm.

"...Oh Mr. Franks did you order any of those sour candy packs we all like to buy when we got a game."

"Oh yeah, that's right it's a good thing you reminded me because I'm just trying to finish up the ordering now. I better get back to it so let me know when you're ready."

"Will do, thanks Mr. Franks."

I watched the old man turn to go into the other room and back to his paper work and when he was out of sight, I walked over and picked the eggs up off the floor of the first aisle where I left them and then went over to the old refrigerator. I could not reach the outlet in the wall, I extended another strip and wrapped it around a portion of the cord and lit it. Then I struck a match and tossed it

on the floor on the lighting strip to race to the kerosene and Mackey. It moved like lightning from each end where I had placed a strip to the flammable substance and his body.

I walked up the aisle to the middle of the store and looked back at Mackey whose clothes had caught the flames, I looked at the refrigerator to notice the old box burning from underneath.

"...Mr. Franks, Mr. Franks the place is on fire."

I screamed, running to the front of the store to grab hold of the old man ensuring the death of the only one deserving. I got to the door with him and made sure he was on his way before I looked back to see if Mackey was still out of sight.

"Fire, there's a fire somebody call the fire department." Mr. Franks yelled.

A few people were across the street but the distance of about half a block away. Mr. Franks cried out to everyone and anyone waving his hands to get their attention. I heard the noise behind me and looked back to see Mackey standing up from behind the aisle. My eyes widened in disbelief that he was still alive, standing and burning before my very eyes.

I reached for the hammer in my back pocket but it was not there, I looked back up and again I was amazed, he was no longer standing there and all I could do was wonder what happened to him.

'Where is he?'

The sparks began to fly and the roaring sounds of the flames grew intensely. Mr. Franks reached back and grabbed hold of my arm, pulling me out of the building. We stood outside together as the fire was consuming the store. People started to gather around to watch the overwhelming amount of smoke escaping the

building. I stood there to what seemed to be an eternity watching the flames engulfs the building. I wanted to know if Mackey would escape the flames and I was looking to see if he somehow got out. Only one exit I had to remind myself but I was unsure if there was another.

'Did he get out or did he burn?' I kept asking myself.

"Oh, Mr. Franks what happened in there." I looked at him with tears in my eyes and as genuinely as possible acted as if I knew nothing about it.

"I don't know young man; did you see where it started?"

"All I saw were flames coming up from behind that old refrigerator in the back."

"That refrigerator, I should have changed it years ago but I always told myself if it ain't broke don't go trying to fix it. I guess I was really telling myself I was being too cheap to buy a new one."

"I don't know if anybody else was in there."

I wanted to know if Mr. Franks was aware of Mackey having entered the store. He turned to me.

"Don't you fret none young man I'm sure you were the last person who came in. Nobody else was in there and it's a good thing you thought to get me out of there or I might have burn to a crisp." He paused.

"...I don't even want to imagine with these old bones if I might have been able to get out of there in time. My God, to think I had the back door boarded up after several burglaries; it has been years since I've seen it. It's possible I would have burned alive, I might not be here now if it hadn't been for you John Chaney."

I looked at the old man as though he was lifeless and nothing

else mattered other than the fact that no one knows and nobody is going to find Mackey inside until they start going through the place. I smiled at Mr. Franks who thought of me as his savior. I was happy knowing that Mackey got what he deserved and no one was going in there to try to save him. Mr. Jake McIntire, Mackey, the school pervert, gone for good and will never harm Sara or anyone else again.

The building was old and the wiring older. All the flammable items inside made it impossible even for the firefighters to get inside. By the time the truck arrived and the men hooked up the hose to the fire hydrant to put it out, it was too late. The fire had spread fast and wild and though the fire department was just around the corner the flames had covered the building in a matter of seconds. The crackling of the flames roared. The top of the building caught fire and the apartment next to the store caught on flames.

The firefighters concentrated on the adjacent building to keep it from burning down to rubble. I thought back to old man Murphy giving me the bag of firecrackers and lighting strips and telling me no one would be able to figure out its use then the words he whispered of how I could start fires and make it look like it was an accident because the strips were a fuse and were capable of disintegrating. I stood next to Mr. Franks understanding Murphy's words, recalling when he opened the door and yelled out to me.

'And that's without a trace.'

As the flames grew more intense, everyone knew that the place was going to burn down to nothing. No one could save it. I wondered about what people would think if they knew I was the

one who burned down Mr. Franks' store, leaving a body beyond recognition. I thought it was a little sad that he had to lose his store but the man has wanted to retire and live out his days fishing in Florida for as long as I could remember.

'So now here's your chance you old fart, get lost and live a happy life.'

Some may say that I am filled with apathy and maybe I am but as I stand here watching the flames, I could see the history of terror Mackey put others and me through. It was all coming back to me how I laid on the floor in the bathroom at the studio in my own feces after what he had done. Everything that tormented my life because of him was now going away and he was the one suffering, and wishing he could have changed the path he had chosen but it is too late for him just as it is too late for Sammy.

It was bad enough what he did to Sammy, not only did he suffer but his mom suffered. She probably had to go to the hospital because of Jake but there was no proof to connect him to her incident either. Sammy's mom never pressed any charges against him but still she definitely had to face the heartache of a mother losing her son because of him and even after touching me, he had gone too far but touching Sara made his sins irreparable.

It was different with her, I could not shake the image of seeing what Brian and he did and it was too much to bear. I thought about the fear he inflicted in her, in all of us but no longer would it be an issue and yet there remains her dad whom I cannot forget because of the stories she told me of him. No one should ever have to feel what Sara was feeling and the words she spoke are haunting to the point that I can still hear them playing repeatedly in my head. This is why my heart aches, why it has

become a heart without remorse, an unforgiving heart and the reasons why I must find her and stop it all from continuing, ultimately stopping her from saying the words she must never again have to repeat…

#

"John, I feel dirty."

MURPHY'S REQUEST

...I left the area to go home, and the clouds rolled in during the evening but the dark was hovering over throughout the heavens as if a cloak covered the ceiling of the skies preventing the remainder of daylight to shine through. I walked in the house as though nothing was wrong and wondered what it was about me that allowed me such a freedom to rid the world of the scum who took advantage of the innocent. I went into the kitchen to put the eggs in the refrigerator when I heard my mother calling out.

"John there's fire trucks at Mr. Frank's store. What on earth is going on, I tell you if it isn't one thing it's another, are you alright?" She said running down the stairs.

"...First I hear on the news someone killed a boy and they found his body over in Jackson Heights, and it was only a few weeks ago and the child wasn't much older than you, and now this, I'm going down the street to the store to see if I can do anything for Mr. Franks."

I went upstairs as she was talking and she continued knowing I had just shut the door to my room.

"...John, come here child let me see you." I went to the top of the stairs.

"I'm fine, mom."

"Were you down there when all this happened?"

I went back down the steps and took her hand to touch my arm, and she took hold of me hugging and kissing my forehead looking at my face and squeezing it and then hugging me close to

her.

"Old man Murphy is dead?"

"What?" She exploded.

"He was shot to death."

"My God child what's happening to this place?" She grabbed her purse and sweater and pulled away to face me before she headed out the door.

"You stay in and lock up I'll be right back."

Clara reached the store and everybody was talking about how John had saved Mr. Franks. Clara Chaney could not believe her ears.

"My John is a hero?" She asked herself softly.

She ran over to Mr. Franks to find out what had happened and after he confirmed what John had done, she was amazed that what she heard was true. She offered her assistance to help where she could be of service to him if any and ran back home.

"...John! John!" She called excitedly. "...Why didn't you tell me you saved Mr. Franks from burning alive, don't you know you could have been trapped in there yourself and to think you took the time to save a man's life? You're a hero John, did you know that you're my brave little hero."

I did not say a word, I just looked at her, what could I have said? I shrugged my shoulders and went back upstairs while she continued to rave. She was happy to call me a hero but was that true? She did not know of the two I had extinguished and the third was only yet to happen that very night. She continued excited about my role in saving Mr. Franks and allowed me to go upstairs while she told me she was going to make me my favorite dinner and bake me my favorite desert, chocolate cake. I let her continue

to think I was a hero and stayed in my room until it was time to join her for dinner and desert.

When she retired for the evening, I made my way back out the window and through the night. The time with Murphy was crucial and I could not afford to waste any with useless delays. I walked up to his house and the door opened.

"Does she know?"

"Know what?"

I walked in closing the door behind me and stood over at the window behind the television gazing into the distance.

"There should be no shame or guilt when the things that are not right in the world are corrected John, and there is still another."

I stared out the window out into the distance.

"Why me?"

"I don't pick the winners John. They pick me, just as you did. It was you crying out for help. I simply heard the cries of your request." Murphy added. "…This is what you were meant to do but it's much more, it's not what you've learned but who you are. Now you must go out into the world correcting everything against justice and put a stop to all those who are trying to prevent you from what you need to accomplish. They must suffer the same fate."

"How did you move the body?"

"You must know deep in the inner core of your being that no one can stop you John, and no more mistakes, no one will clean up your mess. But this alone I'm sure has taught you the importance of covering your tracks."

He knew I wanted to know how he moved Brian's body but ignored my question and continued with his way of enlightening

his protégé, me. His voice began to tremble with excitement, and he was giving me the final stages of what I must do.

"...John it took me years of trial after error to accomplish what you already have in you and you developed within months. To be so young and gifted that's an envy I'm proud to say this old man cherishes and to experience this type of joy knowing that I will have the honor of someone like you succeeding me is unexplainable, John you are truly deserving of the mission you will engulf."

"I don't understand why I have to be this way."

"How are you sleeping?"

"Fine."

"No nightmares, perhaps a hint of guilt?"

"No."

"Then you already understand, now take the reins and soar, John, you're doing society a favor and you will learn that you will come into contact with those far worse than those who ever came into my path. No traces John, is what secures the whole purpose of any of it. Nothing and no one should be allowed to escape and you must finish everything, just as it started in the beginning until it is finished to the end. This is a journey that you will find to be one that is less traveled by the majority; stay on its path and understand it, accept it, and know the outcome before it is completed."

"Is that it?"

"Some choices are not governed by what we want or what we wish could be but simply by the things we nor can anyone else prevent. It's a certain means of existence that is to be established. Many could have done what I am now not asking of you but you have the innate ability to know what you must do and that is why

you're here and it's also, why you will accomplish what has never been spoken. No one else could have foreseen something so desirable, inevitable."

"How did you know, I would understand this?"

"How can I ask someone to do what you naturally possess and that is why the years have been so kind and cruel to me?"

"Will I suffer the same fate?"

"That's your choice."

"But you never asked me, I decided."

"Did you really, you will later see that everything has been arranged and then you'll know. You had to come into my world John because it is a world you've created for yourself. Yes, there were those who were good and had an incredible ability but you John, none had such a gift as what you possess. It is your responsibility to take the place of one who reigned far longer than he desired and be better than he ever was, I have no aspirations and without question I understand even if you don't know the difference that you will uphold it instinctively."

"You know there's more I must learn."

"That's not something I can teach you John, no one can teach it. Justice or injustice, whichever path you take, it is one that no one can teach, the choice is building inside of you and your actions tell which you revere the most it is an unspoken truth and you, the chosen, will be bound by honor."

"Are you sure that either is revered?"

"In your case it doesn't matter because you will know when the time is right how to go about that task. Your subconscious is strong and unmoving, and it's without a doubt that you must continue to strengthen your keen adept ability whichever way you

decide, right or wrong the outcome will be the same to those who get in your way with destructive intentions."

"Who do I go to when things like that of the past come before me?"

"There is nothing more you need from me and you must realize that you are looking at a broken man who has spent many years behind a wall of impenetrable apathy. You have no time to mourn John, it is to be treated the same way the ravaging methods of a wild beast is celebrated when it is killed after having taken the lives of so many innocent people. I only have one thing to correct, all the injustice I myself have created and you, yes you John can fight that same injustice, because it's not an option with you but you haven't realized that just yet. My shortcomings are not something that will curse you. You can give hope to a life once gone too far in a world where nothing more can be done except for that life to allow it to continue through you."

I continued to stare out the window during the entire conversation with a blank expression. There was no way Murphy could have known what I was thinking, but he continued to answer everything I asked or thought about asking without having said a word and when he said it would be instinctual I knew what I had to do.

"When is it to happen?" I turned to face him and his delight was eerie when he smiled as though he himself would be able to get rid of his old bones he had and replace his fragile existence and trade them in to become whom he saw in me. A chill went through my spine.

"You know the answer to that John and I believe you have already prepared yourself for the event."

I turned back to the window to see the reflection through the mirrored pane and the two of us appeared and disappeared as the lightning flashed and still the maniacal grin on Murphy's face was disturbing but the stone cold apathetic look in my eyes revealed my answer as the two of us bounced back and forth off the glass.

Murphy watched me and I silently walked into the kitchen and opened the freezer. The old man turned and went to his chair in the living room knowing the final task had been accomplished. He waited for me to return with the package and when I entered the living room, I had not disappointed him and there was a brown paper bag in my hand. I walked pass him as he sat in his chair, took a magazine out of the rack on the floor next to him, and opened it as my footsteps stealthily made their way out the door. I continued out the house without looking his way nor did I pause and neither of us ever uttered another sound to each other. He continued watching proudly knowing his most accomplished killer would fulfill his final request.

The movements of my steps became more in harmony with the silence hovering in the night air before a storm erupts and I thought back to him naming me the chosen.

BOUND BY HONOR

A dark presence covered the horizon as the shadowy glow from the moon told the tale of mystery through the essence of darkness. Murphy awakened to the sounds of the screen door. He did not secure the door earlier that evening when I left. I watched him get up from his chair and open the door to feel the cold wind blow across his face and body. He returned the latch onto the screen and finally closed the door and locked it. I could tell when he sat down that he noticed my figure looming in the shadows of the corner behind the television closest to the window. The thunder began to roar and lightning flashed outside the windows seen behind my shadow as I moved in closer to the rear of the television. The picture on the screen was covered with the brush of the trees outdoors in the night as the movie showed the lightning flashing almost simultaneously with the lightning happening outside the window of old man Murphy's house. He did not say a word, he only bend down to replace the magazine to his lap, which had fallen to the floor when he got up to lock the door. He adjusted his posture, covered himself with his blanket, and patiently waited. I knew he could feel my movements as he knowingly closed his eyes and I could see his anticipation as he allowed a glimmer of a smirk to appear onto his face. The thunder roared and the sounds reverberated off the walls. Murphy's body lay limp and his eyes quickly popped open as I stood over him and watched the life expire out of the old frail frame. Nothing more was needed.

I went outside, through the back door and picked up the shovel, and began digging in the dark. My arms grew tired and body weak, I was still young but had the will of a stubborn mule. It was a difficult feat but I was able to move the body by using the wheelchair stationed by the kitchen door. I laid several large plastic trash bags in the ground and covered the body with a couple of them. It was easier for me to let the body fall to the ground and then place the feet in one bag and cover as much of the top half of the body with the other bag. I did not think the trash bags were large enough to cover the entire body and was relieved and hauntingly happy when I was able to tie the two ends of each bag together. I looked at the bag with the lifeless being inside and pushed the body until it rolled into the hole and then I commenced with the final chore. Murphy had gallons of containers he used many times in his life and now he had reserved these for my ultimate trial.

I carefully unscrewed the top of the first barrel and then tilted it forward holding onto the edge of the back end of the top portion of it to allow the fluid to escape slowly then I lowered the barrel to the ground and then with the shovel, I hit the top until it broke loose and the substance continued to overflow into the ditch with the plastic bags and the body that lay inside of it. The gases escaping from the barrel was intense and I had to step back to allow it to work and let the incessant fumes escape without allowing them to overwhelm me. I continued until I emptied all the contents from all ten containers into the ditch. Everything dissolved into nothing then carefully the task of covering the hole was my next challenge until all the dirt was finally back into the ground. I put each container back to its original position and I

removed the key from the wall hanging inside, it was my security to have a place to return without anyone knowing Murphy was no longer around. I walked back to my house and climbed up the tree and back into the room.

I had to put all the items worn in a trash bag taken from the other house and hid it in the back of the closet to dispose of it the next day when mom left for work and I was on my way to school. She was completely oblivious to what truly happened and did not know exactly what role I had played in it all. She was not to know, no one was, ever!

LISA'S SECRET

When they all learned about Brian at school, everyone became fearful and the police had no leads, many spoke of how they were glad Brian wasn't going to be around anymore, and others defended him and said they were just hoping he would transfer to another school but never wished him dead.

No one knew what had happened to Jake McIntire and the school found out about him days later. Though the firefighters had found a body in the rubble, they had no idea that a teacher was missing at the school. Everyone was concerned after Brian's death and then the fact that Jake McIntire was missing, surmised that perhaps he was the one who killed Brian and then ran off so he would not face punishment with the law. After a few days, the principal filed a missing report about Mackey and the students murmured amongst themselves that the teacher they all liked was on a police list for missing persons. They thought that he was more than likely a killer until they learned that the police discovered the burnt body they found in Mr. Franks' store was Mackey's and it was ruled as an unfortunate accident.

When the students found out that the teacher was dead they all began to fear that perhaps a serial killer was on the loose and had made Mackey's death look like an accident. A couple more weeks passed and after listening to the concerns of many, the school board thought a field trip to the city would help guide their thoughts in a different direction and was hoping it would get everyone back on track. I was indebted to Lisa but did not realize

that she felt the same about me. I was sure she didn't know who I was until the day she approached me the day I showed up in my very hot suit to impress Sara, I felt I could trust her with such a vital mission.

I decided it would be best to use her as a necessary accomplice because my instincts told me she was not a threat or a traceable factor. I was betting on everything that had happened between her and Brian and I was sure that she perhaps would be the one I could go to with a proposition in order for her to find a way to get Brian to go back into the passageway where it was secluded.

I told Lisa that she and her friends would never have to fear him again and she would be able to walk with her head up high without having to worry about his friends coming after any of them. She was the only one who knew I wanted her to play a part in getting Brian to agree to meet with her and after she learned of his death, she never said a word to me or anyone else about it. She walked the halls in school with Valerie and Roxanne the day they learned Brian was dead and she looked at me as she passed by, the stare was without expression, she winked and kept walking. The police were facing the problem of how to solve the death of Brian but they had no way of finding the killer who had disposed most of the body with acid. Murphy's methods were smooth, precise and unfortunately for his foes, deadly but the message taught me to leave no clues. Lisa was not a part of that scenario.

I was cautious to act on many occasions but I made it my purpose to keep an ear out for the one's deviating from life's arrangements designed for peaceful living and I set a permanent rank for the adversaries in the ever-ending realm of the afterlife.

The field trip happened immediately and the students were in awe when the day was upon us and we all stood in front of one of the many theaters of downtown Manhattan, New York City. December 1973, snow covered the ground and one more year had passed and once again Christmas was upon us. The lights glimmered and shined and the decorations were brilliant in color, glittering and in many ways excessive but truly the mark of the outstanding ostentatious glamour of what Christmas should be in the city that never sleeps. People were out shopping and horns of cars blaring as Christmas songs were heard from every store. Santa Clauses were out on practically every corner ringing their bells, trying to collect money for the needy. There wasn't a store around that didn't have one decoration or another to celebrate the season of winter wonderland. We rode to the city in the school buses and had to stick together in threes. Somehow, I was not part of a group and became the odd one left out. Lisa encouraged the instructors to let me be in her group with Valerie and Roxanne. I thought that perhaps she was going to say something to me about Brian or indicate that her best friends knew about our agreement, but nothing like that occurred; in fact, she was ignoring me. Everything was back to normal in her eyes.

We were going to go see a live performance at one of the smaller theatres a few blocks from Broadway and the day of the event, the teachers started rushing all of us into the atrium because there had been a robbery and brutal rape of an elderly woman and the police was chasing the man down the street. The mugger went by the crowd of people and ducked behind one of the vans double-parked. He slipped pass two of the officers looking for him and made his way around to the back entrance just around the corner of

the same building we entered.

I looked out the window from the lobby of the theatre and saw the man turning the corner while the police were outside milling about back and forth and scratching their heads. I watched for a moment longer, unfeeling to the cops inability to find one man but as I was about to move away I caught sight of what the assailant had done to the face of the woman. More horrifying then that was that the woman was trying to plea for more help because she noticed she was bleeding from a stab wound. She was screaming how she did not realize it at first because of all the clothing and the man had only lift her coat and skirt before ripping her underwear away. She kept screaming, rambling that she thought he punched her and the cop was telling her to calm down because he did not notice the blood and started telling his partner that the woman was telling him the man only punched her when he finished his act of rape.

I watched as the woman turned and I saw that the man had slashed her with a knife from her forehead to the bottom of her chin. She was reaching down to feel the wetness on her hand from the blood staining her coat and losing conscientiousness from racing to get assistance. She collapsed in front of the window where I stood on the inside looking out staring into the eyes of the dead woman. I found myself slipping away from the crowd to the hallway in the direction leading to the side of the street where I saw the man disappear. A door with the words exit and storage was above it and upon opening it; I could see it was leading to a lighting room with sandbags dangling from ropes. The room was for all the excess items that were in need for other shows later.

I entered the room closing the door quietly and started to

make my way through all the equipment until I heard a sound, when everything up until that moment had been quiet. I moved stealthily and found an area close by the door where I waited for another sound. The man entered through the back entrance just after I had closed the door and was unaware someone was in the dark room where he knew he had eluded the police from his trail. He was trying to make his way around the ropes and floor lamps to find another exit.

I removed the knife I used to dive into Mackey's throat and held the blade down then I remembered Murphy's words so I calculated the time it would take to raise the blade and strike. It would probably give the unsuspecting opponent time to combat my limited skills. I changed the position of the knife and grip having figured out a much-needed control of the situation in order to have the advantage from the start just as Murphy had always explained about honing abilities and that it would involve actual situations and it may cause the need to perfect those abilities in a moment's notice.

The man moved carelessly tripping over one of the ropes extending from the ceiling to the floor but caught himself before crashing into some of the breakable lighting fixtures around the room. The room was far enough away from the front entrance and if the man made it out the door, he would have the time to escape out a different exit away from the front. He had given away his position once again. I waited in silence, slowing the pace of my breathing as I squatted low by one of the floodlights, and stayed still. I was close enough to the door to stop the assailant from getting out and far enough away to attack in silence just in case anyone was walking by, it would have been secure that no one

would have heard anything.

The man crept, this time keeping his position silent from anyone outside the room but I could hear his every move with keen listening skills again taught to me from one of the many techniques Murphy showed me. Many times, I felt his training was agonizing and a waste of time but Murphy insisted and emphasized that it was necessary in order to track an opponent. He use to blindfold me and turn on the television or his phonograph and play an album on the turntable, turn up the sound and then drop various items and ask me to identify them.

He wanted me to stay alert and if necessary use skills to make a crucial escape. Now with eyes closed, I could hear the breathing from the assailant who had to get close enough in order for me to execute the attack and take him down. He stood by the flood light where I was hiding down below with the handle of the knife tight in hand, blade facing upward and ready to strike. A sound hit up against the door and the man froze as did I both looking in silence to see if whether someone was going to come in. The sounds of the other students could be heard from a distance as the door was slowing opening and one of the ushers dropped something down just inside of the door and up against the wall and returned the door to its closed position.

For a moment, I looked passed the man who stood above me and saw two figures silhouetted a glow on the wall behind him. The shadow would have revealed one tall and the other crouched low and if the usher had entered, he would have first noticed the man standing some feet away from him.

Luckily, the one who had opened the door was completely unaware of what was to take place inside and it was to his

advantage he did not have to concern himself in being in a life-threatening situation. I was nervous because all the man had to do was look down, but I was ready and would have struck low at the knee first another gift offered by Murphy, if needed, change the rules of attack and get the job done. No longer would anyone have to worry about the unknown assailant for the dark room had one more to store and it would be in the form of the one who had raped, slashed and murdered the helpless elderly woman. I was certain that she was there in my view for the same reason the man had entered the theatre, justice.

The other kids were up front joking around and I gave the usher enough time to get away from the sounds that were about to escape from within. I waited no longer as soon as I thought he was far enough away and it proved the same motive for my unsuspecting opponent, he moved just as I was ready to strike and my attack was as lethal as the blow to Mackey's head, deadly.

The victim had no time at all to realize what was happening and in one sweeping motion, I stood up thrusting forward and upward into the open throat of the unsuspecting villain. I gazed into the eyes of the man staring in complete shock as I twisted the knife once and pushed it further down his throat. The man collapsed to his knees almost toppling over on top of me. I left the knife in place and lowered the man to my own amazement down to his stomach with the strength of an ox I gained in a short period from when I trained with Murphy.

I checked the body of the man to locate the weapon he carried and measured the size of my own blade to that of the one he had on him but they were clearly different in size and shape. I ripped off part of the shirt where I saw it torn from the struggle he more than

likely had with the woman. I removed my weapon, wiping the blade clean of the blood and human tissue of the man staring lifeless up at me and preceded with the second part of the plan.

I maneuvered myself opposite his body and emulated the actions of what I thought might look like a realistic result. After lowering down to a push-up position and simulating the act of a knife in my hand, I looked to see what the possibilities were for the man to fall onto his own weapon. I made sure I did not practice this act with the actual blade in case I made an unfortunate mistake and slipped causing me to land onto it. I went forward slightly reaching over the dead body and saw the alibi.

I put the knife back in the man's hand, closed the grip after using again the corpse's shirt, and wiped away my prints. I put the part of the shirt where I wiped my blade into my pocket because I knew it would be impossible to believe the man removed his own knife from his throat and then in an act of cleanliness decided to clean his own blade from the blood.

'Leave no trace.' Murphy's voice was in my head reminding me.

I used the dead man's hand to force the knife to dig upward and twisted it into his own throat, trying to imagine what the angle and positioning of the outcome of a blade like that would cause if he had tripped and fell onto it. I wrapped one of the ropes from one of the sandbags hanging around his foot so it looked as though that is how he tripped. I walked over to the door and listened to make sure all was clear before walking out. I checked my clothing and hands to make sure they were free of blood then took the chance allotted and slipped into the men's room where I washed them making sure there was nothing splattered on me and if

anyone was looking for me they would have seen me coming out but fortunately I rejoined the group, as they were lead into the theatre to take their seats and no one noticed I was missing.

MOM'S ILLNESS

As time passed and my search continued for Sara, I came across the type of people who needed to reform their ways and to their dismay, there were those who did not take the opportunity to change before they met their tragic and final end. My search consisted within and out of the neighborhood and my memory did not allow me to forget the long legged length I enjoyed seeing as we passed each other in the hallways at school. Days went by and then months and time stood still but it continued and the years past. Several times throughout the years, I would take out a note pad and write down what I remembered to capture her beauty on paper, which only allowed the memorable vision I had of her to take another form.

'She stood tall with pride her shoulders hunch over slightly giving character to her stride with her long legs like an ostrich when she graced us with her presence as she walked into or out of a room. When her neckline is exposed I imagine the sensual taste as my lips gently kiss it as she wears her hair up in a bun. She is older now and I can see her grown in height, but nothing abnormal everything about her body is molded perfectly to the development of her stature. I would gaze into deeper visions of her with fuller lips, developed breasts, which by now have taken the shape of honeydew melons and by no means would her features, be stripped from her beauty. The long line of her cheeks structurally crafted, sculpted is her jaw line and her hair short or long would flow from side to side as a sheet blows lightly into the air as it hangs from a

laundry line outside to dry.

...The undeniably strong features she possess from the descendant of the Cherokee tribe and black heritage on her mother's side of the family and warm creamy complexion combined with the French background she inherited from her father's side, gave her the combination of strength, softness and an outstanding view from others as one looks at the portrait of an angel graced from the heavens. Her family roots would stand out for her beauty is exceptional and there is no other like her.'

Some days I would just walk in hopes of accidentally coming into her view but never the case was my luck inclined to make things that simple. I continued to study hard as each day was nothing more than just another and the days I cherished with the love of my life were only a memory but still I had another love and she was the one I lived for and spending time with her meant a great deal to me. Mom and I would often go to the city to shop at Macy's and Gimbles department stores and most times I would go in hopes that I would see the joy return in that closed area I once vulnerably allowed to shine. I thought of her constantly. I did not know if my mother knew what I was feeling but she did not interfere with my longing and allowed me my right to develop from childhood into manhood.

Occasionally we would go to see a movie on 42nd street. Most of the theatres were old but the seats were comfortable when they weren't actually torn causing any metal to stick out or if the cushion wasn't taken out by any one of the rambunctious acts of the kids. Sometimes the drunks who got mad at the seats for being broken destroyed them altogether. Mom was my pride and joy and the main reason I wanted to continue to do well in school and not

just to get by but to exceed in order to help her have a better quality of life. I had to be cautious because she was never aware I secretly searched the streets during the night in hopes to find the lost love of my life or of the extracurricular activities of murder, I engaged in now and then.

I had a knack as Murphy would categorize differently but during those late night searches, I was obligated to correct the mistakes I believe God forgot to deal with in this lifetime. I continued to use Murphy's place from time to time when it was convenient without anyone's knowledge and I lost an interest to hang out with the rest of the neighborhood kids. The training I had with Murphy increased in some boxing techniques and martial arts with a man who taught some of the kids from other neighborhoods and me over on Northern Boulevard. I was not a graceful fighter but I had become a very skilled one.

My methods were raw as though each sparring match was the first. This trainer was like Murphy in the sense that he too took to me and wanted to help me advance in areas I was not yet skilled but he thought my ability to control the strength I had was outstanding lashing out when necessary and always pulling back before a potentially deadly blow. I controlled the moves made constantly to let the friendly opponent know I could have done irreparable damage. Occasionally I would be in need to show those who defied life's existence when I saw someone attacking others to let them know that theirs was the existence that did not matter. I kept up with the chores or desired requests given to me by my mother and when I was not doing all that I could for her I spent most of that time alone. By the time, I reached seventeen years old and almost out of high school, I would occasionally pass

by the area where Sara and I attended summer school. From time to time, I went onto the school grounds in the park where we use to sit under the tree talking.

Five years had gone by since I had met her but never did I stop looking for her nor did I forget the fate by which her own life was suffering. I couldn't forget no matter how hard I tried and though I wanted to find her sometimes I thought maybe it was best to let her live her life but what kind of life is that for someone so young and without a choice and though she's older, he must pay for all the years he held her captive. Just like all the other individuals who earned their passage right to hear me utter those sacred words, he too deserved to hear them. It was my right to find her and rid her of the father she only knew as a sex, controlling pervert who dominated her and her mother to the point of fear and silence. She would understand that I was doing it for her, and nothing was going to stop me from showing all who deserved the way to a permanent and unforgiving future that I was willing to use methods by any means necessary to rid them out of this universe.

I missed the days with Sara and when mom started getting sick I longed for her more so that she could talk to me, help me and somehow I know she would have been able to guide me through this time of despair. Mom was no longer working after she and some of her co-workers suffered a lay off from the hotel, and though she was a good worker, it was becoming more difficult for her to perform her cleaning duties. The chemicals were affecting her health and she had suffered from bronchitis and asthma in the past. She tried searching for odd jobs where she could find them but there was not enough work to allow her to stay

on for very long.

She wasn't winning this fight, her health continued to get worse and one night she went to the bathroom and slipped, missing the handle of the door and fell.

"John, John--help me." She cried.

I was laying in bed sleep.

"Mom, mom what's wrong?" I jumped up and ran to her.

"Come in here and help me."

I stood looking baffled, thinking she had called me from her bed but when I got there, she was nowhere in sight.

"Where are you?"

"I'm here John, in the bathroom."

I went back out of her room having rushed by so fast I did not notice the light on in the bathroom and had gone straight to her bedroom. I opened the door to see her sitting on the floor. I rushed over to help her up and guided her to sit on the toilet.

"What happened?"

"Oh nothing, I just slipped and missed the seat that's all."

"Are you okay?"

"Yes, I'm okay, baby."

"Are you sure, mom?"

"I'm sure, don't you worry about it, I'm just glad you were here to help me, I don't know what I would have done if you'd been gone."

Her words struck a concern in me because I could not help but wonder if there had been a problem in the past and she called out to me only to find out to her dismay that I was not there. So many nights I had slipped out of my room through the window to undo the faults in others where I thought God had made a mistake in

allowing certain people to live. My duty was to show them that they had an outcome that was inescapable because their prey was the less fortunate but in reality, I had been on a search and the rest was a bonus. I let myself believe it was for the purpose of getting rid of the nefarious that I was patrolling the streets because I knew I was not ready to admit the possibility of not finding her. I had to stop hoping that maybe she would be coming home with her parents from a late night dinner or movie or that perhaps her dad had taken them all out of town on a business trip, which was my favorite excuse to get through the nights.

I used to tell myself that they would be returning home soon enough, one day she would show up at school but after countless months of days gone by turned into years, Sara never showed. I had no choice but to let it go but my stubborn demeanor and determination would never allow me to give her up. I convinced myself that giving up on her was not an option and I was hoping that one day I would come across her. During the silent nights, the walks I took made me become aware of too many different scenarios that were causing chaos in the lives of others. I walked by houses or apartments and I overheard loud arguments only to learn of women or children screaming or crying due to the abuse they had to endure.

The many different stories I heard how some women were getting hooked on drugs by some low life drug dealer or about the many different married women who suffered at the hands of some man blackmailing them because he got into their pants and was now forcing them into prostitution. I was a magnet attracting situations of all these different types in need of justice, was it my justice or what Murphy had instilled in me, non-the-less I felt it

was my duty to appear during the night to the ones who were repeated offenders against the meek.

DAD RETURNS

…The past five years flashed in my mind as I stood gazing at mom contemplating if she knew or recently learned that I had been slipping out of the house or was she genuinely naïve to the countless number of times I had disappeared into the night. Now, practically a man I felt obligated to dedicate my time to her even if it meant dropping out of school. I looked into the eyes of the most loving woman who walked the face of the earth.

"I'm glad I was here too mom, are you sure you're alright?"

"Yes, baby I'm fine thank you, now you go on back to bed and let me see if I can use the restroom without being such a bother."

"Mom, you're never a bother to me, just be careful but don't ever feel like I think you're bothering me."

"I don't baby, I'm just a little frustrated, I guess. Now you go on back to bed, I know I can count on my baby if I need him."

I smiled at her words and left the room only partially closing the door behind me because I was worried and didn't know what it was she wasn't telling me but I could sense that it was something. I looked around the corner of the wall where I could see that she was checking her head.

"Mom!"

"Jesus, John what you doing sneaking up on me like that."

"Did you hit your head?"

"It's nothing, here look for yourself if you want I don't have a bruise and I'm not feeling dizzy so it's nothing, now go on and go

back to bed, you don't have to worry about me."

A few days later, she was feeling better and accepted a job cleaning someone's house. It was fortunate for us that they needed her to stay on longer. Several weeks passes and things were going well until she decided to walk home because the bus was late. She was not expecting it to rain and during her walk, she was hoping a bus would come by in order for her to flag him down if she was not at the next designated stop. Each time she reached the appropriate bus stop she waited in vain.

She decided to wait by the time she had walked up to the third stop but then rain poured down unexpectedly. After several minutes, she thought she would be more successful walking and getting to the next stop instead of standing in the open getting soaked because that area did not have an awning to keep her sheltered. She continued walking and was out of range from the next stop when the bus showed but the driver saw her flagging at him and pulled over to let her get on the bus. He was kind to let her on at an undesignated area but the time between waiting and walking, she was out in the cold for over an hour and a half and then the rain added to her dilemma. When she got home, she peeled out of her clothes to take a warm bath and get herself under the blanket after making a pot of hot tea but it was too late she became very ill.

It seemed like she only had a cold at first and was trying a different over the counter medicine every few days when the one she had tried proved to be unsuccessful. Finally, after a serious series of bad sounding, painful coughs and losing her balance only to stumble into my arms, and seeing that I prevented her from falling to the floor, did she give in to go to the emergency room. I

did all I could do to take care of her but I watched her slowly waste away to nothing.

The doctor was baffled for over a week knowing something more was happening with her other than the pneumonia she suffered. I gave her a cup of water while visiting her in the hospital, her doctor came in to check on her progress but in her case, it was a lack of improvement. She took the cup and drank from it, but before she could lower it from her mouth completely, water squirted out from between her lips as though someone shot the liquid out from a water gun. The doctor stepped up next to me almost impatiently pushing me to the side and took the cup from my hand.

"Here take another sip," He encouraged. She raised the cup and drank again and the same thing happened.

"...Oh my God," He said. "...She's having a stroke."

"What are you talking about she's never had a stroke."

"She's having one now." He ran to the door, "...I need a nurse down here now." He yelled.

Three nurses ran to the door, one from one direction and the other two meeting her in the middle from the other direction. I listened as the doctor requested the nurse to remove the IV from my mother's arm and to get one of the poles to hook up the medication so they could wheel her out of the room. I stood there confused, worried and I did not understand what was happening to her.

"What are you doing, why are you taking that out of her, what's happening?"

"John we need you to leave the room." The Doctor said impatiently. "...Mrs. Chaney, I need you to talk to me. I want you

to repeat after me, dear."

I moved over and away from the doctor but stood slightly to the side of the door next to the wall as they did their job and listened to what the doctor was requesting from my mom.

"Okay." She said.

The doctor did a series of test to see if whether or not her speech was slurred and as she spoke he could see a slight deformity take shape over her face. He immediately ordered the nurse to set up for a CAT scan. His tone seemed harsh but the nurses were all too familiar with the importance of his request. The one nurse rushed out passed me as if I was not there and two other nurses proceeded to help my mother into the wheelchair and take her for the immediate test on her brain.

"Please tell me what's happening to my mom."

I could not control the tears, which affected the doctor and he took me by the arm to walk with him to the elevator.

"We're going to do a CAT scan to see if there's any bleeding on her brain."

"What, why would she have bleeding on her brain?"

"John, don't fall apart its routine when someone falls victim to signs that are indicative to having a stroke and this way we'll know if we can administer the counter-productive drug called TPA. This will reverse the symptoms of a stroke as long as there is no bleeding on her brain. Don't worry, John we're going to do everything possible to see to it that your mom gets the best of care."

One of the nurses met up with us with a portable stand on wheels and another IV and then she attached the needle back into my mom's arm so that the effects of the pneumonia did not get

worse. They took her down for testing and I waited upstairs by the nurse's station because they did not allow me to go down the elevator to the room where they performed the test. Some of the nurses tried offering a kind word to me for the look on my face must have shown the fear I was feeling about the results I might hear but I smiled blankly looking passed them.

One minute seemed like an hour and by the time thirty minutes had passed, I felt as though I had moved into the hospital and was sentenced to wait a lifetime before I could speak with the doctor again. When the testing was over, he came back upstairs where he left me. I saw him get off the elevator and he smiled softly letting me know they could give her the medication and she would be all right.

"John has anything unusual happened to your mother before you brought her here for pneumonia."

"No, she was fine." I said.

"You didn't notice a difference in her speech pattern, or a loss of balance, she didn't seem awkward in any way." He asked.

"Wait, she did fall in the bathroom a couple of weeks ago, but she said she was fine and she did everything the same afterwards until she almost fainted to the floor," He looked at me intensely.

"…I caught her and after that I brought her here but that was right before she took a job and decided to walk home. The bus was late and she was in the downpour of rain we recently had."

"Her fall might have been due to a mild stroke gone untreated for the past few weeks," He paused. "…Honestly, I don't know what caused this to happen and it's possible she may have suffered from multiple strokes without our knowledge but we'll have to do more testing when she's stronger but for right now she's getting all

the proper medication she needs for the stroke and the pneumonia." He said.

"So you're telling me you treated her for pneumonia when she suffered from a stroke."

"No, she definitely has pneumonia but due to having a mild stroke unnoticed the focal point was the pneumonia and without any signs of a stroke there was no way of knowing until I witnessed the involuntary reaction she had after she tried to drink the water." He said.

"You mean to tell me that you guys couldn't test her for stuff like that, I mean what good are you if you can't find out what's going on."

"I'm sorry John but it's almost impossible to test for something where there are no signs showing for any given problem. We could spend hours testing for potential problems, which could take us away from treating the severity of what is actually happening at that given moment. We have to put things in perspective, it would be impossible for anyone to see in advance that someone would have a heart attack when all test results come back showing the individual to have a strong healthy heart. It is an unfortunate reality for the same person to suffer from a heart attack the following week.

...You see, in your mom's case we need to find what caused her to have the stroke. Now we have information regarding her having one and we are going to do all the necessary testing to find out what is going on. It is possible that we made need to call in specialists, but don't worry because we are going to do everything we can to make sure she gets back on the right track. Everything's under control now that we can reverse the potential threat of a

deadly problem."

"What does that mean, do you think she's going to die?"

"It means that we want your mom to be just as healthy as she has been in the past and we want it just as much as you want to see her back to the good health she has always had, so don't worry young man, okay."

The doctor made his way back to the nurse's station where he encountered some of his staff and started giving out his orders as they walked down the corridor. I watched him and the rest of the staff until they were out of sight. I took in a few deep breaths not to alarm my mother and then went into the room and waited for the nurses to bring her back. When they arrived, I put a smile on my face but she was too weak and exhausted to notice. The nurses put her to bed and she went to sleep. Intermittently she would awaken but she did not have a lot of strength. I could see how tired she was, she could barely talk, and after several attempts, which proved to be exhausting, she looked at me lovingly and shook or nodded her head to my inquiries. I didn't leave the hospital and I looked after her with determined dedication making sure everyone did what they needed to do for her and I helped her in every way doing what I could to make things easier for her.

The nurses gave up trying to get me to leave when visiting hours were over because they saw I would hide in the closet, the bathroom or just sit unmoving, emotional and full of love. One of the nurses sometimes watched at the door when she noticed I was fixing the pillow for mom, and straightening her sheets, reading to her or holding her hand to let her know I was still there with her. I once overheard her express the love she saw in me for my mother to the other nurses and tears would well up in her eyes as she

spoke. They all knew Clara Chaney was the light of my world and they all agreed to leave me at her side and let me stay all night whenever I wanted without harassing me. I would only go home to shower and change clothes and I only did that when I realized it was becoming a little bit unbearable even for me to remain in the same clothing. I thought it best to care for mom without telling my dad that she was in the hospital. I remained strong and when she had the strength, she asked me about school. I prepared myself for such a moment and requested the doctor to write me an excuse in order to get the work from classes in advance so that I could turn in all necessary homework and receive a proper grade without having a record of being absent or a penalty for the lack of work I should have completed.

I was out of school for two weeks but had everything I needed to get the work done and in on time including having some returned papers in my possession from the teachers so that I was able to show her in case she wanted to see something from school. She was proud that I had grades reflecting positive outcomes for my efforts.

Many of the teachers showed genuine concern for my situation regarding my mother and would offer me their assistance if there was anything they could do for me to help me during this difficult time. They congratulated me on my ability to focus and accomplish my schoolwork in a timely fashion and accurately to receive the good grades they said they were happy to note.

One day one of the teachers gave the condition about mom to my dad. I guess he had been coming around the house and when I was not there and it looked as if we had moved my dad got in touch with the school and found out everything.

"May I help you sir?"

"Yes, my name is Roger Chaney Clara Chaney's husband and this is her sister Felicia. What room is she in please?"

"Room 403."

"Thank you."

The two rushed to the room and Aunt Felicia broke down into tears. I walked out of the room and dad followed.

"...Why didn't you tell me your mother was in the hospital?"

"Didn't want to burden you with our problems."

"You know John, your mother and I..."

"Save it, I don't want to hear what you have to say."

"Listen up boy, I'm still your father, and you may be growing into a young man, but you're not that grown to stop me from knocking you on your ass."

I was defiant and stared him in the eyes knowing I would choose my time to go up against him but it would mean his death, and then of course the big mouthed, backstabbing whore better known as my aunt, would also have to die or would she? I thought there were too many coincidences to create for both of them to end up dead and for the sake of my mother and making sure I would be able to continue to care for her, I had to come up with something better.

A TIME TO PASS

Dad and my aunt moved right in to stay with me while mom was in the hospital. He showed no respect for his wife, and Aunt Felicia did not seem to have any objections when the two shared the bed where my parents used to sleep. They had their romantic moments all over the house, without shame and with complete disregard to when I would be coming home from school. He also implemented his authority over me and made me return home from the hospital when visiting hours were over.

They drank alcohol on a regular basis and I could see that he wanted me around mainly to use me as their servant, having me clean up the mess made which was often enough. I washed the dinner dishes, pots and pans whether I got the chance to eat or not and dad kept sending me back and forth to the liquor store, something I had been doing with him when he bought alcohol while he was living at home. First he would go into the liquor store with me to get the owner to know who I was and he made sure he told the man that he would always be out in the car if he sent me or to call him at home if he wasn't with me to insure he had sent me on the errand. He would have me go into the store to buy his stash even after he left us and was coming around to pick me up which was not often but when he did he would wait in the car and send me inside to buy his liquor. My father's urge for drinking alcohol was something that bothered me because I never knew what mood he was going to take after he had his fill and now at seventeen I was back to helping him maintain his drunken state

but all I could do for the time being was obey. Many times, he would be down in the living room and not even bother to come upstairs but would yell his orders out to me from the bottom of the steps.

"Did you hear what I said, boy?"

"What!"

"Yeah, I got your what, boy, watch your mouth, you heard what I said, and make sure you bring your aunt some snacks, you know which kind she like."

Aunt Felicia was in the kitchen making dad something to eat.

"You know that's right, baby, he know what to get, and don't be bringing back those nasty coconut balls with the cake inside of them either." She yelled.

Mom came home soon after they moved in because the pneumonia cleared out of her and though she healed from the stroke, the doctors still had no idea why she had suffered from it. She was doing better and so at the demands of her sister and still the man known as her husband they let her return home. The hospital released her after several weeks but she could not do for herself. I spent many days going to school and coming home doing chores, mainly cleaning up the mess my dad and aunt made, running errands two or three times a day with barely enough time to care for my mother and get my homework done. It took me about a month to get a routine down in order to continue to properly care for mom, get the homework completed and maintain my servant hood status for the two but my suspicions were proven right when I believed my aunt was deliberately doing things to make sure I was constantly cleaning up after her. Sometimes after I mopped the kitchen floor, she would go in and as long as she was

telling the story, accidentally spill one thing or another and make some excuse so that I would have to mop the floor over again. When I try to clean the area, where she had spilled either milk or for some unknown reason other than her malicious ways, spilled honey on the floor she would tell me to mop the entire kitchen again in case some splattered on other parts of the floor.

The first time it happened I knew I would be facing my utmost challenge with her living in the house. I would take the trash out clearly, after dad told me to do it to come back and find out later that either the trash was on the back steps from the top of the stairs to the bottom spilled over or the entire bag I took out was back in the kitchen. She always made sure dad saw the defiance she claimed I was committing and he would become violent taking his aggression out on me to prove to my aunt or to himself that he was in control. I never said anything to him or to her but she and I both knew that I knew all the problems were because of something she was the culprit. He took pride in smacking me around and I had to resist fighting back for the sake of my mother. I was still a minor in the eyes of the law and I could not risk leaving her in their care or worse subjecting myself to brutal beatings at the hands of my father. No matter what the situation was when it came to caring for mom, I didn't back down and would be fed up with all the bullshit Aunt Felicia was having me go through but each time I would defend my right to care for my mother.

One day I lost sight of my objective and decided to make a suggestion I thought would be helpful to me, mom and overall the two drunks I had to obey but my tactics lacked the charm of diplomacy. Dad wanted me to go to the store again for his nightly taste and I was completely annoyed.

"Why don't you let me bring you back more than one small bottle of vodka at a time because you know you're gonna drink it all by the time I make mom something to eat." I was angry and it showed in the tone I used but I could not mask my contempt to please the two I was talking to because dad was taking away time I could have been spending with mom and I was sick of being disrespectfully treated and constantly having to deal with the lies told by my aunt.

"Who the hell died and left you boss, boy, you think you grown enough to speak to me like that?"

"Like what?" I snapped.

"Like that!" He bellowed.

"I just want to be able to take care of mom instead of going back and forth to the store unnecessarily for a couple of drunks who don't give a damn about her needs."

"Oh, so what you trying to say, lil man...you don't think I know how to care for my sister without your help, Roger I think this little bastard is trying to tell you how to run your house."

"It's not his house."

"The hell it isn't. So you trying to tell me how to run my household, boy?"

He walked up to me and backslapped me across the face so hard I hit the floor. He rushed me, grabbed me by the throat, and held me up against the wall.

"...You think you man enough to come up against your old man?" He demanded. "...What? You think I'm too old to take care of a piece of shit like you?" He yelled.

"That's right baby, you show him what a real man can do." Aunt Felicia said then she walked right up to him as he held me off

the floor with his hands around my throat. She stopped and gave him a kiss on the cheek and continued into the kitchen. Dad looked into my eyes seeing no emotion knowing I was daring him to finish it. Undeniable wrath was burning inside me. We stared into each other's eyes to rage war with one another, neither releasing the other from his glare until we heard the coughing from mom upstairs and a faint request of me to bring her some water. He let me go, slapped me across the head, pushing me towards the steps when he heard her calling from upstairs.

"Boy you better be lucky your mother still have a breath in her body. You don't know, better ask somebody, I'm warning you, go up against me again." He threatened. I did not trust his intentions and Aunt Felicia proved she was capable of doing almost anything and I did not want them to cause harm to me, which would have left mom without proper care. I managed to keep my temper under control, allowed dad to get away with his violent behavior and decided that I would do what I had to do according to their rules. I knew I could come up with a solution later but until then I wanted to make sure my actions would keep mom safe and the both of us free from his rage.

I went upstairs and stood in front of her door, catching my breath and wiping away the tears of anger. I leaned up against the door and thought for a moment. I stood quietly before entering making sure I would not disturb her with useless worries she could not control. I went inside with a smile in case she was up watching for my entry. She was asleep and I checked her pitcher, filled it again for her as I did a few times daily whether she finished it or not because I wanted to make sure she had clean fresh water throughout the day and night. I poured her a glass full and touched

her shoulder gently to wake her in order to quench her thirst before I went back to my room to let her continue her rest. Most times, I would sit in the room with her but dad and Aunt Felicia were becoming more of nuisance and I did not want to continue the unnecessary traffic in and out of her room.

I thought that he was committing the same acts against my mother and me as to why I disposed of others. It was for mom's sake, dad, was still living but he was living on borrowed time and I had to figure out how to eliminate that time without suspicion but to my dismay, I had no idea the price I had to pay in order to execute such a plan to perfection. When dad was living at home with us, though he still got drunk, he would leave when things got bad only to return after he had time to cool down. Now that he was with Aunt Felicia, I felt that she was more than likely filling his head with ideas of how his life could have been if he did not have any kids and I could only imagine what other lies she may have invented. She too was destined for a serious rude awakening, but timing was the one thing I remembered vividly from all the things Murphy taught me and though at times I felt he was babbling, there were some occasions when what he had to say to me was clear and of significant value.

'Patience allows one to successfully implement all solutions to any problem.'

I went into the kitchen to get something to eat but when I got a plate, took the spoon on the stove, and removed the lid off the pot to fix dinner, Aunt Felicia came into the kitchen.

"Who the hell called you down for dinner, your daddy hasn't eaten yet and neither have I." She picked up the butcher knife and pointed it at me as she spoke and then turned to cut the lettuce she

had left on the table to make a salad.

"...Do you think you're better than anybody else in here that you got to be grabbing spoons and making something to eat, boy you better stop eyeballing me and answer me when I'm talking to you?" She demanded.

I breathed slowly thinking of what I could do but then I would have to come up with a quick and violent solution for my dad but still I enjoyed indulging my thoughts though I knew I wouldn't be able to exercise my current desired wishes.

'I can take her and it would be so easy, and what pleasure it would be to watch her choke, gasping for the last bit of air, unable to hold onto a life not worthy of living.'

My back was to her and I smiled at my thoughts, put the spoon down and returned the plate to the cupboard as she watched my every move. I walked passed her to leave the kitchen to get to the stairs to return to my room.

"...Yeah you better run and stay outta here until somebody calls you out for dinner, and you better not go in there bothering your mother neither with your whining and wetting the bed with your little stank ass self." She yelled.

"I was seven."

"Yeah, you were, and right up until you were twelve, hell now that I think about it, you didn't stop until you were fourteen or fifteen, shit you probably still wet the bed, you grown ass nasty little bastard, you should be ashamed of yourself, seventeen and still wetting the bed."

I could not contain the anger and though I did not say anything further to her, I walked away, went upstairs, and slammed the door to my room making sure she knew I was finished trying to

reason through her asinine allegations. I could hear her from my room deliberately speaking aloud to my dad and laughing about what she said to me. I heard her still talking to my dad as she continued to go back into the kitchen to set the table for dinner. She was evil in my eyes and deserved no mercy when it was time to punish her. I smelled the foul stench of her cigarette rise upstairs when she passed by the steps.

Ten minutes later, I left the room to check in on mom but needed a few moments to breathe deeply so she would not detect that I was angry. She lay in bed looking peaceful but I could see she was perspiring and so I wet a washcloth with some cool water and placed the damp rag across her forehead. I sat with her for forty-five minutes, getting cool water from time to time to wet the rag and placing it back on her forehead after wringing out the excess.

I rubbed her head and held her hand.

"I want you to get better because you mean everything to me. I hope you don't mind that dad is hear because he is concerned about you and I'm sure you hear Aunt Felicia's voice from time to time but she's been helping me with a school play. I joined the theatre class and we have to do a lot of memory exercises." I lied.

"...Don't worry if you think there's arguing because it's not, everything is fine and you only need to get better because I love you, mom."

I sat in the chair by her side as she slept, hoping she heard my words and sorry that I had lied to her about Aunt Felicia but I could not tell her why her sister was there. I picked up one of the six bottles of medication she had and read it, when finished I went downstairs to get her something to eat. Dad and Aunt Felicia were

on the living room couch watching the news and eating fried chicken with rice and vegetables. They both sat glued to the television and ignored me as I walked into the kitchen. I took a plate out of the cupboard to get some food and when I closed the cupboard door Aunt Felicia and dad was standing there in the kitchen watching me.

"I don't recall anyone calling you back down here."

"It's time for mom's medicine, she has to eat something first."

I stared into my father's eyes boldly standing my ground for the right to care for my mother. Dad could see I had his strength and said nothing as he lightly pulled on my aunt's arm to join him back in the living room.

"Her plate is on the stove wrapped up over there and I didn't bother leaving her any fried chicken because she shouldn't be eating that anyway." She said. "…And by the way there wasn't enough food for you so you better try to find some beans or something in there while you're at it." She said laughing.

I ignored her, continued, and took the plate she had made for her sister and went back upstairs to keep her company. I opened the door to see she was still sleeping. She needed her rest, and I did not want to disturb her but she had to take her medication. I went into the room and lightly placed my hand on her shoulder to wake her up. She looked peaceful to me but reality came to me when she woke up, tired, worn out and the frail body was barely able to move and speak.

"Hey John, she said in a whisper, how's my wonder boy? John, I want you to be strong and don't worry about me. You're growing up and you're quite the valiant young man, I had hoped to see you grow to be." She said.

I had to place my ear to her lips to hear the things she wanted to tell me but she was too tired to try to repeat what she had said. She kissed me.

"...I love you so much and I want you to always remember..."

I leaned in waiting to hear what she wanted to say but waited in vain for mom had taken her last breath. I looked up to see that she was no longer breathing.

"No, please don't do this to me mom. Please, please, no, please mom, come back. I'm sorry for all the lies for all the bad things I've done and I'll change, I promise, I'll change, let me prove it to you, please, oh God, please just let me prove it to you." I cried begging her to come back to me. The emotion and the pain was unbearable and the tears more than I thought possible for any human being to shed. I sat begging for her to come back to me but I knew there was nothing I could do or say to bring her back, my mother was gone and my world had crumbled. Murphy did not tell me something like this could happen to me and I did not understand where the tears were coming from as I sat with my head lowering it gently to place on her chest and wept, silently not to alarm dad, because I wanted our last time together to be just that, our time together. I stayed with her silently crying for another hour before getting up, I leaned down to kiss her for the last time on her forehead, went to the door, turned to look at her one last time and smiled through the tears at how peaceful she looked then walked out closing the door gently behind me.

THE SET UP

The doctors found out too late that cancer would take my mom's life. The funeral was simple and my dad and Aunt Felicia wanted a closed casket ceremony. They sat in the front row next to me listening to the preacher as he vibrantly expressed the loss we encountered. Mr. Franks sat next to our neighbor Shirley, who cried uncontrollably with her head in his shoulders. I looked around to see the many who attended the funeral and was honored when I saw mom's friends and the man whom she said was smitten by her all seated near us. Some of the parents of the kids I used to play softball with came and brought additional family who knew her. I could tell the guys who did not want to be there because of the morbid scene and who looked very uncomfortable in the suits they had to wear.

I understood their pain because I too was just as uncomfortable having to wear a tie that was choking me and after service I still had to listen to all the people I didn't know as well as the one's I did know and the reminder of my mother passing on to greener pastures. Some of the things people said sometimes gave me the feeling they were referring to a horse but I understood their concern and my role was to honor my mother and acknowledge those who was with us to share our pain whether I knew them or if they were strangers to me. The fact was that they knew Clara Chaney, my mom, their customer, and friend and they all were there because they wanted to pay their respects. Everyone offered their condolences to him and my aunt and all expressed how they

would miss her beautiful character.

After the ceremony, some asked for a reason to having a closed casket ceremony and I figured dad and Aunt Felicia wanted to cover the guilt they both shared in what they had done to her. I only smiled at their inquest and slowly shook my head because all I could think of was how I did not get to see my mother after the night I was in the room with her when she died. I listened to dad and Aunt Felicia sharing their feelings about their loss and spoke of how wonderful mom was and that she did not deserve to leave this earth so soon. I listened to them feeling nothing except that the two should have thought about what they were doing to her the night he left us for her sister, the night they exposed their betrayal, the night mom truly died.

I felt like a barren desert stripped of all emotions and had to delete any memory of her because I had said goodbye to her in the utmost personal way and believed she would have been pleased with me. I accepted the fact that she was no longer going to be a part of the physical structure in this world. I did not notice at the funeral but Aunt Felicia arranged to have Beanie at the service and I had not seen her but found out as we looked at each other when we were driving away. She stood watching the car pass by and I gave a slow nod acknowledging her presence as she looked at me with a tear falling from her eye and continued to stand looking at the car until it was out of her sight.

I kept quiet in the car as we all went back to the house and when we arrived I went to my room and stayed there for the rest of the night. I had not eaten all day and I had no appetite. Some of the people returned to the house with the family to eat, drink and to reminisce. Dad suggested everyone to leave me alone when some

of the guests asked about me in order to let me have time to absorb the loss of my mother. It was the most humane act he had done for me but I had my own personal service with her alone when she first passed on and now I was constructing a plot of execution. Everyone left the house late and no one bothered me the rest of the night. I was standing at the window looking out into the backyard when I heard the last of the guest leaving. I went over to my bed, lift the mattress, took out the note pad, wrote out a schedule, and quietly continued training in martial arts. I worked hard with the guy from Northern Boulevard during the past two years and continued to do so as I studied programs within the art of defense above my ability. I was not qualified to take such high levels of advance techniques but I needed to strengthen the ability it had to offer for the mind and body that I needed and I needed to do it at an accelerated rate. The instructor seemed more than welcoming to push my endeavors and never tried to forbid me from pushing myself in fact the twinkle in his eyes gave hint that he admired my tenacious endeavors and continued to help me into gaining a personal level of achievement of excellence.

I was seventeen when mom passed away and to honor her I remained in high school to complete my studies. I wanted to disappear but I was still a minor and though I was soon to be eighteen I still had a little over one year left of high school and wouldn't graduate until just before my nineteenth birthday. My life had already trained me at an early age to experience a world far apart from anything like those of my peers and I decided that one more year was only going to help me build a stronger mental capacity for situations I may have to endure for the future. A few days had gone by and I noticed the house was not messy as it had

been in the past. I thought about how my aunt did not do much to keep the place clean when mom was sick and how when I did not clean it, the place remained in disarray but now, it stayed presentable most of the time. I was also aware that the requests from the both of them to send me to the store had almost completely stopped but I had made no complaints and stayed away from all arguments no matter what they were saying to me and I deduced that the death of mom made my dad realize the loss I had suffered. Dad also stopped Aunt Felicia from picking on me with the name-calling she took pride in doing. A noble effort, I thought but one too late for admiring, they both had an appointment to keep with their demise.

I thought it was to my advantage that more and more arguments had erupted between the two of them, and she made it known how she hated the comparisons he was making to her about her sister. Dad's temper was of no surprise to Aunt Felicia and he complained about everything she did or did not do after mom passed away. I endured their quarreling until it was closer to the time for me to graduate, they had not disappointed me in their usual meaningless spats week after week and it almost became daily but now was more crucial, and I needed to set the trap. It was a month before graduation and Aunt Felicia was going to do dad's laundry. I went to the kitchen and emptied almost the entire bottle of fabric softener. I was not worried about her noticing the thin color of the softener when I replaced it with water because she occupied herself with other things to be the most observant person.

The laundry cycle stopped washing and I opened the dryer and sprayed dad's clothes with some starch to help start their feud. I went upstairs making sure I got to my room right before dad was

passing by. I snuck out the house by my usual route down the tree outside my window, went down the block, and made a phone call when I heard the commotion. I got back to the house and they were arguing about Aunt Felicia forgetting to put the fabric softener in the rinse cycle after she had finished the laundry and then he made the mistake of comparing her once again amongst the many other things Aunt Felicia could not do, to her sister. She knew how intense he could act but she never knew of him ever having hit mom and never once thought it would be something she would experience.

"Well if you loved the way she did your laundry so much why don't you go dig up her grave and have her do it for you now. Well, what the hell you looking at, you didn't love her that damn much or you wouldn't have come looking to me. Don't try to get high and mighty on me Roger Chaney cause while she was sick in bed in her own house you were fucking me like she was dead and gone and now she is dead so don't go trying to act like you're a saint to her memory. I know she was my sister but don't try to call a spade a diamond and pretend you don't know the difference. I said it and I meant it, and I'll say it again, she dead, she dead, and I ain't gonna lie to you, I'm glad the bitch is dead."

She crossed the line one time to many for Roger and he charged at her and slapped her across the face. The blow stung her hard and she looked at him as if she was better than the Queen of England and above being the punching bag for any man no matter what came out of her mouth, she reached for the lamp on the side table next to the sofa, and swung it at his head.

His first reaction was to duck causing her to miss but she came back just as fast from the other direction swinging violently.

He had no time to duck but raised his arm up blocking the blow from connecting to his face and snatched the remains of the object out of her hands.

"What the hell is wrong with you woman, you trying to cause damage."

"Damage, did you say damage, motherfucker I'll show you damage." She screamed.

He grabbed hold of her arms.

"Look, I'm sorry."

"No, baby, but you will be, let me go." She demanded. She was no match for his strength but she did not let that stop her from getting free. She raised her knee forcefully into his groin and pushed him off her when he doubled over in pain. She ran into the kitchen mumbling, leaving him in the living room.

She grabbed whatever she thought would serve as a weapon, the butcher knife was first, and then she picked up a steak knife, a paring knife, a butter knife and the long bread knife. She looked over and took hold of the long handled two pronged fork, a wooden salad fork, three dinner forks, a pair of scissors she had left in the kitchen, a spoon, spatula and a pot. She went back into the living room as she continued to mumble and fully armed symbolizing she was ready for war.

"…You want damage, Roger Chaney, oh, I'll give you damage."

He backed away still in pain.

"Wait, wait, wait, baby, it was an accident."

"Yeah, well you're about to have the same kind of accident." She said, emphasizing the word.

"…Like I said, Clara Chaney is dead, you messing with

Felicia Clamrod this day and I will cut your guts out."

A knock at the door.

"It's the police, open up." Roger hobbled over to the door and Felicia remained in the living room.

"COME ON IN!" She yelled.

The police walked in the house to see Felicia standing holding her face which had swollen severely and they noticed the different knives and forks on the coffee table. The male and female officer looked at each other when they saw the woman standing before them to see if they got the same response the other one had as they looked at what was on top of her head, then they saw her face and turned their attention to Roger.

"We got a call about a disturbance. You want to tell us how her face got so swollen, sir." The female officer asked.

She was five foot nine, in good shape at one hundred twenty pounds, and she looked like she would not take shit from anyone. She stood next to her partner confident knowing how she regularly got in the boxing ring with him for techniques she could try out from her training. She was not afraid to go hand-to-hand combat with a male assailant and knew what to do in a hostile situation if one who stood taller and weighed more than she weigh opposed her. The male officer stood six foot, one inch tall and weighed about two hundred and ten pounds.

"Everything's fine here officer she just got in the way when I, well my arm was swinging and..."

"His hand opened just in time to go across my face, is what happened, if you want to know the truth of it."

Both officers looked at the strange sight before them but did not ask any questions regarding what they were looking at when

they looked at her.

"Sir, I'm going to have to ask you to step outside here with me while Officer Hines questions your spouse." The male officer said.

"Can I get my shirt?"

"Your shirt will be there when you come back, sir."

"It's just that it's a little cold out."

The officer looked at Felicia.

"Ma'am, what is your name?"

"Felicia Clamrod, and that's Roger Chaney." She said boldly.

"Thank you, would you be willing to hand Mr. Chaney his shirt?"

"I'm not giving him a damn thing."

"Oh, come on Felicia, its cold out there, I said I was sorry."

"Well now, yes you did, so let me think, oh yeah, I got it now, if sorry removes the bruise on my face I'll give it to you."

She looked at herself in the mirror.

"…Nope, it's still there, take your ass on outside with the man, and it ain't that damn cold this is the month of May, get out of here while I give this young lady my statement."

"Officer Hines, ma'am." The female officer corrected her.

"Yeah, that's alright, but I bet you this, you won't know when it's coming, oh but it's coming baby, it may not be tonight or tomorrow, but you will suffer for the day you put your hands on me I promise you that Mr. Roger Chaney." She ignored the officer telling her how to address a police official and the male officer stepped outside leading Roger to go ahead of him. Roger looked at him.

"And should I call you, Officer Kraft."

"I'm Officer Peters, Mr. Rogers." The officer said sincerely.

"It's Chaney, Roger Chaney."

"Oh yes sir, I do apologize."

"Didn't you get it? I was making a joke."

The officer continued to ignore him while taking out his note pad.

"...If she's Hines, like ketchup, then you must be Kraft, like mayonnaise."

The officer looked up and stared at him blankly.

"So what happened in there Mr. Chaney, have you been drinking?"

"It just got a little out of control that's all, I said some things and she said some things next thing I know I'm in her face with my hand moving away from it, I mean I didn't even realize I had hit her until she kicked me in the balls."

I listened to the two women inside before the officer allowed dad to come back inside the house. The police stayed about thirty minutes and the whole time that I was out of sight, I was still within range to hear everything they were saying.

"Ma'am, I'm inclined to inform you any threats you've made to Mr. Chaney will be recorded and kept on file."

"You do what you gotta do, but he knows what I'm talking about and it ain't no threat, shit. Where's the justice in it all when a man can get away with striking a lady, it don't make any sense to me, but that's alright he'll pay."

"Well ma'am the system works, but so many women refuse to press charges, I've seen it time and time again, the victim feels as though she's the problem and doesn't want to get her spouse in trouble and there's nothing we can do about it. So what's it going

to be ma'am, shall we take him in?"

"I should let him go to jail but he has a son he has to look after and I have my own place, I guess I should just start staying there from now on, he really is a good man." The police officer wrote down what she had to say never bothering to look up at her. Officer Peters and dad came back inside.

"Do we take him?"

"That's a negative. Well ma'am if you have any more problems just give us a call and we'll come back out, and I guarantee you, whether you press charges or not, we will be arresting Mr. Chaney if we come back out here on another call such as this one. Do I make myself clear, Mr. Chaney?"

"That's a ten-four, no reason I'll give you to come back tonight."

The officers left and got to the car.

"Peters, can you tell me why that woman was wearing a pot on her head?"

"You were questioning her, why didn't you ask?"

"Not me, I was afraid of the answer."

They both shook their heads smiling at the ordeal and got in the car. Peters started the car and Hines called dispatch to report their findings and to tell them they were on their way to continue to patrol the streets. Roger stood at the door watching them until the car pulled away and they were no longer in his sight.

'Problem solved, the job done and all that is left is to execute.'

I quietly closed the upstairs door.

GUILTY

I still had to deal with dad and Aunt Felicia arguing and though she went back to her place, she only stayed away for a week and the entire time they were on the phone talking to each other. When she returned, my satisfaction was that I already executed the first part of the plan. The next part was that I had to endure between laying low and taking action. I continued my quest searching for Sara and my efforts only brought me continuous failure and after checking newspaper clippings, the phonebook, and spending countless hours during the night patrolling the streets, I was no closer from the point from which I started but I did not let the failures stop me. I had no desire to give up and Murphy's words played in my head repeatedly.

'You will reach a time when you will have to endure and you will know each failure will bring you closer to your desired goal and know that failure is the alternative to finding another way to bring you to the point of success.'

I persevered and a month later after my dad and aunt had the encounter with the police, the final day at school was upon us and the day of graduation was here at last. It was one more event in life I had to endure before continuing with the plan but all had to seem as normal as possible. Everything had been set and I spoke with counselors and teachers about desires to leave the country. I continued to ask questions and get as much information as possible and wanted them all to be aware of my plans for departure. They were happy for my new life and the adventure I was to embark but

it was all part of my alibi because I wanted to make sure I was giving the police no reason to suspect my involvement of the crime my aunt unknowingly was about to commit.

Dad and Aunt Felicia attended the graduation and for the two of them to arrive there as a couple like it was normal, was an abomination against my mother and I felt as though they were no different from a band of thieves pillaging a sacred village. That is what they did to her. They pillaged her soul and ripped the very core of her happiness out of her when she saw their betrayal and the time for redemption was not something I was going to take lightly. The teachers and board members expressed their excitement for me and asked if I would speak at graduation about my up and coming new venture in life to the graduating class. The end of the ceremony was near, it was one o'clock in the afternoon and the school's vice president and president were next in line to speak but the vice president offered a special addition to the list of speakers.

"This is out of context but before I get started we want you all to know the possibilities of what could be achieved in life if you apply the efforts to accomplish your dreams. There is a young man amongst us who has the goal to go off to Paris, France." She said enthusiastically.

"…And not only is it his dream but he has made it a reality and leaves tonight. I want to introduce to you your fellow graduate of the class of 1979 young Mr. John Chaney."

She applauded as her face gleamed when she turned to face me and urged me to go up the stairs, which caused the audience to explode with cheers. Everyone joined in the applause and there were gasps of surprise and admiration from some of the students. I

looked out into the many faces to see my Dad who sat confused by what he heard. He looked at Aunt Felicia who shrugged her shoulders denying having any knowledge of what was going on. I stepped up to the podium, I wasn't sure what I should say to these people, they were just a blur to me, I looked out to the audience and watched my dad kiss Aunt Felicia on the cheek as they laughed quietly with one another.

I stared down at the two of them infuriated by what I was witnessing.

"Patience allows one to successfully implement all solutions to any problem."

The words were the same words old man Murphy spoke to me and I walked away from the podium. Everyone stared in silence surprised that the speech was so short and seemingly incoherent. They tried to understand the meaning and then a roar of laughter burst from the audience and a thunderous clap of applause followed. Teachers were unsure of what was happening, some nodded, and applauded as if they knew exactly what I meant.

"Um hm, he's right," one woman said but she looked as though she was lost in a daze and had no idea what I meant. I walked down the steps from the stage and students patted me on the back wishing me well and good luck. I confronted my dad as Aunt Felicia walked away leaving the two of us to talk. I did not intend to discuss anything with him and looked into his eyes, and my words shorter than the speech.

"You die, things change." I walked away.

Roger Chaney, husband to my mom Clara Chaney and father to a son full of rage, me while thoughts flooding through my mind as I walked off, I was sure he was wondering if I meant now that mom

was gone, I must take a stand and move on.

"I loved your mother, John." He said.

I was satisfied he had no idea what I meant. I left the school, when I reached the corner I tore up the diploma, threw it in the trash and kept walking. I returned to Murphy's house, it was my new home and no one suspected anything, he was the outcast so whatever took place would seem normal if anyone heard anything. I spent late nights moving things into the house until I was satisfied I would never have to return to my mom's house until it was time. It was June 1979 after graduation and I took a job in the city in a restaurant washing dishes. I accepted wages less than the average dishwasher did in order to get the cash I needed under the table. I ate free and on some rare nights, I stayed in the basement to sleep. The hours were grueling, nine in the morning until nine at night but I would not let it deter me from my ultimate goal. I applied for a passport and when it arrived by mid October I wasted no time continuing forward with the plan. The evidence would be set and it had to be in a place where the police could find it but I wanted it to look as though someone had tried to keep it hidden.

First I had to make it to the airport to finish my plans and met with a fellow who fit my description and gave him some documents and the passport along with the airline ticket, I whispered to the young man and we both went our separate ways. I returned to Murphy's house using the back entrance, where a fence separated the yard by an open lot and I sat in meditation and kept out of sight. Some nights I did not return because I had other priorities and wanted to make sure things were to my standards but often I prowled the night leaving as late as midnight and returning by five in the morning. It was four and a half months after

graduation and it was time to finish what was already in motion.

Felicia was making dinner and Roger decided to go to the corner store to pick up a bottle of vodka. He was accustomed to leaving the door unlocked when he was going to the corner. A figure, camouflaged in the night appeared from behind the tree when Roger turned the other way to walk down the street. It was a windy night, a deadly night. No one was out and most lights in front of the houses on the block were dim or broken. A few days earlier, someone threw a rock, hit a street lamplight in front of the Chaney residence, and blew it out. The block was darker than usual and he climbed the tree and tried to open the window. It was locked. He climbed back down and tried the front door, which was open. He walked in, reached his hand outside the front entrance, and rang the doorbell then quickly got out of sight.

The flames were out and she was satisfied with the results. Felicia had finished cooking and was sitting in the kitchen with a lit cigarette looking at a magazine eating a small cup of the stew she made while waiting for Roger to return. She usually tasted it so often that by the time, it was ready for her to sit and have dinner, she was full but she enjoyed nibbling off his plate after she brought him his food. She heard the doorbell ring, went to the door thinking he might have locked himself out. He watched her from behind the door in the foyer when she walked onto the front porch to open the front door and when she got there; she saw that no one was around. She moved over to the bay window and looked out into the darkness to see if she could see anyone or movement and saw that some branches were on the ground and some were hanging low from the tree in the front yard and thought that perhaps the branch hit the bell when it fell.

The figure slipped passed her from behind the door and moved quickly passed the living and dining rooms and stealthily made his way into the kitchen. He removed a container from his pocket and began sprinkling the substance in the food, watching it dissolve its way into the liquid of the beef stew she made. He saw that there was an ice bucket on the table and nearly knocked it over when he bend down and placed his hand on the table to reach under it. Felicia was returning to the kitchen and he had to slip into the broom closet next to the back door. He closed it as she was opening the swinging door to enter inside and went straight to the pot because she already had Rogers's favorite bowl lined with four slices of bread on the stove.

John looked from between the opening from behind the door of the closet and could see she was getting another bowl and lined it with one slice of bread. He couldn't believe she was making a bowl for herself. The altering of his plan was going to cause questions regarding the motive if she too ended up dead. Roger came home and sat down in the living room, calling out to Felicia as he did when he was ready to eat. She went to the freezer and opened it to take out the ice tray, she filled the ice bucket she had left on the table and noticed the tablecloth bunched up a bit at the corner of the table. She looked at it for a moment trying to decide if she had messed it up then raised her eyebrows in a quick motion thinking she must have done it herself somehow and turned her attention back to her usual routine, got two glasses from the cupboard and headed into the living room for their ritual cocktail. They sat in front of the television watching the news and sipping on their drinks. John thought perhaps while she was gone he could somehow remove it from the pot and only lace the one bowl but it

was too late he had already put the item in the pot of food that was on the stove. This was not like him to make such a mistake that could cause this kind of catastrophe.

It no longer mattered what he was trying to think because Felicia was heading back to the kitchen and he had to get out before she returned. He slipped out the back door and made his way around the side of the house. She entered the kitchen and began scooping the beef stew out of the pot and into both bowls. She gave Roger a healthy amount and only a small portion for herself. She left the kitchen to return to the living room and handed Roger his bowl of stew. She sat down next to him and scooped out a spoon full of stew to put in her mouth.

The doorbell rang and she put the spoon down a bit frustrated.

"You know that happened when you were at the store, and I thought it might have been you but when I went to the door, no one was there." She said.

Roger ignored what she was saying as he watched the television and ate a large amount of the stew while she was getting up to answer the door. He continued with a second and third healthy amount of food that he gorged into his mouth.

Felicia could see some kid waiting with a box in his hands hoping to sell candy. She also saw that inside a car there was a light on when she opened the door and that the boy's parents were waiting for him.

"...Roger some little boy's selling candy, you got three dollars on you? She turned to face the boy. Don't you think that's a little expensive for a box of candy?"

"Yes ma'am, I don't know." The boy said.

"Yes ma'am, you don't know, well which is it, honey, yes

ma'am or you don't know?"

"Yes."

He was frightened and did not want to be there, he turned to walk away. Felicia held up her hand indicating for him to wait and went back into the living room.

"Roger I asked you if you had three dollars, baby didn't you...Oh No, Roger, ROGER WHAT'S WRONG, BABY, ROGER, ANSWER ME!" She screamed.

The little boy heard her scream and ran to the car. John watched the vehicle pull away, made his way down the street, went inside through the back of the house, and closed the door. He closed all the window curtains and sat on the floor in silence. Felicia ran over to Roger to find him on the floor and foaming at the mouth. His body was lifeless and she got on the phone and dialed 911. The ambulance took about fifteen minutes to get there. The police on duty to arrive at the house with the ambulance were the two officers who received the call for the disturbance five months earlier. The EMT pronounced the body dead to the two officers. They watched Felicia get into the ambulance with Roger and decided to hang around.

Neighbors came out to see what all the sirens and lights were about and talked amongst each other. The officers checked around the premises to find nothing out of the ordinary. Hines opened the front door, and they went back inside and looked around to see the food left on the table and another bowl on the floor. They made their way into the kitchen and saw the pot on the stove. Hines looked inside and saw it was the same stuff also in the bowl and on the living room floor. She made her way to the back door. Peters looked and saw a substance of a different color sprinkled on the

side of the stove and on the door handle of the oven. He put a glove on his right hand, wiped the area on the stove lightly, and sniffed his glove.

"Hines, check this out."

She walked over to sniff the matter on his index finger. She looked at him inquisitively. She continued to look around and spotted the same type coloration of substance on the floor by the table. She bend down to find the container partly opened, she got on her hands and knees and reached under the table to get the can. Inside was the same substance that was on the stove, she turned the can around.

"Rat poison, looks like we got ourselves a homicide."

DOCTOR SARA

May 1977 and Sara now fourteen was still missing John but her memory of him was fading and she had no way to get to him because they moved out of town.

"Sara, it's time for bed."

The sound of her dad's voice made her cringe and she was devastated they had moved and she did not have the opportunity to say goodbye to John. He was the only one who understood everything she had been through and she knew things would be better and different just as he promised her but thought how life was not like the movies and she was facing a tough life that no one was able to help her escape.

"I'm going now."

She did not want to go to bed thinking he might want to have his way with her so she sat on the floor a little while longer and thought of her life as a living hell. She also missed Dr. Braddock. It has been a year and two months since their last session and she no longer had the security or protection she felt away from her dad. Sara thought that her home life was horrific and it was causing her a great deal of depression. At times, her depression of having the life she was born into felt meaningless when her memories of the girls who lived in an orphanage came to her thoughts. Her dad took her to see what life was like at a place away from her own home.

He asked some of the girls to share their stories of what it was like to have to live in such a place. Sara was terrified at some

of the stories and the hard core truth of what it was like for them. One girl told her that she would give anything to be in her shoes even if her dad was abusing her. She said she would at least be better off than what she had to do there. It never stopped bothering Sara that the little girl would say such a thing and it frightened her to think that the girl detected that she was the victim of abuse. She wondered if there was a behavior pattern displayed that she, Sara, was unaware she was showing. She did not understand how the girl could detect what she was going through with her dad, or maybe the girl had suffered the same type of horror. Either way it was a thought that made her sick.

The different experiences she encountered with people opened her eyes to a new way of thinking after spending a year with a therapist. Sara thought that perhaps one day she could possibly be a part of helping people restore some order to the things destroyed in their lives.

First, she had to get past her demons and find a way to restore order in her own life. She became more and more recluse, an anti-social, something her father could not understand. He was quite the socialite and considering all the entertaining they had at the house and the different people she met during their time of travel when he had a business trip, he did not think it was possible for his little girl to be rebellious.

She thought back to the school counselor suggesting to her parents that they have her go see a psychologist because she thought Sara's behavior traveled deeper then not wanting to play with the other kids. She sat on the floor remembering a day trip she and her dad took two years earlier and the day she had to meet her therapist. By March 1975 she was on her way to one more

place she thought she didn't want to be a participant but had no choice and went to see the one who was going to be her doctor, the one she referred to as the sicko, psycho.

#

"Hello Sara, I'm Dr. Marilyn Braddock."

At first, the two had a few strenuous moments trying to get to know one another and session after session Sara was becoming a little more annoyed by all the questions. She did not try to involve herself with the therapy and for six months, she rebelled but doctor Braddock saw something more than the regular doctor/patient setting and a rebellious child and wanted to get to know Sara. She watched her display an intelligent behavior she had not seen in any of her other patients and allowed Sara her freedom because immediately Sara started looking at the books on psychoanalysis.

Although Sara began opening up after a few sessions, she kept her responses to a minimum but after months of being around her therapist, she started trying to make things more interesting for herself and began posing questions of her own on a regular basis. The doctor was happy to see Sara showing some form of interest although she knew Sara was trying to be ironic in some situations. She did not let that bother her and saw it as a start on Sara's inner desire to be a part of the therapy. She stayed off the subject of why Sara did not want to get involve with the other students allowing her to bring the matter up on her own but knew that over time and with patience of her own, she was hoping that Sara would bring the subject up. Sometimes she asked Sara for her prognosis regarding their session.

"Well doctor Sara, do you see where there are areas causing you to disconnect yourself from your fellow classmates or do you

feel there is a deeper issue?" Sara had to admit to herself how she got a kick out of Doctor Braddock referring to her as doctor.

"Well, doctor in my professional opinion I think people should have the respect to leave me alone, he should know I don't want to play with them." Sara said.

Doctor Braddock noticed a sadness taking over the warm personality she saw hiding underneath Sara's façade.

"What happened just now Sara, where did you go, whom were you referring to when you said he should know you don't want to play with them."

"The other kids, I guess."

Sara was referring to her dad and his clients but she snapped back to the office of Doctor Braddock and did not want to reveal anything too damaging as she thought of the little girls in the orphanage.

"But you said he should know…care to elaborate on whom it is you're referring to when you said he…"

"I'm sure I was talking about one of the teachers."

"Alright, Braddock said, we'll let it go for now. And what about your teachers, do you think they are bothering you or perhaps you think it's within their rights to request you to join the other kids at recess but don't want to admit it?"

"Well I think we both know I want to say I think they're bothering me." Sara said.

"But…" The doctor inquired.

"But what, there's no but I want to say I think they're bothering me." Sara said perplexed.

Doctor Braddock smiled.

"And why do you feel you should be left alone, Sara?"

"Because they are bothering me, it's not so bad wanting to be left alone you know. I do the class work and I participate in the school activities that pertain to my class work."

"But you don't take it further than that, do you?"

"I don't see the need to go further than that."

"And what about this friend you mentioned to me. Have you been in contact with him recently?"

Sara got quiet and the sadness she had been covering up prevailed. She missed John terribly and she had no way of locating him. Sara spent a little over half a year with Dr. Braddock before she mentioned John and he was her only true friend and the separation was extremely difficult for her.

"There is no one to talk to any more." She said.

"Well now Sara, you have me you can talk to and maybe because you don't feel as if the other kids can identify with you that perhaps you created your friend as an escape." Sara looked at her therapist and shook her head in dismay.

"You're here because of a paycheck and I didn't make him up."

The expression on the face of Doctor Braddock was a combination of truth faces the reality of life and a little bit of disappointment because she had gone further to help those in need without getting paid but she thought there was no way of little Sara knowing such a thing.

"I guess in a way you're right Sara, and there are some things in life money can't buy and somehow I like to try to balance the two, however, it does make things a little more difficult when the one asking you to confide in them is in expectation of a paycheck."

Sara nodded her head as though to tell the doctor I told you so

and Doctor Braddock fully understood what she was conveying and smiled.

"Now, there is another side to it Sara, you see there are people in the world who know of people like me who work in this profession and they know that we are sworn to uphold a doctor/client privacy act."

"You are?" Sara asked intriguingly.

"Oh, absolutely and the people feel more comfortable knowing their dirty laundry of the past won't end up on the six o'clock news and they still feel there is some control in their lives without having to worry about their friends betraying them and divulging their secrets."

"Okay, I guess you're right." Sara said after she thought about it for a moment.

"Why thank you for thinking that I am right and I'll tell you a little secret." She leaned into Sara and Sara did likewise. "...I usually am." She said smiling.

Sara started to grin.

"But I don't have to worry about anything I told John, I know it." She said defensively.

"Wait, did I see, oh no it couldn't be, Sara didn't actually smile did she?"

"Stop it, I'm not smiling." She said with the biggest grin on her face.

"Alright, you're not smiling, whatever you say."

Sara placed her chin in her hand and looked at Doctor Braddock.

"...Are you smiling now?"

"Yeah, but just a little, I don't want you to get carried away

and think that I like you or something."

"Oh no, I wouldn't dare think that, I'm just some old chick trying to get a paycheck."

The two laughed and though she did not think it was possible, Sara began to feel a bond between the two of them.

"But John isn't like that, no matter what I told him he wouldn't tell it to a soul. And that's the way it is…was with us." Sara said.

"And even though you haven't seen him in, what is it now, two years, you still believe he was someone you actually met and not someone you created to escape?"

"Well, I've been with you, in two months will be a year now and it will be only two and a half years since we left and this August will be three years since I've seen him and I was ten but turning eleven that October." Again, a saddened expression won over her face. She paused.

"…Had it been that long," Sara whispered to herself.

"…Well, I think maybe I know if I had a friend who was real or not at ten years old, I mean, it's not like I'm some little kid, you know."

"It's okay Sara, it's just sometimes we create people to escape our own lives when things are traumatic but you're right there are good people in this world like you said and those are the people who are rare in our lives and when we find them it is quite devastating to lose them."

Sara was happy to see that her therapist was not trying to take away her memory of who John was to her and the special bond she shared with him.

"…Tell me about your home life Sara."

A quick glance to the floor caught her attention.

"…Is there something you prefer not to talk about?"

"Yes, I didn't really want to talk about all the parties that go on at the house and sometimes I have to help my mom be the hostess and serve snacks and pick up the trash. I hate picking up after people who throw their trash all over the place. Why can't they just put things in the trash can?" She lied.

A smile quickly came over Dr. Braddock's face and Sara knew she put the therapist's mind at rest.

"Well Sara I'm sure it's a big help to your folks when you help out. Tell me, when do these parties take place."

"On the weekends, Friday and Saturday nights and there have been the occasional get together on Thursdays."

"And what kinds of snacks do you serve? Are you handing them any drinks?" The doctor inquired.

"Oh yes, all the time but my mom only let's me give them bottled water and I do like the snacks because I get to taste them. All sorts of goodies like cupcakes, potato chips, pretzels, and all the good stuff. But I only eat a few because mom makes me eat all my dinner and vegetables so I won't load up on sweets."

"What are your parents like Sara? Do you know how they met or why they wanted to have kids?"

"That's a story I heard more than enough times too."

"What do you mean by too?"

"Oh nothing, I was just remembering something I told John about my parents meeting because I had heard the story of how they met about a million times."

"Well then let's focus on you. Tell me Sara, what do you think your aspirations would be in life?"

"I was thinking about the medical field and help saving lives but I'm not exactly sure if I want to do that."

"Why not, it's quite noble you know and there are ways of doing your job in order to live and take care of your needs and having a practice to help those less fortunate."

"Yes, I suppose you're right but I don't know if I want to be around all the blood and guts pouring out of people."

"Oh, yes I see your dilemma. Your father tells me you're an excellent student and he said by the grades you get in school, it's possible for you to accomplish what you set out to do and if you keep at it, you'll graduate a year early."

"Oh yeah, that, well I figure even though I'll still be sixteen when I graduate I'll be turning seventeen later that same year and maybe I could leave home and start a life somewhere."

"Well that is noble of your endeavors but legally you would have to stay at home until you're eighteen."

"Yeah, somehow I knew there was a catch to it all."

"I want you to know that my door will always be open to you anytime you want, Sara."

"That would be great but even if I get a job, something tells me I might not be able to afford you."

"Well, maybe you could just come by as a guest or like a friend visits another friend."

"Thanks Dr. Braddock but don't worry about me things are going to be different and everything is going to be fine."

She said it remembering the words John spoke to her. The year with Dr. Braddock came and went and Sara was feeling sad that she didn't open up much sooner about John and she liked her therapist deeper than the doctor/patient relationship and realized

that Marilyn Braddock became her friend. It kept her father away from touching her during her time with the therapist but Sara's stay with the doctor lasted only a couple of months after the year was over and in May 1976, Dr. Braddock explained to her that she was heading out west and would be leaving her practice in New York. Sara remained calm and somehow knew the words from the doctor or something similar was going to happen and prepared herself for the news. She thought for a moment and looked at Dr. Braddock.

"Sometimes things have to die out in order for them to change. I guess things can't be different if they don't change."

"What a very insightful way of looking at it Sara, you know, I think you were right when you said to me that you thought everything was going to be alright. I want you to know that if you decide to come out to Los Angeles I want you to look me up."

"I'm going to miss you a lot Dr. Braddock."

"Thank you Sara and I'll miss you too." For the final time Sara heard the one thing she always enjoyed hearing from her therapist. "Goodbye Dr. Sara." She said as she opened her arms to give Sara a hug.

"Goodbye Dr. Braddock." Sara said and pulled away to prevent her tears from flowing and walked across the room, turned to wave goodbye one last time and left gently closing the door. Dr. Braddock waved and watched Sara leave then she continued to put her things into one of the many boxes she had in order to ship her office material to California.

SARA'S NIGHTMARE

... The year seemed to go by fast for all of them especially Sara because she no longer had Dr. Braddock in her life and her dad immediately started approaching her again after she left. James was hoping they all could have stayed in Astoria but he had to move his family away in August 1973 into New Jersey in order to maintain a lifestyle he grew accustomed to living. He always liked to travel and have nice things and when work was slow, the parties and unemployment and the assistance Janie received from the government made it possible for him to continue to some degree a lifestyle he enjoyed. It was a tough time for them but he made Janie give her maiden name and all the information they needed to defraud the county to get assistance for her family as a single mother with a child in order to receive food stamps and money from the government, which qualified them to have the state pay for Sara's therapy.

Once James no longer qualified to receive unemployment, he started taking odd jobs painting and then he switched to door-to-door salesman. He stayed in his sales position a little over a year and by the time, Sara was no longer seeing her therapist he had met an advertising executive who liked his personality and energetic approach to sell a product that the executive offered him a job and he began working for the advertising company. He worked hard when he started out as an apprentice in May 1976 and three years later with the company and having to move from city to city, handling long-term accounts, taking control and initiating

ideas that benefited everyone, had worked his way in becoming one of their best advertising men on the company's management team.

He came across a client that did business with his old boss Mike Peters from the beer corporation. Mike had hired the company James was now working for and was not aware that his old employee had the skills and power to oversee the contract he was expecting. He recalled the time he allowed Mike and Janie to have the time of his ex-boss' life and then two months later when Mike realized he was not going to be able to take Janie away, fired him.

He thought of the times when work was slow for him and how he had to capitalize on the parties he was giving which made up for the loss of income along with the unemployment checks he received and the assistance Janie got from the state. He was presented with the opportunity to do to Mike what was done to him but wanted to keep a low profile, especially since Mike could inform his new boss of the types of private dealings he enjoyed. He decided to give the campaign to one of their junior ad men and authorized the deal in order to keep any potential unfavorable publicity out of his own life.

Sara was thirteen when Dr. Braddock left for the west coast and she was back to doing the same things her dad had started her out doing because he thought there was no chance of getting caught. Her family was moving her from one place to the next, from upstate New York to Ohio and then Detroit and from there to Pennsylvania until in August 1979, they were back in New York exactly six years that month when Sara had to leave without saying goodbye.

They lived in Woodside near 61st street and Roosevelt Boulevard. They lived near plenty of duplexes in that area but James bought a home and again he started his private parties. His job allowed him the opportunity of finding people in and out of his business circle and he used that as his chance to increase his private hobby. Sara thought it was something he would never give up and no matter where they moved he managed to find the type of people who enjoyed his style of entertaining. She graduated in Pennsylvania a year early from the rest of the kids in June 1979 when she was sixteen and by her seventeenth birthday that October she was back in New York by two months and took a job and some courses at the local junior college close to where she lived. She thought of ways to stop her father from forcing himself on her but everything that came to mind ended in her thoughts of feeling that nothing would actually work but she made herself a promise to get free from him. Her job was an escape and by April 1980 she learned of a martial arts course to be offered and she secretly began training at the college she attended when she was not on the schedule to work but could use work as an excuse to get to her defense classes. She thought often about having met John when she was ten and how Dr. Braddock said he was a figment of her imagination but she wanted to believe he was real and no matter how much she thought of him, her memory of what he looked like was becoming more of a faded image in her head. Occasionally she wondered if the doctor was right and if she actually created him to escape her horrific life. She couldn't even remember the location of the school.

She could see that her life was not getting any better and began believing that because of everything she had to endure that

she made John up for herself because it was all one never ending nightmare. She thought of her life as a secret, a horrible disgrace to her existence and John was her only escape because she needed to believe she had the chance of sharing those secrets with someone she trusted. She remembered him saying that he should have been there to protect her but from now on, he would be there for her. As she got older, she believed that John was her alter ego besides why would she divulge such personal information about herself and her family to a complete stranger and now that she has learned some moves in the art of self-defense, she thought perhaps she did create him until it was time for her to become her own protector.

She thought that times were different and that she had to face reality that she needed to do what she could to survive until she could move on. One day in her martial arts class she was instructed to punch the bag to take down an opponent, who was attacking her, she thought of the years of being a victim and when her instructor gave the command, she punched the bag to the point of bruising her wrist and had to keep it wrapped for a few days. James was not happy and told her that she was careless to try to lift something at work that was too heavy, which was the story she gave him but after a few days, he had her back to doing the deals he arranged.

She wished she could take him in hand to hand combat but deep inside knew it was her own fear to go against her father and convinced herself that it was still too soon for her to try to challenge him. The year moved slower than she believed possible and had never known time to be so sluggish. She believed that she needed to have been able to take the classes sooner in order to have

had some sufficient knowledge and technique to execute such a dangerous attempt to challenge her dad. She thought that six months was not enough training and that she still had much more to develop and learn despite the encouragement she received from her instructors.

October 1980 and Sara was making plans for her life but her dad had plans of his own regarding the things she would do for him. He was expecting her to agree to his request and continue to be an asset in his life. She never saw an exchange of currency between him and the people who attended his parties but after his offer, she figured he must have been charging them for her services and realized that her dad was her own personal pimp. She recalled the horrible things he did to her and was waiting the day for her long awaited moment when she would be legal to leave without the chance of him using the legal system against her to hunt her down. She would be of age at the end of the month and able to leave home and get him out of her life.

Sara was planning to take the chance to venture out on her own but things were taking a turn for the worst. She came home from work and felt a blow to the back of her head. Sara fell to the floor and loss consciousness. Later that night James removed the hood from over her head and untied her then pushed her out the door of her bedroom into the living room. The two of them had a brutal argument before she left for work because she refused to accept his terms to become an international prostitute. She was defiant and he could see she had inherited his temper and strong will. James did not continue to argue with her but let her leave for work. He knew he was letting her think the conversation was over but while she was gone; he called his accomplice and made the

deal. Sara did not know that she would be destined to a life of prostitution and thought she would have the opportunity to free herself from her father but without warning, he became monstrous. She wanted to fight him with all her might but she thought of her mother and the abuse he put her through and though her will was strong, she was weak from the head trauma.

She thought that after she suffered the attack to see that it was her father behind her captivity that her mother must have suffered similar attacks and felt she understood why her mother could not protect her. She learned that James had a way of unleashing an unreasonable violent behavior when he did not get his way and he repeatedly told her how she would continue to be engaged in such acts and how she would be satisfying his clients and the source of why he would become a very rich man. Though terrified she was unmoving. He felt helpless and slapped her continuously across the face. He pushed her down to the floor where he began stripping her clothes and punching her mercilessly as she had only seen the after effects of what he had done to her mother. She fought back but his strength overpowered her. He was not concern about her having to try to lie about her looks if he left any bruises because she was no longer in school but was still careful not to damage his property and focused hitting her breasts and thighs. He had no fear of retribution, and he continued to beat, strangle and violently shake his daughter the way an angry child would shake her rag doll, demanding her to submit to his will. He proceeded to rape her then encouraged his accomplice to influence her by using the acts of sodomy on her determined to hear what he wanted her to say.

"What kind of monster are you, how can you do this to me,

what makes you think you're going to get away with something like this, aren't you listening to me. No! Stop it!--Please don't!-- Somebody--help me!" She screamed.

"You will do as I say and there'll be no further discussion on the matter."

Sara was thinking how much worst it would be for her mother if she didn't submit but she remained strong knowing she would get the opportunity to get away and somehow take her mother with her if she made him believe she was submitting to his will. She could not believe what was happening to her and soon everything became hazy, she vowed it was going to stop that very night. Sara thought of it all as a bad dream and suddenly she fell out of consciousness...

#

June 1979 at sixteen, only a few months away from her seventeenth birthday she was valedictorian and prepared to deliver the speech of her life at graduation to the entire school. She was an excellent student but very meek and never spoke up for herself and now she found herself in front of her peers as her mom and dad sat in the audience in chairs outside on the lawn.

They both looked happy together and very proud as their daughter took her place at the podium. She looked out into the audience to see her mom, flashes of her beauty and the woman her dad made her into came in and out of Sara's visions. Janie was a woman who used to be strong and who always came to Sara's defense, a main reason why her dad had beaten her mom so brutally over the years. Although Sara and her mom never talked about the stuff her dad continued to do to them, she had always felt

she was able to grab hold of a strength she saw in her mom that she did not believe she would have been able to tap into if she was someone else.

The day of graduation was to be the first of her conquest in deliberating without fear. She stood at the podium remembering the past as she encouraged her fellow students regarding all of their futures.

"No one should have to suffer at the hands of their own family and that's why I am here today to inform you all of the horror that took place in my life but still I stand before you as this year's student's valedictorian."

Her visions faded away from the podium and she began remembering walking through the living room the first time he grabbed her from behind and started ripping off her clothes. Her visions were vivid as she lay unconscious remembering a distant past. She recalled him flipping her back and forth easily manhandling her, crawling up to her face placing his manhood on top of her lips, and pressing up against her. She remembered him telling her that it did not matter to him if she screamed or not because he enjoyed hitting her in areas, where the bruises were not visible. He beat her on the head so hard and repetitively she would feel the blood oozing out of her nose and mouth. Sara slowly awakened from her unconscious state tears flowing from her eyes to see she was back in her bedroom naked, her arms strapped over her head and tied to the bedposts. Her legs were also over her head and strapped to the posts. She was barely able to focus on the man who stood towering over her and he leaned closer to her and slapped her again across her face. She felt the sting of a whip lashing against her breasts and stomach and then the beatings

started with his belt and he repeatedly beat her ordering her to tell him what he wanted to hear.

"Tell me," He yelled, "...tell me or I'll beat it out of you. You will learn that submission is expected and you will enjoy being obedient. TELL ME!" He screamed.

Sara tried to speak the words he wanted to hear but they stuttered out of her mouth, she was terrified to say anything to encourage his desires further. It made no difference what she was saying because the sound of her voice turned him on insatiably. He moved in closer to her ear.

"I don't care if you scream or not." He whispered. He put himself inside her and pursued his quest to drain his burning needs without mercy. As he continued to enter inside his own daughter, he began ordering her to tell him how much it was hurting and to beg him to stop. He liked the sound of his voice giving her orders. He began to thrust so incredibly wild and hard tears and muffled sounds of her screaming were evident that she was in excruciating pain. It was pleasing him even more and satisfying to his sick desires. When he finished he stood over her then lowered himself down to stick his tongue into her mouth.

She gagged giving him complete understanding she wanted to vomit out everything inside of her system. He stood up looking down at her with disapproving eyes then stooped back down to whisper in her ear but before he could say a word, again, Sara passed out.

Janie was made to tend to her daughter's wounds and the days passed but Sara knew that it all started after she had come home from work and now she could see the full strength of the sun only to suffer over again at the hands of her father and his accomplice

and then to see nightfall and that her mother was once again tending to her wounds. She had no idea how many days and nights passed or what excuses were given to her boss about her lack of appearance but she knew her father was cunning enough to come up with something because his plans was to ship her off to another continent to serve as his private source of income as a call girl. Sara was in pain and then felt a needle injected into her arm.

#

She could see herself as she wore a beautiful peach gown, which was fitting to her waistline exquisitely. Her hair was shining and her deep dark wide set eyes hypnotized all the boys. When she heard her name called out by the announcer, she stood from her place where she sat next to her classmates and approached the steps to the stage, when she reached the top of the landing and started walking toward the podium; the roaring cheers came from the boys in the audience. They caused a raucous for several minutes before the staff could get them to calm down.

Sara had outgrown the goofy look that she saw herself and developed into a raving beauty with long black hair, slender and hourglass shapely figure and she never had a problem getting a date. She thanked them for the extended applause and told everyone how James never liked it when she wanted to have some kind of normal life style with her friends and that he would always display an embarrassing performance to one of her male friends who was picking her up to go to a movie. She continued to express that after several attempts to meet a male friend she thought it best to have all her friends meet her down the street or preferably at the designated spot they would be spending their time together. She told detailed events how his technique was to make

his first attempt at what he used as an excuse of being respectful when he wanted things his way.

"He acted civil when he made a request but then if he did not get the answer he wanted to hear he would slowly begin to change into the monster both me and my mother experienced without compassion." She stood fearless telling them that his demeanor changed so intensely that he would have been unrecognizable to anyone coming in view of his temper…

#

Sara could feel the slaps across her face but they were gentle as her mother tried to revive her to get her to eat some soup.

"How long have I been out?"

"It's been two days this time. You must eat something and get your strength up. He's becoming unbearable."

"Why haven't you tried to leave?"

"He threatened to kill you."

Sara looked at her mother who seemed to be without a fight left within her.

"Look, mom I'll tell him what he wants and when he thinks he has nothing to worry about I'll make a run for it and you can come with me. You don't have to live like this anymore."

"Sara, what else would I do, I have nothing left to offer and soon if he doesn't stop beating on me I'm afraid I'll only have death to look forward to."

Sara silently ate the soup as her mother spoon fed her. She didn't know what else to do or what to think. She finished her meal and watched her mother leave the room and heard the door lock. Sara lay back on her pillow hands and feet bound to the posts of the bed thinking of what she would do but the effects of

the drug had not worn off and without warning Sara went to sleep. She could barely hear what he was saying before she came back to reality.

"Let me tell you a little story, as you know your mother and I have been entertaining people for years and one night some random guy at the party thought he would get away with plowing himself inside of me and then leave thinking he wasn't going to reciprocate to my needs."

Again, he slapped her face.

"Pay attention." He snapped.

"…After I beat the hell out of him with a baseball bat I kept for reasons just for that sort of pleasure I made the bastard play the kind of sick game he started and showed him how the game is really to be played. I took a dump on the floor and forced him about an inch away from it and told him he had the choice of collapsing in it or gritting his teeth and enjoy what I had to offer, needless to say with the help of the other guys holding him down he decided to accept my offer."

He leaned closer to her rubbing his face up against hers and the stench of his aftershave made her cough involuntarily and he knew she was coherent enough to hear what he had to say but she was losing her ability to stay awake and the will to fight. He told her the same story repeatedly to get what he wanted and she was feeling as though she was defeated and began to plead with him for her life and the life of her mother. He ignored her and laughed enjoying his moment of victory. Sara's eyes rolled back into her head and the unconscious vision she experienced took her to where she could see the stunned look of the audience as she continued to speak.

#

"…My eyes grew wide as he grabbed me by the throat and told me not to give him any more problems or my mother would experience the story he had told me so many times before. I nodded helplessly agreeing to his demands because I knew I wasn't going to be fighting against him just for myself. I did what I thought was best at that time so my mother would remain safe from his devious sickness. She and I both knew he had a way of lying to get what he wanted but to describe something like that after what he had done to me made me very cautious as to what he truly would further do to the both of us."

#

Again, Sara could feel the slaps across her face as her dad was trying to bring her out of her unconscious state. Everything was hazy and she realized she was back to reality. She felt sick and began crying helplessly and tried to stop herself but knew it was hopeless as the tears continued to fall. She did not want to listen to her dad's voice but she knew she was going to suffer further and thought how the fight within her was diminishing. Again she felt the sharp prick of a needle and she closed her eyes breathing in slowly taking in even rhythmic breaths until once again she was out cold.

#

…She found herself standing at the podium for the first time to give her speech. Her mom and dad were proud and James couldn't stop taking pictures. She stood before the crowd and began to talk about her high school friends and her classmates and her fellow graduates. She started her story about family and her dad slowly lowered the camera from his face while the look on her

mom's face although surprised this was the moment she chose, was quite sure she knew this day was going to happen.

The crowd listened hanging onto her every word and her father nervously sat still knowing there was no escape. The fathers that were there were a lot bigger than he and they all started looking at him curiously. The mothers frowned as they looked in his direction and he held onto Janie's hand like a cornered child at the zoo trapped by any one of the wild animals ready to pounce on him. Sara stared out into the crowd watching the concern shower their unsuspecting faces. Some sat biting their nails and others stared so hard they were sitting on the edges of their chairs with their mouths open. She began to speak to them as though they were all her closest friends.

#

Days continued to go by and Janie was allowed to tend to her daughter only allowing for her to be conscious when James decided it was time for her to eat which he let happen only twice every other day. Janie was forced to place an adult diaper on Sara and change her while she remained tied to the bed. Finally James decided it was time to make a move and he drenched a rag with ammonia and placed it under Sara's nose and as she came to awareness, the second man was on top of her screaming out in bursts of ecstasy until all at once the explosion released the tension he had build up inside of him. During the time, she was regaining consciousness, she opened her mouth to speak and the words didn't come out as she could see the faces fading away. She could hear the sounds of applause in the background but it was the television with a game show on in the house.

Sara was snapped back to her present situation and could see

both her dad and the man who was his accomplice fixing their clothes and zipping up their zippers. When they finished with her and he convinced himself that she was agreeing to his will, he untied her from the posts to assist her off the bed by reaching out his hand as though he had just witnessed her falling and was offering his assistance. It became clear to her the graduation had already been a success but she was only dreaming of what she wished she could have done when she gave her speech as valedictorian.

It was over and she was a graduate and nothing she imagined in her head during her unconsciousness ever happened. The two men left her bedroom where her father and his partner were keeping her hostage. James started into the bathroom, he stopped and remembered to go into his own bedroom where he had beaten, gagged and tied his wife leaving her in the closet on the floor to wait until he was finished punishing their daughter.

"…If you wasn't such a dried up old bitch I wouldn't have to do this type of stuff. Now go inside and run my bath water before I kick your fucking teeth out." He said.

He untied one of her hands leaving her to loosen the binds herself in order to complete the task for which he had commanded. Janie thought about the time she was as beautiful as their daughter was now but now how she sits in a closet with dried blood on her lips and in her nostrils because she endured regular beatings from her husband. She was sitting in the closet for hours before he came to let her out. She left the room to run his bath water and sat on the edge of the tub feeling hopeless and full of despair. She sat there trying to remember where things had gone wrong. She thought how he used to be very attentive. She recalled first seeing

him when he walked into the room and admired his stature. He stood six feet tall with strong broad shoulders. He was in the U.S. Naval Corp. and strikingly handsome. They met one night while she was performing in a nightclub as a singer but this particular night the drummer was out sick and she got on the drums to play with the band as she sang all of the songs requested and the songs they had come prepared to play. James watched her as she played the drums and admitted to one of the men in the club that her style captivated him. He told her she was slender and sexy and all the curves were in the right places. She remembered him telling her that he didn't think she was as gifted in the breast area when he first saw her and how he had said it in a charmingly joking way as though it didn't matter to him one way or the other. A point he made clear to her and expressed otherwise he wouldn't have been interested. They were married in a courthouse nine months after first meeting and he displayed a very confident demeanor and told her he trusted her and that he was not worried about other men hitting on her while she was out each night performing in nightclubs. He always made things seem lighthearted and convinced her to believe in the two of them and that together they were capable of doing anything and having it all. But now she sat on the edge of the tub thinking, that life didn't always turn out to be the grand fairy tale people were expecting it to be and she too got lost in such dreams. Janie was in love with James to the point of telling him she would have done anything to make him happy and she recalled the first time he had ever come to her with the idea of making money while staying at home.

SARA'S FUTURE

Janie remained on the edge of the tub thinking that she could not believe she was so naïve to have trusted her husband. She knew he took advantage of her innocence and was brutally abusive and understood that there was nothing innocent about her subjecting her daughter to that type of lifestyle. She thought about the time when James was working for the beer corporation with Mike Peters when she became aware of the lustful needs he had and wanted to share those needs with others after he told her about some of his co-workers and the different desires they enjoyed.

She recalled him telling her how he used to listen to all the discussions they would have about the strippers they wanted to submit to them and allow them to explore their sexual fantasies. He told her how he overheard one of the men mentioning how he wanted to stalk one of the young women who worked at the club and get her to please him but he intervened when the man tried to convince a couple of his male workers to join in with him and was able to offer a safer way for the man to get his kicks without the worry of the authorities hunting him down. He thought it was the opportunity for him and Janie to try out his idea. She sat in tears remembering when he came home and approached her with his plan to help them become more of a success…

#

"I know a way we can make a lot of money and stay at home but you got to swear you can trust my opinion and that I would never let anything bad happen to you."

"Of course I trust you, James."

"You know a lot of people who like to stay in the loop of things in the show business world and we can keep them connected. You know how everybody clings to you and how they wish they could get up close to you to get to know you better, and this way we can have them here in our home with whom they consider to be a celebrity." He continued.

"It sounds strange to hear you say I'm a celebrity and it does sound like a good idea. Just think I would be the hostess for all those who are fans." She said proudly.

"We'll invite producers and directors and with the right advertising but nothing elaborate you understand, mostly word of mouth, we could be known as the king and queen of the private parties exclusively for the elite, and who knows how far we could go with this." He said enthusiastically.

#

Janie didn't pay attention as the water continued to rise in the tub and she thought about how pleased James was with his requests but after a few days, she thought to suggest other ideas. She did not know that trying to convince him to find other ways to be more successful would cause him to react violently toward her. She touched her stomach gently and thought back to the time he was infuriated with her and kicked her while they were in the kitchen. She realized then that she had to give in or he would have killed her and the reason why she sat on the floor at his feet and agreed to do whatever he wanted from her. She knew then that she lost her dignity, her identity, and ultimately learning later that it was the precursor causing her to lose her daughter all in one night.

She sat staring into the water remembering how he started

fixing up the basement to their old house in Queens and the night soon after when he came home with two of his friends from work. He introduced them as producers for one of the studios and told her that one of them was a relative to a famous producer who had the same last name. He continued his story telling her that the man was learning the business and already had the connection with a motion picture deal that had big box office success. He planned everything, said the men were in from the west coast to scout locations, and wanted a place that was somewhat remote but where people could still identify and that she was to remain professional. She recalled his words telling her that she was to satisfy them because they did not know anyone in town and that they were paying a lot of money just because they had the extra dough to splurge.

#

"These guys are connected and they have the clout and the cash flow behind them, that's the way it is in this business; it may as well go to us."

#

Janie's tears continued to flow as she thought about James encouraging her to take pills, drink, and maintain a demeanor he could be proud. She remembered him acting animated to get her to smile and that he started telling her of the people they would compare her to and if all went well the producers would use her as the next Hollywood starlet. He was charming and persuasive and said he was going to be right there and no one would ever hurt her. She allowed herself to believe she would never do it again but later realized he wanted her to prostitute herself to all the men and women he would soon have coming over to the house.

He placed her on display and the price was high for the horny men wanting to engage and double if it was a couple wanting to share in the real life fantasy. The key to his success was to get money no matter the method as long as they were meeting his needs. His goal was to have all the things he wanted and by any means necessary to get his name known as a man who could deliver. Janie realized that he was willing to do whatever it took to get his way and it did not matter to him if people knew him for someone willing to sell out his wife. They kept their private entertaining discreet from the neighbors but more people began coming to their soirees and repeatedly he requested his wife to please the many who visited their home. No one made offers in the movie industry as he had promised, and his ability to deliver was only if he was going to gain something from it and as she learned, his intentions were never to help her become famous, at least not the way he implied.

She felt the water hit her thigh as it began to run over the edge of the tub, and quickly she turned it off and grabbed a towel to sop up what had ran onto the floor. She released the stopper to let some of the water drain, and then wrung out the towel from all the excess water then she used the wet towel to cover her face and helplessly she cried into it muffling the sounds so no one would hear her. James went into Sara's bedroom where she sat staring as though she was in the same daze her mother experienced.

"You should go get freshened up and get ready for your departure Sara because we don't want to keep the customers waiting any longer than they have to."

She could not believe how quickly he would dismiss his actions and treat her in his sick demented mind as a loving father

asking her to get ready in a way as though he was taking the family out to dinner. She was emotionally and physically hurt, drained, and without a word, she obeyed him and headed toward the bathroom. She saw her mother's face and the redness in her eyes but there was no sign of remorse or love from her mother who stared at her with a blank expression and then tossed her head sideways indicating Sara to obey her father.

Sara froze as her mother stood still with a glass in one hand and a bottle of scotch in the other. She became more defiant, squinted her eyes in a fury of rage, stormed into the bathroom never uttering a sound. She stayed inside for an hour because she had to tend to her wounds the best way she could, bathed herself carefully for she was in severe agony and full of cuts, bruises and she was bleeding. She mustered the strength to regain her composure to be strong and make her attempt to escape. She heard the sounds of two men and her mother out in the other room and then the sound of a door closing shut that she clearly recognized as the front door. She listened intently and no longer heard any sounds from the room, ten minutes later and not a word, she was sure she was in the house alone and slowly opened the door to peek her head around the wall of the entrance leading to the living room. The room was empty and she went to her room to get dress and retrieve almost four hundred dollars she had been stealing over the past year back from her father.

She did not consider herself a thief but a survivor and if men could pay, the man known to them as, her proprietor to enter their home and do the kind of things they thought was acceptable with a child then she found it perfectly acceptable to be able to compensate herself for the acts they expected her to perform. She

also considered it payback from all the checks she was getting from her job and her dad was taking the cash.

Thinking she could leave undetected, though in the back of her mind she was fearing that she was not alone but at least in a position to get out the door, Sara thought she would be able to outrun anyone on her trail if he or his accomplice spotted her and gave her the chase of her life. She walked out into the living room and saw her dad and his partner standing in the room waiting for her aware of what she was going to do. Sara knew they had set her up and ran in the other direction to make her escape out toward the back where she came face to face with her mother holding a gun pointed at her head. James reached out and snatched her by the hair, as she stopped in amazement at her mother's actions. He threw her up against the wall, after trying to untangle her lock of hair from his ring and then he began punching her in the side until she dropped low, he then dragged her back to the living room and slammed her to the floor where both he and his accomplice held her down and gave her an injection.

She lay shattered and had no clue what was happening or what would happen to her next. A black hood went over her head. When they noticed she was becoming more subdued they picked her up and walked her over to the door, then bound her hands together in front of her and placed a jacket over them. James looked outside to make sure no one was around, his accomplice stopped him as he was starting to take Sara out the door and removed the hood and placed it in his pocket. He and his accomplice headed outside with Sara to take her to the car to go to the airport.

THE DEATH OF A NIGHTMARE

I watched as they stopped at the car to open the door then I rushed up behind the two men that had Sara, pulled out my 32 revolver and shot both men in the head. I took their wallets and started to walk away when she fell up against me. I caught her and laid her gently to the ground. She reacted to the shots but had no idea what had taken place. Everything was foggy and I could see she was not coherent as she moved her head from side to side until she was no longer aware of her surroundings. The neighbors were opening their doors to come out to see what was going on. I left her where she laid but had to look back one more time before I disappeared. I ran and ducked into the yard of one of her neighbors, ran to the back of the house right before a woman opened her door to see what was happening, hopped the fence and headed down the street undetected. I slowed my pace not to seem as though I was rushing, opened the billfolds of the two dead men and saw that I had just killed her father, I felt relieved, it was finally over for her, I removed the money and threw the wallets in a nearby trash bin.

I continued to walk away from the number 7 train where I turned a corner, walked over to 63rd street and headed back up toward the train opposite the street where I left the bodies. I made it back up to Roosevelt Boulevard I turned a corner and proceeded down the block then walked over to 64th street and Roosevelt, got into my car and drove away. Neighbors surrounded Sara as they were all asking questions and trying to help her stay alert. They

were all confused by everything that was happening as they looked at the two men lying on the ground in their own pool of blood.

"Are you alright?" One woman asked.

"What happened to you?" Another inquired.

"Oh my God, Sara is that your dad, who's the man next to him?" A third questioned.

Each one had something to ask, not giving the other person time to get a response. Everything was as if nothing made sense to her, not her surroundings, her neighbors, or the chattering about her father's death. The world around her was shattered and everything was overwhelming to her because of the questions, the events and the betrayal of her mother.

Her father and the man next to him had just finished forcing her into the different sexual acts they enjoyed performing. She began to feel angry at how they pushed, slapped, violently and physically beat her and not only did her mother know about all the things they did but she prevented her escape at gunpoint. Sara could still feel a burning rage inside of her after the numerous times and many years of abuse he inflicted on his own flesh and blood, he was trying to find a way to capitalize on her body even more by selling her into a world of underground prostitution.

The man she was supposed to be able to call daddy for advice, to have as a father figure, to be the stronghold in her fragile life was everything in opposition to what his true role was to imply. It was his job to be her protector. He was the man she presumed she could have trusted undeniably. Instead, he was the man who stole her innocence many years ago, and now he was only a man who had died in her heart, a man she no longer had to fear for he was dead. She thought about how he, his accomplice and her mother,

each tried to carry out an agenda in making his efforts to transport her to another continent and turn her into a prostitute in order to help him become rich had somehow failed and now she lay on the ground confused as she listens to all the chatter and speculations.

One of the neighbors had helped Sara inside the house by the time the police arrived and she was sipping a cup of black coffee. The paramedics, coroners and fire department all arrived. Sara had a very basic check up by one of the paramedics and then released without taking her to the hospital. She never told them or the police what they did for fear that the police would implicate her in the murders. She walked outside accompanied by an officer at his request and stood alone by an undercover police car until a detective arrived and put her in the backseat. No one told her what was happening and she did not bother to question anyone because she was sitting in a police car with an officer knowing she was going to headquarters.

She closed her eyes to get rid of the feeling of being in a dark cave, a maze was what she had to conquer and overcome feelings of being trapped in a cube without an opening to free her from the troubles in life. The ride was not as grueling as her thoughts lead her to believe. She listened to the number 7 train pass by in both directions. One train was heading into the city where they were taking her thinking that only those on the train had the freedom to go to the bright lights of Broadway and the other into Flushing where the home of the baseball team the Mets played at Shea Stadium. She wished she could be on the train to the city with the people who were going to make their way through the hustle and bustle of the New York chaos only she wanted to find seclusion to a life away from her torment.

They arrived and she sat in an interrogation room. The paint was bland cement gray, there was one table and two chairs, a window leading into the hallway, and she could see other police officers walking by and the criminals they brought in. She thought it was not very busy and all she could think about was the people who were committing crimes and getting away with them. She couldn't see opposite the wall across the window to know the craziness of all the people being booked for various crimes until the door opened and she heard all the commotion of voices speaking of police brutality and others demanding justice.

A woman walked in carrying a clipboard with some papers on it and Sara could see she had no personality. She stared at her and Sara thought about the size of the woman's nose and how wide it was to the normal size of someone her stature. Sara's imagination wandered thinking that perhaps it would make one think the big appendage was soft but this one protruded higher than normal and anyone could see inside her nostrils. The woman's nose was clean with no hair or anything else lingering but open to the point that the parting of the red sea would be the first thought. She could tell the woman was apathetic and her first assessment of her was that she seemed to be someone who was uncomfortable in her own skin.

The officer scrunched her face to frown as though she smelled something displeasing to her senses. Sara could not see that the woman had breasts and the pants were tight. She was shapely with some femininity to her move but her pants had the look that she was wearing twill and a polyester combination, the look of something soft until you touch them to feel the roughness of dry leaves. She couldn't help but notice that she had big feet and

anyone looking from the shoes up to the buttocks would have sworn they were about to engage a conversation with a man.

"Miss Plimerpkin I am Detective Allerton. Could you tell me why your dad and a Mr. Yatsu had you bound and from our findings in Mr. Yatsu's pocket, a hood over your head?" Sara remained silent and shook her head.

"…Really, that's curious."

"What makes you think I was bound and why wasn't I taken to the hospital, don't you realize that man gave me some kind of drug?"

The detective looked at her blankly.

"…I don't know." She continued.

She was still feeling the effects of the drug and did not appreciate having to go to the police station.

"I think you do Miss Plimmerkin. Were you aware that this Mr. Yatsu has had trouble in the past with the authorities for being linked to black market prostitution?"

"I'm not a criminal. I don't know anything about that!" She spoke defiantly.

"I think perhaps you're not telling me everything Miss Plimmerkin and the only two men who could tell me are dead."

"No, Detective Allerand, maybe the person who shot them knows a thing or two. Have you tried questioning that guy?"

"It's Allerton." The Detective corrected Sara.

"What?"

"The name is Detective Allerton and how do you know it was a man if the hood was over your head."

"Plimkin, Detective Allerton." She said staring.

The detective raised her eyebrows and gave a curt smile.

"That doesn't make any sense Miss…"

She paused then looked at her papers on the clipboard. "Plimkin."

"I told the officers who were questioning me earlier, the hood was placed over my head in the house but it was removed before I was brought outside."

Again, the detective stared at her.

"…Well I sure as hell didn't kill them. I don't know maybe they were taking me to go see a magic show. I'm telling you I don't know."

"We have had a lead on Mr. Yatsu for some time now and we believe he contacted your dad through a connection given to him a while back, do you know who of your dad's business associates would have this sort of information?"

"Why would I know that detective?"

"Of course, why would you. You see Mr. Yatsu had business dealings with some people who unfortunately got tangled in his operation and then couldn't afford to maintain their, let's say financial agreement. I know that once Yatsu gets his claws into you, it's a lost cause, you become trapped, his property so to speak and those caught in his snare usually end up owing him a great deal of money."

"Well I don't know anything about it." The detective looked at her papers, continued talking, and ignored Sara's response.

"He likes to take it out in the form of favor for a favor and he makes his money back through the young girls or boys he can get his hands on and maybe your dad got mixed in something that was over his head and you became the consolation prize. Maybe your dad and he were in some kind of sorted business deal that went

wrong and your dad agreed to put you on the black market in order for Yatsu to collect his money.

...I'm sorry to make such accusations about your father Sara but for right now that's all we've got and considering the deals Yatsu have made in the past it's more than likely that you were about to be next on his list for payment." She looked at Sara to see if she could see something to give indication that Sara knew more than what she was saying.

"Maybe you have all the answers detective so why are you bothering with me." Sara snapped, her eyes widen and tears came forth.

"...I don't know what you're talking about I don't prostitute myself."

"Most of his girls don't actually choose that as their first profession Miss Plimmerkin but they somehow are forced into it and we think your dad and Mr. Yatsu had some kind of business deal going on and perhaps your dad was in a desperate financial need, maybe he was on the brink of devastation. It's all a mystery to me, I mean who knows why men are willing to sell their kids, but it had to have been for a lot of money owed by your father that he couldn't pay back. Is there any reason you can think of as to why he would put his own daughter up for a black market ring of prostitution?"

'Yeah maybe you left out the fact that Yatsu offered my dad a financial deal that he figured he would get his money back on the investment if my dad was willing to sell me.' "I still don't have an answer for you detective."

"Alright, Miss Plimmerkin," the detective said frustrated.

"...Do you know where we can locate your mother, maybe

she knows something about all of this, do you at least know where she is Miss Plimmerkin?"

"I don't know, no, alright I don't know. All of this was done to me, I was the victim here or did that somehow slip your memory, just leave me alone." Sara cried.

She slipped out of the chair and onto the floor and thought that this was the very thing she used to dream of and now it was real, the only sadness she felt for her dad was that if it happened because of her wishes then she too was as guilty as the man who had taken his life. She was happy that the shame she suffered would remain a secret and she no longer had to concern herself with the sick twisted desires he longed to display at her expense.

The detective left her to cry and gave her time to regain her composure before returning. She walked in the hall and looked through the window to see that Sara was sitting in the chair staring. She opened the door, went inside, and stood opposite where Sara was sitting.

"I am sorry for your loss Miss Plimmerkin and we have no further questions for you but if you can think of anything in the future please don't hesitate to call us."

She stood up to walk pass the detective and looked at the name on the detective's badge.

"The name is Plimkin." Sara said.

The detective thought after the first correction she was saying her name right and now she was embarrassed she had displayed her flippant response to the first time Sara corrected her. She stared at Sara blankly but offered no reaction or verbal response as she left.

SARA'S JOURNEY

Sara walked out of the police station and a few blocks down the street, she looked in both directions and walked over to the train station. People were in a rush everywhere around her, some ran across the street with the traffic heading in the same direction and others rushed across right before cars got to the corner to cross the traffic light. Everywhere she looked, people were around, cars were moving and the noise was overwhelming. She was back in Manhattan on 42nd street and 7th avenue and remembered how crazy she thought things were in the city with all the traffic and people the first time she had ever seen it when she was a child but now a veteran to the orchestrated chaos, she moved in succinct to everything that was around her. Buildings covered every inch of space available on every block and the horns blared. She watched other officers pass by on horses while tourists were riding in carriages pulled by horses as their drivers sat on the top portion of the buggy directing the steps where the horses were to be led.

She went to 42nd and Broadway, down the steps, walked through the long corridor to get the train. She got off at Grand Central and went up the escalator and walked over to the number 7 train, and stood expressionless and void of responding to her feelings when she made it to the platform. She thought about the questions the detective were asking, and satisfied that she was no longer needed in the investigation nor did she care, the unknown killer had done her a favor and she felt it was time to move on in life. She sat on the train thinking about what happened to her and

the betrayal done to her by both her parents. She questioned herself and God as to why she had ever been born. She decided to go home and pick up her things hoping she would not have to face her mother but she also knew that deep inside she wanted answers. She felt that her mother owed it to her to answer the many questions lingering inside of her.

'Why her mother wanted to give birth, why she let a man control her life like she was nothing, why she let that same man abuse both of them, why, why, why?' Sara thought.

She convinced herself that she did not have any more tears to shed and vowed never to be in a position of helplessness again. She went home to find her mother sitting on the couch in the living room smoking a cigarette. There was a bottle of scotch on the table in front of her and an empty bottle of the same spirit lying flat next to the other one.

"I heard about your father. I can't say he didn't have it coming to him. You know he wasn't always like this but I guess people really do change when they see the opportunity to make money and become powerful. I can't make up for what was done to you and somewhere I lost sight of protecting my little girl but I do love you Sara you have to know I do."

"Yeah I know." She said fighting back tears she thought she could no longer shed.

"…Sometimes it isn't enough to know it just because someone says it. It was your choice to live this way; you had no right letting him get me involved in such things. My innocence was taken from me and you chose to ignore all the signs, HELL, YOU EVEN WATCHED!" Sara screamed.

"…What kind of mother are you, is there no remorse, no

regret, are you even aware on this very day you put a gun in my face does that not mean anything to you at all. I didn't know about this stuff, it was your decision to bring me into this world and my right to lean on him and you for safety and security but those things were ripped right out from under me wasn't it? Supposedly, you were to be teaching me the difference between people like, well, people like you, and I was to grow up knowing that I had the right to become the person I know I am to become."

She took in a breath and wiped her tears away.

"…I don't know what that is yet but I'll figure it out. Do you know how many times your husband, my father," She said with a tone of disgust, "…told me how much he loved me? It's not fair mom. Do you hear me? It's not fair. You stole a life I will never know and I'm left holding the mess the two of you created."

Sara gave up frustrated with everything, with trying to get her mother to see what she had done all the years of her life. Janie looked at her helplessly, worn, and beaten.

"…Now I must find a way to sort through and clean up everything in order to have some degree of normalcy if that's even possible now. It's just not fair."

She looked at the swollen face of her mother from where her dad had beaten her repeatedly. Janie's eyes were filling with tears.

"…I've decided to leave."

Janie sat motionless and breathed in trying to keep control of her emotions.

"He's not here anymore, you don't have to go, you know."

"No, you did not just try to make this pathetic excuse suggesting that we try to build our lives together."

"Where will you go?"

"Don't know but I have to go and find my own way apart from all of this."

Janie slowly and quietly nodded her head. An abrupt sound interrupted the tension in the air between the two and a voice came out from the bedroom requesting Janie to return to bed.

She knew her mother had no concept of how to be a real loving mother to her and she couldn't truly blame her for what the man she had known as her father had done to the only type of existence she had ever seen in her mother's life. She looked in the direction of her mother's bedroom when she heard the voice of the man and glanced back at her, shrugged her shoulders in neither an approving nor displeasing manner and turned to go to her own room to pack a bag and leave. She remembered there was a duffle bag in the basement and went down the stairs where she paused as she reached out to open the door, only to recall the horrifying memories. She shook her head to release the saddened reality she once experienced and reminded herself it was a different house and setup, situations were not the same and most importantly, she was an adult about to take on her future.

"No, it's a new day and a better life will be mine." She said.

She opened the door and went inside the room to look for the duffle bag but instead found an oversized backpack. She returned to her room and packed some of her things as she heard the noises coming from her mother's bedroom, again she shook herself from the haunting memories of her past. Sara stopped noticing the dresser draw her mother removed from her room and remembered the additional money she stashed inside of it and slowly walked into the room, Janie and her partner were engrossed under the sheets having their own ritual. She opened the top drawer, reached

her hand up, gently slid it towards the back until she felt the lump, and removed it and quietly left the room, put the wad of cash with what money she had in her jeans pants pocket, and headed out the door.

She started walking vigorously away from a life she was all too eager to leave behind. Her intentions were to walk until her legs gave out forcing her to collapse, for she was determined to get away as far and as fast as she could but she didn't want to take the train she wanted to walk and feel the cool air of the day. She focused on goals that would free her from all the chaos that had been in her life for so many years. She felt free and an inner peace flushed through her body. She was not sure of her destination and started walking toward Roosevelt Boulevard and headed toward the 59th street Bridge. She decided to head west and thought about the sunshine, the beach, the smog, it would all be refreshing and a fresh new start for a life she still had yet to discover. She looked into the streets at the potholes and listened to the sounds of cars. Some were loud from the exhaust and some people were pressing on their horns at other cars, and pedestrians were running across the streets in every direction. She ignored everyone and did not bother to acknowledge those who were screaming obscenities at each other while others were happy and laughing talking with each other and expressing their joy. Owners were outside their shops sweeping the debris away from their storefront and others were receiving deliveries and shouting out orders to their staff, overall for Sara the day was overwhelming but the current hustle of all the happenings surrounding her didn't seem to faze her nor did it pull her attention from her goal. Though there were sounds of people screaming, some were speaking in Spanish and others talking

having general conversations which added to the many sounds around her, she walked past it all glancing at the two men fighting, others trying to separate them, police sirens blaring, and the people trying to get her attention.

"Hey lady, you want to buy a watch?" One vendor asked.

"No, Miss, I got some nice jewelry over here for a pretty lady like you."

"How about this fine lingerie for you to entertain your man," A woman asked as she held up the item.

Everyone had something they wanted to sell but Sara just wanted to leave town and never look back. She walked over to the 59th street Bridge and passed by the Jr. College where she was taking academic and martial arts courses. She thought about going over to talk with the counselor about her decision to leave but wanted a life free from her past and wanted to start fresh toward her new destination and decided to keep walking until she was on the Bridge heading back into the city. She walked as the wind blew across her face picking up force as she continued across the bridge. It was only a few miles long but the narrow width of the walkway for bicyclist and pedestrians of the bridge did concern her because it was still wide enough for other cars to travel and the few that came toward her caused her to stop allowing them to go pass. It was her first time walking over the bridge and she stayed close to the guardrail and though strong, it seemed frail and the experience was new to her and though frightening, still exhilarating. She kept her focus and continued to ignore as many drivers passed her, some slowing down offering to take her where she wanted to go. A cabby stopped and rolled down the window.

"You want a ride?"

"No, I'm going in the opposite direction."

"Don't matter I could take you back to the turning point and bring you into the city."

"No thanks I'd rather walk."

He put the car in park and opened the door to get out Sara stopped eyes widen as he approached and reached out to take her bag. She backed away.

"...I'm okay really."

"How about I make them even better."

He stepped toward and quickly she turned to go in the opposite direction, stopped and kicked with her other leg landing her foot in his stomach. A car pulled up behind the cab.

"Hey what's goin on here, hey lady you need some help or what?"

"I was just offering the lady a ride."

The cabby rushed back to his car and drove away. Sara looked at the man.

"Thanks."

He nodded, got back in his car and drove off. Sara continued until she reached the other side of the bridge only two other cars passed her one man slowing down and pointing to take her back from the direction she left. Sara slowly clutched the straps of her bag and shook her head sending him on his way. When she reached the other end of the bridge, a young man and his girlfriend pulled up to her within seconds after she crossed the street and started to walk toward 42nd street.

"Can we offer you a lift?" The woman asked. Sara felt comfortable hearing the young woman's voice and seeing that the girl was pregnant added a touch of warmth to her disposition.

"Yes, I think I'm going to head out west." She said.

"Well it's out west that we're going and you're welcomed to tag on for the ride."

She could not believe the first ride offered without a perverted intent that she actually paid attention to was heading in the same direction she was going.

"This means it must be fate that I am to go west because I wasn't exactly sure which way to go from here."

"I'm Laura Jean and this here fella is my man Stan. So where out west y'all plan on goin?"

Sara had not noticed the accent until after she was in the car. She looked at the young woman and thought she looked more as if she was just young but she was satisfied and was happy to have a one-time ride to the west coast.

"I don't know at the moment, maybe California. I just need to get out of New York right now because there are too many bad memories growing up here."

"So this where you from?" Stan asked.

"No, not really, I mean I was born in New York but I was very young when we moved but then," Sara thought for a moment remembering her sorted past. "…The man who raised me had a job where we moved from one place to another but then we ended up back in New York."

"Yeah well, we came up here by accident a few months ago during the summer and had to find work and wait fore we could get moving again because the road map genius here drivin decided we should take this wrong tern like I told him he shouldn't have done."

Laura Jean said as she hit Stan across his head.

"...But it ain't that great back home in South Carolina neither cuz its so dang hot ther."

Laura Jean thought she was someone who was wise in the world and on the fast track of life. She checked herself out in the mirror constantly and even asked Sara if she liked the strawberry blonde color of her hair, she told Sara that most people compared her to Marilyn Monroe. Her reality was that she was a hooker looking to swindle everyone she possibly could for her kicks and though Stan was her man, he was her pimp. Stan looked at Laura Jean cutting his eyes at her sharply but Sara did not notice his reaction and she was trying hard not to pay attention to the girl.

She was overwhelmed by the raggedy pile of luggage in the back seat and could only imagine how much more stuff they had in the trunk. She did not have a lot of room cramped in the back with all their stuff and the odor was a bit odd and overwhelming but she did not pay much attention to any of it. She was satisfied with the fact that she was no longer going to be walking carrying a backpack and trying to get one ride after the other until she made her decision about what to do. Laura Jean would not stop talking and Sara was trying to be polite and would occasionally say something just to see if whether or not it could end the talking but it never stopped Laura Jean from her continuous incoherent babbling. Sara gave up understanding that any input on her part would keep fueling Laura Jean's incessant amount of speech.

She continued her non-stop verbal atrocities and Stan never stopped glancing at Sara through his rear view mirror. They drove and drove and Sara looked down to notice a discarded newspaper on top of a pile of clothes and saw the date. Friday, October 31, 1980, the day her father and his business associate raped her, the

day her mother pointed the gun in her face, the day her dad was murdered, and the day of her birth. Sara felt disgusted and turned her head to rest it up against the passenger window and stared out into the crowds of people as Stan drove. She was very tired and didn't realize what direction they were headed, she whispered to herself.

"Oh well, happy birthday."

She closed her eyes, a tear fell, and soon Sara was asleep. Laura Jean took out a piece of cloth, poured something in it, and reached back gently placing the cloth under Sara's nose making sure not to disturb her slumber. Stan turned the car to take a detour. He took the exit in the direction going southeast and they continued to drive into the distance toward Alachua County, Florida unaware to Sara that they were no longer heading to her destination.

John followed at a distance making sure the car ahead never left his sight...

AUTHOR'S NOTE:

"I wish to thank all who have read this book, passed it on, gave it as a gift and/or suggested it to someone to give it a chance. My hope in having written this is that any who may have suffered due to real life events that is used in this book that have been duplicated out of my own life that he or she will take to heart that there is a God and he sees all and knows our pain and struggles and will deliver us for his glory. It is our choice to do good or evil and as a man I chose to be good toward others and as an author allowed creativity to shine and made the character in the book choose a different path. It is my belief that although we suffer heartache, pain and tragedy sometimes due to what has been forced upon us; it is never something that will last forever and we have the strength to move forward by relying on those who are trustworthy and safe and together we can change what is needed to be changed in our lives because of what may have happened in the beginning."

Be strong, have faith and God Bless!

-cortland

Made in the USA
Lexington, KY
24 September 2012